# MURDER BY
# DESIGN

Also by Jon P. Bloch

*Best Murder of the Year*

*Finding Your Leading Man*

# MURDER**BY** DESIGN

## Jon P. Bloch

ST. MARTIN'S MINOTAUR ♒ NEW YORK

Names, characters, places, and incidents, if real, are used fictitiously.

www.minotaurbooks.com

Library of Congress Cataloging-in-Publication Data

Bloch, Jon P.
    Murder by design : a Rick Domino mystery / by Jon P. Bloch.—1st ed.
      p.  cm.
    ISBN 0-312-31312-8
    1. Gossip columnists—Fiction.   2. Television programs—Fiction.
3. Hollywood (Los Angeles, Calif.)—Fiction.   4. Interior decorators—
Crimes against—Fiction.   I. Title.

PS3602.L63M87 2004
813'.6—dc22

                         2003058775

First Edition: March 2004

10  9  8  7  6  5  4  3  2  1

Once again, for Tristan,
whose design for living thankfully includes me

## ACKNOWLEDGMENTS

Thank you to June Clark and Peter Rubie of the Peter Rubie Literary Agency, for guidance and good lunches. And to Keith Kahla and everyone else at St. Martin's, for letting me change horses in midstream.

# MURDER**BY**
# DESIGN

# ONE

MY LIVING ROOM DESPERATELY NEEDED A MAKEOVER.

Gazing forlornly at my pathetically boring Ralph Rapson rocking chair, last year's hand-dyed Jack Lenor Larsen throw cushions, and my tired old Andy Warhol original lithos, I had no choice but to admit that it was all so yesterday's news that I might as well have put up a placard that read: *Monica Lewinsky slept here.*

As fate would have it, however, attending to my den of shame would be—like finding my one true love—easier said than done. On the surface of things, I made an okay living as America's number one gossip columnist. I had my own show on Hollywood Network TV, plus wrote columns and books and things digging up the latest dirt on all the big stars. There was even an online Rick Domino Fan Club in honor of yours truly.

But Rodeo Drive is a harsh mistress. Just the other day I'd received an obnoxious letter from my bank about how in the future would I kindly make certain I had adequate funds to cover the purchases I made. In a world obsessed with numbers and greed, there was no room for free spirits such as myself. I believe spending money to be a wistful, poetical enterprise, part hope, part fancy, and part good taste. It is an art form, really. Add this, balance that—what did they think I was, an accountant? Speaking of which: Subsequent meetings with my accountant and then my business manager proved that the entire universe was all too eager to rain on my parade. My assets literally were frozen until further notice.

"Hmm, frozen," I attempted to joke. "So in other words, I just pop 'em in the microwave and presto, they're all toasty warm again." So much for making sweetness and light in the presence of dim-witted corporate henchmen. By the end of the meeting my hissing, red-faced, clench-toothed accountant resigned in a rage of psycho tears, and my business manager threatened to sue me if I so much as breathed in the direction of a credit card. It was something about "willful desecration of his reputa-tion," whatever that meant.

Yet fate smiled upon me, after all. There I was, struggling gallantly to eke a subsistence out of the meager, mid-range four-figure weekly allowance I was ordered to live on, when my new boss, Max Headroom, proved to be my guardian angel as surely as if Della Reese were breathing down his neck.

Everyone called Max Headroom Max Headroom because he had all the personality and charisma of a computer-generated talking head. We even called him Max Headroom to his square-jawed, pasty face, just to see how far we could push it. He seemed devoid of features, resembling a five-year-old's drawing that had two dots for eyes and one line for a mouth. And his robotic, monotone voice did little to convince one of his humanity. But I guess ol' Max knew how to add two and two, because one day out of nowhere the corporate hot shots plunked him down into the sleek execu-tive suite, where he nurtured what he called the "bottom line."

Anyway, Max called me into his office late one Monday afternoon.

"Rick," he began, his automaton lips parting in imitation of a smile, "how would you like to be a guest on *My House, Your House*?"

"I'd sooner have been a guest on *Queen for a Day*," I shot back. "At least the housewives on that show were honest about begging. And all they had to contend with was the Applause-O-Meter. I mean, really, Max—on *My House, Your House* people work their asses off for two days, and all they have to show for it is some tacky, theme-roomed room that, in order to make inhabitable again, will no doubt cost them far more than the fifty cents they're given to fix up the room in the first place."

"They're given a thousand dollars, not fifty cents," Max replied. "And I've told you not to call me Max. Anyway, it's the number one cable show these days—no offense, Rick—and we thought it would be a real ratings winner if you went on the show while doing a behind-the-scenes look. Kills two birds with one stone—we get free publicity from a rival network for your being on their big hit show, plus we get more viewers for *ourselves* when people tune in to cover your documentary on it."

I scrutinized the framed photo on Max's desk; apparently, he'd borrowed someone's wife and kids to create the illusion that he had an existence independent from his pocket calculator. Because it was impossible to comprehend Max having any sort of personal life.

"Max, this is Rick Domino you're talking to. I interview *stars*. We're talking Julia and Denzel and Halle and Harrison. I don't *do* cable TV." I quickly added, "I mean, except for the slight detail that I'm *on* cable TV. But you know what I mean."

Actually, Max did not know what I meant—or at least not the whole story. True, I was not exactly salivating at the thought of the assignment, but there was more to it than met the lifeless, unblinking gaze of Max's eyes. In reality, I was what you might call a *My House, Your House* widow(er)—or maybe a recovering one. I'd endured long weeks of my now ex-boyfriend holding me hostage on Friday nights when the latest episode would air.


Biff Holden—would you believe it wasn't his real name?—was what I am tempted to call a rising starlet, the very sort of hunky, brainless, heartless clone that had long been my downfall. But I will save all that for my shrink. Underneath all his pseudo *Baywatch*-ish posturing, Biff was just another West Hollywood androgen who went into a state of hyper-orgasm over interior design. And the supreme object of worship for Biff and the rest of his species was none other than *My House, Your House*. There were countless shows on TV about do-it-yourself home repairs—or, as insiders called it, DIY. (In fact, it was but one of many shows on the fledgling Interior Design Network.) Yet something about the gimmick of *My House, Your House* had truly captured America's fancy.

What happened on each episode was that two couples traded houses for two days. During that time, each couple redid a room in the other couple's house, with the help of a designer and carpenter. They had to stay within an incredibly chintzy budget of a thousand bucks per room, as if you can even trim a hangnail for that much anymore. No one got to see the finished result in their own home until the end. Add to the mix a perky, hippie girl host, and somehow it added up to TV magic.

I guess part of the appeal was the soap opera-ness of it all: Would all the work get done in time? What would the couples think of their rooms at the end of the show? But the bulk of the drama sprang from the stable of five designers, each of whom was so different from the others that whichever one got assigned took on a weightiness worthy of Greek tragedy. The couples literally were at the mercy of the designers. Asking a *My House, Your House* designer to compromise on a single element was like asking Britney Spears to hide her navel. Middle East peace talks were a breeze by comparison.

Biff was totally hooked. There it was, Friday night in L.A., and all he wanted out of life was to sit in front of the tube and worry his Kleenex over the latest triumph or disaster in some suburban couple's play room. "I can't *believe* Helena chose *that* fabric for the throw pillows," Biff would decree, as if harshly judging Susan Lucci for not telling her millionth husband about her zillionth affair. "And why oh why did they distress the table top?" Then, after the episode aired, there was the miracle of the Internet, and Biff spent hours online with other *MHYH* addicts, analyzing every last staple and thread.

In protest, I refused to watch the show at all, tempted though I was when my ears tingled over phrases such as "window treatments." The main thing I noticed in the bits and snatches I couldn't help overhearing was a failure of anyone on the show to correctly pronounce "voilà." But glancing over Biff's rock-hard shoulder as he'd urgently peck away at the keyboard, I got the general idea. "Could you BELIEVE Bill's Ceiling Stencil?" one posting would read, while another pondered: "Should Helena Be Arrested For That Mirror Frame?"

As if all this weren't bad enough, Biff sat me down one day to tell me what he described as "wonderful news." By popular demand, the ID Network would now be airing older episodes of *My House, Your House* on Saturday nights. It was what they called their "$H_2M$"—the *My House, Your House* Marathon. So there went *both* weekend nights. "Time for another $H_2M$ Saturday!" Biff would ecstatically announce, rubbing his hands together in delicious anticipation. There were not all that many episodes, and before long Biff was watching the same installment for the third or fourth time. I smilingly suggested that maybe he could record the shows so that we wouldn't have to stay in on Saturday night. "Record them?" Biff scoffed. "You make it sound like I'm some weirdo fanatic. Besides, your DVD recorder corrupts the colors, and the red tones especially are off by several hues. How would I know, then, what the designer was *really* doing?"

Even on those rare occasions when I dragged Biff out of the house, he would hook up with some fellow brainwashed zombie in the bar, and away they would jabber about Basil's color sense or how that couple from Klamath Falls had no business not liking his drapes since they'd had nothing on their windows save for a glorified Wal-Mart pillow case. Once upon a time, gay bars buzzed with sex. Now DIY had replaced KY as the topic of choice. You'd have thought everyone adopted children and had commitment ceremonies just as an excuse to redecorate.

Eventually, Biff and I broke up. I'd like to say it was over something profound, but in point of fact I wanted my weekends back. I wanted to *live*. Well, it was too much for Susan Hayward to ask for, and it appeared that it was also too much for me. Biff took his TV and staple gun with him, while I was left awash in a sea of bitter memories.

Now Max Headroom was telling me to invite into my home the very cause of my recent tumultuous break-up. Besides, even if Biff had never existed (albeit in a way he never really *had*), we still had a problem, Houston. True, I was so intent on getting my living room redesigned I would have eagerly sold my soul or body or whatever to the first bidder. Yet the thought of getting even a broom closet in my home redone for a mere thousand dollars seemed lower than lowest. All the cut-rate MDF coffee tables and bad paint jobs and bathroom hardware as artwork were more than I could have tolerated. And to do it all in public! I might as well have knocked out my two front teeth and gone on the *Jerry Springer Show*.

"Rick, this is not a request," Max scolded. "This is an *assignment*. Do you know what it means to be assigned something? I think not, judging by your recent track record."

Max was no doubt referring to my so-called controversial refusal to participate in a recent special entitled "Psychic Pet Advisors to the Stars."

"I dunno, Max," I thought out loud. "The idea of letting some stranger into my house to completely redo a room. . . ."

Max grinned like a nasty science fiction creature. "Maybe ask a lawyer," he creepily pronounced. "Yes, I think maybe a lawyer would give you the best advice of all."

I may have had pride and taste and dignity, but I could also smell the turpentine.

"Okay, Max, I'll do it. I . . . well, I've been meaning to get some stuff redone anyway." I knew when I was licked; it was time to make the best of things. Take a lemon and turn it into a gin and tonic—that's my motto. Max and I made a gentlemen's handshake that I could pick my work partner, the other couple, and—most important of all—the designers for both houses. Then I set myself down in front of the wide screen TV in my office suite to watch some taped episodes of *MHYH* that were delivered to one of my assistants, as the show's home base was only about five blocks away.

*I hate this*, I kept trying to convince myself. But I rapidly had to admit that I had it all wrong. The show was fabulous. Maybe the problem had been with Biff; it was understandably difficult for me to believe that anything he liked could have had any merit whatsoever. Before long I was on the edge of my seat, wondering what the slipcover made from old drapes would look like on the divan, and if the whitewash on the headboard and matching window seat would look good against the persimmon-and-sea-foam carpet.

But the most suspenseful moment of all came at the beginning, when the couple would be told which designer they would work with, and which designer would work with the *other* couple. Suspiciously seldom was it a good match. A couple wanting something sleek and modern would get a makeover from the designer who specialized in the country look. The other couple, wanting something for their toddler's bedroom, would get their room redone by the designer who specialized in New York sex dungeons. Supposedly, it was all determined by picking names out of a hat, but the frequent utter wrongness of the choices made you wonder if it all wasn't staged for heightened drama. Either that, or the show's producers

6

were atheists determined to convince the masses that there was no God. Of course, the disasters were balanced out by the occasional perfect match. Some of the couples—even some of the big burly straight dudes—would literally burst into tears of joy at how gorgeous it all was.

I actually began to feel good about the whole thing. (Always a mistake, but I am slow to learn certain life lessons.) Indeed, the phrase I chanted to myself almost constantly during those next few days was: *How bad could it be*? Since I got to pick the designer, how bad could it be? Since they only had a thousand bucks to spend, how bad could it be? And if a thousand dollars wasn't enough to totally transform my living room—and I was convinced I should go for broke, and do the living room—then at least it would jump start things in a creative new direction. Max Headroom was right. It *would* be a good ratings booster. Maybe Max wasn't such a bad robot, after all. Maybe in a sitcom-ish way, he knew in advance about my living room, and this was his sly method of trying to win me over.

I eagerly composed a list of plans. First, there was the issue of who to have on the show with me. There had been very few same-sex couples to date, so I figured I would do my bit for the Cause, and round up some young gay stud to partner with. (You could say I had a bit of a hidden agenda here.) And the other couple could be two men or—depending on how politically correct I was feeling—two women. Plus of course they would all have to be celebs, or at least semi-celebs. There were a number of people in the public eye who were out of the closet, so the only obstacle would be finding folks available on such short notice. We were going to start taping in five days.

Most important of all, I needed to pick out which designers to use. Going through the list, the choice was pretty much a no-brainer.

# TWO

THE FIRST DESIGNER I SCRATCHED OFF THE LIST WAS KNOWN SIM-
ply as Aunt Fern. She was a rotund, grandmotherly type who seemed like a
genuinely nice old gal, and there were those who swooned over her work.
But she specialized in country designs that simply were not my cup of
moonshine. Aunt Fern *loved* to crochet, and even ran a mail order business
called Aunt Fern's Homespun Originals. Coincidentally enough, whether
designing a New York loft or a South Beach lanai or an Omaha rumpus
room, somehow a bit of crochet was always just what the room needed.
"We're going to drape some crochet around the fireplace," she would
enthuse, "and I thought we could brighten up the computer hutch with a
nice crocheted printer cover." Aunt Fern would say this with such guileless
sincerity that you'd almost believe she didn't remember doing pretty much
the same thing in the last room she designed.

Or maybe I should really say the last room she changed a few elements
in, because Aunt Fern's rooms looked astonishingly alike in their "before"
and "after" states. Indeed, it all seemed less like "before" and "after" than it
did switching from Cathy to Patty Lane, as it were. I often wondered what
in the finished room cost a thousand bucks, unless all that yarn was made
of spun gold. But Aunt Fern had this strange phobia about rearranging
furniture. You'd have thought it was a felony from the way she carried on,
fanatically measuring with minuscule footsteps to ensure that every last
wastebasket was returned to its *exact* location. Adding to her quirkiness
was the way she'd devised her own method for measurement based on the

perennial kiddie favorite, "giant steps." "This end table goes three baby steps to the right," she would instruct. "And let's put that rocker two giant steps away from the fireplace!"

Aunt Fern claimed she had an ax to grind. "Design is about how you *feel* about an object, *not* where it's placed in the room," she was wont to proclaim. So rather than move the sofa to a different spot, she would do what she called "jazzing it up." This meant gluing little doodads to it, like bows and hand-painted flowers and things.

Besides crocheting, Aunt Fern's other specialty was country themes, and "country" in her mind meant "barnyard." Her finished rooms were enough to tickle the fancy of Elly Mae Clampett at her *cee*ment pond. Aunt Fern was especially fond of MDF cutouts of hound dogs and sheep, which she would adorn with grade school–level paint flourishes that were touted as "folk art," the way you might've said that some bitch who couldn't carry a tune was a "song stylist."

"Sorry to hurt your feelings, Aunt Fern," I muttered to myself, as I drew a red line through her name. I felt like I was saying no to my sweet, well-meaning grandmother when she suggested that my teenaged friends might enjoy some nice Lawrence Welk records.


The next designer I nixed was one Bill McCoy, better known as Shirtless Bill, or the more overtly sexual Bare-Chested Bill. He was famous for taking off his shirt as he sweated away on redesigning his rooms, and indeed he had a sculpted, *café au lait* torso worthy of note. Bill also had a face worthy of a Ralph Lauren model, looking like a cleaner cut version of Eric Benet. But being who I was where I was, a sculpted chest or classically chiseled face was kind of been-there-done-that. And I was more concerned with the state of my living room.

Bill's background was in designing theme parks. In a bizarre conflict-of-interest case settled out of court, he once got in hot water for simultaneously designing a Bugs Bunny Futurama Hutch for Six Flags and a new attraction called Pocahontas's Underwater Nature Nook at Disneyland. As the saying goes, you can take the boy out of the theme park, but you can't take the theme park out of the boy. His rooms were always daring and frequently stunning, but all too often he seemed to forget that some suburban couple's bedroom was never intended to be colossal on a Dumbo scale. He'd say things like: "This bedroom is going to be fire-engine red, and to go with the theme, we'll be turning the *room* into a fire station." You'd half-expect him to add: "It's really going to be fun, boys and girls!" And so there would be a pole you'd have to slide down to get into the bed, and a blaring siren for an alarm clock. Like New York City, Bill's rooms were a nice place to visit but you wouldn't want to live there.

The thing of it was, when the couple working on the room would protest, Shirtless Bill became snootily self-righteous about not altering a single hydrant. The *MHYH* designers were not known for their spirit of compromise, but Bill took stubbornness to new heights. If Aunt Fern seemed to think she was trespassing by being in the people's home at all, Shirtless Bill acted as if each assignment were the Sistine Chapel, and who were these lowly suburbanites to be disagreeing with Michelangelo?

Besides his condescending TV persona, Shirtless Bill had a bad habit of experimenting with new techniques for the first time on the air, with no regard for what a failed experiment might do to the room. "Gee, I guess we didn't follow the directions after all," he'd cheerfully shrug after causing thousands of dollars of damage to someone's dining room walls in a failed attempt to give them texture. "This is a very interesting effect, too. The plaster looks like the bark on a sycamore tree, always unpeeling to new layers. And when it cracks and falls on the floor, that's the beauty of the effect." The couple working on the room would protest, "But they can't go around picking up plaster all the time. They have *kids*." And Bill would haughtily reply, "Who's to say a room has to look the same every day? This way, it will never be boring. Surely that's worth a little extra sweeping."

So, as you can see, it was hardly difficult to sacrifice a look at Bill's bod for higher principles such as sanity. Message boards alternated between contempt for Bill's creations and unabashed crushes on his chest. His fans included both males and females, and Bill chose to be coyly discreet as to his preferences. Officially he was single, if that meant anything anymore. And he was, after all, an interior designer, if *that* meant anything anymore. He was occasionally seen linking arms with this or that actress at a soap award show, and would tell reporters that he was still looking for the right *person* to settle down with. Yet if it's true that the only good news is no news, Bill was no doubt a ratings booster. Sexiness, destruction, power tripping, and angst—what more could a viewer want? Bill was the tortured Heathcliff of DIY.

The next designer to get bumped off the list was Bill's female counterpart. Not that she took off her shirt, though her name was Godiva—specifically, Helena Godiva. The beautiful, regal Helena was like a defiant twin Artemis to Bill's pompous Apollo. And her style was that of a moon goddess in many ways: all cutting edges and visual disruption. Helena would have been ideal for designing, say, an East Village boutique that signaled trend without end. But she didn't exactly play well in Peoria, where things like broken Coke bottles glued to walls were decidedly not regarded as fab. For Helena, a room was like a blank canvas, and she brought an artist's vision to it. Unfortunately for the homeowner, the artist's vision had less in common with Norman Rockwell than it did with Hieronymus Bosch.

Like Shirtless Bill, Helena seemed to have no regard for who she was designing for. But her attitude was even haughtier. Bill did emanate a certain perfunctory niceness, but the super-aloof Helena never even attempted to come across as though she would socialize with the couples outside of the assignment. Making her all the more foreboding was the way her finished results outdid Bill's in the controversy department for pushing the envelope beyond Elmer Fudd and into the realm of *The Story of O*. A couple of her rooms even made national headlines: A living room done up to resemble a giant body-piercing (don't ask), and a bedroom given a swan theme à la Björk's Oscar dress (ditto).

Just as off-putting was her appearance. While other designers sported sensible Nikes and jeans, Helena always wore a variation on a basic white silk dress, complete with pearls and classic white pumps. It seemed to defy common sense, since surely the high heels would get in her way, and the rather diaphanous dress would be covered with sawdust and paint. Yet somehow Helena emerged goddess-perfect at the end of each episode, a kind of Donna Reed with a whip. Her dark hair streaked with platinum blond, she was like an inscrutable angel-demon. As the scandal sheets noted, she'd broken off her wedding engagements to two different Wall Street power magnates. Like the fairy tale about the knights who could not traverse the glass mountain to where the princess dwelt, Helena was tantalizingly untouchable, the designer everyone most loved to hate.

Truth be told, if I could have hired Helena and kept her on a short leash, what she produced might have been amazing. But I couldn't risk using her without having any say. A couple who said, "Do anything but change our carpet," would return to find said carpet cut into little pieces. If your pride and joy was your sofa, you could expect to see it ruined with glued-on feathers. If Bill sometimes caused accidental damage, Helena seemed to purposefully wreck ceilings, floors, and walls, and presumably for no reason other than her personal amusement. As far as my living room was concerned, my attitude toward Helena was let's not and say we did.


I could have accepted either of the other two designers, because they both did decent, solid work. Curtsy Ann Thomas was a gorgeous former Miss Texas with an obsession for symmetry that bordered on certifiable obsessive-compulsive disorder. She spent *hours* with her tape measure and her level to calculate the exact spot a picture should be hung—"exact" meaning *exactly* in the middle—and would add or knock out doors or windows in order for the room to achieve what she called "equilibrium." When couples she worked with questioned her insistence on such precision, the tawny-blond Curtsy Ann would roll her large green eyes and engagingly reply, "Think of it as a teeter-totter," gesturing with her hands to suggest two ends seeking a point of balance. "You have to find that magic place of equilibrium." And then, later in the show, she would wave a scolding finger and admonish: "Remember, y'all—the teeter-totter!"

Curtsy Ann also had an obsession with organza; what crochet was to Aunt Fern, organza window treatments were to Curtsy Ann. Fortunately for her budget, Curtsy Ann seemed to own a virtually bottomless treasure chest of organza gowns from her beauty contest days. When someone would ask where she got the fabric for the curtains, she would sheepishly reply, "This ol' thing? I've had it in my closet for *years*." In a way, she was Scarlett O'Hara in reverse, turning a dress into curtains.

Curtsy Ann's other quirk was that she still seemed to think she was competing for Miss America, and could not resist livening things up with a snippet of song. Atop the step ladder, paint roller in hand, she would burst into a chorus of "Honey Bun" from *South Pacific* or "I Cain't Say No" from *Oklahoma!* or even "Memory" from *Cats*. Part exhibitionist and part modest southern belle, she would sing a few words from a song and then demur, "La de da da da," for the next line or so, to ensure that no one could accuse her of singing a song. This also, of course, avoided copyright infringement. (Her voice was what you'd call Miss America pleasant.)

Still, unlike Aunt Fern, Curtsy Ann really did redesign a room, and unlike Shirtless Bill or Helena, she had this strange, novel idea that a bedroom should have a bed, a kitchen a stove, and so on. I could have accepted Curtsy Ann for my designer, and in fact put her down for the designer of the other room.

But my choice for my own room was Basil Montclair. He was the one designer who had no quirks, no obsessions, and could simply be relied on to do a tasteful, clean, professional job. He was the only one of the lot to whom I felt I could fully entrust my living room with no input from me. There would be no bizarre surprises—or bizarre un-surprises, either. Basil didn't project a particularly strong personality, other than seeming rather fey though supposedly "married." (In one of those ironic little twists, the married-with-children Basil seemed much less butch than the mysterious yet macho Shirtless Bill.) Basil's dark, brooding looks reflected his Cherokee heritage, and like a silent, resolute warrior in the battle against bad taste, he heroically went about giving each couple the handsomest room he could. The colors went together strikingly yet without clashing, the ceiling lights never fell down, the bedspreads were made from bedspread fabrics, the candles were held in candlesticks (as opposed to Goodyear tires or whatnot) and none of the combined elements ever looked out of place. The walls had just enough artwork to look smart. There were no gimmicky themes, no anything that people could not live in absolute comfort with.

But good news equaled no news, and the message boards tended to ignore Basil's fine work in favor of outrage over Helena or Bill's latest debacle. Moreover, like bullied children finding someone else to bully, relatively few TV couples protested the antics of the other designers, yet many were all too quick to jump on Basil for picking a paint shade they felt to be slightly too light, or a tablecloth with slightly too much fringe. Yet next door, Helena would be turning the couple's own kitchen into a sci-fi haberdashery, and at the end of the two days they would force a smile and say, "Well, it certainly is *different*." Maybe people simply had no words for the more outrageous designs, while what Basil did was within the parameters of normal human consciousness, and so they felt they had some control over the situation by criticizing him.

In picking Basil, then, I was not only being kind to my living room. I was also attempting to give him what I felt to be a much-deserved jolt of publicity.

And so, with Basil and Curtsy Ann as the designers of choice, I started a second list: What to find out about the two of them, plus the other members of the team I'd be encountering. After all, I *was* a gossip columnist, and everyone at *MHYH* knew that about me when they asked me to participate. My behind-the-scenes look would, with luck, reveal more than just a crisis over a jammed-up glue gun.

The obvious angle to pursue on Basil was the was-he-or-wasn't-he? bit. I wasn't big on outing people against their will, but occasionally gay celebs had a passive-aggressive way of "confiding" in me when there just happened to be a television camera in the room. As for Curtsy Ann, I was curious to know if she really was all about yardsticks, or if she had a playful side as well. When asked about her personal life, she blushingly told reporters she was a career girl, but of course that sounded a bit too pat, not to mention inadvertently provocative.

The other cast members I'd be dealing with were the host and carpenters.

The host was Koko Yee, a wholesome, perky, Asian-American hippie chick who came across as the sort of person who'd get along famously with anyone. She was *so* smiley-perfect in her postmodern, funky way that I couldn't resist the urge to sniff around for some laundry of hers that was not quite so snuggly soft. Yet offhand, the worst thing about Koko I could come up with was that as a child performer she sang "The Theme from *Mahogany*" on *Star Search* and lost. I mentally considered the headline KOKO YEE'S OBSESSION WITH DIANA ROSS, then thought better of it. Her African-American husband was a fairly successful record producer named J.T. Rex, and she was in fact bulgingly pregnant with their first child.

With true political correctness, one of the show's carpenters was male, and one was female. One was assigned to each show; part of the intrigue was the way the designers fought over the carpenter's time. I didn't have approval as to which would be assigned to my episode, so I wanted to be familiar with them both.

The male carpenter, Brick Edwards, was a hunky heartthrob who competed with Bill in the Bare Chest Division. Brick was an easygoing dude who seemed at least as interested in pulling practical jokes on the set as he was in getting his work done. When he wasn't telling Basil he'd decided to make a requested entertainment center out of egg cartons, or putting wet paint on the seat of a chair Aunt Fern was about to sit on, he was at the very least mugging for the camera in a manner that one assumed was intended to be taken humorously. No doubt about it, Brick was the funniest thing since *Mister Ed.* The message boards waxed gaga over Brick, though the most anyone could get out of him in response was that he had "a girlfriend," and so was spoken for.

The female carpenter was named after her parents' favorite movie star, and Ann-Margret Wochinsky did her best to live up to her namesake. With sass and attitude, she fastened her tool belt under her black leather halter top, climbed onto her Harley, and sped off to her latest gig. With her white lipstick, false eyelashes, and long, big red hair, she was one Black & Decker badass. Yet beneath her hellcat persona, Ann-Margret worked hard to prove that a woman carpenter could be every bit as a good as a man. She was as fanatical about getting things done as Brick was laid back, and seemed to have no personal life at all. But of course, the surface of things could be deceiving.

Yet whatever gossip I dug up on this or that person, I was sure that the whole thing promised to be a dream assignment. Everyone would get lots of publicity, I'd get my new living room, and more than likely work with a hot new hunk in the bargain. As I told myself again and again: *How bad could it be?*

My answer came on Thursday morning, two days before the taping.

# THREE

I SHOULD HAVE KNOWN SOMETHING WAS UP WHEN MAX PERSON-ally called me into his office. Courtesies on the part of bosses always mean they're about to screw you.

Max greeted me by baring his fake-looking squares of teeth. "So Rick, how's it coming with finding the couples?" He meant of course my finding a partner for myself, plus finding the other couple.

"Actually, Max, I haven't much time to chat," I semi-tactfully answered. "I'm expecting call-backs any minute now." It was true; I was awaiting confirmation from both a minor pop star and a minor TV actor who were both kinda sorta known to be gay. I also had not yet heard back from Greg Louganis, Chastity Bono, or k. d. lang.

"Well, I had a talk with the station owners, and they think that it would be best for you to partner with someone . . . you know, from your own backyard." Max mechanically raised an arch eyebrow, as if I should know what he meant.

I could only registered puzzlement. "They want me to use my gardener?"

"No, silly. They want you to give more publicity to HNTV. They want you to pick one of *us*. Or rather, they have generously taken the time to make the choice for you."

It was as if my entire life flashed before me; my panic, outrage, and utter confusion seemed to stretch out toward infinity. "Max, you don't mean—?"

"I'm afraid it's a done deal, Rick. You'll be teaming up with Mitzi."

Respecting my need to be alone with my thoughts, Max sat by patiently for a minute or two while I let fly an impressive assortment of expletives.

The Mitzi in question here was my frequent on-screen co-host and royal pain in the ass, the "lovely" Mitzi McGuire. In between consultations with her cosmetic surgeon, wig stylist, and divorce attorney, the "ageless," nasal Mitzi had swallowed her vowels to TV mediocrity. In her tiny cubicle outside my office suite, she would piece together tacky, supposedly in-depth specials called things like "The True Story Behind 'Pet Psychics to the Stars,'" or allegedly hard-hitting profiles with attention-grabbing titles such as "Marilu Henner: Happy at Last," or "Nancy McKeon: Having It All."

But mostly she tried to steal my job. Every chance she got, Mitzi took a dig at me, so I never had a moment's peace. I always had to decide whether to ignore her or subtly put her in her place while at the same time keeping the broadcast on track. For Mitzi had zero ability to ad lib; the teleprompter was her virtual God. I'd call her amateurish, if the term ironically did not serve to elevate her reputation.

"Now, Rick." Max spoke quietly. "Is it really so bad as that? You work with her all the time, anyway."

"I *know*. That's why I live and breathe for the chance to get away from her. It's like being married. It's *worse* than being married."

"Well, consider it a *fait accompli*. There's really no point in arguing."

I took a deep sigh. "I guess you're right. 'Choose your battles wisely,' and all that." I glanced over at Max's digital clock. "Now, if that's all, I really do have to get back to—"

"Not so fast, Rick. There's more."

"When you say 'more,' you mean I'm like getting a bonus or something, right?"

Max emitted a contrived *ha-ha-ha* that no doubt was intended to pass for laughter. "You're really a card, Rick. Actually, it's about the other team."

"Don't tell me you've picked *them* out, too?"

He leaned back in his swivel chair. "Of course not. That would be impinging on your turf. It's just that, well . . . we were thinking."

"I see." I stood with my chin jutting out in defiance.

"Relax, Rick. You do get to pick the team. It's just that we'd like it to be someone more . . . well, *you know*, than what you might have had in mind."

"And 'you know' means straight?"

Max feigned a cough, of the sort that wouldn't convince a parent that their eight-year-old should stay home from school. "Not at all. But aren't there some gay people out there who are more like regular folk? A working class gay man, let's say, who's just making ends meet. To contrast with your palatial digs. The producers of *My House, Your House* were a little concerned. Their viewers want to see at least one home they can relate to."

"I would hardly call fifteen rooms a palace," I sternly corrected, damned if I'd let this corporate honcho create the absurdly false impression that I was not grossly underpaid. "But I suppose I can see their point. I'd expect that some of the struggling performers I've been in contact with—"

"No performers, Rick. Just a working stiff." Max hastily added: "If you'll pardon the expression."

I had to think fast. "Tell you what, Max. I'll see what I can do. There is one average-type guy I'm thinking of. But if he can't do it on such short notice, we're back to the not-so-average young hunks on my list." I sportingly offered my hand. "Deal?"

Max tapped his well-jointed fingers together, computing the information. "Very well, Rick. That sounds like a reasonable compromise." He stiffly extended his arm to shake my hand.


Of course, little did Max know that the blue-collar guy I planned on calling was a junior detective for the LAPD named Terry Zane. Through a series of misadventures, the affable, bearish Terry had partnered up with me to solve a high-profile murder a while back, and he came out as gay in the bargain.

Terry and I had *nothing* in common. Still, we sort of became friends around the murder thingie (trust me, long story). Moreover, Terry understandably looked up to me as a mentor, given my effortless sophistication. And so I'd been nobly attempting to make a bona-fide gay man out of him.

But Henry Higgins's task was a breeze by comparison. If only all Terry had to learn was the where the rain fell in Spain.

As a husky, six-four bear of a cop with a buzz cut, dark brown eyes and expressive Elvis eyebrows, Terry had no trouble setting hearts a-fantasizing. The problem was that, in typical good-guy form, Terry came out in an "after-school special" sort of way. He did it because it was the Honest Thing to Do. He was always bemoaning how West Hollywood just wasn't how they did things back in Artichoke Valley or wherever he was from. He wanted to meet a nice, simple guy before he went All the Way. Since your average West Hollywood Joe was neither nice nor simple and hardly hesitated to go All the Way and Then Some, Terry was spending an inordinately long time stuck at first base, so to speak. This can make even the most good-natured bears cranky. Probably he needed to find some other gay guy who lived in Redneck Heights (or wherever it was he lived), if in fact there was any such animal.

But if his old-fashioned values were strike one against Terry's success on the gay circuit, his taste—or rather, lack of it—amounted to strikes two and three. Terry could not be relied on to pick out *socks* without supervision. Left to his own devices, he thought nothing of wearing, say, a plaid jacket with a paisley shirt—as in, he didn't intuitively grasp what the problem was. I'd never been to his home, but I could just imagine. There was little reason to doubt that the predominant motif was gun-rack-and-spittoon.

So I figured, what the heck? I'd cheer Terry up or flatter him or whatnot by inviting him on the show, knowing perfectly well he'd politely refuse. Terry would never have even heard of *My House, Your House*. Besides, his natural modesty would never in a million years permit him to be a guest on a TV show. And even if he *wanted* to accept, he sadly wouldn't be able to think of anyone to partner with, and that would be rubbing too much salt in the wound. Since he maintained his essential working-class ethic about the sanctity of marriage, Terry felt more than a little ashamed about being single, as if he somehow was not pulling his weight in the larger scheme of life. So I was confident that a call to Terry would render me right back where I wanted to be—holding out for the cute pop singer or the cute TV actor.

"So, who is this person you want to invite on the show?" Max inquired.

I briefly described salt-of-the-earth, Lava soap–squeaky clean Terry.

"And he's *single*, you say?" Max enthused. "That's even better. Kind of poignant and all that." He carefully pressed his index finger on the intercom, instructing his executive secretary to call Terry.

"Fine," I shrugged. I knew that Max didn't quite trust me here, so I played right along as though I had nothing to hide. But I knew that Terry was even less likely to accept an invitation from someone he didn't know.

"Now then, Max, if that really is all . . ." I turned to take my leave.

"Not quite, Rick. There's also the matter of the designers."

I stopped dead in my tracks.

"And what, pray tell, about the designers?"

Truth be told, I'd always wanted to say "pray tell," but it was small, defiant comfort for what I was fearing. Every time I tried to do something nice at this cheesy dump of a network, some nitwit would fuck it all up. Now I was probably going to be told that Basil was insisting I not ask about his personal life, or that Curtsy Ann had to use her own tape measure or some other nonsense.

"I hope you don't mind, Rick, but there's been a slight amendment made to the plan. Neither Basil nor Curtsy Ann are available this weekend. They both said they were too busy planning their next assignments. You know how those creative types are—they don't like to be interrupted when the juices get going."

"Oh, so we're shooting next weekend, then? Actually, that's good news. It'll give me more time to—"

"Oh, we're shooting this weekend, all right. But with different designers."

Suddenly, I felt like I'd been sentenced to the guillotine. "Max, what the fuck is—"

"Helena Godiva and Aunt Fern!" Max blurted out, as if, like HAL in *2001*, his power source was about to die. "Don't be mad, Rick, but they were the only ones available."

Frantically trying to salvage things in my mind, I told myself it didn't have to be so bad. "Okay, so I'll get Helena. She does some pretty out-there designs, but maybe I'll like what she comes up with in an in-your-face way. And if Terry accepts"—I knew of course he wouldn't, but I needed to play along—"he might actually enjoy Aunt Fern's old-fashioned homey touches."

The secretary buzzed Max. "Yes," he pronounced into the phone with his monotone voice. "Yes, yes, very good, excellent, yes."

Hanging up the phone, Max swerved his head back in my direction. "Your friend Terry Zane has accepted. He said he's a huge fan of the show and never misses an episode. He enjoys correcting the carpenters as they go along. He said to thank you very much."

I rolled my eyes toward heaven. "It figures."

"Oh, and he already picked out his partner. It seems he's the best of friends with his former wife, Darla Sue. Sounds like they've got that *Will and Grace* thing happening."

"I wouldn't know. I've never met Darla Sue. Though I hear she's the belle of the trailer park."

Max emitted another hollow *ha-ha-ha*. "Cheer up, Rick. They should make a nice contrast to you and Mitzi. Oh, and one more thing. Aunt Fern and Helena already drew lots for their assignments, though of course they were calling them 'Rick' and 'Other.' It seems that Terry's room will get redone by Helena, and your room will get made over by Aunt Fern."

There were several more minutes of banter, but it all went by in a haze. At some point I made cognizance of being back in my office. And as I got my bearings, there came a troubling, paranoid thought: The whole thing had been orchestrated from the start, and I was really just a dupe in the ratings sweep. My trendy Bel Air digs would get revamped by country-fried Aunt Fern, while Terry's modest clapboard cottage in the boonies would get worked over by the dangerously hip Helena. It would be the biggest thing yet on *My House, Your House.* Everyone but me was smiling. *How bad could it be?* Well, pretty much as bad as it could possibly be.

I called home to instruct the major domo to put Post-its *everywhere* in the living room saying things like: NO SHEEP, NO HOUND DOGS, NO ANIMALS, NO CREATURES, NO ZOOLATRY, NO ARTWORK, NO CRAFTS, NO JAZZING UP, NO CROCHETS, and REALLY NO CROCHETS. There was no guarantee that Aunt Fern or (I could still scarcely believe it) Terry or Darla Sue would take my not-so-subtle hints when they redid my beautiful living room however they felt like, but I figured it didn't hurt to try. Then I left my office, ignored Mitzi's titters as I walked past her cubicle, and drove to the nearest bar for a double vodka Martini.

# FOUR

I SMILED INTO THE TV CAMERA AND READ FROM THE CUE CARD. "I'm Rick Domino, reporting for the Hollywood Network," I began. "And I'm here on the set of *My House, Your House,* the do-it-yourself show that has become all the rage." I gestured appropriately at the ladders and paint cans surrounding me. "Now, this is one set I know very well. Because you see, it's my living room"—I registered the proper look of bemused puzzlement—"or at least it *used* to be my living room. But now it will be given a whole new look by the top-level design team of *My House, Your House.* I'm as excited as I am on Christmas, or Oscar night."

"And *I'm* Mitzi McGuire," proclaimed my lesser half, thrusting forth her alimony-from-my-last-husband boobs, rather like Fran introducing us all to Kukla and Ollie. Ever desperate to steal my thunder, Mitzi had elected to wear a clingy, hot pink sequinned number and a platinum, polyester wig while I was in industrial coveralls. I felt like Eddie Albert to her Eva Gabor.

"I will be going behind the scenes," Mitzi continued—though she was supposed to have said "we" instead of "I"—"to see what *really* happens when two couples trade houses for two days, and redo a room in each other's homes." She solemnly stepped ever closer into the camera, so close that you'd have thought she was a talking nose job. "Two of Rick's dearest friends will be redoing his living room, while Rick and I redo *their* room. You know, Rick, I was thrilled beyond words when you asked me to be your partner today, because I *never* miss an episode of *My House, Your House.*"

"Plus, let's not forget, Mitzi," I genially interjected, turning to face her so that she needed to step back to her marks. "We'll do it all on a budget so minuscule that—"

Mitzi stole my line. "That you know, Rick, it truly is a *miracle* that they can achieve such *awesome* designs in so short a period of time."

"Amen to that," I replied, taking *her* line, and playing right along. For I knew what was coming.

"As we all know," Mitzi brightly carried on, "do-it-yourself, or DIY, is the new drug of choice. It's *tons* safer than LSD, and us hairy-chested butch guys are just as big fans as the women are."

Mitzi, of course, was far too ditzy to improvise, and so she read the lines intended for me pell-mell. It was already a joke for me to be saying it—my being gay was not exactly the world's best-kept secret—but Mitzi's bewigged, sequined obliviousness made it an instant classic, blooper-wise. But then, no one put the T-A-C-K-Y in "tacky" quite like Mitzi.

The HNTV crew, always eager to see Mitzi get hers, broke up laughing. Mitzi pretended that she was in on the joke, and gave a playful punch to my chest—though her idea of playful would have made her a favorite with the Manson family. Probing my chest for what hurt enough to signal numerous broken ribs, I began the same spiel all over again. Temporarily humbled, Mitzi stuck to the script, and this time we nailed the innocuous little scene.

I then sauntered toward the other crew—the one from the ID Network—to participate in the actual *MHYH* episode. Mitzi trembled with confusion as she mumbled some assy New Age affirmation to herself; it was hard for her to do two things at the same time.

Actually, our shooting schedule made perfect sense. We had to get a bunch of footage of Mitzi and me at my pad for both shows, so it was logical to shoot it all at once. It was like filming a movie, where the scenes were shot out of sequence due to the locales. Next up was the usual opening scene for *My House, Your House*, in which Mitzi and I would talk about my living room and what "we" wanted to see done to it. (When the episode was edited together, our words would be interspersed with views of my "before" living room.) As we took our seats on my white silk divan in the silvery entryway, an original David Hockney pool scene hanging overhead, Mitzi could hardly wait to offer her friendly suggestions.

"I would like to see Rick's recreation room—excuse me, *living* room—imbued with an injection of elegance and taste," Mitzi confided for the benefit of the TV millions. "I am a *huge* fan of Aunt Fern, and I feel that as one of our nation's *leading* folk artists, she is *just* the designer to give the room this much-needed injection of subtlety, elegance, and taste while also bringing to it . . . well, an injection of *warmth*. I would like to see the room radiate with happiness, as if to create the impression that a kind and happy person lives here. That it is a home filled with love, and not rejection and bitterness. I think that *aging single* people so often fall into the trap of over-decorating their homes to compensate for what is lacking in their lives in so many other ways." She ever-so-sweetly patted my knee. "Now, I wouldn't suggest in a *million* years that Rick's living room reflects this negative sentiment, but just that the more . . . well, showcase-y aspects of it are perhaps leaning just a wee bit in that direction." She winked into the camera for good measure.

I patted her knee in return. "Mitzi, I really appreciate your advice, given your personal experience with injections and makeovers. And I know that you were the one to move out after your last divorce, so I suspect you've been indulging in a bit of showcasing yourself."

Mitzi subtly jabbed me with her elbow. "Well, Rick, I do *so* appreciate your kind words. I truly cannot *wait* to see what Terry and Darla Sue do to the room. I just know you must have *such* confidence in them."

And so it went.

The instant the shooting wrapped at my place, we left for Terry's bear hollow in the boondocks. The town was only an hour or so out of L.A. proper, yet it looked like something out of *The Grapes of Wrath*. "Downtown" consisted of a gas station, plus a trailer for a post office. As we drove up to a typically modest, old-movie type of house—the kind of house you could picture being along railroad tracks—I spied Terry on the small front lawn, waiting in eager anticipation to welcome us. In his denim overalls, he looked like a giant Teddy. Terry broke into a big, infectious, crinkly eyed smile as I stepped out of the car, running toward me to warmly touch my shoulder while shaking my hand.

"Thanks so much, Rick. I still can't believe that out of everyone you know, you picked *me* to exchange rooms with."

"My pleasure, Terry."

"My, my," Mitzi rudely interjected. "Rick is blushing."

"It's the heat," I quickly offered. After all, I certainly didn't want to hurt Terry's feelings by explaining that I was more than a little embarrassed to be so far out of my element—which of course was the logical explanation for my flustering.

"I'm Mitzi McGuire, and *you* must be Terry." She leaned forward in an air kiss, though Terry, not knowing about these sorts of things, took her literally, and got a mouthful of thick foundation for pecking her cheek.

"You know me pretty well, Rick," Terry elaborated, subtly wiping a million dollars' worth of makeup off his lips. "I mean, you can understand what I mean when I say I want a bedroom I can be proud of." He quickly added, "You know, something I can bring someone home to. I mean, like, if I met someone—"

"I *know* what you mean, Terry. Jesus H. Christ, give it a rest." The last thing I needed was to be held accountable for whether or not he found a partner on the basis of what I did to his room. Especially when I was going to be at the mercy of Helena Godiva's latest sadomasochistic flight of fancy. Plus, I was just plain tired of hearing his wistful longing for a partner. He was like Cinderella by the fire, singing "In My Own Little Corner."

"Jeez, Rick. You always get so snippy over nothing." Terry knitted his big, thick eyebrows in hurt; he had large eyes, a large head, and large hands and feet.

"We *all* have to make certain adjustments when we let Rick into our lives," Mitzi generously contributed.

"Ah, Rick's a good guy," Terry good-naturedly countered, playfully slapping me on the back.

After I fought to maintain my balance from the force of his friendly nudge, Terry gave us the grand tour. The house, I noticed, boasted some okay landscaping, in a hedge-and-rosebush sort of way. And Terry had built, brick by brick, a handsome barbecue pit out in back. Otherwise, there was nothing to be said about the house, including the room we'd be redesigning—Terry's bedroom, as it happened. It was a small, utterly nondescript room featuring a *single* bed with a headboard and matching bedroom set that looked like something out of a local discount furniture store commercial. The closest thing to art was the L.A. Lakers pennant on the wall. There was a generic Wal-Mart window shade and a typically overdone ceiling fan, its light fixture embellished by the silhouettes of numerous dead moths. In sum, Terry was just the man to be working on my designer living room.

"The bedroom set was a steal," Terry proudly informed us as we walked back outside. "Fifty percent off, if you can believe it."

"I believe it," I replied forthrightly.

"Gee, thanks, Rick," Terry responded, obviously missing the point. "Hey, look—here comes Darla Sue!" He pointed across the street, where a woman was emerging from a corroded pickup truck.

I had never met Terry's ex-wife, but from the way he went on about her, I expected Dolly Parton crossed with Joan of Arc. He described her as a laugh riot and great sport with aspirations to make it as a country singer. I figured she was the sort of woman who, in a different world, simply would have been his best friend rather than making the mistake of getting married to him. Terry might not have been the brightest strobe light at the disco, but he was a man of high character, and I figured anyone whom he'd been close to all his life would be made of similarly fine stuff.

The Darla Sue who now stood before me looked like she'd been rejected by the *Jerry Springer Show* for being too trashy. At some point between birth and the present moment she possibly was not actively engaged in smoking a More menthol, but from the general nicotine stench that surrounded her like a nimbus, it was difficult to imagine when such a moment might have been. I didn't think she was anorexic, because that would have suggested the presence of complex psychology; it was more like she simply was not bright enough to know she should eat once in a while. Her skin had that prematurely shriveled quality, especially around her jowls, neck and bony chin, like a deflated balloon. With bad teeth and hair like a dirty industrial mop, Darla Sue could not afford to wear a midriff with Daisy Mae cut-offs, yet that was precisely what she was doing. Apparently, she saw herself as one hot and cheesy Whopper.

"I'm Rick Domino." I forced a kind smile as I offered my hand.

"Who?" Darla Sue croaked, puffing away indifferently, like a kid in school too dumb to even know that school was for learning things.

As I took back my unshaken hand, Terry frowned with concern. "It's *Rick*, remember? We worked on the case together that got me promoted to junior detective. Rick's on TV. And he's *why* we're on the show."

"Aw, I don't watch all that smart, fancy stuff." She laughed in a cackling, self-satisfied manner, as if light-years superior to those who indulged in said smart, fancy stuff.

"What do you watch instead, reruns of *The Dukes of Hazzard*?" I inquired, trying—but barely managing—to be civil.

"Naw, that gets too deep for me." She lit a smoke with a smoke.

"Uh, Mitzi McGuire," offered my teammate, baring her capped teeth in a phony smile.

Darla Sue hawked and spat on the ground in response. I had to admit, it was a fitting way of responding to Mitzi's countenance.

"We goin' to that fancy house, Terry? The one you said had a pool and sauna and seven crappers?"

"In a *minute*, Darla Sue," he patiently replied. I imagined that Terry was embarrassed in a thousand different ways. He was embarrassed by the reality of Darla Sue, embarrassed that I knew he'd been married to her, and also embarrassed that she was the best he could come up with to be his partner. Apparently, a lot of his old cop friends, though technically "supportive," weren't exactly standing in line to hang out with him since he'd come out as gay. And as I was saying not a moment ago, he also wasn't having much luck forming a new crowd of uptown friends, since his idea of chic was bean dip with extra hot sauce.

Koko Yee approached with the *MHYH* cameraman and director. After some quick, polite introductions, Mitzi and I were filmed as we commented on Terry's bedroom—or rather, as Mitzi did, since I once again could barely get in a word edgewise.

"Terry's bedroom, like his entire home, is *utterly* charming," Mitzi explained. "It's a real *guy's* kind of place. The contrast with Rick's rather overwrought domicile frankly could *not* be more dramatic. Now, Helena is just *so* imaginative and creative, which is *why* Rick and I wanted to work with her. She is *exactly* the designer needed to give Terry's bedroom just the right bit of oomph." Mitzi's chest emphasized her point. "Terry's single and on the move, and his bedroom should be a place where he can bring back friends, bring back dates—men, women, whatever."

"Hmm," I considered. "'Men, women, whatever'—I believe that's your motto, Mitzi."

"Why, you silly bumpkin!" She smilingly pulled on my earlobe—so hard that I thought she'd rip it off.

Finally, the Big Moment came to switch keys. The genial Koko Yee stood in the middle, with Terry and Darla Sue on one side, Mitzi and me on the other. "Do you all understand the rules?" Koko posed rhetorically, as she proceeded to explain them. For *MHYH* addicts, this was the equivalent of having to hear the rules for the Academy Awards at the start of the ceremony. It only took a few seconds, but it seemed to last forever as millions champed at the bit for entry into DIY heaven. At long last, Koko instructed: "Okay, teams—switch keys!" Par for the course, we all obediently called out in unison: "My House, Your House!" as I tossed my keys to Terry, and he tossed his to me.

"Cut," called the director. "You on the end—out with the cigarette."

"Shit." Darla Sue reluctantly threw her latest More menthol to the ground and mashed it out with her Payless sandal.

"And *join in* this time," the director scolded. "You didn't even mouth the words."

"Yeah, yeah, yeah." Darla Sue stretched her smelly, skinny arms and yawned.

"My House, Your House!" We tossed the keys, only this time Mitzi couldn't resist reaching up to catch them, whereby my elbow jabbed into her right boob. Darla Sue snorted through her nose in amusement as the director called for take three.

Take twenty-seven was a wrap. By this time, the director was wearing the expression of one who could maybe, just maybe, survive for a few more seconds without a drink.

As it happened, we made *MHYH* history of sorts, in that we were the first episode to get assigned *both* carpenters, given the geographic distance between Terry's place and mine. Brick, the class clown charmer, would be working at my place, no doubt planning on spray-painting graffiti through the halls just for a good *hyuk*.

Ann-Margret would be working with my team, and sure enough, she pulled up on her Harley, enthusiastically shaking hands with Mitzi and me. "Wait till you meet Helena," she told us with a wink, bending down into her bike mirror to apply more white lipstick and purple eye shadow. "She's a trip if I've ever taken one. And believe you me, I've had a few rides around the block." She tied her tool belt to her hip-hugging black leather pants, and adjusted her skimpy halter top. "Tomorrow night we drink. Helena always picks up the tab to make up for all her diva crap during the shoot, so make sure you order something expensive." We overheard Koko laughing as she genially told the director, "It's a good thing I've got my running shoes on. I have to go back and forth between houses like a jillion times." She cheerfully patted her very pregnant belly, and launched into a goofy little dance step that was all the goofier for her condition. "Koko's a peach," Ann-Margret remarked. "A real sweetie." I couldn't tell if she was being sarcastic or sincere, but before I could find out, she squeezed my hand and strode off in her tall, high-heeled boots.

At the sight of Terry, she stopped dead in her tracks. "Oh, my God," she exclaimed, her arms held open. "It's Baby Cousin Terry!"

As Ann-Margret ran toward him, Terry recognized her and lifted her off the ground. The camera crews for both networks hurried over to start filming this spontaneous bit of high drama.

"I was saving it for a surprise," Terry told her. "I figured you'd get a kick out of it."

"God, I haven't seen you since Cousin Sheila's wedding. Did you know that she and Brad are expecting twins?"

"Did I know? I'm going to be godfather."

"Oh, and how is your mom's back? I know she saw that specialist last week."

"She's doing much better. You know Mom—she's a feisty one."

Darla Sue gave a derisive sputter; Terry had told me that Darla Sue and his mother had never gotten along. Otherwise, Darla Sue just stood there off to the side, smoking away. For a flicker of an instant, she sort of nodded at Ann-Margret with the corners of her mouth upturned.

"It would be helpful to know what's going on," I suggested, approaching the ecstatic twosome.

"Rick, I didn't want to say anything ahead of time," Terry explained, "but one reason I always watch the show is because Ann-Margret here is my mother's sister's daughter. My cousin. We're all just *so* proud of her."

"I was more or less figuring that out. But what's with the Baby Cousin Terry bit?" I didn't want to say it, but frankly it was hard to believe that Ann-Margret was older than Terry. I'm a young-as-you-feel forty, and Terry is about my age. Ann-Margret, though, looked maybe about twenty-five.

"Oh, that," Ann-Margret laughed, brushing a long wisp of bright red hair from her face. "See, I was born a lot later than my brothers and sisters."

"But until *this one* came along"—Terry gave her nose a playful pinch—"I was always the baby of the family among all the cousins." Terry, I knew, was an only child who had lost his father when he was twelve, so I guessed that his cousins and things meant a lot to him.

"So when I was growing up," Ann Margret continued, "he was always called Baby Cousin Terry."

"Sort of like Baby Huey," I commented.

"Who?" Ann-Margret asked cheerfully.

I guessed my age was showing. "Never mind."

After a few more Kodak-worthy moments, Terry left with Darla Sue for my place, where Aunt Fern awaited. (I wasn't scheduled to meet the old witch until the end of the weekend.) Ann-Margret waved good-bye to them like a cheerleader on a sugar jag, then strode off to the house, her biker chick attitude in full flourish. Seeing her with Terry, I was reminded of some of the "bad" girls back at my high school, who, at the drop of a hat, could suddenly seem as wholesome as a Nabisco vanilla wafer. Something about the fluidity of their personalities had fascinated me.

A white limo pulled up behind the massive *MHYH* trailer.

The car looked all the more imperial for being so out of place amongst all the Ford pickup trucks that dotted the neighborhood. The driver opened the back door, remembering to tip his hat; out stepped a tall, statuesque woman all in white. From the way she held her nose in the air, you'd have thought Helena Godiva was on her way to a charity fashion show instead of embarking on two vigorous days of DIY.

"La Godiva has arrived," I heard one of the *MHYH* crew members mutter, as the director rushed forward to kiss both her cheeks, in the manner of an ancient Roman whose very survival depended upon not offending Caligula. Another crew member whispered to Mitzi and me: "You guys better get over to the bedroom. Helena insists on making a star entrance." Obediently, Mitzi and I followed him toward the house.

But just as we walked past Helena, it was clear from the intensity of the voices that more was going on than DIY. I told Mitzi I'd catch up to her in a second; as she scampered off obliviously, I heard the director tell Helena, "But we have no control over Aunt Fern. Not in that way." And Helena responded, "You tell Granny Clampett to keep her Beverly Hillbilly mouth shut. You tell her if she says *one word* about this, if she even drops a single hint on camera, I'll stuff those fucking knitting needles down her throat."

# FIVE

"SO, MITZI AND RICK," HELENA BEGAN, WITH HER USUAL FROSTY, preoccupied smile, "What did you have in mind for Terry's bedroom?" She asked for our opinions with all the interest of an executioner asking a condemned man if he *really* wanted his head chopped off.

"It needs oomph," Mitzi declared, too unimaginative to resist repeating her earlier remark.

"It needs a king-sized bed," I offered. Mitzi threw her head back in a fake spasm of laughter; her dementia was such that she fancied herself a kind of Martini-dry Lauren Bacall.

Helena didn't even attempt to draw our comments into her plans. "What we'll be doing," she decreed, "is creating a bedroom worthy of L.A.'s Finest. Terry is going to have a police station bedroom. I've bought yards and yards of dark blue fabric that is exactly what LAPD uniforms are made out of, and we'll be gluing it to the walls and ceiling. Then we'll take hundreds of fake but authentic-looking police badges and fasten them to the ceiling and walls. The room will have this gorgeous contrast between the matte finish of the near-black walls and the shiny badges."

Mitzi pretended to lose her breath in excitement as she clasped her hands together. "Oh Helena, it will be like looking at the Milky Way."

"Uh-huh," Helena briefly condescended to note. "And *then* we'll be making end tables and lamps out of officer's clubs. I have blowups of FBI posters from the post office that we'll be gluing onto the closet door and dresser. We'll lift up the carpeting to reveal the stark concrete floor, which we'll spray paint with graffiti. Then we'll take down the ceiling fan—I'm sure you *know* how I feel about ceiling fans—and instead use a police siren as a light fixture. *And*—well, I was going to leave it as the big surprise, but I guess I'll tell you now—we'll be making the bed into a prison cell. I have iron bars for Ann-Margret to drill into the floor and ceiling, and we'll also have her build us a bunk bed, just like they have in jail. We'll spray-paint it to look like iron."

"Like hell we will," I replied. My outrage was such that I scarcely knew where to begin. "What makes you think a cop wants to come home and stare at blowups of scumbag criminals? And he needs a *bigger* bed, not a bunk. He's single. He lives alone. What's he going to do with an extra twin mattress?"

Helena scoffed at my protest. "What do you mean, what's he going to do? He can sleep on one bunk, and then the other. You know—variety. And if he doesn't want to look at the criminals, he can shut his eyes. It is a *bed*-room, after all."

"*I* think it all sounds marvelous," Mitzi enthused.

"And I say you can all fuck off. I won't do it."

"*Cut!*" yelled the director. "Rick, watch your language. A little disagreement with Helena is expected, but don't take the act over the top."

"Who's acting? Damn it, Terry is a good guy, and I'm not going to damage his floors and ceiling and walls. This will go no further. And I mean it."

Helena yawned, brushing my words away. "The guy already sleeps on a single bed. What's the big deal?"

"He sleeps on a single bed because he's shy and just coming out and he's sweet and just about as green as they come. He needs to get over it. And anyway, it's not just the bed, it's everything."

The director sighed. "Mr. Domino, this kind of thing has come up before. You signed a contract. You would be held liable—in fact, I suspect your network would be held liable—if you do not cooperate with the terms you agreed to cooperate with, and I'm afraid that . . ."

I walked off the set, so I never heard the rest of it, but I assumed it was more of the same crapola about how I had no choice but to compromise everything I believed in because of a certain dotted line that bore my signature. I called my attorney. I called Max Headroom. The upshot was that I had to take a deep breath, return to the set, and follow Helena's plan. I could make a suggestion, and Helena could follow it if she chose, but she could also choose not to. As my attorney pointed out, I could always offer to reimburse Terry for the expense of getting his room brought back to normal. Which I felt was the least I could do under the circumstances, even if it meant wreaking havoc on my stupid weekly allowance.

And so we filmed another take. Helena again went on and on about making the room into a bondage and discipline fun house, only this time I got all wide-eyed as I asked: "Gee, Helena, are you *sure* Terry will like it?" And Helena replied, "Rick, trust me. When it's all done, he'll *love* it."

I felt a little better when it came time to move out the furniture. On TV, this happens in sped-up motion, so it only takes a few seconds and looks easy, but in real life it's a chore. In fact, it was Mitzi's turn to pull a tantrum, because she refused to help with the moving. "I'm not some . . . some furniture mover!" she wittily hissed.

"Surely you knew this was coming," I pointed out. "Assuming that you really have watched the show before. After all, Mitzi, when in a million years have you said something less than absolutely true?"

"Afraid to break a nail?" teased Helena, her cat eyes glancing over at me for approval. I got the impression that, in a perverse way, she liked me for giving it back to her as good as she dished it out, whereas Mitzi just seemed like a silly prima donna. I smiled at Helena, and she smiled back—more warmly, I had to admit, than she came across on TV.

"My nails are indestructible," Mitzi replied with utter seriousness, as if Helena had been genuinely concerned for their well-being. "It's the principle of the thing. I won't move furniture. I just *won't!*" She stamped her ultra-high heel for emphasis.

Well, Mitzi stormed off the set, called Max Headroom, called her lawyer, and soon was back among us. She condescended to move lightweight items such as the wall pennant (which she did with a spastic mock cheerleader move), and the table lamps. But in fast motion you couldn't tell that she wasn't moving anything heavy.

"Now then," Helena commanded, "I'll get Ann-Margret to start blow-torching the prison bars while you two get busy gluing the fabric to the ceiling and walls."

Attempting so arduous a task with Mitzi was no Fourth of July picnic, to say the least. But finally, after many hissy fits on her part, we stumbled onto a routine that worked: Mitzi mastered how to brush on the glue, and, after she did so, I would smooth down a swatch of dark blue fabric. It sounds most elementary, but we worked together so poorly that it took us about two hours to get to that point of cooperation. Even the good-natured Koko, after watching us for a few minutes, grimaced and decided, "I think I'll drive over to Terry and Darla Sue."

In the meanwhile, I managed to pull Ann-Margret aside to ask her—off-camera—what Helena might have meant when she'd earlier talked about Aunt Fern not saying something or even hinting at it on TV.

Lifting up her welding mask, Ann-Margret burst out laughing. "That's just Helena being melodramatic. We're planning an on-camera baby shower for Koko. Aunt Fern is such a dear. She hates surprises. I think a relative of hers once had a heart attack being given a surprise birthday party. So she wants us to tell Koko about it in advance. But the whole idea was Helena's brainchild. She's trying to—you know—come across a wee bit nicer on TV." She nudged me with her elbow conspiratorially. "So as you can imagine, Helena doesn't much appreciate Aunt Fern sticking her finger into the pie. But don't worry. They're great pals. And Aunt Fern's a tough old gal in her way. Did you know that some crazed fan once threatened to off her if she didn't go out with him? Aunt Fern set up a mock date, called the cops, and actually asked if she could handcuff the SOB herself."

"What happened?"

"The cops let her do it. And as they led the sleazebag away, Aunt Fern lifted up her skirt and told him, 'Take a good look, Buster. You ain't getting one of these where *you're* going.' "

It wasn't exactly the biggest scandal since Liz and Dick, but I was getting the impression that on this assignment I'd have to make a meal out of nothing, gossip-wise.

"Thanks, Ann-Margret. Let me know if anything happens with the baby shower."

"Will do, Rick. Sometime I'll have to tell you *everything* about Terry when he was a kid. But I better get cracking on those billy clubs. We don't want Helena to get . . . well, you know. She's a great kid underneath it all, but she has zippo sense of humor when it comes to getting her rooms done." Ann-Margret absently tapped a club against the palm of her hand, deep in thought. "It's funny, but I watch Helena sometimes and think: Why isn't she happier than she is?" Shrugging, she laughed and added: "Anyway, back to work. Later, handsome."

An hour or so later, Ann-Margret entered the bedroom carrying an armload of billy clubs, the large holes properly—if insanely—drilled into them as ordered. "For Your Majesty's inspection," she called out merrily to Helena, who was perched atop a ladder like it was a throne. Helena's hatred of ceiling fans was practically worth a Ph.D. dissertation in behavioral psychology, and at the moment she was resolutely about to start unscrewing Terry's.

"Leave the wood with my *servants*, if you please." Helena gestured with mock grandeur at Mitzi and me. There in the same room with her, I could see she was kidding, but I already imagined millions across America taking offense at her haughtiness. Oddly enough, I found myself feeling a little sorry for her.

"Oh my God, Helena—stop!" Ann-Margret dropped the clubs in alarm, and they fell to the floor like a cacophony of bowling pins. "The power's not turned off."

Helena cupped her hands to her face. "What do you mean? I thought I'd—"

"There's only one circuit breaker per room. Since the power's still on in here, the ceiling fan's live."

"Are you *sure*? I could've sworn I turned it off." Her long, tapered fingers trembled as she clutched her pearls.

I wondered if this was a contrived little drama enacted to give the episode some punch—as well as remind all those DIY freaks watching to always put safety first, and blah-blah-blah. But both women swore it was spontaneous.

On camera, they made light of it all. "I saved your life," Ann-Margret mock-bragged, while Helena made a tentative gesture with her hand. "Well, maybe a little."

But off camera, I saw Helena in the garage, weeping as she hugged Ann-Margret in gratitude. "It's like *everything* is out to get me," Helena wailed. "I ask so little out of life, and all it does is tell me no. No matter how many rooms I do, I can't get rid of this feeling."

It was a vulnerable side of Helena that the public never got to see. Ann-Margret held her and soothingly whispered, "Let it go, sweetie. Just forget it."

"I get these dreams, you know? I'm trying to paint a room, and this man just keeps beating me and beating me."

"Sounds horrible. But it's only a *dream*, honey. And you have everything to live for."

Helena forced herself to smile. "You're right. I was just being silly."


Meanwhile, Aunt Fern was having a regular barn dance with Terry and Darla Sue.

Of course, I didn't know at the time what was going on, but when I later saw the tape, I learned that what happened was approximately the following:

Aunt Fern arrived in one of her plump, matronly polka-dot dresses— though she wore it with Nikes and white socks. In a homey touch, she first took notice not of the room itself, but of my deplorable black cat, Dasher.

Just as there are some criminals so bad they really should never be let out of prison, Dasher had done much to convince me that certain animals in the pound do not deserve to be rescued. I'd brought him home as part of a fundraiser for animal shelters, and he'd been nothing but trouble ever since. While still a kitten, his antics had had a certain *Rebel Without a Cause* panache. But over the years he'd graduated into a sleazo hardened thug, reminiscent of Joe Pesci in *GoodFellas*. I should never have granted him parole.

"My, what have we here?" Aunt Fern enthused, stooping down to make kitty-kitty sounds. Predictably enough, Dasher utterly ignored her. Not content to let His Majesty be, she saw fit to lift him up to her ample lap. Dasher meowed loudly with indignation. "I never met a kitty that I didn't just love to oodles." Aunt Fern lifted her plump hand to pet him, but before she could do so, he spat at her.

"Such a spirited kitty," Aunt Fern pronounced, as Dasher jumped free—hissing for good measure.

One could only hope Aunt Fern would be more successful at making friends with my living room. As Darla Sue and Terry filed in, I could tell that Aunt Fern was like a bean pot ready to boil over with ideas.

"My, this is already such a lovely room," she commented modestly. "I don't know that there's much of anything I can do to make it better, but I'll give it my honest injun best. Now then, children—tell your Aunt Fern what you'd like to see us accomplish in here."

She passed around a canister of homemade peanut brittle. Terry got wide-eyed as a child as he helped himself to a generous block, but Darla Sue chose to ignore it, and instead added another stick of nicotine gum to what was already a walnut-sized wad in her mouth.

As he crunched away on the savory treat, Terry searched for the right words. "Rick's room is very . . ."

"Full of itself," contributed Darla Sue, cracking her gum. "It's like, where's the TV? Where can you put your feet up and chill? It's like there's *chairs* and things, but who'd want to sit on any of them?"

As if latching onto her comments for want of knowing what else to do, Terry added, "Yeah, and what about beer? With all this expensive stuff in the room, you'd think he could have a small fridge to keep beer in." As he gestured with his hand, he almost knocked over one of my Armani lamps.

"And [censored word]," interjected Darla Sue, "most of this junk looks like [censored] I can get at Goodwill." She pointed ruefully at my Kennith Edwards antler table. "And *this*," she continued, looking sadly at my original Lichtenstein. "I mean, the funny pages on the wall? If you have like art stuff, it should be pretty. Trees and flowers, or those cute little kids with big eyes. What were they called again—Smurfs?"

"There's no recliner!" Terry cried. "What's a living room without a La-Z-Boy?"

Aunt Fern laughed jollily. "My, you certainly do have a lot of ideas. I can see we're going to be very, *very* busy these next two days. I think many of your ideas are good as gummy bears. A room *should* look lived in. And especially a living room should have that real 'howdy neighbor' feeling. Now, we'll keep things pretty much in the same place in the room, but we'll jazz it all up. We'll get that big strong Brick to help us put some stuffing and upholstery on the chairs to make them nice and comfy. I found the most wonderful thing to use for stuffing—baby-sized alphabet macaroni. You won't *believe* how soft it feels when you've got bags and bags of it. We'll take down *all* the artwork and make our own. Now, don't be shy if you've never made art before. I have a paint-by-numbers pattern that will be easy as chocolate cream pie to follow. It's a wall-sized mural of chickens in a coop, with a rooster wearing glasses, who's writing something with one of his tail feathers. Get it? Rick is a famous writer. And we'll paint the walls a nice warm color called margarine yellow, and add on a cow bell stencil in pink and baby blue." She lowered her voice to a stage whisper. "That's to symbolize that very modern kind of androgyny that I think Rick admires." Then, departing from her brief detour into the Unmentionables, she continued with her usual twinkle: "We *can* add a small refrigerator, which we'll cover with some crochet that I brought along. Plus some crochet on the swizzle stick holder. And Brick can turn one of those abstract-looking chairs into a recliner, which we'll cover with this gingham-and-fencepost fabric that I just love—that will be for *you*, Terry. And some pretty flounces on the windows held together with those corn-on-the-cob-shaped prongs that you use to eat corn on the cob. Plus lots of crocheted animal throw pillows, and a patchwork carpet on the floor." She rather touchingly clasped her hands together in glee. "And let's say for good measure we *do* move in a TV from one of the other rooms."

"It's going to be beautiful," predicted Darla Sue.

"Sounds okay," Terry agreed, "okay" being guy talk for "splendidly magnificent."

Aunt Fern started taking down all the strategically placed Post-its. "Oh, wasn't Rick just the sweetest thing to tell us not to make a big fuss? But we'll show him that we don't mind a little good old-fashioned hard work. Not when we're doing our bodacious best to give him a beautiful new living room."

"You know, Aunt Fern," Terry proudly declared. "Ann-Margret Wochinsky is my cousin." He said this like a kid in school who thought he'd done something to deserve an A.

"Well, don't we all just live in the coziest little world?" She affectionately patted his wrist. "Family is the most important thing of all, isn't it? Now then, children—to work! And remember, let's not spoil our appetites with too much peanut brittle!"

The entire discourse was enough to make me die a thousand deaths. But I didn't know exactly what was being done at the time. I assumed the worst—and would hardly be disappointed—but I mostly was concentrating on Terry's room. In a way, I was reminded of Alec Guiness in *The Bridge on the River Kwai*, a prisoner of war who gets so into building a bridge for the enemy that he loses sight of the bigger picture. I didn't want to be doing all this to Terry's bedroom, but since I had no choice, I was determined to be finished by the following afternoon and to do as good a job as possible.

Besides, as much as I hated to admit it, I had warmed up to Helena. We understood each other as fellow snobs who mean well underneath it all. I got the impression that she was uncomfortable when meeting people for the first time—especially on camera—and as so often happens, her shyness came across as superiority or diffidence. The room itself truly was looking . . . well, *different*, in a way that reflected real vision and style. I still didn't think it was right for Terry, but maybe he'd at least appreciate the effort. At one point, Helena actually asked my opinion about whether to put an extra gloss of varnish on the end tables made of police clubs. I told her that we should put it on the top half of the clubs only, and she warmly patted my hand and told me, "What a smashing idea."

I looked forward to interviewing Helena over our lunch break and was disappointed when I was told she'd be busy. In fact, diva that she was, Helena did not return right after lunch, leaving Mitzi and me to keep gluing on our own. When she finally did arrive about an hour late, she was moody and distant. I greeted her, but she did not even answer. The director had to prompt her to comment on the "great job" we were doing, and when

I asked her a question about the police badges her initial response was: "What badges?" A brief scene with Koko over how long it was going to take to fasten on the badges took several takes, because Helena simply couldn't concentrate.

It was hardly the first time I had encountered mood swings in a celebrity. In fact, I wondered right off the top if maybe she was on something—or had gone *off* something, as the case might have been. But I was disappointed that the progress toward friendliness we'd made over the morning had apparently come to naught.

Late in the afternoon, she absentmindedly dropped a slip of paper, and when I picked it up to hand it to her, she didn't thank me. That little slip of paper somehow struck me as the essence of Helena. It had THINGS TO DO TODAY printed across the top, with an arch cartoon of a harried cat. Her penmanship was *perfect*; her handwriting almost looked like typesetting. She'd written KOKO in big letters—presumably referring to the impending baby shower—and then underneath I read, "5' × 7½' tablecloth, M&Ms (blue and beige ONLY), food—let caterer do," and "Dr. M"—which was neatly crossed out, but then she'd carefully written OK next to it. I found it amusing that she would fuss over the exact size of the tablecloth or the color of the M&Ms to be served, and then leave the real food totally up to the caterer. Whoever "Dr. M" was, even her indecision over him or her reflected Helena's determinedly orderly way of doing things, as though her life were actually chaos but she didn't want anyone to know.

At the end of the day, Helena gave us her characteristically enormous amount of homework to do. We had to fasten all the police badges to the walls and ceiling, plus pull up the wall-to-wall carpet, scrub the concrete floor underneath, and then spray-paint it with graffiti. If you'd told me in advance that I'd cooperate with doing all this, I'd have said you were nuts, but I set myself to all my tasks like a good Boy Scout.

Needless to say, Mitzi was impossible the entire evening, but after a while I just ignored her tears and bitchery and kept us on task. None of the homework time ever appears in the *MHYH* episode, but the HNTV camera guy and his assistant stuck around in case there was anything worth using for the behind-the-scenes documentary. They resisted the temptation to help out, which would have been cheating. But I was grateful that they were there, since being alone with Mitzi was hardly my highest aspiration in life. At about four in the morning, the walls and floors were finally done. Needless to say, everyone was ready to collapse. Terry's one bedroom was of course not fit for sleeping in, but there was the living room sofa plus some room here and there on the floor. Us guys chivalrously gave Mitzi the sofa and stretched out on the floor with sleeping bags. It wasn't comfortable by any means, but we were all so zombied out with exhaustion, it didn't matter.

Bright and early at seven A.M., Ann-Margret tapped me on the shoulder and whispered, "Rick, I need you."

I always wake up fast. Even in an unfamiliar setting, I instantly get my bearings. "Did the fabric come loose?" I sat up and stretched, the adrenaline of the apparent crisis making up for my lack of sleep.

"No, it's something else. Please, get dressed and come with me."

Moments later, we both put on helmets as she revved up her Harley. I climbed on the back and clutched Ann-Margret's waist, feeling like the sex toy of a dominatrix as she sped off.

"By the way, do you mind telling me where we're going?" I shouted at her.

"You're obviously competent, Rick," Ann-Margret shouted back. "And, despite the impression you try to create, a nice guy. Cousin Terry thinks you're the greatest. So I figured better you than the other dudes hanging around." We glided around a hairpin corner. "And certainly better you than Mitzi."

"Did that stalker finally catch up to Aunt Fern?"

"Don't even joke about such a thing."

In only about another minute, we stopped in front of a motel. "Helena and I crashed here rather than drive back home," Ann-Margret explained as we dismounted. "It gives us a nice early start, plus the show picks up the tab." I followed her along the row of motel rooms.

"Here it is, Helena's room. Sleeping Beauty has done it again."

"Done what again?"

"Had a princess of a night, to say the least." When I registered puzzlement, Ann-Margret added, "She got ploughed. Plastered. Get it? Now I can't wake her up. I didn't want to get the motel manager. I figured he'd spread it all over town." She frowned as she knocked on the door, then banged on it.

"So instead you figured you could trust a gossip columnist?"

"Perverse as it sounds, yes. I could tell that you *like* Helena. You understand what makes her tick. I don't think you'll rat her out."

I looked at Ann-Margret shrewdly. "Plus, you figured that telling me first, and flattering me with your confidence, was better than having me figure it out on my own. In which case I might just, as you say, rat her out."

Ann-Margret dimpled. "You give me an awful lot of credit, Rick Domino. Actually, I just figured you'd know how to nurse a hangover."

I laughed. "Somehow, I get the impression it's not the first time this has happened."

"No comment, Mr. Reporter." Irritated by now, she banged on the door with all her might. "C'mon, Rick. Help out a little."

I banged away at the door with Ann-Margret, pounding with my fists and the sole of my work boots. As she joined in with her spike-heeled boots, we both started laughing. Somehow, we brought out the mischievous kid in each other.

"After I get a good's night sleep, let's go dancing," I told her.

"It's a deal," she replied. "We'll divvy up the hot guys between us."

Finally, the door flung open.

"Okay, Miss Thang," Ann-Margret cheerfully scolded. "Time to—"

Her scream gave way to a deluge of tears. Helena's dead body swung from the ceiling fan like the tongue of a clanging bell. Bolts of bright gold material were tightly entwined around her torso, and as the sudden morning sun shone in on it, the reflected light in the room made it seem eerily festive. There was a hideous translucent coating over Helena's face that looked like some sort of sealant or glaze. It was as if it wasn't her real body, but a wax museum likeness. But of course it was her real body, and clearly, this was neither an accident nor a suicide—someone had murdered her.

# SIX

AS ANN-MARGRET SCREAMED WITH HYSTERIA, RAGE AND GRIEF, I
put my finger in my ear and called 911. Then I led us back outside, discreetly closing the door. I held her in a Cary Grant sort of way while she
softly whimpered. A couple of motel guests looked outside to see what the
commotion was; I waved at them and smiled that everything was fine.

A couple of ragtag, local cops arrived—in separate cars—to cut down
the body. I got the impression there was no love lost between them. One
guy had orders to drive the corpse now if not sooner to the LAPD crime
lab for an autopsy. But the other cop had conflicting orders to deliver the
body to the local station. After some intense phone calls, I got the impression that L.A.—big surprise—had won out. The corpse would be sent over
to a bona-fide crime lab, while the local peace officers would content themselves with chasing skunks off Main Street. From what little else I could
gather, the cause of death was not immediately known.

Soon the L.A. cops appeared—replete with sirens, ambulance, and
motorcade, as if to show these local yokels how it was done. The big city
pros swiftly loaded up the corpse, told everyone to stay in their rooms—
nobody did—and pulled Ann-Margret and me aside to question us sepa-
rately. My complex history with the LAPD compelled them to treat me
with kid gloves and then some. Besides which, I hadn't much to say. I
barely knew Helena, and there were witnesses aplenty as to my whereabouts the night before. But poor Ann-Margret was in a neat little jam. She
knew Helena very well indeed—and was apparently the last person to see

her alive. Moreover, her own motel room was across the parking lot, so she couldn't say she heard anyone going in or out of Helena's room. She couldn't point the finger elsewhere. The cops didn't arrest her on the spot, but they made it clear that her leaving town would be about as wise a move as spray-painting without a face mask.

I hadn't heard much of Ann-Margret's story at this point. Yet unless she was the world's greatest actress, she couldn't possibly have had anything to do with Helena's murder.

"She was my *friend*, for fucking crying out loud." She wiped the tears from her face as I led her across the dusty parking lot—which by now had crowded up with cops, motel guests in their bathrobes, and curious locals. I noticed she had freckles underneath her heavy foundation. "Can't they give me five seconds before . . . Oh Rick, they think I did it, don't they?"

"What exactly did you tell them?" I replied, skirting the issue.

"The *truth*. Ever hear of it before?"

"Once or twice. But if we get out of here alive, I'd enjoy the chance to get reacquainted with the concept."

"I just wish I could talk to Baby Cousin Terry. He'd know what to tell me. Damn that fucking contract."

She was of course referring to the fact that by contract none of us could have any contact with the people working on the other house. Even in the case of an emergency, the most we could do was use an intermediary. Obviously, though, the present circumstances signaled an exception, to put it mildly.

"Uh, somehow I don't think the show will go on," I told her as gently as possible. Clearly, the poor kid was in such a state of shock she wasn't thinking logically. I mean, imagine continuing with the taping after a *murder*. I could just imagine Koko cheerfully saying something like: "Meanwhile, the gang at Terry's house is in a real bind. How will they finish in time when Helena croaked?" But then again, maybe Ann-Margret was just clinging to her everyday routine for some semblance of sanity.

"Maybe it's best not to do anything just yet," I suggested. "Or if you *do* talk to someone, make it a lawyer."

"Gotcha." She sadly rubbed my arm. "Still, I wish Terry were here. He'd know just what to do. He *is* a junior detective, you know."

47

"I can tell you're very proud of him."

The nitwit desk clerk—one of those guys who at twenty had the mental agility of a grandfather in the last throes of Alzheimer's—managed to saunter over. He took the toothpick out of both his teeth long enough to ask, "Everything okay here?"

"Ducky," I assured him. "One of your guests has been murdered."

"Well, if that ain't somethin'." He looked over my shoulder toward the motel room where all the commotion was.

"The cops are already on it," I assured him.

"Okay, then." He spat on the ground, and managed to elbow his way back to his office. It was a pity that video cameras couldn't have recorded his swift and caring response as a testament to the professionalism of the establishment he managed.

Not much time had elapsed between my calling the police and being questioned by them, but it was time enough for reporters to arrive at the crime scene. In fact, like a sudden hailstorm, reporters were everywhere, their cars, vans, and trucks jamming up the already crowded parking lot as if it were Oscar night or the O.J. trial. I had no idea how the story got leaked, but once it had, it made no difference. I knew that Ann-Margret's life would never be the same.

Max Headroom called me on my cell phone to tell me that legally-shmegally I was to say *nothing* on the air about finding the body, and in fact they were sending some other network whore over to cover the story at the motel. He told me to hang tight for further instructions.

I'd barely hung up when he called me back.

"I have, well . . . *interesting* news, Rick. We're going to continue with the taping."

Unexpected tragedy hits people in funny ways. Helena's bizarre murder hadn't really sunk in for me yet, but being told that we were going to keep filming the episode made me feel like I'd been kicked in the stomach.

"Tell me, Max, that you didn't just say that."

"Now, don't get all bent out of shape," Max offered in his unaffected monotone. "It makes perfect sense, if you think about it. The cops would just as soon have everyone in one place. And the ID folks feel it's a fitting tribute to Helena. She would want the room to be finished. They'll be sending in another designer to supervise. Be reserved, hardworking, respectful. I'm sure we can count on you, Rick, to maintain the proper decorum."

I moved away from the clamor to hear better. "And I suppose the fact that the ratings will go through the roof never entered into it. Damn it, Max, the woman's been murdered. Can't we just—"

"Rick, I've already told you what's happening. Now, if the press asks you anything, tell them all to watch our own upcoming tribute to Helena. That'll give us a good plug. I'll call Mitzi and the camera crew. All you have to do is—"

"Fuck you, Max." I turned off my phone.

Sometimes I truly hated my line of work, and this was one of them.

I put my arm around Ann-Margret's shoulder and led her through the pack of reporters. "Ms. Wochinsky is devastated," I told them on her behalf. "Please give her some space." After all, I couldn't very well say "No comment," or "Away with you, you pack of locusts," given that I was one of them. In my way, I try not to be hypocritical. So I gave them just enough to chew on while still protecting Ann-Margret.

"I can't believe it, but we have to go back to work," I muttered under my breath, as we mounted her Harley. "It's just as well," she whispered back, drying the last of her tears to rev up the engine. "Just give me a circular saw to chase away the blues." I couldn't tell if she was being sincere or sardonic. "By the way, I think I'll take you up on your suggestion about the lawyer bit."

"Sounds good to me."

A caravan of press cars lined up behind us, but we pretended not to notice as we motored back to Terry's house. We headed there not out of corporate loyalty, but because we honestly couldn't think of where else to go. Being filmed against your will for the benefit of millions can make you a little indecisive.

At a red light, I murmured, "Talk about feeling like you're in a goldfish bowl."

Ann-Margret reached over to squeeze my hand. "My bike used to make me feel free. I wonder if it ever will again."

We pulled into Terry's garage, and swiftly closed the door behind us. "We'll have to get all the work done in here," Ann-Margret affirmed as we dismounted. "No way am I letting those reporters film me in the backyard like some sort of zoo hyena."

The *MHYH* director and crew came forward for a long, silent group hug with Ann-Margret. I felt awkward and out of place, so I went inside to Terry's kitchen. The HNTV camera guy and his assistant nodded at me with unspoken understanding, while Mitzi approached with sweepingly open arms, like we were long-lost siblings on a talk show. She frowned as much as her last shot of Botox permitted.

"Oh, my Rick, what are we to do?" She drew me close to her hard, plastic breast. "Such a *loss*, to the design world as well as on a personal level."

"Cut the crap, Mitzi." I pulled away, never more repulsed by her phoniness. "You know nothing about design, you barely knew Helena, and you wouldn't know how to like someone if your life depended on it, which unfortunately has never been the case. Do what you have to do to convince America that your wig is in mourning, or whatever it is you're trying to prove. Tell it to the vodka bottle or call boy or shrink or whatever you do to get through another day in your pathetic life. But leave me out of it."

For someone supposedly devastated, it didn't take much for Mitzi to shift gears. "*Fine*, Rick," she replied, in a voice so icy it would have chilled a chocolate mousse. "I was only trying to show my concern." Her cell phone rang; she cleared her throat before answering, in order to achieve the proper grieving tone. "Yes?" she answered softly. "Oh right, yes. Uh-huh, *Terrific*." Grinning from incision to incision, Mitzi could hardly wait to tell me the good news. "That was my agent. I'm to write an *exclusive* piece for *Us* magazine entitled 'Helena's Final Day.' It might get picked up for syndication." She punched numbers into her phone. "I *have* to call Max to tell him the good news."

As Mitzi twittered off to wheel and deal, Ann-Margret came into the kitchen and poured herself a cup of coffee. "I heard the whole thing," she informed me, smiling with a gentle sorrow. Though the shades were pulled down, a phantom ray of morning light brought out the subtle gold in her red hair. I noticed she had repaired her makeup. "Helena would've liked you just now."

I got myself a black coffee and practically inhaled it. My mighty ten seconds of sleep the night before were catching up with me. "Thanks."

Swallowing back a fresh wave of tears, she stirred three packets of Cremora and four packets of NutraSweet into her coffee. "We all loved Helena. Hard as it might be to believe, she was a *real* person. The white dress and all that other stuff was just to draw attention. She and I did the girl-talk thing whenever we were in the same location for the show."

"Did you always get soused?"

She shrugged wryly. "We weren't teetotalers. Helena is—I mean, *was* such a controlled, disciplined person. She used to joke that it was her English sense of order coming out—her grandparents, I think it was, came to the United States from England. So she liked knowing she could kick back every now and then. But last night was different. She really outdid herself. She just kept on pouring Scotch into this ugly little motel drinking glass, smiling to herself, but looking really worried about something."

"I assume you asked her if anything was wrong?"

Ann-Margret stared into her steaming mug of coffee. "Once. That's how Helena was. You didn't push the issue with her. She insisted everything was fine, and I let it go at that."

"And you're *sure* she said nothing else important?"

"Well, it's possible I missed something, since I was feeling no pain myself. But she pretty much just carried on about the baby shower. She ordered a tablecloth. She left a voice message with the caterer. Also with Koko's obstetrician, a woman named Dr. Mallory, I think. I know Koko liked her doctor a lot, so Helena figured she'd invite her. And something about a custom order of M&Ms. All those fussy, silly details that now seem so—" She quietly sobbed. "Maybe if I'd . . . well, I guess I'll never know."

Right to the end, I thought to myself, Helena resolutely checked off each item on her list of things to do. And what did any of it matter now?

I resisted the urge to grab the remaining pot of coffee and drink it down in one gulp, and settled for a polite second cup. "What about when she left the power on in Terry's bedroom? Was that staged?"

"Not at all. You know, crazy as it sounds, I'd practically forgotten about that. It seems like it happened a hundred years ago. But as I think of it, she was pretty out of it all day long, wasn't she?"

There was a package of stale-looking mini-donuts on the counter, such as you would buy at a 7-Eleven. I gave in to the urge to eat one; when you're hungry enough, food is food.

"Actually, Helena seemed much more out of it after lunch. Though I assumed it was her normal personality to be a little out of it."

"No, never. Helena was always extremely *present*." She looked toward the window in thought. "But yesterday, the way she kept spacing out on the set, or at the motel, going through that stupid list of things to do, almost like it was her last will and testament. Like she—" She put her hand to her face, as if shocked by her own words.

"Like she knew she was going to die?"

Ann-Margret turned around to face me. "It's probably just my imagination running wild. The thing of it was, Helena was a pretty hard read. She was kind to the people she let in, but she never really opened up much about herself. So you couldn't help but wonder about her."

"And this is what you told the police?"

"More or less. I think they think I'm hiding something, though."

"Are you?"

She drank her pale, sweet coffee and considered the question. "What could there possibly be to hide?"

A weighty question to say the least, but I wouldn't get an answer to it anytime soon.

"I need to get to work," Ann-Margret informed me. "We all do. God, poor Aunt Fern. She's always awake all night after the first day working on a new room—a nervous wreck, but she hides it so well. She'll make a huge production out of finding just the right fabric, then panic at the last minute and drive around all night trying to replace it. And now, to have to hear about this . . . I just wish I could be with her. She must be bouncing off the walls."

"Remember, those are *my* walls," I couldn't resist quipping. "Let's hope she doesn't make a mess of them." Though of course this actually was not a joke at all.

"Rick, you're incorrigible." She managed a faint smile. "But you have nothing to worry about. As you well know, the finished product is always superb."

Actually, the finished product often stank to high heaven, but I didn't think it tactful to say as much. "You're right," I amiably agreed. "I have nothing to fear but my social status."

"Oh, *you*." She gave me a half-hearted nudge.

I ate another stale little donut. "Do you think Helena was killed in her sleep?"

Ann-Margret sighed deeply. "Helena was *very* drunk by the time I left. Common sense would say she passed out at some point. On the other hand, she could be a real insomniac herself during a shooting. We all are, actually. On TV, you see us going merrily on our way to leave the couples doing their homework. But we're all pretty nervous about screwing up. We look over our plans for the millionth time, we wonder what to do if something or another doesn't turn out right. So it's hard to say."

She was right about one thing, however—it was time to roll up our sleeves. The police would be questioning everyone, but they still didn't even know the cause of death, and for now our priority was to finish the room.

Since the producers couldn't trust us lowly workers to get the job done on our own, Shirtless Bill McCoy had generously volunteered—or been recruited—to oversee our efforts. He was the logical replacement, given that his style was nearly as outrageous as Helena's had been.

Bill looked about the same in person as he did on TV, only he was wearing a white shirt and tie instead of his customary T-shirt, I presumed out of respect for Helena. When I stepped forward to shake his hand, he drew me toward him in a sort of half-hug. "It's nice to meet you, Rick, but I wish it could've been under nicer circumstances." He seemed to mean it. In fact, the more we talked, Bill struck me as a much nicer guy in person than the uppity persona he adopted on TV. But then, who could say what was an act and what was real? I'd known him for all of five minutes.

For the benefit of the TV cameras, Bill sat on the floor of the bedroom with Mitzi and me to go over the plans for the room. "I love what Helena has done," he told us. "But she always believed that a designer had to be true to his or her vision, so I think she would approve when I say that we're going to make a couple of changes."

With a grim flourish, as if he were a submarine commander pulling out his war orders, Bill showed us his drawings. "Instead of blown-up photos of the Ten Most Wanted, I thought Terry might like pictures of famous law enforcement heroes, like Elliott Ness and Wyatt Earp. And instead of a mock prison, I thought Terry might like a bed that was made to look like a police car. Then I thought, why not take the concept up a notch, and make his bed into a Batmobile?"

Sure enough, Bill had designed an MDF frame with cool shiny fins and a headboard made to resemble the masked face of Batman.

I had to hand it to Bill. Terry would definitely have preferred to have pics of heroes instead of villains staring at him in bed each night. Indeed, I ventured that anyone would have, save for the criminally insane. And if the Batmobile wasn't exactly making me turn green with envy for not having one in my own bedroom, at least the design called for a full-size mattress. Terry was, after all, a simple kind of guy, and maybe he'd think it was cool in its theme park way. In any case, the pervading sentiment was a British sort of let's-just-get-to-work-and-not-make-a-fuss. So I wasn't about to protest. Yet though I approved of the changes, I wasn't sure of Bill's motive—was it the worst kind of egotism, or was it a sincere gesture aimed at trying to make the best possible room?

In general, I was getting the impression that interior designers could be every bit as enigmatic as movie stars. Supposedly, my gaydar is second to none, yet I honestly couldn't tell if Bill was straight or gay or bi or even none of the above.

Koko Yee came in to see how we were holding up. Her red eyes indicated that she'd been crying hard. "Before you guys get going," she told us, "I just wanted the world to know how much Helena meant to me. So let's do the best job we can, for Helena." Clutching her pregnant belly, she sobbed on camera. "I'm sorry," she managed to sputter, before leaving the room with an understated dignity.

And so we got to work. Any time there was a question or a problem, it was handled with a decided lack of hysteria. Shirtless Bill most solemnly kept his shirt on. The constant subtext was that we were doing it for Helena. Of course, we were also semi-destroying someone's bedroom, but in the moment, our actions felt noble enough to be worthy of *Mrs. Miniver*.

---

Meanwhile—as I would later learn—over at my place, Aunt Fern was conducting her own memorial service of sorts with Terry and Darla Sue. I already knew from the director that Aunt Fern bawled like a baby upon hearing the news, and even said she didn't think she could continue. But trouper that she was, she pulled herself together.

Of course, Terry and Darla Sue had never met Helena. But I knew that as a cop, Terry didn't much cotton to murder. Moreover, as a junior detective whose true passion was working on homicides—and who was stuck doing penny ante stuff like busting illegal fireworks dealers—he no doubt was champing at the bit to get a piece of the action. But besides not having seniority, he was related to Ann-Margret. They probably would've told him his objectivity would be compromised if he were assigned the case. And speaking of Ann-Margret, Terry knew enough about how murder investigations unfold to probably already be nervous about her well-being. I was certain that only his firm sense of sticking to the rules prevented him from calling to see how she was.

But Terry was used to disappointment on the job, as well as conquering it through perseverance. The tape I later watched showed him being a predictably good sport when it came to finishing my living room. Aunt Fern started the day off by asking Terry and Darla Sue and Brick to join hands for a moment of silence in honor of Helena—though the silence was quickly interrupted by Aunt Fern's own eager prayer for Helena's soul. "Please, Lord," she beseeched with closed eyes. "Accept thy daughter Helena into thy Kingdom. Watch over her and let thine light shine upon her always. This we ask of you, Lord. Amen."

Darla Sue was silent and respectful throughout. Whatever her limitations, she'd been a cop's wife for years, and no doubt had a very basic idea of right and wrong underneath the smoke cloud.

They all worked on my living room with the same subdued dedication as we adopted while working on Terry's bedroom. Again, you got the impression that they felt they were doing more than just redesigning a room.

Dasher, needless to say, could be counted on to destroy the mood. To cheer things up, the irrepressible Brick set the feline loose in the room. Aunt Fern was not about to admit she'd been defeated when it came to making friends with an animal, so she welcomed him with open arms.

"Oh, kitty, you're back again to say hello," she warmly commented. As if knowing exactly what he was doing, Dasher headed straight for the largest piece of crochet in the room—the refrigerator cover—and demolished it with his claws in nothing flat. Utterly pleased with himself, he crinkled up his eyes with pleasure while luxuriantly wetting his paws to clean his own regal face. Terry was the one person Dasher (sort of) took to, and he actually kind of rubbed himself against him for a moment or two.

"Oh, you can't help but love Dasher," Aunt Fern decreed. "Even if he is just one naughty little kitty." As Dasher marched off, beaming with pride, Aunt Fern and her crew continued with the important task before them, doing their very best to get it all done in time. She even had another piece of crochet for the refrigerator. (It was my impression that she carried a reserve supply with her everywhere.) There was a minor crisis about a bolt of fabric not showing up—as Ann-Margret predicted, Aunt Fern had made a last-minute switch—but show up it did, and they all managed to hammer and sew away. Terry even took a turn at the sewing machine, and helped to whip up my new yellow gingham throw pillows, to complement the margarine-colored walls and various animal patterns that Aunt Fern had made.

The day seemed to stretch on forever, but finally, it was time to finish up. I guess there's nothing like a brutal murder to keep people on a DIY show in line.

Mitzi and I were driven to my house, where I would see my finished room. Koko Yee guided us into the living room with our eyes closed. "Okay," she announced, with less pizzazz than usual, "open your eyes."

"I'm too nervous," Mitzi informed us. "I just can't." It wasn't even her house, for God's sake, but she couldn't resist a chance to steal the show.

Well, I opened *my* eyes to see what looked like the set of a Walton's reunion TV movie. Looking back, I'd say that in its way, it was very well done. My designer chairs indeed had been made to look like something out of an old Sears, Roebuck catalog. The walls truly took on the look of Country Crock spread, as planned. The paint was evenly applied, and the cowbell stenciling was executed with virtually no mistakes. The paint-by-numbers mural was all that one would expect of its genre. The patchwork carpet looked like it would hold together pretty well, completely covering up my parquet floors and the mother-of-pearl inlay. The recliner actually worked, and was indeed conveniently located in terms of the beer refrigerator and the TV. The corn-on-the-cob window treatments were enough to make you reach for the nearest bib. And, of course, Aunt Fern certainly did know how to crochet. There was crochet, crochet everywhere. As always, she kept things in the same spot, so I didn't have to worry about tripping over something unfamiliar in the middle of the night. Moreover, they had done it all for a thousand dollars, and in two days.

But then and there my heart sank down to my feet. The room looked like it had been designed by Ma Kettle. I felt like I was back in my horrific hometown in Iowa, and, needless to say, that was not number one on my list of preferred sensations.

"It's beautiful," I pronounced, as Darla Sue knowingly nudged Terry, who breathed a contented sigh of relief. Aunt Fern cried a little as she gave me a hug. "Bless you, child," she murmured. "Enjoy your new room. And *live*."

We then drove over to Terry's place.

Koko did her usual open-your-eyes bit, and Darla Sue yelped with joy while Terry literally wept. "It's so great," he proclaimed. "I love it. I'm not changing anything." He looked around the room in awe, gazing at the fabric walls and concrete, graffiti'd floor as if he'd stumbled into King Tut's tomb. "It's . . . well, it's a bedroom I can be proud of."

His response was as sincere as mine had been fake, but both were convincingly appropriate to the moment. Terry gave me a huge hug and muttered, "Thank you, buddy." In fact, he hugged everyone. Koko Yee said her usual good-bye into the camera, though us couples did not smile and wave as was the norm, but just sort of solemnly stood there. The designers and carpenters stepped forward to join us—which also was not the usual procedure—and Koko asked us to all join hands. "For Helena," she simply declared, and we all joined in to repeat, "For Helena." Holding hands with Mitzi was not my idea of a good time, yet even as such I was alarmed to feel her middle finger pointedly rubbing a subliminal message against my palm.

And so it was done.

Not more than thirty seconds after the director yelled "Cut," the police stepped forward to arrest Ann-Margret Wochinsky for the murder of Helena Godiva.

# SEVEN

IN THE HARRIED MOMENTS FOLLOWING ANN-MARGRET'S ARREST, Terry pulled me aside. "You know what we have to do, don't you?"

It was all that needed to be said. "Let's do it," I affirmed.

Solving the murder would be the scoop of the year, and there were worse fates to befall a reporter. Plus, I knew that Terry could help me figure out where to dig.

But more important, my guts were practically screaming at me that Ann-Margret was no murderer. And I don't just mean out of loyalty to Terry, who would of course have wanted to believe his cousin didn't do it. It made no sense that Ann-Margret would save Helena from electrocution only to bump her off a few hours later. In a devil's advocate way, I supposed it was possible that the ceiling fan episode was staged by Ann-Margret just to throw everyone off her scent. But in that case, why not let Helena fry right then and there? Surely it left fewer possible clues than the elaborate display in the motel room. I also had to ask myself if maybe something had happened between the afternoon and the wee hours to make Ann-Margret do a total about-face and suddenly hate Helena's guts so badly that she killed her. But Ann-Margret wasn't at all upset when she got me to go to the motel room—not even in a telltale, nervous sort of way. Her tears and rage upon finding the body were utterly genuine.

I personally knew the jolly experience of being falsely accused of a crime, and now I had the chance to help someone else it was happening to.

And if it *did* turn out that sweet little Ann-Margret was guilty as all get-out . . . then I'd still have a story to tell.

As for Terry, it was just as I'd suspected. He'd all but offered to put out for a chance to get officially assigned the case. And as I'd also guessed, he'd been turned down.

But Terry wasn't taking no for an answer. Any chance that he'd patiently wait for the next case to prove his mettle died the moment he saw those handcuffs placed on Ann-Margret's trembling wrists.

I'd use my reporter's sense of smell to track down the killer, but I'd need to do it on the QT. I'd have to be low key at work for a while, taking as much time off as possible. Fortunately, it was a reruns week, so I didn't have to film a new weekly show—although this wasn't all that fortuitous, since there'd been an alarmingly high number of reruns that season. (Max Headroom had this strange fetish for so-called "necessary budget adjustments." Saying he was a cheapskate would be like saying that Julia Roberts quite possibly had teeth.)

And so, for not the first time in my life, I found myself waiting in my Jeep Cherokee outside LAPD headquarters. Given Terry's status as a junior detective, he was able to contrive a reason to be at police headquarters and in a by-the-way manner learn what he could about Helena's death and Ann-Margret's subsequent arrest. While I waited for Terry to tell me what his fellow officers told him, I gazed out at the ton of TV and newspaper reporters clamoring outside the front doors. On my own, I would have been clamoring beside them, but Terry, as an officer, could go in and out through a special side entrance. He might not have been the King of Style, but if you wanted to solve a murder, it never hurt to have him as a friend.

"C'mon, Rick." Terry tapped at my window.

I followed him toward the police station. I barely had a moment to notice that it was one of those rare, fresh-smelling nights in L.A., in which a tinge of ocean breeze seemed to mingle with some sort of invisible honeysuckle in the air. Yet the vivid image of Helena swinging from the ceiling fan made it all seem pointless, like a beautiful perfume sprayed over a graveyard.

"Are we going to see Ann-Margret?"

Terry yawned. "Not exactly. But there's someone else who wants to talk to us."

"And you're keeping it a surprise? Terry, you're such a tease."

"Look, it's Aunt Fern, okay? She's here to see Ann-Margret, too. She's been trying to bribe the desk sergeant into letting her in with a jar of her homemade rosemary jelly."

"Must be pretty mean jelly if she thinks she can make some stupid cop—" I stopped myself. "Sorry, I forgot."

"No sweat, Rick. Believe me, in these instances I share some of your frustration. As for Aunt Fern, I like her a lot, but we need to be careful. She's a real gossip. A busybody if I ever saw one. And not like you, Rick. She doesn't know when to keep her trap shut."

In a charitable mood, I decided to take his remark as a compliment. "I know what you mean. Let's not tell her much."

Terry started to open the glass front door, then paused. "I know Ann-Margret could never have done this in a million years. But they must have *something* on her other than that she was the last one to see Helena alive."

"Well, if all we do is stand here by the door, we'll never find out, will we?"

"Rick, you're really a smartass sometimes." He opened the door. "Say, wasn't there some movie star named Ann-Margret? I think she starred in that movie about the chauffeur."

One of Terry's least endearing traits was his total obliviousness to movies and showbiz. On those rare occasions when you'd force him to watch a movie, he'd forget the title or who was in it almost immediately. Then he'd drop some obscure clue like "that movie about the chauffeur," and you had to play Twenty Questions to figure out what he meant.

This time, though, I already knew what he meant, based on a previous conversation.

"No, that wasn't Ann-Margret, that was Jessica Tandy. And the movie was called *Driving Miss Daisy*."

"Oh, right. I knew it was one of those people."

The ammonia smell of the police station hit me hard as we stepped unnoticed down the busy corridor. Seated on a bench at the far end of the reception area, Aunt Fern tearfully held out her hands to us as if she had just lost her husband and we were her sons. I got the impression that it was but an added bonus that I was a gossip columnist and Terry was a cop; we could've both been ditch diggers and she would have reacted to us just the same. As far as Aunt Fern was concerned, we existed to *help*.

"Oh boys, isn't this just the most dreadful thing?" She clasped our hands ever more tightly for support. "Now they tell me I can't even see the sweet girl. And it is all so *wrong*. Why, if Ann-Margret murdered Helena, I am Playmate of the Year."

"I see your point," I offered, ignoring Terry's frown at my apparent impertinence. Aunt Fern, though, was on a mission and not about to be derailed.

"I'm right in assuming that this is why you're here, am I not? You boys know as well as I do that she's innocent."

"What makes you so sure she didn't do it?" Terry asked, sidestepping her question.

"What a thing to say about your own cousin." She slapped his hand. "She's a *good* girl. A little wild, maybe, but nothing that marriage and babies won't cure. Did you know she spends every Thanksgiving cooking at a homeless shelter?"

"Aunt Fern, please don't misunderstand me. I know she didn't do it," Terry countered. "But I'm also a police officer, and I'm trying to tell you how police have to think about these things. I'm afraid her being a 'good girl' isn't much of a defense. The police know from experience that in a moment of weakness, or anger—"

"But they were *friends*." She took a frilly handkerchief from her purse to dab her nose. "It's all just too ridiculous. You worked with Ann-Margret, Rick. Now you tell me—do you think she could have done this?"

"The police must have evidence," I replied judiciously. "Even if it's only circumstantial."

Some sort of screaming junkie pimp was led right by us, the handcuffs he wore doing little to convince one that he didn't pose a threat to society.

"The poor young man." Aunt Fern shook her head sadly. "But you still haven't answered my question, Rick. Do you believe in your heart-of-heart-of-hearts that our lovely Ann-Margret could have done such a horrible thing?"

"No. But I also believe that she's hiding something."

"Well then, what are we waiting for?" Aunt Fern stood up spiritedly, pulling on her polka-dot dress for its static cling. "You're a police officer, Terry. Why don't you start acting like one? Get us to her cell so we can find out what the poor frightened child is hiding."

Terry laughed in spite of himself. "It's not that simple, Aunt Fern. You can't just—"

He was interrupted by the sudden clamor at the entryway. The chief investigator for the case, a woman lieutenant in full uniform, strode importantly down the hall to a podium on the front steps. We could tell that a press conference was about to begin. The three of us got up to scoot over to the glass doors in order to hear.

"I am here with you this evening to report the coroner's findings in the murder of Helena Godiva," the lieutenant began. Talk about a catchy opening. Flashbulbs popped and TV cameras whirred, but she remained square-jawed and resolute.

"A credit to lesbians everywhere." I nudged Terry, who pretended not to hear me.

"It is the coroner's finding that Ms. Godiva died at approximately four o'clock this morning. The cause of death was suffocation caused by forcefully holding Ms. Godiva's head in what must have been a large vat of a substance identified as an acrylic primer."

There was instant pandemonium among the press. The lieutenant ordered everyone to clam up, and she was so forcefully bulldyke-ish about the whole thing that even the pushiest of reporters instantly obeyed.

"In a post-mortem state, she then was wrapped in wads of material and hung from the ceiling fan of her motel room."

A million reporters asked questions all at once. Out of the mishmash, the lieutenant managed a response: "As you know, we have arrested Ms. Ann-Margret Wochinsky for the murder of Ms. Godiva. That is all I am at liberty to say at this time."

There was another wave of shouting voices, but the lieutenant was having none of it. She stepped away from the podium. As an afterthought, she zigzagged over to smile sideways and thank the reporters for their time, and then forthrightly strode inside.

For a minute or so, the three of us just stood there in silence. A ludicrous thought occurred to me, and was possibly occurring to millions of other people as well: The bizarre cause of death, the fabric her body was wrapped in, and the way she was hung from the ceiling fan all signaled that Helena had been murdered because somebody out there *really* didn't like her designs. It seemed ridiculous. And yet in a world in which people got murdered over a pair of sunglasses, it was possible that Helena was murdered because of her theme rooms. Dead is dead, yet I found myself hoping that this wasn't true. That at least she was murdered over something more important. Then I reminded myself that even if Helena made Leona Helmsley look like Mother Teresa, she didn't deserve to be murdered, because nobody does.

"I must say, I don't like that lieutenant one bit," Aunt Fern finally stated, in the manner of someone finding the nearest target on which to vent her myriad feelings. "She's too sure of herself. I find that an unattractive quality."

"I know her a little, and she's by the book," Terry stated in the lieutenant's defense. "She would never take any sort of premature action."

"*Exactly,*" Aunt Fern concurred, totally misunderstanding Terry's point. "Well, we'll see if she and her glorified hoodlums are sitting quite so pretty when we find the real killer." She looked up at Terry and me for assurance. "You boys will be cracking the case, won't you?"

"Aunt Fern, if Terry and I do any snooping around—and I'm not promising we will—we have to go where it leads us. And if what we come up with points to Ann-Margret, well then, even Terry, though he's her cousin . . ."

"I know what you're doing, Rick, and I respect that. You need to be professional, and jitterbug-whoopty-do. But what I'm saying is that none of the evidence *will* point to Ann-Margret, and you already know perfectly well that it won't. Look, I'm not a rich woman, but if you'd like, I'll redecorate your entire home free of charge."

A coughing spasm came over me. "That's perfectly all right, Aunt Fern. You don't have to pay us anything. We'll go digging around as a matter of course. And if Ann-Margret really is innocent, then so much the better."

"From what I've gathered, she'll probably make bail tomorrow," Terry added helpfully. "So the best thing to do, Aunt Fern, is to go home and get a good night's rest. Pray for her, too. Never hurts."

"You boys are so sweet." She drew us toward her in a hug. "You remind me so much of my son, Leo. Now, be brave but be careful. It's a good way to stay alive. And you let your Aunt Fern know if she can help."

"She kind of reminds me of my grandmother," Terry commented as we watched her leave the station.

"Speaking of which—what gives with Darla Sue?"

Terry frowned in confusion. "What does Darla Sue have to do with Aunt Fern?"

"You know what I mean. Your ideas about women are baffling, to say the least. You told me that Darla Sue was this sweet, funny woman whom I'd take to like a fly to dog shit."

He looked genuinely hurt and puzzled. "You mean you don't *like* her, Rick?"

"'Like' is not even the point. Terry, maybe it's none of my business, but how did you stay married all those years to . . . well, to *that*? I know you said there wasn't much physical between you, but my God. Gay, straight, whatever, the idea of touching her at all is just—"

"Is just what? Not up to your snooty Hollywood standards? Look Rick, I want to work on this case with you, and I even like you, but if this is what you have to say about Darla Sue, I insist that you drop it. As in, right now."

"But Terry, she's so—"

"I mean it, Rick. I will not tolerate anyone saying bad things about Darla Sue." Terry the Teddy Bear suddenly looked more like a pissed off Grizzly Adams. It was one of the few times I felt intimidated by the force of his anger, even as it simmered just below the surface. I guess we all have our blind spots, and evidently Darla Sue was one of Terry's.

"Okay, okay, I'll drop it."

"Good. Now then, let's follow our own advice and get out of here. I should call my mom and her sister, to tell them everything's okay."

"But what about Ann-Margret?"

"They're taking okay care of her. And she *will* make bail tomorrow, I'm sure of it." He led the way back outside.

"But what if we still can't get to her?"

"I don't think that will be a problem. I got a note sent over to her that she should meet us at your place in the afternoon. I'm pretty sure she'll want to, seeing as how she'll be needing all the friends she can get."

"Terry, I have to say that if you're not a genius, you're not special ed material, either." I got into the driver's side of the Cherokee and turned on the ignition.

"Gee, thanks." He looked down at his watch. "It's Sunday night. Any chance of you taking me out to a club to meet someone? Hopefully not one of those pickup joints, but a nice place where people go to make friends."

"Terry, how many millions of times do I have to tell you that—" He looked so hopeful and vulnerable that I couldn't refuse him. "Okay, sure. We'll go out someplace. I know you like to dance, so the night won't be a total waste."

"Cool!" His face lit up with a thousand-watt smile. "Listen, Rick— please promise me you won't just go home with the first sleazebag who asks you. I . . . well, I worry about you."

"Yes, mother." I drove us back toward Wiltshire.

"I mean it, Rick. You deserve much better than what you let yourself have."

I chose to ignore him, and turned on the radio for news about the murder. It was all just a rehash of the press conference, but I listened just in case. After about a decade's worth of commercials, a song came on—Steve and Eydie's version of "Dancing Queen." "Just what we've all been waiting to hear," I remarked sardonically, changing the station. But Terry was having none of it. "Wait, Rick. I think I like this song." I sighed and let the dynamic duo do their Catskill thing.

Terry started singing along, though it was yet another of his quirks to never know the real words to a song. And so at the refrain he pleaded: "You want to dance with me . . ." He had a rather nice tenor voice, such as you might hear in a policemen's barbershop quartet; I encouraged him at one point to audition for the gay men's chorus, but Terry claimed he suffered from stage fright.

"Actually, it's not the original version," I politely noted.

"Are you *sure*? How can you tell?"

I couldn't bring myself to answer. Where would I have even begun?

Terry put his hands behind his head and closed his eyes. "Maybe someday soon, Rick, you and I will get married."

"I beg your pardon?" I damn near lost control of the wheel at the shock of what he'd said.

"Oh, not to each other, bud. But maybe we could have one of those joint ceremonies."

"Sounds delish."

"Don't be like that, Rick. You're always so cynical." He snapped his fingers to the urgent Steve and Eydie beat.

"I'm just . . . I'm just not you, Terry."

The deejay came on the air. "This just in: Ann-Margret Wochinsky has escaped from her holding cell at L.A. Police Headquarters. Yes, you have heard correctly. We expect to hear official confirmation at any moment that the suspect arrested in the slaying of Helena Godiva has escaped to whereabouts unknown. Please stay tuned for information as to—"

"So much for dancing our way to wedded bliss. What should we do, Terry?"

"I guess go to your place. Just in case she shows up, or sends word or something."

# EIGHT

I TACTFULLY TRIED TO STEER CLEAR OF MY LIVING ROOM, TELLING Terry that I didn't want to spoil my pleasure in it by associating it too much with all this murder stuff. But Terry encouraged me to get past all that and to appreciate the beauty of the room at this time of turmoil and upheaval. I poured myself a *tall* glass of single-malt Scotch, and—at Terry's insistence—leaned back into my new recliner. I had to admit it was comfortable. Perched on my new pasta-filled sofa, Terry told me that to get the full effect, we should turn on the TV—which, thoughtfully enough, had a long cable attached to it, so I could watch all kinds of channels. "Oh boy, *D.A. McCoy*," Terry enthused, after a moment of channel surfing with the remote. Translation: it was an episode of *Law and Order*. But Terry had his own funny names for things. Helping himself to a Budweiser from the fridge, he informed me: "I like the older episodes of *D.A. McCoy*, too. Before he was on the show."

I decided to let that one slide—I had my mental health to consider. All through our police station interlude, he'd worn the stylish black leather jacket I'd picked out for him, so I'd forgotten that he was still wearing overalls. Given the country décor of the room, he made me think we were at a hoedown. "Mind if I put my feet up?" Terry asked eagerly, as if to drive home the fact that my new and improved living room was a place of comfort.

"Not at all." What did I care if he got scuff marks on my new Chiquita Banana crate coffee table?

"Great." As an afterthought, he took off his size fourteen work boots and socks. Watching Terry wiggle his thick toes, I realized that I had achieved a complete Appalachian ambiance in my living room. And without even trying.

I thought about Ann-Margret's escape. Though I didn't understand why she did it, I figured she must have looked pretty cool sneaking her way out, in a kitten-with-a-whip sort of way. She was probably in her prison threads, but I pictured her in spike heels and black leather, giving a strategically placed karate kick to some dim-witted guard. I didn't condone breaking the law, yet I couldn't help smiling.

I was starting to doze. The recliner—and the Scotch—was making it easy to do so. I told myself that Terry's nonstop babble about the *Law and Order* episode—"You tell 'em, McCoy," and so forth—was just so much white noise.


The doorbell made me sit up with a start.

Terry was snoring on the sofa, several empty Budweiser beer cans surrounding him. I roused him awake, and repaired to the front door.

No one was there.

The bell rang again, and I realized it was coming from the back door.

A moment later, I opened my abstract-themed wrought iron back door to Ann-Margret, out of breath and a bit the worse for wear, but full of energy. She had changed back into her civilian biker-babe attire. Her skin responded strongly to the weather, and she seemed to carry in with her the coolness of the night air, which mingled with her powerful perfume.

Oddly, standing next to her was none other than Aunt Fern.

"What the . . . but how did you . . . ?"

"I climbed your security wall," Ann-Margret explained. "Then I opened the gate for Aunt Fern."

Making a mental note to get a better security system first thing in the morning, I hurried them both into the living room.

Ann-Margret ran to Terry's arms. Aunt Fern joined her—on purpose, I thought, to keep Terry from saying anything too extreme. Glad as he was to see his cousin alive, to an equal measure he was distressed that she would break out of jail. And simple guys like Terry often don't deal well with having two or more emotions at once.

Ann-Margret walked over to the rooster mural. "Hey, great job. Tell me how you did it." She stepped away from the colorful wall with a discerning squint, as though this were purely a social visit.

"Oh, it was easier than Matthew, Mark, and Luke," Aunt Fern modestly insisted.

"We started with a paint-by-numbers," Terry elaborated. "Then to create a distressed look, we gave it a thin coat of white and beige paint, which we sponged on, and then wiped with a *dry* sponge in order to—"

"Enough about the room," I interrupted, hoping the displeasure in my voice didn't give away how I really felt about it. Even under less pressing circumstances, I hardly would have wished to dwell on how its many wondrous effects had been achieved.

"You're right, Rick. Sorry, I just got carried away."

"Oh, DIY can be quite habit forming," Aunt Fern sympathetically enthused. "Take it from one who knows." She sat herself down in one of the plump country chairs. "Now then, boys. Please say you'll help us."

"Unfortunately, the answer has to be no," Terry sensibly replied. It was encouraging to see that his lapse into Roosterville had subsided. "Obviously, I have no choice but to arrest you both and call for backup. Ann-Margret, I hope you know how much I don't want to do this. But it's for your own good, believe me."

"I'm so sorry, Baby Cousin Terry." Ann-Margret lowered her head in shame.

Terry looked more than a little angry. I was sure he resented being placed in such an awkward predicament. But there was an air of familiarity to his ire, as though he was long accustomed to feeling put upon by family members.

"I'll give you *one minute* to explain," he reluctantly added.

Ann-Margret started to speak, but Aunt Fern cut her off. "It's all my doing, dear. I might as well own up to it. After I said goodnight to you boys, I'm afraid I did a very naughty thing. I snuck back inside. This time, I took out the Bible from my purse—I always carry the Good Book with me, you know. I told this guard and that one that I was there to spread the word of the Lord. I've volunteered at many a prison to teach crochet, so I happened to know that there were always people giving Bible lessons to inmates. So they let me in. Once I got to Ann-Margret's cell, I saw that she was talking to her lawyer. A *vile* man, I must say."

"Now, Aunt Fern, he's very good." Ann-Margret reached into her pocket for a business card. "Have you heard of him, Rick?"

I looked at the unfamiliar name. "No, I'm afraid I haven't."

"I hired him earlier in the day, when you told me to lawyer up. He was highly recommended by Bill. Anyway, my lawyer dude had bummer news. He said the D.A.'s office would *not* be recommending bail, even though they earlier claimed they would. It had something to do with the heinous nature of the crime."

"Isn't that just the most dreadful thing you ever heard in your life?" Aunt Fern shook her head and shuddered. "The idea of this poor child spending days, weeks, months in jail. I just couldn't let it happen."

Terry and I spoke at the same time: "But Aunt Fern—" I let Terry finish the thought.

"That's just a tactic, Aunt Fern," he explained. "The D.A. was instructed not to show Ann-Margret favoritism. That's when Ann-Margret's lawyer would argue in *favor* of bail. Since Ann-Margret has no priors, the judge will probably grant it just the same. Or at least the judge *would* have, before the defendant presented a flight risk. You do both realize that Ann-Margret now faces additional charges, even if found not guilty of murder?"

"Then they can put me in jail instead, since I'm the one who started it," Aunt Fern gallantly offered. Ann-Margret reached over to pat her hand.

"It doesn't work that way," Terry told them. "You're both going to be in trouble for it. But anyway, you still haven't told us how you escaped."

Distant headlights winding up the steep road below shot a beam of light through the curtains. Both women shuddered, then realized it was nothing.

"Well, that hot-shot do-nothing attorney left," Aunt Fern conveyed. "No doubt to go home to his gold-plated yacht. Then, to make matters worse, this awful prison guard was making wolf's eyes at Ann-Margret. I feared for her safety more than ever. The poor girl was crying on my shoulder. Then I got my idea. I asked the guard to let us go down the hall for what we all call a lady's day." She winked for emphasis. "You know—to a dispenser. So the guard unlocked the door. I then asked him, 'Would you be a dear and look here in my purse for my glasses? I just can't find them.' The guard stepped inside, and lickety-split, I grabbed Ann-Margret, and locked the horrible man in the cell. This dear young thing protested that I shouldn't get myself in trouble, but I was having none of it. Especially when the guard . . . well, let us just say that he used language I would not repeat as to what he was going to do to both of us. Then I *knew* there was no turning back."

"I was just plain terrified," Ann-Margret explained. "So much was happening at once."

"So we took off down the corridor," Aunt Fern continued. "There was an exit door. We opened it, which set off an alarm. But my car was parked close by. Ann-Margret got down in the backseat. A very polite and handsome young police officer stopped me as I started to drive off, but I convinced him I knew nothing. My Bible on the dashboard didn't hurt matters any, not only as a source of inspiration, but—you know—as a way of making me look legit."

The crazy thing was, Aunt Fern seemed to have no idea what a difficult feat she'd just pulled off. You'd have thought she'd been describing how she'd talked a salesperson into giving her the discount price on floor tiles when the sale was already over.

"And so you drove here?" I asked, not knowing what else to say.

"Of course, silly," Aunt Fern scolded. "How else do you think we got here—by sprouting wings? Honestly, Rick. You have no more sense than a doodlebug."

For a minute or so, no one said anything. Aunt Fern and Ann-Margret seemed to be hoping against hope that we would tell them there was some magical solution to it all, while Terry and I simply were wondering how to handle things without being too cruel about it.

"The judge should take all the factors into account," Terry finally offered. "But as a police officer, I still have no choice but to tell you both that you're under arrest." In his bare feet, he padded over to his black leather jacket for a pair of handcuffs. "I always carry a spare set, just in case." Walking toward the reluctant fugitive, he sighed deeply and announced: "Ann-Margret Wochinsky, you are under arrest for escaping from state custody. You have the right to remain silent—"

All at once, the power in the room went dead. Before he could cuff her, Ann-Margret slithered free of Terry's grip. In pitch blackness, I heard Aunt Fern cry out, "Sorry, boys," and the sound of rapid scuffling about. (I also heard a most distinctive meow and hiss, followed by the sensation of cat claws on my leg.) The living room had been the only room with the lights turned on, so the whole house was in darkness. By the time I got to the circuit breakers and turned the lights back on, the two women had disappeared. A handmade hassock had been overturned, and was leaking a bit of alphabet pasta, which Dasher pawed contentedly. Terry and I listened in vain as we heard a car speeding off.

"Damn it, she knew about the fuse box behind the Jasper Johns," I complained, shooing the cat away to set the hassock upright. "Or at least where the Jasper Johns used to be before you guys made that . . . *lovely* MDF puddle duck."

"The old gal's got a mean karate chop," Terry added, rubbing and flexing his wrist. "I can't believe they got away from me, but they did."

"Maybe you *let* them get away. Maybe you just didn't want to harm an old lady out of respect. Not to mention that you'd rather not have Ann-Margret left alone with that total slime bucket guard. So you subconsciously—"

"Rick, I do my job, and do it to the best of my ability." Terry looked at me sternly, yet I could have sworn I saw a slight grin at the corners of his mouth.

"Anyway, I have to report what happened. Jesus, I don't even know what kind of car Aunt Fern drives, do you?"

"Nope."

He took out his cell phone, then paused. "Say, what's this?" He reached down and picked up a folded piece of paper. "It's a note." Opening it up, he read it out loud:

*Dear Terry and Rick,*

    *I am writing fast and furious in the back seat of Aunt Fern's car, in anticipation of possibly having to make a quick getaway.*

We are hoping that you'll be able to help us, but if not, Aunt Fern agreed that it was good to set down what I have to say.

My attorney has told me that they found my fingerprints on some discarded containers of acrylic primer, along with a big stirring pot, that were lying in a dumpster not far from Terry's house. Then they found traces of primer on my hands. As you know, Rick, I helped to prime the Batmobile, but that answer was not good enough for them.

They also found my diary, and there was a recent entry that said something about how I could kill Helena for stealing Bill McCoy away from me. Well, as I explained to them, this was all just a joke. It was only about some friendly trip to the movies. I invited Bill to go with me, but he'd already promised to have dinner with Helena. I swear that is all there was to it. The problem was, they gave me a polygraph, and it seems that I failed an important question. According to the machine, I am in love with Bill. (No comment, okay?) According to my lawyer, they found other "inconsistencies," but he won't tell me what that means. He said the less I know, the better. I guess I was just so nervous, they didn't know how to read the answers. But since there was the one supposedly important lie, they must have decided not to give me the benefit of the doubt.

The final trumped-up piece of evidence is that the motel clerk says he heard shouting coming from Helena's room, and that one of the voices was mine. Sure, Helena and I were kind of whooping it up for a while, laughing and singing along to her CD player, but that was about it. The guy must have an overactive imagination.

Anyway, that's what I have to say for now.

Aunt Fern and I both know full well that Cousin Terry might have to do what he has to do, and Aunt Fern wants me to emphasize that she bears neither of you any bad feelings. But she hopes you also understand that we needed to escape.

Lots of love,
Ann-Margret Wochinsky

*PS: Aunt Fern says you think I am holding something back.*
*Believe me when I say I am not.*

"Not much of a case," Terry commented upon finishing the note. "Maybe they're just playing mind games. They're assuming that she *is* holding back, and they can scare her into cracking."

"If that's true, then she's blown it royally. She's made herself look as guilty as Son of Sam."

"I need to find out what these inconsistencies were in the polygraph. I'll ask around." Terry folded the note and stuck it in his jacket. "Boy, poor Aunt Fern. I just hope they don't get roughed up before being brought into custody. She is *way* out of her league."

I nudged him good-naturedly. "Though apparently not out of *our* league, huh? I mean, she did manage to outsmart you, officer."

The glower in Terry's dark eyes told me not to keep going there, but I couldn't resist. "What are you going to say? That an old lady whipped your butt?"

"If this is a ploy to get me to not report them, it won't work. I'm reporting everything. Including the note."

Terry dialed the police. As he was being connected, a news flash came on the TV: Aunt Fern had turned herself in at a gas station for her role in helping with the breakout. She said she'd sent Ann-Margret on her way, and claimed to have no idea where she was.

# NINE

TERRY HUNG UP THE PHONE, AND WE DROVE BACK TO POLICE headquarters.

But it was déjà vu all over again. Predictably enough, Terry was told it was too late to see Aunt Fern. However, Aunt Fern herself called Terry on his cell phone to say that she would stay up all night so that none of the guards went near her, so he wasn't to worry. Almost as an afterthought, she asked him to find her a *good, decent, hardworking* lawyer, not like that shyster who was robbing Ann-Margret blind. Terry told her that as a police officer he'd best not get involved but he'd be happy to refer the matter to me. I'd had my share of bad luck with lawyers, but through Biff Holden I'd met a rising young attorney named Boxer Jones who seemed on the level. He also emitted a powerful gay vibe, which gave his sharp, irregular features a veneer of sexiness. Boxer had the sort of face that would have been considered homely on a woman, yet passed for virile and handsome on a man. His well-shaped shaved head signaled a masculine premature baldness, and his pecs went on for days.

Unfortunately, I had to call Biff to get Boxer's home number. I was barraged with several minutes of hysteria on Biff's part over my being on *MHYH*. He actually said he was sorry he'd broken up with me (!) because he missed his chance to be on the show. He didn't even mention that Helena had been murdered, but that was Biff for you.

Ultimately, I got the friggin' phone number. After playing matchmaker for Aunt Fern and Boxer, I was ready to call it a night. Also, Terry was anxious to get home to his new bedroom—though he added that he wasn't going to sleep well with Aunt Fern in jail.

"Did I tell you, Rick, that she reminds me a lot of my grandmother?"

"Did I tell you, Terry, that you have an extremely irritating habit of repeating yourself?" After all, it was at least the billionth time in the last twenty-four hours that he had told me this. Maybe it's just the business I'm in, but I have this total-recall memory for who said what when. I've never understood it when someone confides something seemingly important, and then ten seconds later can't remember having done so.

"Jeez, Rick. There's always gotta be something for you to pounce on."

If there's a ever a time I wish I weren't gay, it's when men pull that moody, hurtful, stone-cold silence routine that there's just no getting past. Terry was pulling it now, as we drove back to my place in mummy-like silence. Of course, Terry and I were hardly a couple, yet just being around him when he got that way was enough to remind me of any number of failed relationships.

"See you tomorrow," Terry managed to mutter as he climbed into his ratty old pickup truck to go home.

"Fuck you," I genially replied, shooting him the finger for good measure.

First thing in the morning, Terry called in a personal leave day. I, in turn, canceled my interview with a sitcom second banana trying for a comeback in a promising new series about a talking ferret, as well as my usual Monday appointments with my shrink and my pedicurist. Terry swung by my place, and after I nibbled on an almond–white chocolate croissant and Terry consumed several jelly donuts, we arrived at the courthouse for Aunt Fern's arraignment. Picketers carried signs that read things like: FREE AUNT FERN and DON'T PUNISH THE NICE. After elbowing our way through the crowd, we sat in rapt attention at the arraignment.

With Boxer at her side, Aunt Fern listened as the charges against her were read: obstruction of justice and aiding and abetting a fugitive. In a louder voice than she seemed to realize, she muttered to Boxer: "Fancy-schmancy stuff, huh?" When asked how she pleaded, she replied, "You got me, judge. I am one guilty old gal." She started to say something else, but Boxer, as her attorney, literally placed his hand over her mouth. He spoke about how Aunt Fern had always been a model citizen, and it was but motherly concern for Ann-Margret that caused her to commit what he called an heroic act of sacrifice.

Boxer's speech—not to mention Aunt Fern herself—would've made life tough for any prosecutor. But when I realized the Assistant D.A. handling the case was one Marion Goober, I knew that Aunt Fern was home free. Following a period of suspension related to a case a while back involving *moi*, it appeared that Mr. Goober was back on the job, ready to trip over his dick all over again. Marion Goober was so devoid of anything approaching humanity or a personality that he made Max Headroom seem warm blooded by comparison. Young Mr. Goober looked like a bleached earthworm, a living and breathing blank.

He also was a smarmy, sloppy, underhanded skunk of a lawyer.

"Yo, Marion," I called out in a loud whisper, unable to resist tormenting him. Normally, I wasn't the kind of person who said "yo," but Marion Goober brought out the rebellious punk in me. He turned around, and as I waved at him and smiled, his anemic face paled to a kind of ultra-white. Hissily, he feigned an absorption in his paperwork, and turned back around.

Not about to risk getting stoned to death by an angry mob, Marion Goober was happy to let Aunt Fern off with a fine and community service, provided that she immediately report any knowledge of Ann-Margret's whereabouts. Talking with his hands in his pockets in a bad imitation of Gary Cooper, he tried to make it sound like he was a nice guy who loved dear old Aunt Fern as much as everyone else. The judge agreed to the terms, and the filled-to-capacity courtroom erupted in applause.

On the way out, Aunt Fern turned to Terry and me and muttered, "We'll be in touch, boys," in the style of someone who'd seen too many spy movies. The strong, handsome Boxer surprised me by touching my shoulder. "Call me sometime, Rick," he encouraged with a wink. "And thanks for the new client."

On the courthouse steps, Aunt Fern eagerly met with the press. She emphasized Ann-Margret's innocence, then turned things over to Boxer when the questions became what she called "too technical."

In spite of all the high drama, I felt a bit giddy. "Well, it just goes to show that not everything in this rotten world goes badly."

"The system is just," Terry affirmed. "Jail is no place for Aunt Fern."

"Who said anything about Aunt Fern? I meant Boxer, you dope. It looks like yours truly has a date."

"A *date*? I guess that's one word for it." We stepped outside into the glaring morning sun of downtown L.A.

"Meaning what?"

"Meaning that Boxer strikes me as a guy with real values. I doubt very much that he'll be nearly as casual about . . . well, certain things."

"And by 'certain things,' I assume you mean the dreaded S-word?" I impatiently pushed the Walk button at the corner of Temple and Spring. "And by that I don't mean 'sushi.' Just because I don't require light-years of acquaintanceship before compromising my virtue doesn't mean I'm the whore of Babylon."

"No, you're just the whore of West Hollywood." Terry chuckled, quite pleased with his little witticism.

"Look, I've lived with a number of different guys. That's more than you can say."

He intuitively held out a restraining arm when a car illegally sped round the corner. "You live with guys the same way you pick up tricks. I can't explain it—something serious and mature is missing. That's why you always end up—"

"Look, drop it, okay? You say you became a cop because you wanted to help people. But you're off duty, officer. You can't write me a ticket for picking the wrong men."

My cell phone rang. "Who the fuck is it?" I heard myself shout upon answering.

"Why Rick," scolded the lilting voice at the other end, "you have no more manners than a moose. It's Curtsy Ann Thomas. You know—from *My House, Your House*. You *are* coming to the memorial service today for Helena, I assume?"

"Uh, sure." Actually, I hadn't heard of it before, but it sounded like a good place to be.

"Oh, Rick, isn't it all just too awful? And now, poor, poor Aunt Fern . . . They certainly never taught us in design school that it would be like this. You try to do what you can to make things better for your fellow man, and so you pick out your fabrics and paints and go about your business, and then something like this just ruins everything." Her bitter wailing reflected her keen perception of the tragedy at hand.

"Can I help you in some way, Curtsy Ann?" I softly asked after a discreet interval.

"I . . . I wanted to talk to you. About the Helena that I knew."

"I understand. You're hoping that by sharing your feelings, you'll feel better." It might sound crazy, but in a mixed-up town like Hollywood, some people actually took me for a shrink or father confessor. They'd cry and hug me when it was over, and then be outraged when I went public with what they gave me to go public with.

"I'm hoping for an *exclusive*," she answered curtly. "What did you think—I wanted a warm fuzzy moment?"

"I can see how devastated you are."

"Oh, I *am*, Rick. But if a single girl doesn't look out for herself, who in this wide, wide world will? I *know* it's what Helena would have wanted."

"You're right, I can practically hear her spirit cooing approval. Okay, then. An exclusive. Right after the memorial."

And so Terry and I readied ourselves for the deeply moving tribute to Helena that was about to transpire. In our dark suits and L.A. shades, we looked like the Blues Brothers.

I have to say that memorials and I have never gotten along. Supposedly they're for the deceased, yet I've never been to one that wasn't more about the people left behind. And the misbegotten service for Helena would hardly break the mold.

Helena's memorial was held at Forest Lawn in Glendale, where you can visit the crypts of all sorts of major and minor stars. To outsiders, it probably sounds psycho to have a cemetery with a museum, automated guided tours, and a gift shop. But Forest Lawn, in its bizarre way, was a normal part of the entertainment industry. It was horrifically tasteless, and yet all sorts of people with perfectly good taste chose to rest in peace within its glittery pastures. Being at Forest Lawn made you believe that even in heaven there was a Hollywood.

The ceremony took place beneath the massive shadow of the scale replica of Michelangelo's *David*. No doubt a handful of the several thousand gawkers were there that morning to see the patriotic museum exhibit on American Presidents, but most had come to pay tribute to Helena Godiva. To say that many of the mourners were gay men was like saying that there were a lot of bras at Victoria's Secret. Peddlers were selling shadowbox replicas of Helena's most famous creations, such as the body piercing room and the swanlike Björk room. There was also a contingent of humanoids called the Helena Society, a small group of both sexes dressed in Helena-like white dresses with pearls. Several of the men made no effort to pass for a woman—they had full beards and no makeup—and their solemn countenance made me wonder if they weren't transvestites but some bizarre new religious cult.

On the basis of my press credentials, Terry and I were let in past the ropes to the seating area, joining about two hundred others. I recognized most everyone as either a member of the press, a member of the *MHYH* production team, or a celebrity. (I spotted Janet Reno, Darla Hahn and David Lee Roth, among others.) Yet there was a highly conspicuous absence of any sort of family member, significant other, or even personal friend. It was as if Helena's entire existence had been *My House, Your House.*

I spied Mitzi off to the side, beneath the mighty cheeks of David's marble ass, as she covered the proceedings for the network. Contractually, she had to do grunt work while I got to sniff around for news. She *hated* this annoying little fact of life, yet gave each yeoman assignment her Daytime Emmy–best. As this was a Sad Occasion, the Kleenex was never far from Mitzi's surgically corrected septum. Her tears were so crocodile you could have made a handbag from them and still had enough left over for a smart pair of pumps.

The service was emceed by Koko Yee. Only her simple black maternity dress signaled that this was not just another weekly episode of the show. "Helena Godiva gave her entire heart and soul to endowing our lives with beauty," she explained, offering an interesting spin indeed on Helena's penchant for things like jailhouse beds. "Now God will design a special room in heaven for Helena." A smarmy New Age guru then took the podium, and, with extended arms, informed us that Helena did much more than design rooms—she enriched our souls, and so on.

Next up was none other than our own Curtsy Ann, who, we were told, would be sharing her feelings toward her spiritual sister, Helena. She wore a ruffled, full-skirted black dress with a long black veil, which she dramatically lifted as she spoke into the microphone. "I can only give what is in my humble heart," she told us. "And in my heart, there is music." She signaled to someone off to the side, and started trilling a sort of karaoke version of "Wind Beneath My Wings." As is often the case with beauty contest singers, her voice had a tendency to go flat when aiming for the big, high notes. That last little "*w-e-e-e-e-n-g-s*" she gave us went particularly sour, inspiring numerous chi-chi, beribboned lap dogs among the mourners to join in with considerable enthusiasm. Nonetheless, the crowd gave her a thunderous ovation. Presumably my exclusive scoop would be more revealing, lest I was reduced to telling the world something along the lines of: CURTSY ANN SEZ HELENA WAS HER HERO.

Keeping the general mood in check was the next speaker, Bill McCoy. He was appropriately angst-ridden in a black suit with a trendy black shirt and tie. If Curtsy Ann intermittently sounded like so many fingernails on a chalkboard, then I felt like Bill turned the entire universe into a grimace when he told us he would read a poem composed in honor of Helena. As if that weren't bad enough, he would accompany himself on the *guitar*.

"What is this, *Star Search*?" I whispered to Terry, who admonished me to be quiet.

As his fingers muddled through what was probably supposed to be "Twinkle Twinkle Little Star" with as few mistakes as could charitably be expected, Bill let loose the turmoil of his soul with all the torrential force of a premature ejaculation. The poem—if you could call it a poem—was a long, *long* piece, but a couple of snippets stood out for their lyrical gift:

> *And so Helena, you have left us all*
> *Alone to run, run with the ball . . .*

"See Dick run," I murmured to Terry, who knitted his brow distractedly, as if I were ruining the profound profundity of the mood. One could only hope he was still able to appreciate Bill's concluding lines:

> *You started with your brilliant eye*
> *For colors brighter than the sky*

*And themes to make Walt Disney weep*
*In heaven where your soul will keep . . .*

The simpleton rhyme scheme—not to mention the airheadish actual words—made Bill's nimbus cloud ambiance seem like so much ado over nothing. It was if a mad scientist announced from his lightning-bolted tower that he was going to create a wind-up puppy. Bill's voice actually choked up at the Walt Disney bit—which, for what it was worth, struck me as a shade narcissistic, since it was Bill himself and not Helena that was the Disneyite. Yet people of various sexes swooned when he was finished, grief-stricken though they were.

"Thank you *so* much, Bill," Koko told him, on behalf of us all. "We could all feel how those powerful words were wrenched from the depths of your heart."

Next on the program was Brick Edwards, who significantly was introduced as *the* carpenter on the show. No mention at all was being made of Ann-Margret, for obvious reasons—and yet as far as I could tell, she was possibly the best friend Helena had had on the set. Brick stepped forward in a white suit, presumably because he was mellowly impervious to things like funeral colors.

"Some people say it with flowers," Brick told the masses, "but I wanted to say it through my carpentry." Of course saying it with flowers was intended for things like Valentine's Day, but in today's slobbo world no one knew the difference, and the crowd appropriately oohed and aahed as Brick presented his visual tribute to Helena. It could have been the audience on *The Price is Right*. Brick had constructed a kind of 3D painting, the symbolic meanings in which he explained to us as he went along. It was a depiction of a house, only the house was also supposed to be Helena's face.

The roof was made of braided electrical cord to resemble the streaks in her hair. For, as Brick explicated, "Helena's hair gleamed like a solar panel, letting in the light."

Guiding us further along what was starting to seem like an especially intense acid trip, Brick told us that the windows of the house were—big surprise—Helena's eyes. The windows had been cleverly devised out of sardine cans, which, as Brick demonstrated, could open and close just like window shades. "I heard Bill once say that the eyes are the windows to the soul," Brick elucidated, apparently believing that the notion had originated with Bill. "And windows are strong and fragile at the same time, just like Helena's womanly soul."

Not content to leave unwell enough alone, Brick had painted little TV screens in the middle of each eye to look like pupils. He importantly told us that he wanted the house to look "realistic," so it made but common sense that the people inside the house would be watching TV.

For a mouth, poor Helena had to make do with the door to the house, which was fashioned out of the rubber bottom of a toilet plunger. The subtle irony thereof seemed lost on the cluelessly sincere Brick. The rubber disk had been cut in half and attached to hinges, so that it opened and closed. According to Brick, this was Helena's mouth because doors were entryways, and to talk to Helena was to experience "everything colorful and magical about life." As he insistently pointed with his extended index finger at this most prominent orifice, the mind could not help but wander. Brick winked in conclusion, adding an Elvis touch to the proceedings as some of the female mourners—despite their devastating loss—squealed out their repressed sexual energy. (Brick, I observed, had less of a gay following than Bill.)

Aunt Fern was up next, and she was greeted with a standing ovation. On the surface of things, it made no sense; why cheer the one who had aided Helena's supposed murderer? But in an unspoken way, everyone *knew* Ann-Margret couldn't have done it, and Aunt Fern was being but a good Mommy in shielding her baby sparrow from the mouths of predators. "I loved Helena like my own daughter," she pronounced, her voice choking on the word "daughter" while she punched her ample bosom for good measure. "All of us at *My House, Your House* are a family, and like all good families we love and protect each other." After *another* standing ovation subsided, Aunt Fern got to her main point: "I find it unforgivable— unforgivable!—that no mention has been made of a second victim in this tragedy, whose very life might well end as surely and as wrongly as Helena's. I am speaking of course of our own Ann—"

Conveniently, the microphone went dead—an uncannily common coincidence, I had found, at Hollywood memorials. The crowd began to chant: "Let Aunt Fern speak." The platform itself was a veritable football huddle of whispers, involving Aunt Fern, Koko, and several people whom I assumed to be producers. After a minute or so, Aunt Fern returned to the microphone—to yet another standing O. "You have to hand it to the old gal," Terry commented to me. Yet given the self-promoting nature of the *MHYH* gang—they were after all on a highly rated TV show—I couldn't help wondering if Aunt Fern was milking the high drama for all it was worth.

"As I *started to say*," she continued, with glaring eye toward the producers, "Ann-Margret Wochinsky is innocent!" From the way the crowd erupted, you'd have thought she'd just announced that Jesus was appearing at Wal-Mart. "It is in memory of Helena Godiva and all she stood for that we must make certain that the *real* killer be found!"

It was anticlimactic, to say the least, when Aunt Fern finally departed the stage and poor Basil Montclair was left to wing it alone. Always one to hide his light under a bushel, Basil quietly stepped forward with Native American reserve, dressed in a proper dark suit.

"Helena, I love you," he simply stated. But rather than leave well enough alone, he took out his hand-made ceramic drum, placed it between his legs, and proceeded to drum out a beat so monotonous that a busy signal was symphonic by comparison. At the same time, he wailed out something or other that sounded like a porcupine mating call. Everyone sat in rapt attention; some closed their eyes as if in a deep state of meditation. Indeed, I knew better than to dare to interrupt Terry a second time when he was in the throes of a truly transcendental experience. I'd have sooner sung "The Laverne and Shirley Theme" in the middle of sex.

When Basil finished—and it felt like hours before he did—a long stream of silvery fabric began unfurling down the aisles. Everyone was to take hold of it as part of what Basil termed the Circle of Life, though as such we were more accurately creating the Zigzag of Life.

Out of nowhere, a mighty gust of wind swept over Forest Lawn, causing the long shiny bolt of fabric to get tangled up on the microphone. Needless to say, everyone chattered away about how this was Helena's spirit swooping down on us all. Given the chaotic look of the tangles of material, it did seem a credible possibility.

Koko Yee told us to toss the fabric toward the sky and cry out "Helena, we love you," though as the silvery threads flopped down on everyone's faces our words became somewhat difficult to decipher. Before you knew it, everybody was hugging everybody. My discomfort with the entire enterprise must have been palpable, because Terry nudged me and whispered, "Death is hard to deal with. They're just doing their best to say good-bye."

"Bullshit. You can't convince me that any of them gave a damn about her."

"I disagree. I think they're sincere. And certainly Aunt Fern is devastated."

"You're right, except Aunt Fern," I amended, annoyed as always when Terry corrected me. "Oh, well, at least it's finally over."

But it seemed that I spoke tragically too soon. No release from purgatory was to be forthcoming. Someone or another in their infinite wisdom arranged for what was announced as "top-drawer celebrities" to now pay a special musical tribute to their dearest friend, Helena Godiva. Actually, from the audience's perspective, a voice without a body made the announcement, since whoever the voice belonged to apparently was afraid of getting the raspberry.

First up was Danny Bonaduce, who, upon apologizing to the crowd that he was very nervous about singing in public, proceeded to croon, "Isn't She Lovely?" Or, as was more befitting the tragedy of the occasion, "*Wasn't* She Lovely?" At the second chorus, Danny went down to the audience to encourage people to clap their hands and sing along, shoving the mike into this or that person's mouth whether they liked it or not. Finishing to hearty, Vegas-style applause, Danny appointed himself *de facto* emcee. Looking up with what one could only assumed to have been mock intimidation at the David statue, he asked if everyone could feel Helena's spirit there at Forest Lawn. The answer—big surprise—was a resounding yes.

Danny introduced the next act, a high-school marching band visiting L.A. for some sort of world champion glockenspiel tournament, or whatever. "I *know* you'll make them feel right at home," Danny predicted, gesturing out at the cemetery. As the tinny musicians and leggy baton twirlers high-stepped away to what after several minutes was faintly recognizable as "Aquarius/Let the Sun Shine In," a kind of paper house on wheels appeared on the stage. For a pregnantly long amount of time the house just sat there, obfuscating one's view of the piccolo section altogether. But judging from the crowd's response, the wait was worth it when finally, out from the roof of the house, there appeared Louise Mandrell herself. "There she is," Danny enthused, "One of the talented and beautiful Mandrell sisters." It was evident that Louise had learned a thing or two about how to milk a crowd from the way she scampered about the stage urging us all to indeed let the sun shine in so that "Helena can hear us from her cloud in heaven."

Impressive as the show was, clearly the natives were growing restless. People began to talk and mill about, giving the proceedings a county fair ambiance. Tragically, just as Danny introduced a duet between Fabian and Peter Frampton, I was distracted by the sight of Curtsy Ann patting the blubbery wrist of none other than the ever more rotund Chauncey Riggs, my main competition in the gossip racket. Not even Peter and Fabian's tuneful harmonies on "You Are So Beautiful to Me" could assuage my painful curiosity as to what was transpiring.

Predictably enough—in the way that you would predict that a vulture would circle a rotting corpse—Mitzi McGuire couldn't resist joining the little huddle, armed to the teeth with her usual counterfeit piety. Mitzi and Chauncey had an ongoing conspiracy of sorts to all but inject me with cyanide. Each of them had their reasons for thinking me their archrival, and, as they say in the mafia, your enemy's enemy is your friend. Though by far the more ladylike of the two, Chauncey did not suffer fools gladly. While Mitzi simply got on my nerves, I was always vaguely scared of Chauncey. He was a silly, ruthless old queen who'd neglected to take his conscience along for the ride. Since clearly no one would have sex with him without being paid for it—and paid a *lot*, I would imagine—Chauncey compensated by finding other ways of screwing people.

As usual, Chauncey was sweating so profusely he should have been sent to those starving desert nations as irrigation. Patting the highly unattractive three strands of hair combed over his ever-widening bald spot with a rumpled handkerchief, Chauncey listened to whatever Curtsy Ann was saying with an intense, asthmatic breathing and a mildly twitchy eye that told me he was trying to beat me to the latest scoop. As was so often the case, I wasn't sure if he was doing it within eyeshot of me on purpose, or through sheer sloppiness.

What the hell, I decided. I walked over to them.

"Why, *Rick*," Chauncey brightly declared, as though oh-so-pleasantly surprised to see me. "Isn't this just the most *marvelous* tribute? Have you met Curtsy Ann Thomas? She's one of the designers, you know, from *My House, Your House*."

Typical Chauncey—his catty little query was insulting on about a hundred levels at once. He knew that I'd been on the show, he knew that I'd just sat through the same memorial he had, and—even more basic—he knew that it was my job to know who's who in the industry.

He didn't wait for my reply. "It's really quite moving to see how important designers are to people," he pontificated. "Of course, I've never used one myself. I've done all three of my homes to date without a smidgen of outside help, and they've *all* been given featured spreads in magazines."

I did not doubt it for moment, assuming that one could conjecture which magazines. My personal guesses were along the lines of *Bordello Beautiful* or *Tacky Homes & Gardens*. Chauncey's tastes ran to the rococo—at about the speed of light. His rooms were so over-the-top with garish, gilt-edged crap that the homes of Barbara Cartland or Liberace looked like Zen monasteries by comparison. He didn't decorate a room; he did it up in drag.

"I'm sure your homes have all been scrumptious," Curtsy Ann contributed. "And if truth be told, Rick and I are old buddies." She linked arms with me and smiled winningly. Of course, we weren't old buddies at all— we'd never even officially met—but I liked that she didn't let Chauncey get away with devouring the universe.

"How fascinating," Mitzi offered, as the high-school band launched into a spirited rendition of "I've Got to Be Me." "I wouldn't have thought you'd be Rick's kind of person, Curtsy Ann. You're such a sweet, kind, decent girl."

"Occasionally, I lower my standards," I explained.

Mitzi and Chauncey pretended to laugh, while Curtsy Ann legitimately chortled as she gave me a little teasing push.

The microphone gave out a high-pitched squeak that did not please the crowd one bit. Thankfully, the next act was Barry Williams, who was already coaxing Louise Mandrell into singing a duet version of "I Can't Smile Without You," so the crowd wouldn't be unhappy for long.

Even more fortuitous, the grief-stricken Mitzi and Chauncey were soon in hot pursuit of Aunt Fern. A little of either or both went a long way to desecrate what was left of my overall mental and physical health. I introduced Curtsy Ann to Terry, with whom she exchanged a few perfunctory pleasantries over his being on the show, and wasn't it sad about Helena?

"Now then, boys," Curtsy Ann told us. "Let's have us a long talk. I need to set the record straight before someone sets it straight for me."

Curtsy Ann was new to celebrityhood, and so didn't seem to realize that telling a reporter "to set the record straight" was the equivalent of someone saying they read *Playboy* for the articles or attended a high-profile charity gala because they cared about the cause.

"What record is there to set straight?" I asked.

"Oh, just a couple of li'l ol' things that happened between Helena and me." She crinkled her nose and bent her wrist. "Nothing to write home about, as they say."

"You realize that Terry is a cop—I mean, police officer?" He nudged me and I amended: "A junior detective."

"And what a good thing it is that you serve and protect us, big fella." She stroked Terry's arm in a chummy way.

"I'm not assigned to the case," Terry informed her. "I'm just kind of . . . you know, hanging out with Rick."

"Oh, I *see.*" She gave us a wise, downturned smile that emphasized her fine cheekbones. "You boys are *special* friends. I think it's so beautiful that you do everything together."

"Actually, we're *just* friends," I corrected. "And barely that."

Terry glowered at me. "Ann-Margret is my cousin."

"Now I really do see." Curtsy Ann cringed ever so slightly through her smile, as though Ann-Margret were the proverbial elephant in the room, and she regretted that this distasteful matter would have to spoil our otherwise congenial time together.

"Well, I suppose we should get going." She gave a resigned sigh as she glanced at her watch. "Darn it all, I'm going to miss Lee Meriwether. I heard she was next on the bill. To me, she has set *such* a standard of excellence for Miss Americas." As a former Miss Texas, Curtsy Ann evidently maintained her pageant-centric outlook on the cosmos. She looked hurt beyond anything to do with Helena when Terry innocently asked who Lee Meriwether *was*.

A rapid change of subject seemed in order. "You do need to realize, Curtsy Ann, that anything you say—"

"I know how it works, Rick. That's just fine with me, because I have nothing to hide. I mean, sure as a sugar plum, I had my reasons to want Helena deader than a roadkill possum. But I swear, I had nothing to do with it."

# TEN

Her humble abode was as big as Tara, yet by the way her eyes lit up at the sight of it, she seemed to think it was Barbie's Dream House. It was a gleaming white structure with flawless Georgian pillars and tasteful, tasteful landscaping that was absolutely matched on each side of the front brick pathway, right down to the last pansy.

On the way the front door, Curtsy Ann stopped and cried, "Oh, no! No, no, no, no!"

Her horror was such that I thought she must have spied a corpse on her property. But we soon learned she had in fact spied a stray pine needle daring to litter her lawn some ten feet away. Stopping to pick it up, she tried to make light of the whole thing. "These naughty pine needles," she laughed. "They're *always* spoiling my lawn." Her extremely green lawn was trimmed so meticulously I wondered if Curtsy Ann had commissioned Vidal Sassoon for the job.

"This silly old house has so many rooms," she declared dismissively, as though owning a mansion put one at a disadvantage. "I was *such* a goofball to buy it."

A Mexican maid met us at the door. Curtsy Ann handed the maid her hat and veil—briefly fussing to straighten the veil—and took off her black high heels, placing them neatly on the shoe rack in the entryway. "Your shoes, fellas," she instructed with a self-conscious smile. We obediently took off our filth-carrying shoes, and placed them beside hers. I noted that the only other pair of shoes on the rack were Reeboks that I assumed belonged to the maid; Curtsy Ann put everything in its proper place all the time. I had half a mind to ask, *So tell us, Miss Crawford, about the wire hangers.*

The maid flip-flopped over in terry cloth slippers à la Baby Jane Hudson as she directed us to a room called the "east parlor."

"Here's about as theme room-ish as I get," Curtsy Ann told us as we stood in what appeared to be a sort of beauty contest museum. The ruffles of her extravagantly perfumed black dress made a swishing sound as she gave us the grand tour.

In the exact center of one wall was a glass case that housed the gown she wore the night of her crowing as Miss Texas. Precisely centered over it was a smaller glass case, which held her rhinestone crown. To either side of the glass cases were four full-color photographs with matching frames, each the exact same size. The photos were a veritable story in pictures as to how she clinched the Miss Texas crown. One photo showed her in the talent competition, wearing a tiara while warbling, "How Do You Solve a Problem Like Maria?" from *The Sound of Music.* Another photo was from the evening gown competition, in which she wore so many layers of yellow organza she would've made Marie Antoinette seem naked by comparison. In a third photo she competed in the question-and-answer segment. As Curtsy Ann solemnly explained to us, she stood there in her form-fitting gold swimsuit and spiked heels, one leg bent in front of the other, while she answered the question: "If you were to speak before the United Nations General Assembly, what would be the title of your speech, and why?" Curtsy Ann told us she replied: "My speech would be called, 'Let's Put Children First,' because I firmly believe that the children of today are the future of tomorrow." In the fourth and final photo, a wide-eyed Curtsy Ann put her hands to her face in a pose reminiscent of the *Home Alone* poster as she was proclaimed the new Miss Texas. The runner-up was hugging her and wishing her well—as if Curtsy Ann gave a rat's ass.

"There you have it, boys." She toyed with the small silver crucifix around her neck. "I started off as li'l Miss Abeline, and the next thing I knew I was whisked off to Atlantic City. It was just like Dorothy going to Oz."

"What happened in Atlantic City?" I did my best to make the question sound innocent. I noticed there was a decided lack of Atlantic City paraphernalia in the room, and could only guess that the judges at the national pageant hadn't exactly salaamed before her.

"They didn't like my platform." Evident in her collegial face was an undercurrent of bitterness that the years had done little to soothe.

"What's a platform?" Terry asked. "Do you mean the shoes you had to wear?"

It was such an inane question that Curtsy Ann assumed that the guileless Terry was joking. "No, silly." She playfully slapped his arm. "You know—each state contestant has a platform. Some major social issue that she promises to raise public awareness about if she's chosen Miss America."

"Gee, that's really impressive," the deep-thinking Terry concluded. "And here I always thought Miss America was just a beauty contest."

"It is not a beauty contest at *all*," Curtsy Ann corrected. "Anyway, my platform was called 'Harmony Through Interior Design.' I argued that by designing rooms that reflected harmony through color and fabric and the placement of objects, we could become a more harmonious people, nation and world."

"So your platform was world peace through better interior composition," I summarized.

"Exactly!" Curtsy Ann enthused. "But the judges were a grim bunch that year. The girl who won wanted to find a cure for cancer."

"*B-o-r-i-n-g,*" I empathized, feigning a yawn for good measure.

She smiled wryly. "Anyway, I never even made it to the semi-finals. Though I did win a special talent commendation, and came in fourth for Miss Congeniality."

"I notice that the photos don't match," I commented.

"Don't *match*?" Curtsy Ann wore a look of alarm.

"Relax. I just meant that they were not all the same photo, or the same on each side."

"Oh, I get it. You're pulling my leg." She absently straightened one of the frames. "People tease me about that all the time. But really, I'm *not* obsessed with symmetry." Frowning, she made a flicking motion with her wrist, and out popped a metal tape measure as handily as a sawed-off handgun flung out of Robert DeNiro's sleeve in *Taxi Driver*.

"I invented this myself," she told us, absorbed in realigning the frame a fraction of an inch. "The patent is pending. I call it the Handi-Measure. Actually, I was going to call it the Expandable Inchworm, but my business manager said that was too fanciful, whatever that meant. I think all designers should have one. It is *so* convenient."

Satisfied that the picture hung evenly, she sat us down on the sofa, and took one of the two matching chairs for herself. The furniture was upholstered in a shade she'd patented. It was called Miss Texas Yellow in honor of the gown she wore. (As Curtsy Ann explained, she'd made as much money off of Miss Texas Yellow as she had off of her designs.) The coffee table was studded with tiara-like rhinestones. Copies of the past few issues of *Pageant Digest* were artfully displayed across the tabletop, for those who were interested. The matching yellow walls featured a silvery stencil of the crown, executed with precision. She had also created a kind of false pillar in the corner of the room so that the pattern could end evenly with the opposite wall. The window treatments featured the same yellow organza, with gold banners proclaiming MISS TEXAS streaming down the sides.

Still, the room was far less over the top than it would have been had Helena or Bill designed it—in which case the floor might have been turned into a giant rhinestone, or some such thing. If you squinted and ignored all the beauty pageant stuff, it simply looked like a thoughtfully appointed sitting room.

The maid brought us tall glasses of iced lemonade.

"It matches the walls." I held up my glass for scrutiny.

"Do you *think*?" Curtsy Ann pondered. "I'm not sure, Rick. To my eye it seems three or four shades paler. Maybe if I added just a few drops of vegetable dye—say, two drops red and crazy as it sounds a drop of blue—" She stopped herself, and gazed at me knowingly. "They warned me about you. I better hurry up and get used to all your ribbing."

"There's *no* getting used to it," Terry confided. "It's nonstop."

I took no small offense at Terry's comments. It was hardly the case that

I gave him or anyone else a bad time of it, and in fact knew myself to have a highly agreeable nature. But this didn't seem the time or place to go into it.

Terry took a hefty swallow of lemonade. "Say, this is *good*."

"I use fresh lemons," Curtsy Ann confided. "It's the only way."

"Tell me honestly, Curtsy Ann. Do you think my cousin is guilty?"

She took a dainty sip of lemonade. "About as guilty as a goldfish would be of starting World War Three."

"Huh?" Terry didn't get it.

"I mean that you have nothing to fear from me. I know that Ann-Margret never, ever, *ever* could have done this. I am just appalled that she is being made to suffer through such an ordeal. She must have *so* much courage."

"Any idea where she might be?"

Curtsy Ann forced a frosty smile. "If I knew, don't you think I would have called the police? Don't get me wrong, Terry. I think your cousin is a fine person. But I'm afraid we don't pal around much. She didn't confide in me."

"So what were you saying back at Forest Lawn about wanting Helena dead?"

I saw no reason not to ask this, but Terry's wary expression told me I'd done something wrong. My guess was that I'd interrupted his grand performance as "good cop," but I had an understandably low threshold for this type of pomposity.

Curtsy Ann patted her Miss Texas chest; a sip of lemonade had gone down the wrong pipe. "Excuse me, fellas. My, it *is* an unsettling day. But you're right—I asked you here to talk about Helena, and so we will. It's just that . . . I'm finding it easier said than done."

"What did she do?" Terry gently asked.

"She ruined my life, of course." Curtsy Ann set down her glass, then distractedly moved it slightly over. "Here, let me show you something."

She reached under the table to detach a remote from its hidden Velcro holder—as Curtsy Ann explained, she found things like remotes to be eyesores. As she aimed the remote at the wall opposite the museum cases, we saw the silvery doors of a cabinet slide open to a wide-screen TV.

"I'm sure she was on her best behavior when she worked with you,

Rick. But how'd you like to see some outtakes? Here is the *real* Helena Godiva we all grew to love."

The opening of *MHYH* episodes often introduced the designers by showing them arriving on the scene, or swimming in the pool of the cul-de-sac where they were filming, or what have you. In this video of outtakes, we first saw Helena and Curtsy Ann walking up a sidewalk in one of the more upscale residential neighborhoods in Vermillion, South Dakota. Only instead of just walking along in a chatty, fifty-fifty sort of way, Helena was pulling a full-scale Mitzi McGuire and smilingly trying to force Curtsy Ann out of frame. Several takes were required before Helena agreed to cooperate.

"You can imagine what a *delightful* experience it was to work with her," Curtsy Ann reflected.

"So the bitch upstaged you," I replied. "Surely that wasn't enough to wish her dead." (Actually, my experience with Mitzi in this regard taught me otherwise, but it was the sort of thing you never admitted out loud.)

"Oh, I promise you—we're just getting started."

In the next outtake, Brick dared to tell Helena he didn't think he could finish an armoire to her specifications within the remaining time, and Helena just about had a nervous breakdown on the spot. "Why do you do this to me?" she wailed in desperation. "It's because I dropped you, isn't it? It's your pathetic way of getting back at me."

"Now just a second, Helena," Brick suggested. "We may have fooled around a little—"

"A *little*? We do it like every other minute, and then you say it was a *little*." In a fit of anger, she gave him a shove.

"Okay, so we fooled around a lot. But we never had anything to break up from. Look, I know you're sore because I stopped returning your calls, but to twist it all up—"

She slapped him hard across the face. "I'm the designer, and you'll do as I say. I want an armoire done in the shape of Mount Rushmore, and I want it done *now*."

"Okay, okay." Brick smarted from the slap. "Christ, you're a fucking bitch. A fucking *psycho* bitch," he added for good measure.

Helena burst into tears. "You're beyond cruel," she managed to stammer, her chin quivering. The camera followed her as she ran up the stairs of the suburban home, like so many teenaged daughters in fifties sitcoms.

"Why would Helena and Brick have permitted all of that to be filmed?" I asked.

"They didn't. We used a hidden camera. You know, as a practical joke." Curtsy Ann emitted an ironic laugh. "Some joke."

It would seem that the drama was just getting warmed up. The camera operator followed Brick upstairs, where—in the best Robert Young tradition—he knocked on the bedroom door, was told to go away, then knocked again and was let inside. There was a cut in the film; I assumed the camera operator simply stood outside the door for a few minutes or so. But then Helena and Brick emerged—looking, as they say, none the worse for wear. Over soft little afterglow kisses Brick affirmed his promise to make extra furniture for Helena's room, even if it meant not finishing his stuff for Curtsy Ann.

"Charming, wasn't she?" Curtsy Ann ruefully noted.

"And who shot all this film?"

She fussed over the gold fringe on a throw pillow. "Oh, just the usual camera guys."

But something in her sidelong glance made me wonder if the cinematographer hadn't been Curtsy Ann herself.

There were more of the same kind of shenanigans in various locales all across the USA—Helena and, by extension, Brick seeming hell bent on sabotaging Curtsy Ann down to the last curtain rod as they carried on what might generously be termed a relationship. Then I noticed something else.

"This is Helena's body piercing room, right?" I had never actually seen the legendary episode—let alone rare outtakes from it. I found myself experiencing that little jolt of pleasure that a kid would get when encountering a sought-after baseball card or comic book; this was *the* all-time disaster room for *MHYH* addicts. (Of course, under the circumstances, I did not express my approbation to Curtsy Ann.)

"That it is, I'm afraid." Curtsy Ann rolled her eyes. "Can you imagine actually doing that to someone's living room? Let alone . . . well, other things."

In this infamous room in an otherwise respectable Hollywood home, Helena first glued flesh-colored ultra-suede to the ceiling and walls—to resemble human skin. She then methodically fastened two thousand screw-eyes into the suede to look like body piercings. The floor was covered in hand-painted "tattoos." Furniture included her famous "whip chair," in which she Super-glued sex fantasy whips to an authentic Eames chair. The finishing touch was a ten-foot papier mache sculpture of an ear with twenty wire coat hangers for "earrings."

But I could see that there was more to it all than Helena's questionable taste.

"Hey, that's Fernando San Marcos," I commented, recognizing the semi-struggling actor who, it would seem, had the singular pleasure of owning the notorious living room. I say "semi-struggling" because his was one of those odd cases of technically making it while not making it at all. On the one hand, Fernando was in his fourth season of steady work as a supporting character in the hit detective series, *Badges of Philly*. On a show that featured Emmy-winning, angst-ridden hamminess and so-called "groundbreaking" dialogue (i.e., people said the "F" word), Fernando played the one yawnish, stalwart, "clean" detective who more or less blended in with the wallpaper. He played him so well, in fact, that he fought hard for roles as evil, sexually harassing bosses or evil stalker cops in TV movies starring Melissa Gilbert or Judith Light. ("*Badges of Philly*'s Fernando San Marcos as you've never seen him," the promo ads would promise.) Indeed, it was a tribute to Fernando's un-fame that the body piercing room was better known than he was. My educated guess was that when *Badges of Philly* had run its course he'd turn up as the host of some reality cop show, or reality ESP show, or some such. It would pay the bills, but it wasn't exactly why Mom sacrificed for all those tap-dancing lessons.

"Fernando was so sweet to work with," Curtsy Ann reflected wistfully. "He's even nicer in real life than he is as Detective Bob Garcia."

"*That's* Detective Garcia?" Terry suddenly lit up; predictably enough, he hadn't recognized Fernando out of uniform, so to speak. "You mean from *Badges of Philly*? That's just too cool. Of all the guys on the show, I really relate to him."

Of course, leave it to Terry to relate to the one vanilla character on a show full of potty mouths. Although for once he at least got the name of a TV show right.

"I like him, too," Curtsy Ann concurred, perhaps a bit too magnanimously. After all, there wasn't much about Detective Bob Garcia to like *or* dislike. "Of course, poor Fernando would have to deal with that monstrosity of a room that Helena created. When she wasn't behaving like a common whore, that is."

"I never saw the reveal at the end, but didn't he at least act like—"

"Here was his *real* reaction, Rick." With an impatient press on the Fast Forward button, Curtsy Ann showed us Koko telling Fernando and his teammate to open their eyes. Fernando was, as they say, a bachelor, and his partner on the show was a kind of arranged date with a sweet airhead starlet named Taffy Something-or-Another. The Taffy starlets of this world come and go, yet one could not help but be affected by Fernando's first glimpse of his new and improved living room.

"That motherfucking cunt bitch!" he enthused. "What's she trying to do, out me to the world as a leather queen?"

Now *there* was a response worthy of headlines. Fernando wasn't the kind of actor whom the press followed like a pack of hounds. But as such, if he really wanted to punch up his image he could have shared with the world that he was gay, kinky, and proud.

On the video clip, Koko Yee attempted to calm the poor guy. "Now Fernando, I don't think that people will assume *anything*. It's just a fun room. Kind of, you know . . . different."

"Different? *Different?*" Fernando pondered rhetorically. "Is that the only word you people know? The bitch destroys my home and my good name, and all you people have to say is, 'Well, it certainly is different.' What did you think of Adolf Hitler? Well, he certainly was *different.*" He shook his head with tragedy. "My Eames chair! My favorite whip! All ruined. Who did she think she was, snooping through my personal things? I'll bet she even found my slave collar." He looked about the room with panic. "Where is it? How did that twat incorporate it into her swell design?"

"Detective Garcia is into . . . those things?" Terry was crestfallen. Being around anything too overtly sexual—gay or straight—caused him anxiety, let alone discovering that his role model as a no-personality detective was considerably more exotic offscreen.

"Leather-wise, he's more Ginger than Fred," Curtsy Ann matter-of-factly noted. "Which, by the by, fellas—you should know that contrary to rumors galore, both Bill and Basil are straight. Basil is *married*. He has three beautiful children. And Bill is a real lady killer."

The mind reeled with questions, not the least of which was my desire to know if Bill had done any lady-killing in the direction of Helena—not to mention Curtsy Ann herself. But for the time being, I was more absorbed by what Fernando was saying on the tape as he paced the floors like a determined, subversive Iago.

"I'll sue, that's what I'll do," Fernando vowed. "Then I'll put a hit on her. I'll take her for every dime she's worth, and then when she's homeless and starving and eating old cans of Little Friskies out of dumpsters, I'll have her killed."

"*Interesting*," I observed with relish. "Curtsy Ann, if you ever get bored with designing, you could make a pretty penny hawking volumes of *My House, Your House* outtakes."

"They are fun, aren't they?" She turned off the TV. "But as you can see, Helena, though a great actress if there ever was one, was unlikely to be honored with the Jean Hersholt Humanitarian Award by the members of the Academy."

"What exactly happened with Fernando? I mean, about the room."

"Well, after he calmed down—which took about an hour, as I recall—they filmed another take of the reveal." She took out a frilly hanky to wipe a drop of lemonade off the table top.

"And . . . ?"

She raised a sarcastic eyebrow. "He said it certainly was different."

"Rick, you're not going print all this, uh, *stuff* about Detective Garcia, are you?" Terry urgently wanted to know.

"Of course not. Or at least not yet," I amended. "And his name isn't 'Detective Garcia.' He's an *actor*. That's a *part* he plays."

If I were only a humble reporter on my beat, I'd have been in seventh heaven—or at least fourth or fifth heaven, given that Fernando wasn't exactly headline news unto himself. But we were in the midst of a much bigger story, with a possibly innocent person's fate on the line, and discretion, as they say, is the better part of street smarts.

"You know what I mean," Terry protested. "Of course I know he's an actor."

Curtsy Ann laughed nervously. "Please don't misunderstand, guys. I didn't bring you over here to out Fernando San Marcos to the world. I only wanted to show what made Helena tick. So I'm glad, Rick, if you aren't going to . . . well, you know what I mean." She cleared her throat and gave us her best Miss Texas shoulders-back-chest-out posture. "Because otherwise, I might have to deny that such a tape ever existed, and we wouldn't want to go there, would we?"

Suddenly I was confused. Her threat meant little to me, but the point of our visit was, like Chauncey Rigg's forehead, not altogether clear. "I could care less if Fernando San Marcos likes to do it with a snapping turtle. But if you didn't bring us over here to teach me the finer points about his brilliant career as a leather slave, what exactly was this tumultuously exclusive scoop? That Helena and Brick screwed around?"

"Oh, silly me!" She gave a coy slap to her noggin. "I must have bats in my belfry. Did I forget to mention that Brick and I were once engaged?"

"We all have a lot on our minds," I sympathized. "But let me guess—did the engagement break up over Helena?"

"Boy, did it ever," she replied, as if I'd asked her if a window valence done in braided velvet achieved the desired look. "You see, guys, once upon a time, I was just another unknown designer, and Brick was merely a struggling carpenter whom I hired to do a fireplace for a house out in Burbank. He was trying to break into stunt work in the movies. I'm afraid I was the one who talked him out of that dream. I said I would be so worried for him all the time, so he finally gave up on it. Was it wrong of me? I'll never know. Because in the meantime, we got hired for this marvelous new cable show called *My House, Your House*, and that was when Brick met Helena." She gazed moodily at her Miss Texas crown. "I'd say it was like something out of *Days of Our Lives*, if it still didn't hurt so damn much."

"Gee, that's a tough break, Curtsy Ann," Terry pronounced. "But that would have been a few years ago, right? You've had time to get over it, haven't you?"

I didn't know if this was some subtle detective ploy on Terry's part, or if he did in fact seem to think he was a character on *Days of Our Lives*.

"Maybe for some people, but not me. You see, I was taught to believe in happy endings." Curtsy Ann gazed dreamily about her Miss Texas room. Given the yellow, yellow everywhere, her dutiful funeral black dress seemed to heighten the melodrama of it all. "When I was a little girl, I even thought I was a princess."

I gave her my best serious expression, but underneath it all I thought, *Good grief, here it comes, the I-thought-I-was-a-princess bit*. If I had a nickel for every dummy who told me that when she was four years old she thought she'd grow up to be Audrey Hepburn in *Roman Holiday* or Grace Kelly in real life, I would have been able to buy up a continent or two by now. Still, I reminded myself that if no one bought into the princess fantasy anymore, there'd be no one to serve as beauty queens, which is dirty work but someone has to do it.

Curtsy Ann made a point of urgently clasping our hands for the profundity of what she was about to share, though needless to say it was obvious what was coming. "I thought I'd grow up, and all my dreams would be right there, ready and waiting. But most of all, I was sure I would meet Prince Charming."

"Wow," Terry articulated. "That's really profound." (Unfortunately, I think he was being sincere.)

"Profound? Or just pathetic." Curtsy Ann bravely fought back a sniffle. "You see, I thought I'd met my Prince Charming in Brick Edwards. Maybe I should have compromised myself, and—you know—moved in with him before getting married. But I couldn't betray everything I was raised to believe."

I could scarcely believe my ears. "You mean to tell me that you never—"

"I never said *never*. What did you think, Rick, that I was one of those abstinence beauty queens?" She gave a dismissive, mean-spirited chortle.

"I have to admit, you gave me quite a scare."

"What a joke all *that* is, let me tell you. Why, some of those holier-than-thou, second runner-up—" Curtsy Ann stopped herself, and smiled. "Anyway, all I meant was that I could never 'live in sin,' as they say, with the man I was going to marry. My parents were very Old School about these things. It would've broken their hearts. Besides, Brick was such a ladies man, I figured that by keeping the goods just a teensy bit out of reach . . ." She let me finish the sentence, as if too delicate a flower to do it herself.

"Oh, I see." Though I really didn't, other than to conclude it was some sort of bizarre southern custom to feign instant virginity when it came to getting married. Maybe this was why her discourse on the whole episode struck me as missing a certain vital dimension, as though she were play-acting at being in love and brokenhearted. Take it from one who knew many times over: *True* love and *real* heartbreak were nothing to play-act about. It took me days, if not weeks, to get over Biff Holden, to cite just one example.

"It must be hard for you to hold onto your values," Terry admiringly gushed, "when you get exposed to so many people with no values at all."

"Well, I do work in television," she philosophized, with a resigned frown. "I'm afraid it comes with the territory."

"It is strange how these things work, isn't it?" I reflected. "A major film actress who shall remain anonymous once told me how when she was growing up, she had a stepsister who kept having all these hunky boyfriends while she herself was lucky if some loser nerd gave her a stick of Dentyne. 'I'm just as pretty as she is,' she'd angrily tell herself. 'Why does *she* always get the guys?' Well, come to find out, ol' stepsis was putting out like there was no tomorrow. I knew this gay guy once who was homely as sin, yet it turned out he had the biggest—"

"That's quite enough, Rick." Terry looked genuinely displeased. "I mean, *really.*"

"Just trying to lighten things up," I replied.

"That's okay, Terry. I know how Rick likes to joke." Curtsy Ann daintily sniffled into her hanky. "The thing of it was, Helena never even pretended to honor what Brick and I had. Right there in front of the entire crew, she made her move and that was that."

"Did Brick try to be discreet?"

"Not really. 'Within a matter of days after being hired, he broke off our engagement. Over lunch hour, can you imagine? And he didn't even spend the entire time with me. He went off to Helena for more fun and games. At that point, I wondered about, well, you *know*, beating Helena at her own game. But the thought of giving myself to Brick under such sleazy circumstances seemed like a lose-lose proposition. I certainly did not have Helena's experience, and all I would've accomplished was reducing myself to another notch in his belt. All I could do was hope against hope that he'd come back to me."

"Why was none of this ever publicized?" I asked.

"Clauses in our contracts." She tugged at the ruffles on her black sleeves. "We're supposed to be one big happy family. Now, if Brick and I got married like we were supposed to, it would've been all right. But to have affairs or break up with each other—*that* was a no-no."

"What did the other people on the show think?" Terry inquired.

"The women were very meowy. They all kept saying, 'Well you know, you *do* have to keep a man happy.' Like it was my fault for not playing a better hand of cards. They were jealous, pure and simple. I do have to say for all the talk about woman's lib, the men were much more there for me. Basil invited me over for dinner and let me play with his kids. He even did this Cherokee healing ritual with me, where he waved smoking sage over my body—my fully-clothed body, of course."

"Of course," I agreed.

"And as for Bill, well . . . Bill is just a sweetheart."

"You mean that you and Bill—?"

"Oh, no, nothing like that. But he'd take me to dinner or for long walks in the hills, and just let me talk. More than once I cried on his shoulder. Literally."

"Well, anyone who could give me a Batmobile for my bedroom must be an all right guy," Terry decreed.

"But you see," Curtsy Ann undauntedly continued, "to answer your question—no, I haven't been able to get over it. Brick was supposed to be *mine*. The one love of my life. Things like Helena weren't supposed to happen to me."

"But it sounds like Brick was no picnic on a Sunday afternoon for

Helena, either," I noted. "On tape, it looked like she had her own unrequited feelings for him."

Curtsy Ann's eyes flared with southern-belle rage. "Of course, she meant nothing to him. Her kind of woman never means anything to a man. She made it so that everyone lost. A broken heart—if she even *had* a heart— was too good for her. It was a small price to pay after what she did to me."

The force of her words went beyond anything she'd said thus far. Besides the mere technical possibility of it, I seriously began to wonder if she in fact *had* murdered Helena.

But obviously it would do little good to ask her outright. So I compromised:

"You know, this probably sounds silly, but just where were you on Saturday night between the hours of—"

"I was home alone, as always. Actually, I take that back. The maid was here. She can vouch for me. I have trouble sleeping, and play solitaire until all hours."

A quick look from Terry told me not to pursue this matter any further for the time being—and even if I'd wanted to, my cell phone was ringing.

"Hello, Rick? It's Boxer Jones."

"Why Boxer, I was just thinking of you," I answered brightly. Not exactly a bad omen when someone gives you his number and then calls you himself. Especially when he's someone you'd very much like to know better. His telephone voice was, if anything, sexier than his face-to-face voice—full of deep, quavering hormones.

"That's nice. Listen, Rick. It's about Aunt Fern. I was wondering if we could meet with you guys as quickly as possible."

"I don't see why not," I melodiously agreed. In a way, it seemed old-fashioned cute that he was contriving a meeting for us that would involve both Aunt Fern and Terry so as to not seem too obvious in his intentions. It could very well have been that Aunt Fern wanted to meet with Terry and me, but it was doubtful to say the least that the dear old thing would have anything of substance to offer. If anything, I expected that she wanted to milk *us* for info, in which case Terry and I would have to be careful to offer her a little bit of something, but not all that much.

"Splendid," Boxer remarked, with an excitement in his voice that proved contagious. "I think—no, I'm certain she knows where Ann-Margret is and is sneaking off to meet with her. Aunt Fern keeps going on about you guys, so I thought that you might be able to talk some sense into her. Especially with Terry being a cop. She's awfully stubborn."

"So I've noticed." We both laughed. I thought to myself, *Our first laugh together*. Let the Terrys and the Curtsy Anns of the world stick to their naïve principles. *I* knew how the game of love was played.

"Oh, and Rick . . . ?" Boxer added, like a shy, slightly contrived after-thought. "When I gave you my phone number, I was trying to—"

I laughed again. "Say no more, Boxer. I'm not in a position to get into it, but I know what you're getting at."

"You do? That's terrific, Rick. Tell me everything you know about Terry. Is he single? Would he like to go out with me?"

# ELEVEN

"ARE YOU *SURE* NOTHING'S BUGGING YOU, RICK?"

Terry drove us to Boxer's woefully pretentious, *nouveau riche* address while I stared out at the ugly sprawl of L.A. and brooded.

"Couldn't be better," I insisted. "Oh, by the way, Boxer mentioned something about wanting to go out with you."

Terry uncharacteristically honked the horn for no apparent reason besides approbation. "I knew it," he affirmed, raising his fisted arm in a cheer. "I could *tell* that he—" He stopped himself. "Oh, gee, sorry, Rick."

"About *what*?" Before he could answer, I added, "We're going to need a hell of a lot more to get the charges dropped against Ann-Margret than wishful thinking cross-pollinated with gut instinct. There's a clear list of suspects forming. Curtsy Ann, Fernando San Marcos, and—who knows?—maybe the entire cast of the show. Helena wasn't exactly Maria von Trapp, and if her memorial was any indicator, the show was pretty much where she did her dirty work. I suppose technically there's even Aunt Fern to consider, though to put it mildly I doubt that she ever could have or would have—"

"Rick, stop it." Terry pulled the Cherokee over to the shoulder.

"What? Are you mad because of what I said about Ann-Margret?"

He nervously tapped at the steering wheel. "Rick, playing dumb doesn't suit you. You *know* you mentioned something about being interested in Boxer. If you have any problem at all with my going out with him, I won't do it. It's that simple." He looked at me with his thick eyebrows radiating earnestness. "Tell me the truth, Rick. Does it bother you?"

"Jesus, Terry. You're as bad as Curtsy Ann, blathering on like Erica Kane. Okay, Boxer looked like a decent lay. He probably would have bored me to death if he's—" I stopped myself before I said: *He probably would have bored me to death if he's interested in you.*

"If he's what? Interested in someone like me?"

"Of course not."

"*What*, then? Tell me why anything to do with two people just trying to have a nice, normal time so totally grosses you out."

"Look, go out with the whiny little shit, okay? If you don't think I have better things to do than worry about your stupid, smarmy, sophomoric crush on some full-of-himself lawyer with nothing better to do than represent some lonely old woman with nothing better to do than befriend accused murderers, then you know nothing about me. So go ahead and fantasize about picking out the china pattern just because he's asked you out. No wait, I forgot—you wouldn't know *how* to pick out china. You probably don't even know what china is."

We both sat there, staring straight ahead, the hum of the engine and the roar of the passing traffic the only sounds.

"Anyway," I finally decided, "let's talk about our suspects."

"Agreed," Terry concurred, yet he shook his head sadly for some reason as he drove back into the traffic. "I think your list, so far, sounds pretty good. We can meet with Boxer and Aunt Fern, and then look up Detective Garcia—I mean, Fernando San Marcos. Then all the other people from *My House, Your House.*"

"Somehow I have the feeling they'll be contacting me." I touched Terry's knee good-naturedly. "You know, to set the record straight."

His eyes crinkled up into an appealing, face-splitting grin. "Those showbiz folks sure do spend a lot of time setting the record straight."

"If you want any help or anything with your date, you know that I'd be happy to . . ."

"I know, Rick. Thanks." We were at a red light; he reached over to give me a light peck on the cheek. I was surprised by how sweet and touching the gesture seemed. I even felt myself blush a little.

"Anyway, back to business. It seems to lil' ol' me anyway that Curtsy Ann's obsession with exact measurements doesn't exactly bode well. Perfectionism and the killer instinct have been known to go together like a horse and carriage, or at least according to all that Freudian rigmarole." I hastily explained, " 'Freudian' means coming from Sigmund Freud, who was a famous—"

"I *know* who he was, Rick." He distractedly honked at a driver who'd changed lanes without using his turn signal; I could tell that Terry was contemplating pulling the driver over. "I should have known better. You did your ten seconds of niceness, so you had to point out your intellectual superiority by assuming I'm a total moron. I've got news for you, Smarty Pants. All sorts of perfectly normal people are particular about measuring things. I myself use a level to hang a picture."

I resisted the urge to comment.

"But it is true," Terry continued, "that Curtsy Ann has some strange sort of anger thing when it comes to Helena. It's like it consumes her, yet she's not even aware of it. Not a good omen."

"She's as pissed off about Brick and Helena as if it happened yesterday," I agreed. "Which, come to think of it, just might be true, more or less. She could've caught them together again, and bingo—the straw that broke the camel's back."

"Plus maids can be paid to lie," Terry interjected.

"Still, when you look at her neatsy streak in a different way . . . I dunno." We drove past a huge billboard bragging that the latest exclusive on Helena's murder could be acquired only by watching Chauncey Riggs on the rival cable network. Rather than feature a photo of Chauncey, there was a caricature of him aimed to make him like a loveable old curmudgeon. My first impulse was to call Max Headroom and kvetch, but I reminded myself that the less network interference, the better off I'd be.

"You mean she might have wanted Helena dead, but she wouldn't have been so messy about it? But think about it, Rick: As murders go, it *wasn't* a mess. Helena's body was wrapped in fabric—*gold* fabric, no less—and she was drowned, which is a relatively unmessy way to go. They say it's even relatively painless. And then that glaze—creepy as all get out, but neat and tidy."

"You do have a point."

Brainwise, Terry was not always the flashiest towel at the bathhouse, but it was fun to see how homicides brought out this profiler side of him. In fact, I found myself disappointed when we arrived at Boxer's trendy but uninviting office, and had to put our conversation on hold. Which, among other things, told me that I really was over my bizarre, mild infatuation with Boxer. Some have called me fickle, but when it comes to letting go of situations that will do nothing but hurt other people, fickle ain't such a bad thing to be.

In fact, now that the proverbial worm had turned, I saw Boxer for what he was: A full-of-himself, balding attorney determined to do anything short of counterfeiting to make a buck. In some subterranean way, I knew that he knew about my what-was-I-thinking crush and was disappointed to see it gone. He was the type who no doubt got off on having one guy ache with jealousy while the other ached with unrequited love.

Of course, nothing was said about any of this. It was all strictly business as Terry and I sat down in Boxer's pseudo-upscale office. The fake plants, fake wood desk, and fake leatherette furniture were redeemed only by the fact that it was all spanking new and so radiated a certain pleasant cleanliness. The hazy L.A. sun angled in through the blinds, casting shadowy stripes over Boxer's dome of a head as he pretentiously sat behind his glorified Formica desk.

"I've decided that the best thing to do with Aunt Fern is humor her," Boxer told us, leaning back in his pompous swivel chair. "Let's give her something to do. Something that keeps her out of trouble."

"If you think she's sneaking off to see Ann-Margret, why not shadow her instead?" I helped myself to an upscale, chewy Swiss candy.

"My *job*," Boxer lectured, "is to protect my client. I can't have her breaking the law."

"You lawyers," I snorted contemptuously. "You're all alike. Who cares what does the most good, so long as you're racking up the hourly fees? Isn't that right, Terry?" Since Terry was extremely worried about his cousin, I figured he'd appreciate my forthright opposition to Boxer's tactic.

Talk about dialing the wrong number. Not only did Terry not value my effort, but he felt compelled to pick up where Boxer left off in this impromptu little lesson in Civics 101.

"Actually, I understand perfectly why Boxer is doing what he's doing," Terry patronizingly preached. "He's absolutely right. If he doesn't strive to protect his client, the system doesn't work."

"And what about finding Ann-Margret, oh Wise One?"

Terry's eyes met Boxer's like they were in on some cute conspiracy together. "There's no need for sarcasm, Rick. Of course I want my cousin to turn up safely more than anything. But not like this. Aunt Fern means well, but she's a naïve old lady. She can wind up hurting herself. Or getting Ann-Margret hurt, and who knows who else."

Boxer's smug, smarmy face brightened like a pink balloon. "Thanks, Terry. I'm glad you see things my way." Of course, he was really saying more than that, the arch subtlety of which was hardly lost on Terry, who got fairly disgustingly giddy as he smiled back at Boxer.

After going over his silly little scheme to dupe Aunt Fern, Boxer told us he would bring her in.

"Where have you been hiding her, the medicine chest?"

Everyone ignored me as Boxer left the room. I could hear Aunt Fern's voice through the wall, complaining that it was about time he had come to get her.

A few moments later, Aunt Fern entered, Boxer gallantly escorting her in on his arm. At the sight of us, she registered a joyous anticipation of back-fence secrets to be divulged. "So boys, watcha got?" Sitting down in a squat, neutral-toned chair, she sounded like Shelley Winters as Ma Barker.

"Oh, not too much," Terry replied, with the proper tone of vagueness.

"You see, Mr. Fancy McShmancy Lawyer, Rick and Terry and I are like the Three Musketeers." She girlishly crossed her legs. "We are living and breathing to get Ann-Margret home where she belongs. *Tell* him, boys."

"Aunt Fern is correct," I affirmed. "We're on a quest to set an innocent girl free."

"That we are," Terry agreed. "In fact, Aunt Fern, we have a special job for you. Assuming it's okay with *you*, Boxer."

Like a lot of cops, Terry was a born actor in some situations, rattling off a bunch of BS without batting an eye. But when *asked* to give a little performance, he resorted to grade-school Christmas play woodenness and long "A" sounds. In telling Aunt Fern about "a special job," he was about as convincing as the average episode of *Baywatch*.

Boxer twirled a pencil in his fingers. "Let's hear what you have to say."

"Say," Aunt Fern protested. "Since when is it okay with you that I get involved?"

"I haven't said it was okay, I just said I wanted to hear what they had up their sleeves."

"Oh." Aunt Fern looked disappointed; I got the impression that, like a lot of grandmotherly types, she relished minor fights and was saddened when the promise of one gave way to a perfectly reasonable answer.

"We want Aunt Fern to use her media savvy," Terry explained. "She's to listen morning, noon, and night to everything she can on TV or radio about the case. At the slightest inaccuracy or inconsistency, she's on the phone to us." He took out his police badge, breathed on it, and polished it on his T-shirt to make her assignment seem all the more official.

In an instant, Aunt Fern's expression changed from elation to devastation to resignation. Like a lot of older people, she seemed quick to give up hope that she'd ever be a real part of things. "But boys, I . . . oh, very well then. I suppose I can't say no to a handsome police officer. But only on one condition."

"You name it," Terry magnanimously agreed.

"You tell me what the hell's been going on." Aunt Fern rose from her chair, her palms flat on the Formica tabletop. Boxer, who'd been contentedly leaning back in his chair, suddenly sat up straight.

"Stop diddling around with me like I'm some senile old piece of nothing. I may be a little bit country, boys, but I can rock and roll with the best of them. So you level with me, and you level with me *now*."

"Don't say anything, guys," Boxer told us, as though *we* were his clients and Aunt Fern some merciless, hardball D.A. "Now, Aunt Fern. This has got to stop. You are neither a police officer nor a reporter. All you'll do is get yourself and some other well-meaning people in trouble if you insist on—"

Aunt Fern started crying. We all gathered round to comfort her, like sons for whom blood was thicker than sleuthing.

"I'm sorry, boys," she finally told us, wiping her eyes to recover herself. "But having innocent people in jail just isn't right."

"You're absolutely correct," Boxer soothed.

"Oh, stop talking down to me."

After we let her cry some more, Terry softly told her, "We spoke to Curtsy Ann, if that makes you feel better. You can probably guess what she told us." He was careful to be both vague and chummy.

Aunt Fern loudly blew her nose. "Poor Curtsy Ann. We were all so hard on her. But who could blame her, really? Why, if I were thirty—excuse me, ten years younger, I'd have gone after Brick myself."

"She did say you tended to side with Helena when Brick broke off the engagement," I shared. "But I'm sure she doesn't hold it against you." Actually, I didn't think that was true at all, but it sounded nice.

Aunt Fern looked perplexed. "She said Brick called it off? *Brick*?" Her tears subsided as quickly as they gushed. Nothing like a little gossip to get the adrenaline going.

"You know, when he started, uh, dating Helena," Terry responded patiently. Aunt Fern apparently got easily confused.

"Let me tell you something, boys. All Curtsy Ann *did* when they were engaged was nag-nag-nag. Brick had to dress better, eat better, speak better, probably do everything but you-know-what better. And behind his back, she bored us to tears with her endless litany of all the things he was not."

"You mean that Curtsy Ann—"

"She lives in a fantasy world, Terry. Almost like those whatever-you-call-it people. The ones who can play poker or play Mozart or what have you, but can't tie their own shoes. She measures away and obsesses over her designs—which frankly are rather like a broken record, are they not, boys? Seen one, and you've seen 'em all." Aunt Fern rummaged through her purse, as if searching for some important legal document. "As a pampered little beauty queen, she no doubt thought that getting a man was like picking out a prom dress. And if you don't like the sash, you tell the dressmaker to change it. So she thought she could turn poor Brick into this, that, the other. Now, Brick may have been the one to finally call it quits—I frankly have no idea and could care less. But it was Little Miss Curtsy Ann who really called it quits every single minute of every single day. If it wasn't for her insane jealousy toward Helena, she would've made whoopty-do all over town for being free of him. She wasn't crushed by losing Brick—she was crushed that Helena stole him fair and square."

"Well, that certainly is a different interpretation of events," I could not help noting.

"And to think dear Helena isn't even here to defend herself. No, boys—take it from one who was there. Helena was the only one who loved Brick. It was only after Helena realized that Brick would never commit himself that she went after those fiancés, and whatnot. They were like traveling businessmen. They barely even knew her." She finally stopped fussing through her purse, and produced a roll of butterscotch LifeSavers. "Candy, anyone?"

As I thought of it, there was nothing in the video clips that contradicted anything Aunt Fern said. Helena had indeed seemed troubled over her relationship with Brick, and the only mention made of Curtsy Ann was of wanting to steal her thunder. Which, if even half of what Aunt Fern was saying were true, seemed understandable. Not admirable, maybe, but one way of telling a third wheel to bug off.

Aunt Fern sucked contentedly on her butterscotch candy. "*Still* think I'm just a senile old wind bag, boys?"

Rather than answer her, I thought it politic to pose another question. "It is true that Helena was—shall we say—active in extracurricular pursuits?"

"Shame on you, Rick." She reached over to slap my hand. "Honestly, the cavalier way you young people discuss these things."

I tried a different tactic. "What about Fernando San Marcos?"

"He plays a police officer on a TV show. I have to say I don't care for him—or the program—one bit."

"Oh, really?" Terry evidently took offense at her appraisal. "You don't think that Detective Garcia makes a fine example of what an officer should be?"

"It's all too violent," Aunt Fern opined. "I like nice shows."

"But don't you think that when the violence teaches a moral lesson—"

"Put a lid on it, Terry. Save it for CNN."

"Oh, sorry, Rick. I just get a little carried away sometimes."

"Anyway, as I was saying, Aunt Fern. Curtsy Ann showed a tape of Fernando having a very strong reaction to his body piercing room. As in, he wanted to do all sorts of crummy things to Helena. What did you hear about this?"

"Oh, *that* Fernando San Marcos. Is he the same one as on the cop show?" I nodded affirmatively.

"Huh, isn't that funny. I wonder if anyone recognized him. But yes, of course I heard all about it. He *liked* the room, as I recall."

"But what about the tape we saw?" Terry wanted to know.

"Well, he's an actor, right? And we do joke around an awful lot on the set. So probably he was just pretending to hate it."

"Are you *sure*?" I asked.

"Listen, boys. If there's trouble in paradise, believe you me we *all* get wind of it. We would have all been called in to the producer's office and given a no-nonsense lecture about avoiding lawsuits and looking over our shoulders, and I don't know what all. Not to mention we all would've been talking about it. Koko would've told us, Brick would've told us. And most of all, Little Miss Panhandle herself would've told us. She would've pounced on *any* chance to badmouth Helena. Certainly *someone* would've told Helena about it, and she would've confided in Ann-Margret or me."

Boxer's desk phone rang. "Damn it, I told them to hold my calls." Glancing at the caller ID, he sighed for the gravity of the decision before him. "To hell with it," he importantly decreed.

"Really, Mr. Jones," Aunt Fern scolded. "I should hope you do not use such language in the presence of less agreeable clients." With a hand to the side of her mouth, she pretended to whisper: "He thinks I sneak off to see Ann-Margret."

"Do you?" Terry asked, in his best cop voice. "If so, it means more of the same. You know—sheltering a fugitive, not to mention obstruction of justice. Sound familiar?"

"Terry, I knew my legal ABCs while you were still playing with water pistols. Even if I wanted to help her now, Ann-Margret would refuse. Such an unselfish girl. Just like Florence Nightingale."

"Well, do you have any wild guesses where she might be found?" Terry asked.

Aunt Fern reopened her purse; she took out a freshly minted square of crochet, which she proceeded to embellish with her hook. "Oh, I don't keep up with you young people and the places you like to go." I knew nothing about crocheting, yet I guessed that the speed and precision with which she worked was worthy of the *Guinness Book of World Records*. It was amazing how much larger the square became right before our eyes; even as you watched her do it, you couldn't see how it was done.

"Now do you understand what it's like?" Boxer complained. "Obviously, she's hiding something."

Aunt Fern stared into her yarn with a determined tranquility. "I'm sure I have no idea what you mean, Mr. Jones."

Terry got down on one knee, as if proposing marriage. "Aunt Fern, we suspect you gave your word to Ann-Margret not to tell anyone where she is. But look at it this way: If she really is innocent, then whoever did it is out there someplace. And this person, whoever he or she is, might just want to make sure that Ann-Margret doesn't stumble upon the truth."

Aunt Fern looked up from her hook and yarn, and stared straight ahead in thought.

"Please, Aunt Fern. For Ann-Margret's own safety, tell us where she is. I'll personally make sure no harm comes to her in jail."

"Plus, if some dopey cop finds her on the lam and she makes a run for it," I helpfully added, "he might shoot her, for want of knowing what else to do."

Terry gave me an evil stare.

"You boys are right," Aunt Fern decided. "But you see, I really don't know *where* she might be." She looked at us with a poignant earnestness. "She really didn't tell me where she was going. You have to believe me."

"Aunt Fern—"

Terry touched my shoulder, signaling me to give things a rest. "Never mind," I decided.

"So, do you have a big family?" Terry cheerfully asked her.

"I'm afraid not." She put her crocheting back in her purse. "I lost my dear husband years ago."

"Didn't you say you have a son?" I asked.

"My Leo. My special pet. Killed by a drunk driver seven years ago next month. He was such a promising young man."

"Aunt Fern, we're so sorry." Terry patted her soft hand.

She dabbed her nose with her lace hanky. "The Lord works in mysterious ways. *'Thy* will be done.' But at least I have my life as Aunt Fern. I *so* need to still feel like a mother in some way, shape, or form."

All at once, I felt guilty for every sarcastic remark I'd ever said about the old battleax. "What happened to the drunk driver?" I gently asked.

"They jailed the hooligan who was behind the wheel. But ever since, I've been . . . well, funny about these things. I just get so upset when I hear about someone being killed, or the wrong person going to jail."

"That's very understandable," Terry affirmed. "Don't worry. We'll get this all straightened out."

"Oh, bless you both. You, too, Mr. Jones." She urged us to come toward her in a group hug. Probably there are things in this world that embarrass me more than a group hug, but I'd be hard pressed to think of what they might be. Still, I felt like I had no choice but to join in.

After a minute or so of dull pleasantries—where I went to college, and so forth—Terry and I made our excuses to leave.

"Rick, don't you worry," Aunt Fern stated on our way out of the office.

"Worry about what?"

"About not finding someone special. I just know you will. Oh, and Boxer—is it all right if I call you that? Make sure you're a gentleman with Terry, because he has a very good heart."

The three of us guys looked at one other, then back at Aunt Fern. "What the . . . how the heck did you—?" Boxer managed to sputter, while Terry's large face turned red as a traffic light. There had been no furtive little asides between Terry and Boxer, not even—as far as I could tell—any sort of telltale eye contact once Aunt Fern came into the room.

"When you get to be my age, boys, you begin to notice things."

# TWELVE

"I JUST HOPE I'VE MADE THE RIGHT DECISION." TERRY WORRIEDLY paced the floors while continually glancing at his watch. "I've never tried something like this before."

"Trust me," I promised. "You'll accomplish everything you need by sticking to my plan of attack."

"But are you *sure*, Rick?"

I sighed with exasperation. "Okay, fine, then. *Wear* that stupid pirate shirt with your 501s, for all I care. But I'm telling you, the simple white T will make the point so much stronger."

"I paid a lot of money for this pirate shirt," Terry countered, holding up a kind of seventies-era ruffled rayon monstrosity that made you think of a nightmare version of *Saturday Night Fever*. "I'll have you know it came from a *catalog*."

After we repaired to my place for much-needed naps, Terry was readying himself for his dinner date with Boxer Jones. Ironically, the longer I thought about it, the more I decided that Boxer was not worthy of Terry. The more I considered Boxer's shiny dome of a head and his lame, put-upon smile—not to mention the fact that he was a lawyer—the less I trusted the creep. But since this was Terry's First Real Date (i.e. dinner and a movie) since coming out, I tried my best to be supportive.

My changing room had recently been redone to give it a theatrical twist, featuring mammoth-size original posters of movies about the theater: *All About Eve*, *Stage Door*, and *Noises Off*. There also was a stage dresser with lots of lights, and my clothes were kept on these costume racks that slid in and out of the closet. The fanciful designer even put a star with my name on it on the outside of the door. *Ray of Light* by Madonna was thumping away on the CD player, providing the perfect getting-ready-for-a-hot-date background music, and Terry, despite his anxiety, somewhat worriedly bopped along.

"But is a T-shirt fancy enough?" Terry asked me, for about the millionth time.

"Have him take you to one of those upscale retro fifties places. You should have food you're comfortable with, and be yourself."

"But—"

"I'm sorry, Terry. But that other shirt is ugly, plain and simple. Trust me. Besides, your great asset is your naturalness. Just be true to who you are, and you'll stand out like . . . like June Allyson at a burlesque house."

"Huh?" Some gay men don't appreciate fem-type teasing, but Terry was cut from a different cloth—he just plain didn't get it.

He studied his reflection in the full-length mirror. "I hope you're right, Rick."

The doorbell rang. "That's probably the flowers," Terry explained. The look on my face must have indicated incredulousness, because he quickly elaborated, "You know, for Boxer."

"Oh, how nice." I managed to smile, but I was thinking to myself: *Poor Terry, he's really going to get hurt.*

Terry thundered down the stairs, then thundered back up. "Well, Rick, what do you think?"

Just as I feared, he'd ordered a dozen red roses. Gay courtship etiquette might still be a work in progress, but surely one's sensibilities indicated that this was too much for a first date.

"They look great, Terry."

"I sure hope Boxer likes them."

*I sure hope Boxer doesn't stand you up*, I found myself thinking.

Well, Boxer arrived *exactly* on time, like a true gentleman caller, with—I could scarcely believe it—a dozen red roses for *Terry*. In that repulsive way that new daters have of reading hidden meanings into everything, they of course couldn't wax enough on the profundity of getting each other the same dozen flowers. It was as if they truly believed themselves to be the first people in history to think of giving someone red roses. I mean, okay—so they both had a) no imagination, and b) no taste, but was it really worth going ape shit over?

"It *is* amusing, isn't it?" I sportingly offered, sipping an extra-dry vodka martini while the two of them just kept laughing and clearly getting more obnoxiously cross-eyed over each other by the millisecond. Above and beyond red roses, there seemed to be a litany of items that surely should have landed them a featured segment on *Ripley's Believe It or Not*:

"I like to channel surf with the TV remote," Boxer blushingly gushed.

"Me, *too*," Terry breathlessly enthused. "Do you by any chance like to watch sports games?"

"With beer and potato chips," Boxer gingerly admitted.

"This is so weird," Terry decreed. "*Me*, too. But I *hate* taking out the garbage, or dusting and mopping. Or when my car breaks down."

"Me, too!" Boxer trilled, overcome by the heavenly ecstasy of it all.

Their haughty, coy eye contact made me feel so ignored in my own home that I might as well have been an amoeba. Which actually would have been preferable under the circumstances.

"On your way now, children," I merrily scolded. "I'll be waiting up."

"Actually, Rick, I won't be coming back here."

"Why Terry, aren't you just *full* of surprises?" For some reason, I almost felt ill.

"I'm going *home*," he informed me. "I have a big work day ahead of me."

"Well, I'm sure that as a criminal defense attorney and a cop, you'll have *so* much in common. Didn't I read about some major drug dealer that you got off on a technicality, Boxer?"

I don't think they even heard me. They were doing a full *West Side Story*. It was as if they were the only two people in the world.

Even when they left, I noticed that they spent a long time in Boxer's car before driving off. Whatever they were doing was none of my business, of course—and besides, in the dark, at that angle, I couldn't see a thing.

I was on my third or fifth drink—and was playing "Is That All There Is?" by Peggy Lee for about the hundredth time—when the phone rang.

"Rick, can you hear me?" I recognized Ann-Margret's purring yet aggressive voice.

"Holy shit, where are you?" Talk about sobering up fast.

"Like I'm going to tell you. Listen, and listen tight. I remembered something important. Helena, in the motel room that night, said something like, 'That goddamn white room—I knew it would come back to bite me on the ass.' I asked her what she meant, and she acted all innocent and denied even having said it. She said I must've been hearing things, and went on about how much I'd had to drink. But I know she said it."

"Do you have any idea what she meant?"

There was a pause. "Listen, Rick, I gotta fly. Do what you can. Later." She made a *kiss-kiss* sound into the receiver, and hung up.

I dialed the number on my caller ID and got no answer; obviously, it was just a pay phone, but it might help to at least know where it was. I saw no choice but to call Terry on his cell phone and thereby interrupt his cute little date. Still, the fact that it pleasured me to do so made me feel duplicitous, as if I were a soap opera villain.

"I'll be right there," he informed me after I explained what happened.

"But aren't you guys, you know, like . . . doing something?"

"We're just now finishing up our banana splits. I mean, I am. Boxer chickened out and got one scoop of frozen custard. We're at one of those fifties places, just like you suggested, Rick. I've had—I mean, we've had a great time."

"So you really were just going to go home?"

"Listen, Rick. I can't hear very well. I'll say good night to Boxer, and be there before you know it."

Minutes later, he called back. From the background noise, I guessed he was on the freeway. "Rick, I called in the number you gave me. It's at a gas station on Interstate 80."

"Did Ann-Margret by any chance use a credit card?" On TV shows, people were always getting caught by the cops by using their credit cards.

Terry laughed. "One step ahead of you, Buddy. Nope, she's a smart cookie. Or smart enough, anyway. I even had them check on Aunt Fern, just to make sure. The detectives on the case thanked me for the tip, and then told me in a nice way to bug off."

It must have been the vodka, but I found myself wanting to make the house cheery for Terry, and lit a fire in what I was starting to call the Aunt Fern room. I still couldn't stand it, but I knew that Terry would feel more at home there than anyplace else in the house.

"So, how's the stud?" I joked, upon his entrance.

"Say, a fire. That's nice, Rick." He smiled at me. In his black leather jacket, white T-shirt and 501s, he looked like more like a biker dude than a cop.

"I really didn't mean to cut your date short. I just thought—"

"You did the right thing, Rick. No sweat, we were getting ready to say good night, anyway."

"How was the movie?"

Terry's forehead creased for the effort of concentration. "Movie? Oh, yeah, right. We saw, like, this old movie. It was in black and white and everything. Kind of fit where we went to dinner."

Was it sadism or masochism that inspired what I said next?

"Do you remember the name of the movie?"

As Terry unlaced his workman boots, his face signaled that he was ever more deeply enmeshed in the troubling waters of thought. "Something about . . . it's like there was this guy and a girl. Two guys, actually, only the one was way cooler than the other. Only the girl ends up with the one who isn't as cool, on account of it being World War Two. The guy's name was . . . that's right, it was Rick. Small world, huh? Is there a movie called *Rick's Café?*"

"Oh, so you saw *Casablanca.*" As always, I tried to sound nonchalant.

"Right. That was it. Boxer said it was one of his favorites. Like I said, the lead guy was really cool. The girl I'm not so sure about. She was pretty and all, but the way she couldn't figure out her own feelings, and so she strings these guys along—it's just not right, you know?"

Terry had difficulty sympathizing with adultery even in a movie. I figured it was best to change the subject. "Do you think you'll see Boxer again?"

He sat down in the recliner, and helped himself to a beer. "Sure, why wouldn't I?"

"Yeah, you're right. Why wouldn't you?" For some reason or another—some illogical lingering crush on Boxer, perhaps?—I was having a rough time accepting that Terry and Boxer might become an item. But I couldn't let Terry know this—especially not after lecturing him all this time about how he needed to get out there and meet someone.

"So, I guess Ann-Margret is way gone by now," I concluded.

"The phone was on the northbound side, if that means anything. Any ideas about the white room?"

I reached over for my laptop. "I looked up Helena's rooms on the *My House, Your House* homepage. Helena being Helena, she'd only done one room in her entire career in anything so traditional as white. Although needless to say, that was the only thing traditional about it." I clicked on a link. "Presenting for your enjoyment: the Swan Room."

The headline-making disaster in question was inspired by a casual remark to the effect that the owner of the bedroom liked the singer Björk. As I explained to Terry, she especially thought that the swan dress worn by Björk to the Oscars was fab. And so hundreds of white feathers were carefully Super-glued to the ceiling and walls. The antique nineteenth-century sleigh bed was cut up and painted to resemble a swan's beak. Plaster was applied to contorted Slinky toys to make curved, swan's-neck lamps. An Eastlake chest of drawers was splattered with white paint to simulate droppings. And to enter the room, one had to walk across a small bridge, beneath which Helena had created a miniature pond, tearing up the parquet floors to do so.

The lucky homeowner was a rising young standup comic named Tippi Finklestein, whose very name seemed intended to be the equivalent of the roguish little drum roll that so often followed one-liners in boozed-out night clubs. In point of fact, Tippi's act was considerably more original than the take-my-wife variety of humor. She was actually a kind of impressionist comic, and would do bits like "Barbra Streisand visits her shrink," or "What if Pamela Anderson were a NASA scientist?" She appeared now and then on the *Tonight Show*, but the nature of her talents hadn't yielded her, say, her own sitcom—unless maybe she could have starred in a comedy about someone with multiple personality disorder. And so she was staying stuck at that kind of B+ level of success. Still, Tippi did well enough to have a small but attractive home in Van Nuys. Or at least it was attractive until Helena got hold of it.

Unlike the body piercing room, I had actually seen the swan room episode. Tippi jumped up and down, shaking her hands as hot tears shot out from her eyes, as if she'd just won a prize. But it was no secret that the very next day the entire room was taken apart. Yet this publicity-hungry young woman always offered "no comment" to the press when queried about the room—and, curiously, she'd yet to develop any routines about it for her act.

"Who knows?" I pondered aloud. "Surely no one would actually kill another person just because they hated how their room was decorated. But with Fernando, the charming body-piercing motif stood for his charmingly kinky sex life, so maybe, just maybe, there *is* something there. Maybe the swan crapola revealed a secret about Tippi. Or at least Tippi thought it did."

"And when were these shows filmed?"

"They were both about a year ago. But it takes time to plot a murder, no?"

Terry scratched his buzz cut. "A successful murder, yes. Were there other really not-so-nice rooms Helena designed?"

"I think every room she ever did had its detractors," I tactfully observed. "But these rooms were really the Big Two. And besides, they were both in L.A. The only other rooms she did in our fair city were to regular, unknown folk who surely would have had nothing at stake but a hefty bill to repair the damage she caused. But Fernando and Tippi are more or less celebrities who can't afford to have any dirty laundry aired."

Terry mentally weighed what I'd said. "Sounds like a good place to start, then. Plus of course there's still Curtsy Ann."

"Not to mention Basil and Bill and Brick, and maybe even Koko," I added.

"So we start going through the list until we find a winner. *Plus* we find Ann-Margret and check in with Aunt Fern to see that she's alive and well. Anything else?"

"A large fries and a medium coke." I did a web search on Tippi and got a number of hits about the notorious swan episode, her club dates, and the to-be-expected homepage. But there was another, unexpected listing: Something about Tippi being seen at a premiere with a rising Dreamworks exec named Hoover Swann. Then I did another web search, and hit the proverbial jackpot.

"Bingo." I turned the screen to face Terry. It seemed that Hoover Swann was a former Wall Street player who'd once been engaged to Helena.

"So there's more to it than Björk," I commented, dumbfounded as to how life had led me to saying such an absurd thing.

"Just where does this Tippi Finklehoff live?" Terry inquired.

"I told you, Van Nuys, and her name is Finkle*stein*. She's in *show* business. You should know her."

"Do you think she'll meet with us? Tonight, if possible."

It was only about ten o'clock. "I know she's in town. I'll bet she's starting her second show right now at the Pink Hightop."

"At the *what*?"

"The hip new comedy club on the strip."

Terry rubbed his hands together and cracked his knuckles in eagerness. "Well, then, what are we waiting for? C'mon."

But I wasn't quite ready to go—or more to the point, we weren't. Something about Terry was occurring to me, and the more it occurred to me the more intently I stared at him.

"You know, Terry, I was just thinking. You remember how, when we worked together before, I had to pass you off as my assistant?"

"Actually, it was as your bodyguard."

"Whatever. Anyway, I bought you all those nice clothes, some of which you even occasionally wear instead of . . . other things." I was trying to be diplomatic, but I could tell I'd hit a nerve. Terry didn't like it when I criticized his taste—if you could say that he had any.

"Of course, the reason we did that," I continued, "was to put everyone at ease. There's this funny way people have of not wanting to tell everything they know to cops."

Terry regarded me with suspicion, as though he knew what was coming but wanted to avoid it if at all possible. "And your point is . . . ?"

"My point is that the people from *My House, Your House* already know who you are. When we meet with them, we have no choice but to remind them you're a cop, and hope for the best. But Tippi Finklestein is trying for the big time. Same with Fernando San Marcos. And they *don't* know who you are. And they're going to be very uptight about saying anything to a cop that might get them into even a *soupçon* of trouble."

A log in the fireplace sparked and crackled as it split in two; I grabbed the poker to shove the logs over a bit.

"But Rick, they'll know who I am soon enough. The episode will be airing next week. And if they have a connection to the people on the show, they'll find out anyway."

I set aside the poker, and brushed the residue of soot from my hands. "True enough. But right here and now, we can get the straight dope from them *without* them knowing who you are. And as for what they think next week . . . well, as we both know from past experience, an awful lot can happen in a week."

"What are you saying?"

"I'm saying that I think it would never hurt to disguise you a little. Last time we gave you that very upscale casual look. We should go for something different this time, just in case."

Terry groaned. "Rick, I *hate* disguising myself. I'm no good at that stuff at all."

"C'mon. You know we have to do this."

I dragged him off to my master bath. About forty-five minutes later, he emerged with his buzz cut dyed pale blond and spiked into desperate little tufts. I then gave him a non-prescription pair of nerdy-looking glasses that I'd worn once at a costume party—Terry could barely squeeze them onto his large, round head, but they did the job. Plus there was a handsome suit I'd bought him that still hung in my guest closet after having been placed there, unworn, during our last case. All suited up, he looked like a dweeby businessman trying—and failing—to achieve a post-punk cool.

"So, you're Terry, my personal secretary." I did what had to be done, but I had to admit to gloating a little at Terry's displeasure, in light of what had happened to my living room.

"Oh brother." He rolled his eyes. "I hate what you did to my hair. And these stupid glasses . . ." He was so frustrated, I almost thought he was going to cry. "I just don't think—"

"Look, what choice do we have? We just have to hope it works."

# THIRTEEN

THE PINK HIGHTOP WAS SITUATED IN AN OLD WAREHOUSE THAT had been through numerous incarnations before finally clicking as a comedy spot. It featured hanging ferns, dim lights, a rickety stage, and watered-down drinks. Tippi, a razor-thin, nervous, frizzy-haired brunette in a flashy black sequined pantsuit, was holding her inebriated audience of about two hundred in the veritable palm of her hand. In a Boris-and-Natasha sort of way, she was mysteriously beautiful, but her kooky personality somewhat detracted from her looks.

"And so then I say to the salesclerk," she told the audience, while adopting the proper look of befuddlement, " 'Is this bra on sale, or not?' And the salesclerk gives me the once-over *like this . . .*" Tippi uncannily registered the appropriate disdain of the salesclerk, who seemed the sort of woman who clipped a chain to her eyeglasses. After letting the audience laugh, Tippi got to her punchline: "And this salesclerk lady says to me, 'The bra's on sale all right, and tits are half off on Aisle Seven.'" The audience roared with guffaws as Tippi looked down at her chest, shrugged, smiled, and delightedly tried—and failed—to interject her next bit before the crowd had calmed down.

"Now I'd like to do . . . Now I'd like to do . . . my impersonation of Hillary Rodham Clinton having tea with Anna Nicole Smith." The audience burst into applause; Tippi did a mean Hillary impersonation.

Tippi quite uncannily captured Hillary's nonjudgmental liberal niceness and Anna Nicole's zombiness as the former asked the latter what she would like in her tea, and the latter replied, "Crack." The ever eager-to-please Hilary answered, "One lump or two?" The audience was all but literally rolling in the aisles, yet Terry whispered over to me, "What's so funny about making fun of people? I think it's mean." I knew he felt doubly out of place for having to sport the suit and glasses and dyed hair.

"Lighten up, Terry. It's just a *joke*."

"Drug addiction is nothing to joke about."

"She's just making it up. Who knows how Anna Nicole spends her billions?"

"Well, I just don't get it." Still, he politely applauded at the end of the bit.

"Now, ladies and gentlemen, I'd like to do a brand-new routine." The microphone gave off a high-pitched squeak; the audience appropriately moaned. "Easy there, fella." She scolded the mike with a tiny slap. "Frisky little devil, huh?" She winked to the audience. "A brand-new routine, ladies and gentlemen, ripped from today's headlines. My impersonation of Ann-Margret Wochinsky and Helena Godiva, alone in a motel room."

An urgent mumble swept through the audience; a number of people got up and left, while several others booed. Tippi looked pleased by the strong response, as though she'd out-Lenny-Bruce'd Lenny Bruce.

"Thank you, come again." She bowed to the people getting up to leave. Turning to the remaining audience, she raised her fist in the air and shouted: "The few, the proud." Everyone applauded, as though it were a testament to one's integrity to be willing to listen to what promised to be an exercise in sickness and depravity. Terry no doubt would have left himself, had it not been for his cop's curiosity to hear what Tippi had to say.

The misbegotten routine opened with Tippi standing with legs bent to signify riding a Harley—if not something else. In an Ann-Margret Wochinsky voice, she said to the imaginary Helena: "How's about a nice vat of gin?" Then she impersonated Helena scooting over with a rather exaggerated femininity to her walk. She made a point of putting her hand near her neck. "Mustn't get my pearls wet," she told the audience, which tittered nervously. She bent down into the imaginary vat as Helena, then turned herself back into Ann-Margret, holding down "Helena" while shouting at her: "Take *that* for the swan room! Take that and that and that!"

Then she switched back to Helena, struggling for air with her arms flailing about. Tippi had the good taste, if it can be called that, to end it there, and not depict the actual moment of death. The routine ended to confused, perfunctory applause.

Following her encore piece about flying on Budweiser Babe Airlines, I repaired to the minuscule dressing room backstage with an agitated, bespectacled Terry, who had not been amused by the skit. A weddings-and-bar-mitzvahs caliber house band launched into a sluggish, garage-sounding version of "Stairway to Heaven."

Upon introducing ourselves, Tippi thought for a moment, and then sarcastically bowed and waved us in. "Enter, your royal pain in the asses." It wasn't exactly the strongest vote of confidence I'd ever been given.

"Uh, maybe we could go to the bar?" I looked dubiously about the microscopic dressing room, noting that an outhouse would have been palatial by comparison. A single bare light bulb fizzled from the ceiling like a trapped fly, providing the only light in the musty brick room.

"No way," Tippi replied with mean grin. "Bars have ears. Not to mention big mouths."

Of course, since I was a reporter, whether anyone heard what she told me was pretty much a moot point. But I sensed that she really wanted to meet in the cramped dressing room simply to get rid of us as quickly as possible.

As it was, Tippi, sitting with her slim back to the pockmarked dressing table, didn't have enough room to uncross her legs without rubbing them against mine. The enormous Terry was more or less pinned against a pointy umbrella stand, where a feather boa tickled his nose. "So, *you're* Rick Domino, that tacky reporter," Tippi reflected, tightening the silk knot around her dressing gown. "Ruin anyone's life today?"

"I don't write like that, and you know it." I was slightly put off by her attitude, but not much. As a cutting-edge comic, she needed to project an image of haughty indifference when it came to anything so establishment as the press.

"Look, let's just get straight to the point. I think you're a ruthless prick, and you think I'm a pretentious cunt. But if I don't let you interview me, a half-dozen assholes who think they run my life will be all over me for letting such a golden opportunity pass me by. So let's just do it and get it over with." She looked at Terry disdainfully. "And you're Rick's *secretary*? Funny, but to me you look like a cop."

As Terry blew with his lower lip at the ever-present boa, his glasses worn crooked across his face, I pointed at him with sublime confidence and stated: "Him, a cop? You gotta be kidding."

She giggled like a schoolyard bully. "Yeah, I guess I see your point. So why do you keep him around, Ricky boy? Is he *that* good a lay?"

Terry's deep blush could only confirm in her mind that she'd been on the money.

I was eager to change the subject. "You've been straight with us, so we'll return the favor. We know Ann-Margret didn't kill Helena."

Tippi burst out laughing. We waited for her to recover herself. "Of course she didn't. Only the cops are stupid enough to think she did."

I had to hand it to Terry. He didn't betray the slightest flicker of anger over her words.

"Well, at the risk of sounding corny, we're looking for the real killer. Will you tell us everything you know?"

"Sure, Rick. Why not? I have absolutely nothing to hide."

It was a familiar enough claim, having just heard it from Curtsy Ann—not to mention a million other showbiz types who over the years had told me for one reason or another that they were brutally honest people who never held anything back.

"Great act, Tippi," Terry contributed, trying to win her over.

"I'm glad you enjoyed what little you saw of it." She took out an emery board to file her nails. "Who was the critic who said that less of me was more?" She shrugged indifferently. "Anyway, thanks, I guess."

"That swan room sketch was especially clever," Terry shared, wincing in annoyance at the feather boa.

"Swan room? Oh, you mean the death of Helena." She reached for a bottle of purple nail polish. "It's odd you should say that, because I watch my audience carefully, and you didn't laugh at all during the sketch. You looked very uncomfortable."

As was typical of a certain kind of comic, Tippi seemed to consider herself an officer in the hypocrisy police. Perfunctory niceties that other people let slip by were pounced on by Tippi with the moral aggressiveness of a cop entrapping a serial killer.

"Let's just get to the point, okay?" Tippi studied the shiny purple nail polish as she applied it to each nail. "If you care at all, Rick: I was born an only child in Brooklyn thirty-one years ago. Two years at Hunter College. Math major. Dropped out to follow my dream. Three times on the *Tonight Show*. Lived with my nobody boyfriend for six years. I'm straight, but frequently wish I weren't, since men are such fucks. I speak to my psychotic parents about once every three years. And here I am."

"What about the swan room?" Terry asked.

"Oh right, I almost forgot. You guys don't care about me at all unless I killed Helena. Well, I guess we'll never get cozy, guys, because I didn't kill the bitch. I'm a *vegetarian*, for chrissake. And anyway, I was home alone, reading a good book." She blew on her nails, then frowned, as if not liking the color after all. "My agent said it would be good free publicity to be on the stupid design show. So I figured, what the hell? Well, hell was too good a word for it. Did you *see* what she did to my bedroom?"

I nodded affirmatively. "It must have been quite a shock."

"Shock doesn't even begin to say it. On TV, the millions saw me do my happy, jerky oh-my-God-there's-David-Cassidy impression, but my real first reaction was to cry. I bawled like I hadn't since I was ten years old. In a way, it was all very cathartic. Very cleansing. Helena cost me a horrendous repair job on my bedroom. I swear, I haven't been able to afford so much as a new pot holder since I got the room put back to normal. But it probably balanced out in shrink bills. I can't *tell* you how many years my shrink has been trying to get me to cry."

It was intended to be a funny shtick, but Terry's clueless perplexity killed any chance for merriment. "Why would he want you to cry? I thought doctors were supposed to make patients feel *better*."

Tippi clasped her hands together in laughter. "God, you're too much . . . Terry, right? You *have* to give me permission to use that in a sketch."

"You're making fun of me, aren't you?"

"Not at all. You have this unusual quality. I just don't know how to put it in words. You're. . . . It's a kind of. . . ."

"Honesty?" I offered.

She pointed at me like a queen holding court. "Yes, that is it exactly. *Honesty*. God, whoda thunk it? And in L.A., of all places. I guess Dorothy was right. There *is* no place like home." Tippi laughed some more, genuinely amusing herself, while I kind of smiled and nodded politely and Terry stared self-consciously at the dirty floor.

"Anyway," I interjected, "what about the swan room? As in, Hoover Swann?"

Abruptly, Tippi stopped laughing. "Hoover Swann is dead."

"I'm sorry to hear that," I quietly stated. The house band proceeded to butcher "Go Your Own Way," by Fleetwood Mac.

"Why? You didn't know him." Now moody and sullen, she reached for the hand brush, and attacked her thick mane, the tangles making electricity. "It was a suicide. He jumped from his New York penthouse, twenty stories down."

"Does anyone know why?" Terry inquired.

"Guess he was having a bad day." Irritated, she winced to disentangle a knot in her hair.

"We both know you can do better than that," I scolded.

"Fair enough." She set down the brush. "Coincidentally, it was shortly after Helena dumped him. He asked her to marry him. She said she didn't love him any further than a snake could throw a stick, but she had the deepest respect for his money, and would that be enough? He said yes. Then she changed her mind and said, 'La-de-dah, even with all your money, I still don't like you.' Or words to that effect."

"That must've really smarted," Terry commented.

"I guess a shrinkie would say that it went much deeper than that. That Helena's rejection symbolized rejection from his mother or all women or all people or whatever. But I guess it doesn't matter once you're dead."

"Did you date Hoover Swann?" I asked.

"A few times. In a manner of speaking."

"You mean that you—"

"In theory, Rick. But theory doesn't get you there. I think the lowly boy made his billions to compensate for something else. He didn't have much to work with, if you know what I mean. And adding insult to injury, he couldn't work it up to anything much." She pulled her hair back with an elastic tie, frowned, and let it fall loose again.

"Huh?" Terry registered puzzlement.

"The guy was impotent," I explained, somewhat impatiently.

"And *tiny*," Tippi added. "I mean, we're talking getting out the magnifying glass and still mistaking it for a toenail clipping. We're talking—"

"Okay, I get it," Terry assured us.

"Then why the swan room? What was Helena trying to say to you—or to the world?"

She squeezed past me to step behind the changing screen. "I really do believe that was a coincidence. That it had to do with my propensity for all things Björk. I think my all-time favorites are 'Bachelorette,' 'Pagan Poetry' and 'Venus as a Boy.' I *really* love 'Venus as a Boy.' She just has this way of *saying* it, you know?"

"Indubitably," I agreed, in my best showbiz-affirmative voice.

"Did Björk do that song, 'The Night the Lights Went Out in Georgia'?" Terry asked.

Neither Tippi nor I wanted to go there.

"*Anyway,*" she continued, her voice betraying an exasperated sigh, "as I told you, I hated the room, but who wouldn't have?"

"We have access to outtakes from the show," Terry lied. "If you're hiding anything, it will only make you look worse."

We waited for her to respond.

Finally, Tippi emerged from behind the screen, wearing a plain white blouse and French jeans. "Okay, so you got me. I didn't just cry because I hated the room. I cried because the room was all about Hoover. I *loved* him, okay?" She neatly folded back the cuffs on the blouse.

"I thought you said he couldn't make you happy."

Tippi inspected her image in the flecked mirror. "Look, this is completely off the record. I have my reputation to think of. But there's other things more important than making it when I make it. I know that sounds very un-liberated of me, but them's the breaks."

"And you're sure Helena never loved him?"

"Don't make me laugh. Don't make me cry. You should have seen them together. She treated him like a bug. I saw him beg on his knees, literally *begging* for her to give him another chance. And she laughed and said, 'But I keep telling you I don't love you.'"

"Sounds like a very personal situation for you to have been privy to," I commented.

"Okay, so I followed them a few times. Big deal."

"Do you make a habit of stalking people?" Terry vainly attempted to shoo a feather from his face.

Tippi shrugged. "Only when it serves my masochistic need to feel rejected. The thing was, Hoover would've traded a lifetime of devotion from me for five seconds of her depraved indifference. I was like the whore with a heart of gold in those old Shirley MacLaine movies. Good for a lay and a laugh when the real love hurt him all over again. Helena and I had met only briefly before she did my room. We were like ice cubes toward each other, but civil. The room was after Hoover had died. When I saw it . . . it felt like someone telling you the person you loved most just died, and then slapping you across the face. Which was pretty much what *did* happen."

She turned away from us to cry, clearly not trusting us enough for support. She knocked a clip-on fan over in the process, but didn't seem to notice. As she stood there crying, I was struck by how the masks of comedy and tragedy so often seemed to be not opposite each other but near-identical twins. There was nothing schizoid or inconsistent with Tippi's abrupt changes of mood; it all just seemed part of the same highly strung temperament.

I also found myself wondering how many more of Helena's "masterpieces" had some hidden meanings attached to them. If maybe she found out some sort of dirt on all the people whose rooms she designed, and then found some symbolic way of expressing it in her chosen theme. Sometimes people complained that Helena's themes were—among much else—obscure. What made her give that nice couple from Tallahassee a room with a bald eagle theme? Well, maybe it wasn't just her nutty sense of style. Maybe it because she knew something about them that the bald eagle would symbolize—and the couple in question, knowing perfectly well what she meant by it, could only force a smile and say that the room certainly looked different.

If this were true, I couldn't even begin to guess what insanity possessed her to do it. To desecrate a room in someone's house on national TV while furtively revealing some skeleton in their closet—and getting *paid* to do it—was so passive-aggressive and yet so unapologetically sadistic that surely even the spendiest shrink in Beverly Hills would be stumped.

"Tippi, I know this is hard for you, but as far as you knew, was Helena in love with someone else?"

She turned round to face us, reaching for a Kleenex to pat her red nose. "I believe you got what you came for, Rick. Now please go."

I started to repeat my question, but Terry's eyes told me not to push it. Clearly, it was too difficult for her to consider that Helena might have suffered out of all this, too—suffered guilt over Hoover Swann, plus her own unrequited feeling for Brick, which turned the proverbial tables and then some. Not to mention the trivial detail that she'd been murdered.

Terry and I repaired back to the main room of the club to plot our next move.

"So she stalks people," I remarked. "I'm sure she's a sweet girl underneath it all."

"And that bedroom Helena designed sure was . . . well, *white*," Terry added.

Before I could reply, something caught our attention: Brick Edwards was headed straight toward Tippi's dressing room. He was carrying a large bouquet of yellow tulips. At the doorway, he paused for a moment to nervously straighten his tie.

"I guess I'll have to go in without you," I told Terry. After all, Brick knew who Terry really was.

He put a restraining hand on my arm. "Let Brick get into the room first." After an infinitely long minute, I walked back to the dressing room. I knocked on the door, knocked again, then opened it.

No one was inside. The one window, located behind the changing screen and looking out to an ugly brick alleyway, was flung open.

# FOURTEEN

OUR SEARCH FOR TIPPI AND BRICK PROVED ABOUT AS SUCCESSFUL as a *Gilligan's Island* reunion movie. We looked all around the alleyway, but there was no sign of either of them, save for a rumpled program from Tippi's show that could've belonged to anyone. Perhaps they simply wanted to get away from a pushy reporter on general principle, but for the time being, we could only speculate that it must have been more than that. Obviously, the notion that Tippi was dating Brick did much to implicate either or both of them in Helena's demise. If nothing else, there was the weird, seemingly unnecessary secrecy of the whole thing.

Terry ended up crashing in one of my guest rooms, and by early the next morning we were ready to make our next move. While Terry took another personal leave day, I canceled my appointments with the cable producer of new game show entitled *Did I Say That?*, a lowlife from QVC salivating to convince me to do an infomercial endorsing a line of deodorant soap on a rope, and Angelina Jolie.

I called Tippi and Brick at various numbers. No one had seen them yet today, but I thanked everyone anyway. It seemed best not to leave any messages. The sooner they felt I'd stopped hanging around, the sooner they would reappear.

Fortunately for Terry and me, it *was* another working day on the set of *Badges of Philly*, and so we were likely to meet Fernando San Marcos whether he liked it or not. His was absolutely not the "white room" that Helena so cryptically and so drunkenly talked about with Ann-Margret, but clearly he'd been mighty PO'd at Helena. And anyway who could say what Helena really meant by the "white room," or what it really told us about the case?

Supposedly, it was a closed set, whereby the *extremely* serious, method-trained actors could find their true inner essence or whatnot. But once I mentioned the word "publicity," the set opened unto me like an oyster giving me its pearl. We pretended to get chummy with the script people and gofers and gaffers and light technicians as I asked them innocuous questions about whether they liked working on the set—amazingly, they all told me they loved it—or was it true that this or that coworker was a jokester.

Terry had never been on a set before, and he was as tickled pink as a twelve-year-old, staring with wonder-lit eyes at all the booms and lights and catwalks and things. Everyone accepted that Terry was my secretary, and he even pretended to take notes. Still, a couple of people gave him a suspicious once-over, and then looked at me as if to say: *Rick, why did you pick such a dweeb?*

We watched as the assistant director ordered about the extras, and the director herself—yes, Virginia, there are women directors—set up a big confrontation scene between the good, the bad, and the ugly. She was slight, soft-spoken and rather mousy looking, and prefaced what she called her friendly suggestions with the word "please."

"Action," stated the director.

The hero of the series grabbed the bad guy by the scruff of the neck and banged his head against the wall until a plastic blood pellet burst open to simulate blood.

The hero hissed with intensity: "Okay, motherfucker, tell me where she is!"

"Cut," the director decreed. Approaching the actors—who had closed their eyes in concentration so as not to lose the moment—she instructed, "That was just great. I got goose bumpy-tingly all over. But could I please make just a teensy little friendly suggestion? On the word, 'motherfucker,' could you please bang him so hard that he shoots blood into your eye?" She turned to shout to the crew: "I'm afraid we need more blood down here, please!"

The scene continued pretty much the same way it started. This one was going to stick his foot up that one's ass, that one was going to be served this one's dick on a silver platter, and so on. Finally, the bad guy died—though not before spitting in the hero's face, not to mention shooting him in the shoulder. Amidst all the highly photogenic blood and guts, Fernando's character, Detective Garcia, entered the scene in his crisp, clean, bland white shirt and trench coat. He was technically handsome and completely uninteresting.

"Good work, Officer," he stalwartly pronounced in his deep, bland voice. Then, intently speaking into his cell phone: "Officer down. Ambulance needed."

"Cut, print!" called the director.

A flunky handed Fernando a towel with which to wipe his brow after all that hard work. Spotting me, Fernando put on his best showbiz smile and walked over to shake hands.

"Welcome to the set, Rick." He looked quickly at Terry, then looked at him again, no doubt sensing that beneath the thick glasses there just might be the cherished butch master of his dreams. "And who have we *here*?"

As they shook hands, I was impressed by what a good job Terry had been doing of acting appropriately Clark Kent-ish. But then I wondered if part of it was simply the falseness of disguise itself, which couldn't help but make him feel physically unsure of himself.

"Actually, I'm here—*we're* here—to talk about Helena Godiva."

Fernando furtively glanced about the busy sound stage. "I have nothing to say. Besides, I'm needed on the set."

"I checked the script. You're not needed for another twenty pages."

"But I—"

"Look, we'll snoop around anyway," I warned. "So if you have anything to tell us, better we hear it from you than for us to draw our own conclusions."

"Look, guys—" He took a deep sigh. "Let's go somewhere we can talk, okay?"

Fernando told us that his dressing room was being "redone," which probably meant that he was embarrassed that it wasn't bigger or nicer. So the somewhere to talk turned out to be a dark, empty stage in back of the main lot. The only lighting was that which angled in from the set. Otherwise, you could walk so far into the darkness you couldn't see your hand in front of your face. Someone had left a broom, an industrial-sized bucket, and a stand-up fan on the floor—for how many decades was anyone's guess.

"I don't want everyone and their mother knowing about my personal life," Fernando warned. It was as if he cared more about staying closeted than whether or not I thought he was a murderer. But, sadly enough, a lot of people in Hollywood were the same way.

"No one's here to listen except the broom," I observed. "And I'll bet it's a very liberal, tolerant broom."

"We saw a tape of you getting very upset when you first saw your, uh, exotic new living room," Terry shared.

"For an assistant, he's awfully nosy." Fernando eyed Terry like Detective Garcia looking over a suspect.

I made a point of laughing. "I'm training Terry to handle interviews. Don't worry, Fernando. He's family." By "family," I of course meant Terry was gay.

"Okay, so I enjoy being dominated in bed," Fernando told us. "It's just the way I am. It doesn't hurt anyone. But I don't exactly want it to be a *TV Guide* cover story. So yes, I was very, very pissed off when I saw what Helena did to my living room. And you have to remember: It was my *living* room, not even my *bedroom*, which at least is more private."

"But there's something puzzling," Terry continued. "Someone connected with *My House, Your House* claims it was all an act. That you were just kidding. Because if you were really all that upset, the cast members of the show would've heard about it."

Fernando slammed his fist into his hand, barely controlling his anger. "The *reason* they never heard about it was Helena. She pulled such a hysterical scene with the producers, they decided to hush things up as best they could and never mention it again. That was Helena in action—she screwed you over, then turned herself into the victim."

We could hear the sound of fake gunshots and sirens coming from the filming. An actress probably playing a hooker or a junkie or a hooker junkie let out a bloodcurdling scream.

"But if you kept your personal life under lock and key—if you'll pardon the expression—then how did Helena even know about it?" I inquired. "I assume you didn't leave the latest issues of *Fun with Torture* on the coffee table."

Fernando walked about the dark, barren set in his white shirt and tie, his footsteps making echoes. "I knew Helena. I knew her very well, in fact."

"Did you meet her at some kinky sex club?" I asked in a moment of pure jest.

He looked at me warily. "How did you know?"

"Uh, just psychic, I guess."

Fernando leaned against the wall, the diagonal of light crossing over his body. "Actually, we knew each other way before that. Years ago, when I first came to L.A. She claimed she was the descendent of some sort of English lord. But for the time being, she pretty much had her hands full as a cocktail waitress. In a singles dive, where I was bartender. She claimed to have been this honor student in design school, and had all these fancy plans to design movie sets. Helena was gorgeous enough to be in the movies herself, but she was very firm that she didn't want to act. Of course, as a Grade-A, first-class bitch-and-a-half, she gave far greater performances than any Oscar winner in history." He nervously tapped his foot. "We had a few misadventures back then. You know—stealing booze from the bar. Scoring weed. Rescuing each other after hitting on the wrong guy. The usual kid stuff."

Terry studied his own hand as he moved it back and forth from darkness to light; I imagined that as a child it took very little to amuse him. "So what happened?"

Fernando laughed. "What could have happened? Not much. We went our separate ways. I just figured she was another lying little twat trying to get someplace in this dirty lowdown world. Some make it, some don't. When she made a name for herself on *My House, Your House* I just figured, 'Okay, so she made it.' "

"Just how *did* she make it?" I asked.

Fernando laughed even harder, his head tilting back in a roar that reverberated through the cavernous set. "Looking at some of her designs, you can't help but wonder. Oh, I'm sorry—she was 'cutting edge.' The epitome of style. Actually, as I recall, some rich old biddy took her under her wing. Helena was always saying how she had to do some work for Mrs. Symington-Smithers, or whatever the snooty old bag's name was. I guess one gig led to another."

"But she never—"

"How the hell should I know? You think I'd have gotten off hearing about some straight chick putting out for a job? It was bad enough dealing with her pawing all over me, batting her eyelashes while asking in that ever-so-sweet little voice if just this once I'd slam it up her ying-yang."

I couldn't help but wonder how Detective Garcia's fans would have felt to see him talking far more in the manner of his fellow cast members off-screen. Terry, for one, shook his head sadly for what I could only take to be his disillusionment.

"So, as you say, you lost touch, and . . . ?"

"And then about a hundred and fifty million years later, Rick, I'm at this leather sex convention thingamajig, and who should pop up but Helena. Turns out she did this full dominatrix routine. Spiked heels, whips, sticking candles . . . well, anyway, you get the idea. Straight guys were her slaves—the more macho and powerful, the more she got off. It was all very hush-hush, of course. Everyone protected everyone else's privacy, and even when you recognized someone from the regular world, you weren't sup-posed to talk about it. So in the moment, we just sort of winked at each other. Then—what, a year later?—they want me on the DIY show, and Helena sends me an eau de cologne note about how much fun it will be to see each other again, and how she pulled a few strings to be my designer."

"It must have been quite a shock, then, to see what she did to your room," Terry offered sympathetically. "There she was, breaking the sacred trust by telling the world you were into the leather scene, when she was just as into it as you were. And to top it off, she requested the privilege of doing it to you, and for no good reason in the world. Other than maybe spite, for not sleeping with her."

"And so I offed the bitch?" Fernando flashed a shrewd grin. "Sorry to disappoint you, Terry. I know that would be quite a scoop for you. But nice try."

"You have to admit, you don't exactly seem devastated by the loss," I contributed. "And you have what might conservatively be thought of as a motive."

"Motive, shmotive. You don't know the half of it." He stared at us with the defiance of someone who hadn't meant to spill the proverbial beans, but realized there was no turning back.

"What don't we know?" Terry calmly asked.

"Several choice details. Way back when, Helena was inconvenienced by pregnancy. Or so she claimed."

"Not exactly a sympathetic way of putting it," I noted.

Fernando laughed coldly. "Believe me, with Helena, it was always all about *her*. She'd quit her job waitressing or got fired—I can't even remember —and was starting to get a gig or two as a designer. She dropped by the bar, and said she needed to talk to me. Turns out she wanted me to go with her to the clinic, to take care of things. She had some typical Helena story about how the father had raped her, and how I had to take her word for it that she couldn't go to the cops. But by that time . . . I can't explain it, but I sat there listening to her and she even cried real tears and said how maybe she couldn't go through with it, and yet I wondered if the whole thing was an act. You know—to get attention, to get me to never leave her, and all that crap. All I could think of was that I wanted her out of my life."

"So what happened?" Terry queried.

"I figured I'd hear from her the next day, but didn't. Or the day after that, either. I didn't bother calling. I just figured she took care of it on her own, or met someone else, or did whatever she did. Then suddenly, about a month later, she pops up in the bar, looking like she just came back from Tahiti. Call me stupid, but I couldn't resist asking her if everything turned out okay. She laughed and said, 'Oh, *that*! Everything's just fine, Fernando. The father took care of it.' Now, that made about as much sense as hearing that Custer's Last Stand happened in San Francisco. I mean, supposedly some rapist merrily took care of things for her? Did she blackmail him? Or was I right in the first place—she was making the whole thing up? Whatever it was, I figured that was the end of it. But then, as she left with some guy she picked up, she whispered in my ear: 'I never forget who my friends really are.' She flashed that smile of hers—the one where you never knew if she was mocking you or liking you. I think with Helena, it was all pretty much the same thing." As he walked around, his shadow loomed large across the floor. "Then as a sweet little afterthought, she added that she'd get me back one day and I'd wish I'd never been born."

From the set there came the sound of a ghetto blaster playing some hard-edged rap, while two people—a cop and a junkie or else two junkies— had a minor difference of opinion that resulted in one of them getting shot.

"Was that the last time you saw her?" I asked. "Until the sex club thing, I mean."

"I guess. There was so much dope and booze back then, it's hard to remember if she was ever at some lowlife party I went to. But then, years later, when she did that to my room . . ." He looked at us beseechingly, as though unable to finish the sentence.

"Sounds like she really knew how to carry a grudge," I offered.

"Yeah. Guess you could say that."

"What about the leather . . . uh, social club?" Terry inquired. "Anyone have her on their short list of enemies?"

He loosened the knot in his tie. "I doubt it. She was in her element. The lousier she treated her kinky intimates, the more they liked her. From what I could gather, her life was that damn TV show. They seemed like a nice enough bunch, though they had a real blind spot when it came to Helena. Like they thought she was *nice*, or something."

"Do you know Tippi Finkelstein?"

Fernando shrugged. "I've seen her act, Rick. She's funny. I probably said hi to her. Maybe posed for one of those stupid showbiz pics where I'm smiling next to her at her opening night. Who can remember?"

Terry absently toyed with the mop handle. "But you've never known her better than that?"

"Not as far as I know. There could be a Kevin Bacon thing, I suppose, where she's friends with the great-uncle of my sex master. But why this obsession with B-list comics?"

"She suffered from the same affliction as you—a bad case of the Helena Blues. Ever hear of her swan room?"

He glanced at his watch. "Vaguely. I don't watch *My House, Your House*. The memory of the whole thing is pretty painful. But I can imagine. Hey, if Tippi bumped her off, I'd say all the more power to her."

I wasn't sure I bought Fernando's protestations about not knowing Tippi. Clearly, he was capable of pulling the ol' oh-did-I-forget-to-mention-she-was-my-long-lost-sister routine.

"Well, in the off-chance that you hear from her, let us know."

"Brick Edwards, too," Terry added.

"Brick? Oh, right, the carpenter guy. Sure, I'll let you guys know."

"Oh, and one more thing." I scrunched my nose to signal how silly I felt even asking it. "Where were you the night of the murder?"

"I was . . . indisposed. Yes, if the cops ever asked me, I can provide a witness. But let's just leave it at that, okay?"

There was a loud, echoing knocking.

"Anyone home?" The virile yet genial star of the show appeared, one of those actors who specialized in ruthless characters but in real life was described by coworkers as being gentle as fabric softener. "Oh, it's you, Rick." He stepped forward to shake my hand. "Welcome to the set."

I introduced him to Terry. The star firmly shook his hand and gushed: "It's a privilege and honor to have you as our guest."

Even in the dim lighting I could see Terry's face redden. "Aw, shucks."

"Fernando, I was wondering if you'd help me with a scene," the star explained. "Let's read our lines so I can get the right mood."

I couldn't help noticing that he said it was so *he* could get the right mood, and not the two of them. It didn't come across as hogging the spotlight, though. It just seemed an honest appraisal of what they needed to do to give the scene some snap. Because all eyes and ears would be focused upon the intense, no-nonsense star, and if he wasn't at his best at all times, the entire cast might soon be out of a job.

"Uh, sure," Fernando agreed. "Assuming, that is, that we're done here?"

"I think I have what I need for my interview."

And so we followed them back out into the hustle and bustle of the main set.

Just as we were taking our leave back out to the car, I stopped in a sudden panic. "Did we make it clear to Fernando to *not* tell Tippi that we spoke with him?"

"I *think* we said . . . maybe we should go back in and make sure he understands."

And so we walked briskly back onto the set, and headed straight to Fernando's dressing room. We knocked on the door and called his name; it sounded like he said "Come in." We opened the door to find Fernando, naked as a show dog, handcuffed on his knees, with a studded collar and leash around his neck. Fernando had pierced nipples, a pierced navel, and an additional piercing dangling from another prominent appendage on his body. The macho star of the show, in full cop uniform, evidently had commanded him to perform an act known to give pleasure to the recipient. The star's manner was indeed soft spoken; he seemed to have a knack for maintaining a certain calm or even gentleness while performing his role as a sex master, as if a whisper could be far more forceful than a shout.

"Oh! Um, pardon us."

"We thought you said—"

"He said, 'One minute,'" the star explained, making little effort to hide his irritation and embarrassment. "This is fucking bullshit."

"Maybe the collar is a bit too tight," I joked. "That might tend to muffle speech."

"An honest mistake," agreed Terry.

"Well?" the star asked us.

"Uh . . . we'll call you later, Fernando."

"Don't even think about printing this," the star warned in his toughest TV show voice. "I'll sue you for every crooked dime you've ever made."

I shrugged with indifference. "Why should I write about it? Everyone already knows."

"You fucking prick."

"Whatever." My cell phone was ringing. "Oh, great," I commented after hanging up.

"Who was that?" Terry asked.

"Brick," I answered. "He's willing to talk."

"Well, that's good news, isn't it?"

"He's willing to talk for a price. Plus we have to agree not to interview Tippi anymore. He said we made her nervous. Fucking oxygen makes her nervous."

"We pay, but we don't cave on Tippi."

"My sentiments exactly."

"I guess we'll have to come clean about . . . you know." And I did know what he meant: The jig was up on Terry being my assistant.

"No sweat. We're paying him, remember, so the whole thing's pretty jaded anyway. And there's no love to be lost between Tippi and us."

*"Excuse me!"* the star called out, while Fernando stated a far less polite equivalent of the same sentiment.

"Oh, sorry, guys." Terry and I had both forgotten that we were still standing in the dressing room, inadvertently causing what might be termed *handcuffedus interruptus*.

"Carry on."

# FIFTEEN

WE MET BRICK EDWARDS AT HIS HOME IN THE OUTSKIRTS OF VEN-
ice. He lived in a ramshackle hippie-to-white-trash enclave that had taken
on a rural ambiance more through human neglect than force of nature—a
weedy flatlands dominated by rusted trailers and remnants of bonfires
from illicit drug parties. However, Brick's abode was the legendary palace
of the neighborhood. Starting with a simple trailer, he had impressively
built on to it with his own two hands. His house wouldn't have seemed like
much in Beverly Hills, but in its alternative-lifestyle way it was a clever
menagerie of rooms and lofts and varying levels, as if designed by an imaginative child using his Tinker Toy set for inspiration. Going from one room
to another not only often required going up or down a few steps, but
sometimes going up or down a ladder.

Considering his hostile disappearance the night before—let alone his
insistence that he be paid for his time—Brick couldn't have been in jollier
spirits. In his open Hawaiian shirt and trendy shades, he took a lion-like
pride in showing us the house, explaining in more detail than I could keep
up with how he constructed or fastened this or that. Terry, though,
couldn't hear enough, and was full of both questions and advice about
epoxy and drill bits and beveled edges.

Certainly, for the DIY enthusiast, it was like dying and going to heaven.
An old car engine had been fashioned into a footstool. The kitchen table
was made from an old headboard whose surface was a mosaic of broken

glass, the sharp edges painstakingly sanded down for safety. The bathtub was an old wine vat that he had sealed with many coats of an acrylic gloss.

At the uppermost level was the master bedroom—which, psychologically speaking, was telling insofar as how Brick saw himself. His king-size bed frame hung suspended from the ceiling. It faced the swimming pool, which was entered through handmade French doors. This meant that from one side of the entire house you looked out into the lower depths of the pool, sort of like being at a marine world. Brick told us that he enjoyed inviting "ladies" over, having them wait in the living room, and then surprising them by swimming naked underwater through the pool, tapping on the living room window like a male mermaid.

After what felt like hours, Brick finally seated us around the pool, from which vantage point we could see the rather scrawny scrub oaks and sagebrush that dotted the vista. It was the kind of bright sunny day that made you squint even with your sunglasses on. He slipped off his open shirt, wiggled out of his baggy shorts to reveal his striped bikini briefs, and kicked off his flip-flops. With a satisfied sigh, he eased down into a cushy lounge chair. "Seat yourselves, guys," he chipperly told us.

Terry made a point of sitting up crosswise, like a patient in a shrink's office refusing to lie down on the couch, and I figured I should follow suit. I guess all the murder stuff was getting to me, because the proximity of Brick's buff bod seemed neither here nor there. If anything, it struck me as something Mamie Van Doren might've done. Brick would never have admitted it in a million years, but I think he figured he could razzle-dazzle these gay guys with his lean, mean physique, and so fool us into believing something we shouldn't. But of course, it's also possible he was simply oblivious about these things, and thought nothing of showing off his body to anyone at any time.

"Up here, babe," Brick called out from his lounge chair, and there instantaneously appeared a bikini-clad lass whose platinum blonde hair color was doubtless about as natural as her gargantuan bra size. Brick told us her name (Amber? Tawny? Melody?) and went on to explain that he was giving her a place to crash while she eked out her God-given destiny as a car show model or some such.

Brick put his arm around her waist in that knowing way that guys of all persuasions often do, like it's a real accomplishment that he knows what turns him on and he gets it in spades.

"Babe, get these gentlemen some ice-cold brewskies."

The babe in question giggled her desire to be obedient in this regard, and went scampering off. I'd like to be politically correct and say that underneath her bimbo exterior there lurked a rocket scientist, but from what I could tell, what you saw was what you got.

"You know, Brick, there's something we need to clear up right away. When we met with Tippi—"

"You told her Terry worked for you." He smiled agreeably, laying back to soak up the sunshine. "Listen, guys. I know that sometimes you just have to do what has to be done. Hell, I lie all the time."

"So Tippi knows the truth?" Terry queried.

"It was no big deal. I told her that Ann-Margret was your cousin. Not that it did much good. The thing is, Tippi's great, but she's got this humungous chip on her shoulder. She thinks everyone's out to get her, and she likes to be right. So in a way it made her happy that you lied. It gave her more reason to hate you guys."

"Speaking of which," I interjected, "I assume that Tippi doesn't know about your housemate?"

"What can I say, guys? Tippi's a real lady. I treat her like a queen. Then there are girls, who I treat, well, like queens in a different way." He put his hands behind his head in relaxed self-satisfaction, luxuriating in the sweet, balmy breeze that wafted across the pool.

Actually, Tippi, with her R- to X-rated jokes, wasn't in the conventional sense all that much of a lady, but I let it slide. I guess by Brick's standards being a lady meant that it took a couple of extra compliments to bag her.

"Do you think Ann-Margret did it?" I asked instead.

"I think Ann-Margret is the victim of a conspiracy." Brick nodded solemnly, with a conspiracy theorist's conviction. "I think that there are rich and powerful forces out there trying to silence her for some reason. Get her taken out of general circulation."

I of course greeted his opinion with the proper seriousness. "What do you think it is that Ann-Margret knows that puts her in so much danger?"

"I haven't quite figured that out yet. But it must be something. The thing is, once they go after you, there's nothing you can do about it. Except run like hell. I gotta hand it to her for taking off like that. I'd do the same thing in her place."

"Do you have any idea where she is?" Terry inquired.

"Nope."

"Just why did you take off through the window last night?" Terry asked. "Was it only because Tippi said we made her nervous?"

Brick considered. "That was part of it, sure. But it was fun. Kind of romantic. I wanted to be alone with her. I didn't feel like answering any questions. I still don't, without some do-re-mi to sweeten things up. Dwelling on Helena, murder, all that kind of stuff—I don't like it. Life should be a good time, you know?"

The bikini lass appeared with three frosty bottles of beer. "Thanks, babe." Brick gave her a zestful pat on the ass. "Now, let us guys talk."

She tittered as she scampered off.

"Cheers." Brick sat up, raising his beer in a toast. Truth be told, I wasn't much of a beer drinker, but when in Rome . . . Our three beers clicked, and Brick took a long, satisfying swallow. "Life sure is a pisser," he philosophized, shaking his head in amusement.

"Some people have suggested that Helena was in love with you. Ain't that a pisser?"

Brick chuckled. "Helena was a great gal, Rick. I'm really sorry she's gone."

"I can tell. Just what *was* there between you two?"

He thought about it. "I guess we did have a very special sexual chemistry. Maybe that's what viewers responded to. We got a lot of fan mail speculating that there was something between us."

"Brick, I didn't mean what gave you that Gable-and-Lombard magic. I meant, were you guys seriously involved, or what? When did Tippi figure into all this? What about Curtsy Ann? Was there a reason—"

"Whoa," Brick interrupted. "One thing at a time, cowboy. Let's just relax. It's a beautiful day." He eased back into the lounge chair, relishing the rays of sun that were deepening his tan. "Helena was strictly about having fun. We laughed up a storm. We could tell each other anything. Nothing was off limits, including other people we were seeing. Now, she might have had a girly moment or two when she wanted more out of me, but she pretty much knew the kind of guy I was. That I'm just not built for settling down."

"Actually, we saw a tape of you and Helena having what you might call words. During the filming of the pierced-body room."

"Oh?"

I nodded affirmatively. "Frankly, she seemed to be having more than a girly moment."

"Well, she had her good days and bad days, like any other broad." He looked pleased with his answer.

"What about her kinky days?" I asked.

Brick sat up and lowered his sunglasses. "Say what?"

"Did Helena ever get into her dominatrix stuff with you?"

He nervously reached for his beer. "I heard a little something about it, I guess."

"And did you *do* a little something about it as well?" After all, it clearly was not beyond Helena to share other people's foibles with the world, especially when they'd royally screwed her over. And if Brick was into kinky stuff himself, it didn't exactly take Stephen Hawking to figure out that he might have deemed it a good idea to off the bitch.

"Helena was a class act," Brick blandly replied. "I never paid attention to those kinds of rumors. And neither should you, Rick." He eased back into his tanning position; tiny beads of sweat were forming on his rippled arms. "And that's all I'm going to say about it." He quickly sat up. "I meant, all I would say about that kinky stuff. Not that the interview was over."

Indeed, we had paid him for a certain period of time that had yet to expire. "We know what you mean, Brick," I assured him. "We know you have integrity when it comes to business arrangements."

"Cool." He grinned and lay back down.

Terry took a thoughtful swallow of beer. "Did Helena ever talk to you about her past? Ever mention some rich old lady who helped set her up?"

"Helena never talked about the past. At least not with me. In fact, I guess you could say she didn't talk much at *all* when she was with me." He guffawed knowingly.

"So Helena basically understood about your need to be a free man. Does Tippi also possess this wise womanly knowledge?"

Brick polished off his beer like a true connoisseur. "You seem awfully concerned about her, Rick, considering she hates your guts."

"I'm sentimental. I turn to mush when I think of how she called me a ruthless prick."

He snorted, reaching over to give me a friendly punch. "Say, you're okay, Rick. It's true that Tippi is a serious gal. I think that's why she's a comic. Because she doesn't really think anything's funny at all. Does that make sense?"

I had to admit that it did.

"Anyway, I know that Tippi wants to, like—you know—get married and all that stuff. And I have to say, if I ever would sacrifice my freedom, she's come closer than anyone else to making me want to do it. But I've told her that she can't expect me to be more than I am. That I need my space."

Terry set down his empty beer. "Did she ever talk about Helena?"

"Nope. Whenever I tried to bring her up, Tippi would change the subject PDQ. I can't remember the details, but I guess they both had the hots for some dude who died. You know how women get—always up for a catfight." He did a kind of pantomime with his hands to simulate gabby little puppets fighting. "I met Tippi, as a matter of fact, when Helena was doing her room. Man, that was some assignment. Helena had me build that bridge over the fake pond. I had to bolt it down from the underside of the floor."

"*Really*? Did you do it with dowels?" Terry wanted to know.

"Yeah, but I had to make anchors for them. On the lathe."

"I bet you could have done it on the jigsaw. Just around the head of each end."

Brick snapped his fingers with regret. "Damn, I never thought to do it that way, but you're probably right. With a lip to enjoin it."

"Either that, or if you drilled in from behind and—" The look on my face apparently compelled Terry to stop mid-sentence. "Well, anyway. As you were saying, Brick, about Tippi."

"Tippi?" He frowned in his confusion; having gotten carried away talking about carpentry, it was a struggle to reorient himself. "Oh, right. She hated what Helena did to her room, but I guess she got the last word, because later that night she was drowning her sorrows here in my pool, if you know what I mean."

"Did you ever think that you were Tippi's way of getting back at Helena?"

Brick rubbed his stubbly, tanned chin in thought. "Well, Rick, if I was, who cares? I think it would be kind of cool, to be used as a love weapon. But it seems to me that Tippi is a pretty genuine sort of person."

"There's one thing that keeps bothering me." I took an indifferent sip of beer. "Why would Tippi not tell us about you?"

"Probably because it's private. Why *should* she tell you everything about herself?"

"Bravo." I gave him a mock round of applause. "You've brought back chivalry, Brick. Defending Tippi's honor while telling us all sorts of tacky things about the exquisite, fragile princess, to the tune of four figures."

"I gamble. I'm short on cash. I swear I did it for Tippi. To show her a good time."

"And here I thought the best things in life were free."

The look in Brick's eyes made me think he was going to take a punch at me. But I *was* paying him, and the customer—as a wise old hooker once told me—is always right.

"Say, Rick, buddy. Go easy on me, okay? I'm not a clever guy like you are. What can I say? I do my best."

"Did Helena ever mention something about a white room?" Terry asked—in part, I think, to change the subject. "Other than Tippi's room, that is."

Brick shrugged. "It's possible. She was a designer. Why?"

"Never mind," Terry decided, trying instead for a different tactic. "What about you and Curtsy Ann?"

"Why, what did she say about us?"

"Nothing much," I assured him. "Just that you were engaged, and then you ran off—albeit not very far—with Helena."

Brick sat up to scratch his neck. "If that's what Curtsy Ann said, then it's true."

"Well, what if she had said you were her identical twin?"

"I don't mean it like that, Rick. But Curtsy Ann is a sensitive, lovely and highly moral gal. I'm sorry if I hurt her feelings. If this is how she sees it, I'll accept it."

I picked at the label of my beer. "But you *could* see it differently, I take it?"

"We all have our own truth," Brick pronounced, wrinkling his brow for the depth of his thoughts. "Didn't somebody once say something like, 'There are many roads to China?'"

"Also to New Jersey," I pointed out. "But this is not Philosophy 101. Aunt Fern told us Curtsy Ann drove you away, even though she blames Helena."

"Aunt Fern is very wise. I won't say anything against her. And Curtsy Ann helped me get hired on *My House, Your House*. I've never had to do another dry wall job again. I owe her a lot."

"Would you have broken up with the bitch or not if Helena hadn't come along?"

Brick stared down at the terra cotta tiles, as if unable to look either of us in the eye. "You're asking an unfair question, Rick. I mean, in the gay world it must be the same way—sometimes things just happen. Am I right?"

"And for some of us, I guess more things tend to happen than others."

"You got it, buddy." Brick grinned like a tomcat.

I set aside my beer; it was still half full. "I think we get the picture."

Brick rolled over to tan his smooth, sculpted back. "You gay guys think you can judge me. But let me tell you something. You're just as bad. Except you do it to each other, instead of to girls."

"Not *all* of us," Terry put in defensively.

I supposed Brick had a point, but I wasn't about to commiserate with him on the many horrors of the West Hollywood scene. "That's right. Terry is so upright and moral, it's as if he's not a man at all."

Brick thought my remark was hilarious, though Terry, needless to say, was less than charmed.

"Just a sec." Brick's cell phone was ringing to the tune of "Born To Be Wild." "Yep," we heard him say. "Sure, babe."

He hung up the phone. "Tippi's coming over." He turned to shout in the direction of the house. "Hey, babe. Get up here." He whispered to us conspiratorially, "I'll have to ask my housemate to take a hike for a few hours."

The phone rang again. "Oh, hey there, babe. Long time no see." He mouthed to us that it was Curtsy Ann. Apparently, the opportunity to brag about a conquest was far too tempting to resist, even if it meant arousing suspicion.

"Yeah, great to hear from you. I can't remember the last time . . . Oh, so it has been that long? Whoa, you know the exact number of *days*? You're really amazing, babe. You'd like to *what* now? Well, let me see . . . What about now? I have an hour or two before I'm expecting company. Oh, you know—just some of the guys. I'd invite you to hang around, but you'd be bored out of your mind." He winked at us, like we were utterly rooting for him to fool her. "Okay, sure. For an hour or so."

As he hung up the phone, Brick looked deeply content, like a general who just won the war, or an architect who just won a commission to build the world's tallest building.

"Curtsy Ann," he stated aloud, as though we hadn't gotten it already. "We get together every now and then. I guess I kind of cheer her up. I'm a fun kind of guy, you know. That's why I play all those practical jokes." He stood up to stretch and yawn, flexing his muscular arms. "But I'll tell you, I sure do know a lot of unhappy women. Must be a hormone thing."

Terry pretended to laugh. "Say Brick, I know this sounds dumb, but do you remember where you were when Helena was being murdered?"

"I was where I always am at that hour. In bed with a gal pal."

"Do you remember which one?"

"I'd have to think about it, Terry."

He dove into the pool like a happy porpoise, gliding with a grace that seemed to bespeak his prowess and virility. As the bikini foundling pranced over to join us, he stepped from the pool, dripping wet and breathless. "I need privacy this afternoon, babe."

"And what if I don't feel like going?" She thrust forth her chest, as if to say, "Remember, if I go, these go with me."

"Oh, you're going, all right." He pushed her into the pool, then comically held his nose and jumped in after her. They paddled around while Brick kept saying, "You're leaving," and she kept saying, "No, I'm staying," and they kept laughing and splashing and dunking each other under water. As her top came undone and Brick started kissing one of her bare breasts, Terry nudged me. "I guess it's time to go."

"Are you kidding? And miss Curtsy Ann's arrival?"

Glancing back over at the pool, I noticed they both were naked. "Okay, so maybe it *is* time to go at that."

As we turned to leave, Brick leapt out of the water, grabbing a towel to drape around his dripping wet torso. "Hey guys, where are you—"

"Don't worry, Brick. I'll leave your check on the kitchen table."

"Thanks, man." He made a point of shaking both our hands. "And hey—stay out of trouble, okay?" With his free arm, he kind of tweaked my nose in a buddy-buddy way.

We heard the French doors open.

"Curtsy Ann, it's been too long." Brick towel-dried his hair, smiling as though genuinely glad to see her. "I didn't realize you were quite so nearby." As he attempted to mildly embrace her, he forgot himself, and the towel around his waist fell to the ground. "Oops," he sheepishly grinned, making no effort to cover himself up. Somehow, the dimples in his ass reminded me of a smirk. (PS: Brick was uncircumcised, and, as my farmer grandpa used to say, "fair to middlin'.")

Curtsy Ann, though, was more focused on the naked houseguest in the pool, who was doing all these Esther Williams–style dips and spins in the water.

Ever devout in her conservative family values, Curtsy Ann managed to articulate: "Why, you cocksucking piece of shit."

"It's not my fault you're early," Brick pointed out.

"Um, maybe we should go now?" Terry suggested.

"Just a minute." I waved him away. "I know it's tacky, but this might be important."

Curtsy Ann shoved Brick into the pool. "I'm *two* minutes early," she hissed, her green eyes narrowing. "Can't you even *pretend* to be something other than a total prick? After all these years, after all we've been through. After I've even . . ." She stopped herself from saying any more. Dismissing him with her hands, she ran back inside, her high heels clacking on the wooden floors. The sound of screeching tires told us she had driven off.

For a moment, no one said anything. Then Brick, after diving underwater and coming back up for air, told us, "Now do you see why I wouldn't marry her?"

We didn't answer, but as we were dropping off the check on the glass mosaic kitchen table, we noticed a different check. It was from Tippi, it was dated the day before, and it was made out to Brick for a cool ten grand.

# SIXTEEN

NEEDLESS TO SAY, BRICK INSISTED THAT HE HAD NO IDEA WHATSO-
ever what Curtsy Ann was getting at before she stopped talking in mid-
sentence. As for the check for ten G's, he told us it was payment for
remodeling he did on Tippi's house. When I mentioned that Tippi claimed
that nothing had been done on her house since repairing Helena's fiasco,
Brick stated—without missing a beat—that what he'd meant to say was
that it was a down payment on future work. We could only guess as to
whether Helena's more exotic sexual entrees had found their way to Brick's
palate. As for Curtsy Ann, she was, according to the maid who answered
the phone, indisposed for the rest of the day with what was termed a
"headache."

We were bordering on a standstill of sorts. Ann-Margret was still on
the run, and Aunt Fern was still acting like a glorified pain in the ass. She
called and called, wanting to know our every move, as if we worked for her.
True, she had her sagelike moments and she made me feel sorry for her and
was in general an enthusiastic gossiper—which can be useful—but she
nagged and I hate to feel nagged at. (Terry, of course, liked her rather better
than I did. But then, he hadn't had his living room desecrated by all her
folksy appointments.) After a while, we stopped answering when she
called, deciding instead to meet with her prudently, with a specific list of
questions—if in fact we would need to meet with her at all. Tippi, Curtsy
Ann, Brick and Fernando were not exactly bending over backwards to help

us—though collectively, there seemed to be a fair amount of bending over to achieve other purposes.

Sometimes trouble finds you, but sometimes you have to find it yourself. So Terry and I figured it was an opportune time to track down Koko Yee and the remaining designers to see what they had up their sleeves.

Surprisingly, setting up an interview with mellow, pixie-ish Koko Yee proved as daunting as trying to gain access to top-secret Pentagon files, or maybe even wrangling through the contract clauses regarding camera angles when interviewing Streisand. After about forty-five minutes of getting put on hold, disconnected, and explaining everything from scratch all over again to some other *My House, Your House* flunky, I yelled at someone or another that I was not, repeat not, asking to have my utilities kept on even though I drank up the welfare check. Rather, I was the reputable Hollywood columnist Rick Domino, who was just on the show, and was even doing a documentary on the show, and all I wanted to do was speak to Koko Yee.

"You're *who* again?" asked the ninny on the other end of the phone.

"I'm President George W. Bush," I finally declared in exasperation. "I want to talk to Koko Yee."

"Koko's pregnant," explained the mentally enfeebled assistant.

"Look, she'll *want* to talk to me."

"Koko asked me to hold all calls."

"Go to the dictionary, and look up 'go fuck yourself.' "

With that friendly piece of advice, I hung up the phone. I figured I could always reach Koko through the back door, so to speak: Her husband, J.T. Rex, had actually been contacting my office to plug a new recording artist he produced. Indeed, the receptionist at J.T.'s studio was much more mentally alert—who wouldn't have been?—but alas, J.T. was out of town until the following day.

Next, we figured we'd try Shirtless Bill, who lived closer into town than Basil Montclair.

Bill, however, told us he would need to consult his lawyer before agreeing to even clear his throat in my presence. "You know how it is, Rick," he kept insisting. "I can't just . . . well, you know." Actually, I didn't know, yet

I had no choice but to cheerfully agree to wait. No sense making the paranoid feel more paranoid.

When I called Basil Montclair, he needed to be reminded who I was. Once his memory was jogged, he was cordial, if remote. I got the impression that he let very few people into his inner circle. True, there might have been a cultural proclivity for him to be rather introspective, but I didn't see what that would've had to do with not remembering who I was. Even if he didn't know the Hollywood scene, I'd actually contacted his office a few ancient days earlier about using him as the designer for my living room.

"I don't watch TV," Basil conveyed. "I don't keep up with all that."

"You don't even watch *My House, Your House*?"

"I especially never watch *My House, Your House*. And especially when I'm on. I'm very uncomfortable seeing myself on TV."

"I don't see why," I gushed. "I truly admire your designs, Basil. You're the best." I avoided any discussion of what was indeed his decided lack of on-camera charisma.

After an interminably long pause, he replied, "That's nice."

"Well, I did want to talk to you about Helena, if that's okay. Plus, bring along my friend, Terry. You'd like him. He was just on the show. He's a cop. He's Ann-Margret's cousin, and we'd both like to help clear her name." I figured I might as well be upfront. No point driving all the way out there, only to get the door slammed in our faces.

But I couldn't help noticing that something about Basil's quiet demeanor made me inclined to frame things on this noble, lofty-purpose level. From the way I carried on about how we were trying to help an innocent person, you'd have thought that later today we'd be picketing to save the whales. Somehow it wouldn't do to tell Basil something like, "So give us the dirt on Helena."

When I finished my spiel, there was *another* long pause.

"Hello, Basil?"

"Yes, Rick?"

"Well, would it be all right if Terry and I met with you?"

"I live out by San Bernardino. Silver Lake."

I couldn't tell if that meant yes or no. "Are you saying—"

"What time will you be here?"

"Um, maybe in a couple of hours."

"Fine. Why not join us for a late lunch?"

"Great," I decreed, which similarly insincere assessment I had voiced to my last sexual encounter. "We'll see you then."

Basil struck me as one of those ultra-liberal types for whom waxing on about social ills came far easier than connecting to people one-on-one. Probably he was at his most engaging during a crisis. Once the person with the broken leg or whatnot got to the hospital, his mind would drift back to the misty gray clouds it normally inhabited.

I still thought Basil was the best designer on the show. Doubtless I would've found his design preferable (to put it mildly) to what I actually got. Still, I couldn't help thinking that two days with Basil would have been mighty long days for Terry, especially since Darla Sue was no Barbara Walters in her ability to draw people out.

Sometimes life seemed like one great big trade-off. The nicest person on the show was probably Aunt Fern, while the hardest to get to know was Basil, yet when it came to wanting them to design my house, the order would have been reversed. Life was never set up where the best designer would also be the nicest one. Extending the analogy, people who were most agile behind closed doors were all too often the biggest shits in other ways, while the nicest people usually sucked—if you'll pardon the expression— in matters of the boudoir. And so it went.

Driving out to Basil's, I looked over at Terry as he frowned with sincere concentration behind the wheel, and I couldn't help wondering what sort of trade-off he would've been when it came to being a life partner. Not that I had any interest in him in that way; he was such an odd bird. Sometimes you get a sense of how someone might be in bed. But Terry seemed to give off no vibes whatsoever about any of that stuff, other than an intense desire to not remain single on general principle. It was as if something he didn't like about being gay would be cosmically erased if he had a partner.

"Thinking about something, Rick?"

"Just the murder." I turned on the radio. "I'm wondering all over again if Tippi might have paid off Brick to kill Helena. She probably didn't think she could breathe with Helena still alive, she hated the bitch so damn much."

The radio station was playing "Tammy" by Debbie Reynolds. Terry whistled along, then sang—as usual, contorting the lyrics. Instead of Tammy being in love, Terry crooned that "Bambi's the one." I refused to explore the visual images flashing before me.

"I'm really starting to worry about my cousin," Terry shared. "She acts all street smart, but she's really just a sweet kid. Her parents had a lot of problems by the time she was born, and her older brothers were all long gone and married."

"What sort of problems?"

"Her mom got real sick. Then her dad. She had to work after school from a really young age. Never complained, though. Just sort of grew up before her time."

"Maybe she wanted to compensate for being so much younger than everyone else," I reflected.

Terry maneuvered into the exit lane. "Maybe. But I don't go for all that easy-breezy psychology rigmarole. It's suffering over *real* stuff that messes people up."

I didn't feel like arguing with him. Odd little impasses came up that signaled some larger difference between us that neither of us ever quite took the time to explore.

"Fine. Whatever."

"I know the sound of that 'fine, whatever.' It means nothing's fine or whatever at all."

"Look, Terry, we're almost at Basil's. Give it a rest, okay? I know that you think I'm this incredibly fucked-up, uptight, bitchy person who wouldn't know happiness if it came in my pants. But I do what I can."

"Rick, you puzzle me. You're the most *hostile* nice guy I've ever met."

I hated it when people analyzed me in that smarmy, superior way, like they knew something I didn't but weren't about to share it. I felt like I did when I was a kid, and I'd ask if I could have something and the grown-ups would say *Maybe* before deciding *No.* Like they held all the cards, and weren't about to let me forget it.

"Maybe it's because people are always hassling me to be something other than who I am. Maybe it's because I can't say 'black' without someone saying 'white.' Maybe it's because all I've ever wanted from anyone is to be left the fuck alone."

I guess I shouted louder than I'd realized, because Terry was visibly shaken as he drove along the winding, woodsy road to Silver Lake.

After about ten minutes of silence, he remarked: "It's pretty out here."

"Lots of trees and shit," I genially agreed.

Seldom was I more relieved to get out of a car than when we pulled up at Basil's. From Terry's sullen countenance, you'd have thought we'd been carrying the remains of the Queen Mother.

Getting out of the car, Terry ran his fingers over his bristly blond scalp. "I can't wait for my hair to grow out."

His hair was so short that surely it would take no more than a few weeks for the blond to get buzzed off. But like a dog who can't stand wearing a ribbon on Christmas, Terry felt utterly encumbered by dyed hair.

"I think it's very becoming."

"Can it, Rick."

Basil's home was at the end of a sandy, wooded road not far from Silver Lake. You had to look carefully to spot it, though, because it was built underground. There was a naturalistic landscaping of pine trees, scrub oaks, and artfully arranged rocks. Behind a dramatically tall, pointed slice of granite, you could see a triangle of solar panels jutting out and a glass doorway. This led down to the subterranean home. The panels served to give considerable light to the house down below. Still, it meant that Basil's own home was not appointed with any of the sleek, ultra-trendy window treatments that he gave to the rooms he designed on TV.

Basil greeted us at the bottom of the entryway, sporting a mixture of the ecological and the stylish: a hemp summer dress jacket that—from a distance—looked like linen, a black V-neck, button-down 501s with an elaborate turquoise belt, and woven sandals. Both ears sported small silver hoops. His jet black hair was slicked back with gel, though an artful forelock was trained to curl down his forehead. Basil was handsome to the point of being girl-pretty—a kind of Cherokee Jim Morrison—though his best feature, his dazzling smile, was featured all too seldom.

Indeed, Basil gave us a gravely serious tour of the house, pointing out the energy-efficient function served by every last doorknob. He recited a litany of facts and figures as to the average temperature of his home, its natural candlepower, and so on. Even the aesthetic appeal of this or that tapestry or throw pillow was subsumed within the larger issue of creating a habitat that minimized exploitation of the environment. When I mentioned how much I liked the stripes on a throw rug, Basil nodded in agreement and stated: "Yes, it's made from natural fibers and dyes," as though we were making the same point.

Still, Basil's keen eye for style was everywhere. The rooms were done in yellows and golds to make them all the brighter, with sumptuous satin and velvet throw pillows on sturdy, oak-framed beds, sofas and chairs. The overall effect was simultaneously elegant and hippie-natural. Basil's own artwork was featured on the walls—what he called interplanetary landscapes, serious-looking oils done somewhat in the style of Cézanne, yet depicting the surfaces of Mars and Jupiter and Saturn. It sounds like an odd mix, yet it worked. He also was a talented wood spinner, and had crafted the dinner plates and serving bowls, along with numerous more showy art pieces that aligned the mantles and end tables. Some of his decorative bowls and abstract shapes were so delicate and glistening it was hard to believe they were wood.

Basil himself came across as stressfully sensitive, all darting eyes and expressively fluttering fingers, with a voice that had never quite lost its adolescent crack. In photos, he could look intensely masculine, in a hip sort of way. But the moment he spoke or moved, his naturally fey demeanor took over, and if he weren't married, *no one* would have taken him for straight. When Curtsy Ann staunchly defended his heterosexuality, I wondered if she was being naïve or perfunctory.

By contrast, Basil's wife, Tarragon, was a study in butchdom. Introducing herself upon coming inside after chopping wood, she wore a Pendleton, overalls, and hiking boots. A no-frills surplus store bandana framed her Dick Tracy jaw line, tying back her nondescript hair—a short haircut left to grow out for want of knowing what else to do with it. After vigorously shaking our hands, she admonished Basil to have snacks ready for the kids when they came home from their alternative, multilingual school. Upon registering obedience, Basil announced he would make us his special blend of herb tea, and serve veggie sandwiches made with his homemade bread *and* homemade mayo. "It takes all of a minute to make fresh mayonnaise," he lectured, somewhat testily. "And there's simply *no* comparison between the store-bought impostor and the real thing."

"Abso-fucking-*lutely*," Tarragon asserted in her hearty baritone, slamming her fist on the heavy kitchen table for emphasis. "My Basil is the best goddamn cook—I mean, chef—this side of Albuquerque. I tell ya, guys—he cooks, he sews, he decorates, he's *great* with the kids. He's my fella."

"Aw, my little bear paw." Presumably, this was his affectionate nickname for her, given that he proceeded to give her cheek a light peck. "Tarragon is even more handy around the house than I am. Right now she's building us a stone fence, plus a toolshed."

"Gee, I don't think I've ever had homemade mayonnaise before," Terry shared.

"Well, you're in for a rare treat," I affirmed. "It's even better than an orgasm."

Terry shot me one of his nasty looks of displeasure, but Tarragon slapped her knee to guffaw.

"I run my own contracting firm," Tarragon told us. "Built most of this house with my own two hands, after Basil did the specs."

"And the decorating," he put in, dead seriously. "We're a real fifty-fifty couple. Everything is shared right down the middle."

He said this as though Terry and I were the politically correct police, ready to levy the stiffest of penalties at the slightest indication of gender stereotyping within the household.

"You have what I want," Terry remarked insipidly. "A real fifty-fifty kind of thing."

"So who takes care of the kids?" I asked, with no small amount of curiosity.

Just as Basil proclaimed, "I do," Tarragon uttered, "He does." They laughed in merriment over saying more or less the same thing at the same time, nudging their foreheads together. The only thing more irritating than couples bickering over how opposite they were was when they twittered over how much they had in common. For me, anyway, the effect was always just the opposite of what was intended: A couple's moments of discord made me see how unconsciously alike they were, while their expressions of commonality seemed pathetic attempts to run from the fact that they were painfully unsuited for each other.

"Adopting children was the greatest thing we ever did." Tarragon clasped Basil's hand within her firm, wrestler-like grip.

"I would agree," Basil nodded, as though reaching the same conclusion through lengthy philosophical exploration. "Ben, Marley, and Shiva are the light of our lives." His voice rather poignantly cracked, as though swept up with emotion.

Of course, anything was possible now. Ann-Margret, for one, did carpentry work and no one questioned her straightness. And whatever the details of their marriage, it was clear that Basil and Tarragon genuinely cared for each other. Still, even the most naïve and least catty person in the world would've wondered if this marriage hid a few home truths from the world—and hid them not all that well.

"You know, I can't resist asking. Is Tarragon your original name?" Personally, I never much warmed up to the idea of naming people after herbs. But I was curious to know if she'd given the name to herself—no doubt after some sort of earth-goddess equinox thing—or if her parents did, no doubt after some sort of earth-goddess equinox thing.

"Nope. I renamed myself at a spiritual retreat." She rolled up her sleeves, revealing her thick, furry arms.

"She doesn't discuss her original name," Basil informed us, his raised eyebrows signaling that he was making light of a mighty sensitive subject.

Tarragon warmly clasped our hands as she excused herself. "Gotta get back to my hatchet," she explained.

"My wife—I think I'll keep her." Basil sliced up generously homey portions of bread.

"She seems real nice," Terry commented. "Down to earth. A lot like my ex-wife."

Basil flicked handfuls of sprouts onto the bread. "Oh, so you were *married*, Terry?" From the way he said this, you'd have thought it was the one possible grounds by which they had something in common.

I couldn't help but roll my eyes. "*Anyway,*" I put in quickly, before Basil and Terry could wax on the finer points of marriage, "we did want to talk about Helena."

"And so we shall." Basil laid out a spread of festively presented sandwiches and tea that probably looked much better than it tasted. Health food and I were not exactly bosom buddies.

"It all looks too good to eat," I protested, but Basil insisted that we sit at the rustic table and dig in. (Thankfully, we were spared any sort of spiritual ritual before eating.) The rabbit-food sandwiches were innocuous, tasting of flavorless greens. The bread was slightly dry to my palate—it had too many grains in it—but there was indeed a hint of a rich, honey-and-garlic–flavored mayonnaise.

"Great mayo," I commented, taking just enough bites to seem appreciative.

"I didn't know you could put cucumbers in a sandwich," Terry revealed.

"Just goes to show, you learn something new every day," I contributed. "Cucumber sandwiches are practically the ambrosia of dull old society matrons who think food is for showing off how rich you are, or pretentious younger—" I caught myself. "I think you were starting to say something, Basil."

He quietly sat down to join us. "I wasn't. But I sense your impatience, Rick. You're like a cigarette smoker having a nicotine fit. The *story*. It's all about the next story, isn't it?"

Basil was strangely nonjudgmental when he said all this, so I felt comfortable to respond with a matching frankness.

"Yes, it is. That's my life."

"You're honest. That's important." With a large wooden spoon, he helped himself to a homemade salad that looked like tabouli but was something else. "Gentlemen?" I took a polite spoonful, while Terry favored a big helping. We forced a few minutes of small talk, made all the more excruciating by none of us being remotely interested in what anyone else had to say.

Basil laughed out loud, startling us with his brilliant, unexpected smile. "Poor Rick. You really do need to get to the point, don't you?"

"It would be nice," I admitted.

"Very well, then. *Helena and I*, by Basil Montclair." He stared down into his steaming tea as though it were a magic potion. "You know, it's the strangest thing. But one of those awful tabloids called me this morning. Seems they're running a spread on Helena's murder. They wanted to know if it was true that I always resented her."

"Did you?" Terry asked.

"Of course not. According to this reporter, I was jealous that my own designs always played second fiddle to Helena's . . . shall we say, more ambitious creations? That I did these marvelously tasteful rooms that got ignored, because people were so busy having nervous breakdowns over Helena."

It occurred to me that Basil—like so many other misguided souls—wanted to speak to me to set the record straight once and for all.

"And you want to set the record straight?"

"Exactly, Rick. You see, I'm comfortable where I am. I'm busy raising my children. I wouldn't want more clients than the ones I have. The show has given me enough publicity. And if Helena's the one who brings in the ratings, then that's great." He distractedly played with a crumb of bread on the table. "Or should I say Helena *brought* in the ratings?"

"Dumb question: Are you sad?"

Basil took a philosophical sip of tea. "Obviously, I'm sorry she was murdered, Rick. My belief is that murder is just not meant to be—it is brought about by human folly, and so it cuts short the spiritual journey of the victim. Helena will not get the opportunity to finish what she came here to accomplish."

"Well, if you're spiritual," Terry suggested, "you must believe in some form of afterlife."

"No. There is none." Basil set down his heavy ceramic cup with finality. "Only when we're living can we manifest the spirit. It dies when we die. All that lingers is the sorrow and loss. Helena's soul will be wailing from now into infinity."

"You mean like a ghost?" Terry helped himself to a plate of sliced tomatoes. I could not tell if he was playing along to win Basil's trust, or if he actually thought he could learn from him.

"No, not a ghost. Just . . . like a tremor in the wind, or the snap of a twig. It's there late at night, when no one is even listening. That aloneness that knows no peace."

"Say, anyone catch that MTV special last week, *The Hundred Rockingest TV Commercials of All Time*?" I put in brightly. "Would you believe that they ranked the Doublemint Twins *below* Speedy Alka-Seltzer?"

Clearly, Basil was doing a full-scale Morticia Adams, and I found it excessive, to put it mildly. Besides, if you really wanted to get into all that meaning-of-life jazz, didn't it count for *something* to solve the murder?

"*Rick,*" Terry admonished. "I was very interested in hearing more about Basil's beliefs."

Basil emitted a melancholy laugh as he stood up to tie on his apron and start collecting plates, very much the resolute homemaker. "Don't worry, Terry. Rick is apparently uncomfortable dwelling on the more mysterious aspects of life. So we'll keep things all sweetness and light." He raised a sardonic eyebrow. "Helena had real passion. She was so very deeply *engaged* in everything. Some people, you know, just sort of eat, sleep, and shit. But Helena was one of those cursed types who thought it all meant something. When things went wrong for her, it wasn't just a matter of ouch-that-hurt. It was more like, 'Why is God punishing me?' Not that she was religious in a church-on-Sunday way. But she did believe that everything happened for a reason. That there was some sort of guiding master plan to existence, and she grappled with trying to figure out what it was."

I took a polite sip of bitter-tasting tea. "Plus, she liked to fuck."

"Very funny, Rick," Terry scolded.

"Oh, but don't we all?" Basil's down-turned grin gave him an androgynous quality. "Rick is right. Helena was spirited. Unafraid of life. Or at least until Brick. She was different after that."

"What do you mean?" I asked.

"Brick never understood Helena. He was incapable of understanding her. And when you give your power away to someone who doesn't understand you . . . well, after a while, she lost her nerve."

"I don't think Curtsy Ann exactly minded when Helena got hurt."

Basil wiped off the table with a slightly dampened sponge. "You have an interesting way of putting things, Rick. It's true that Helena more or less stole Brick from Curtsy Ann. We all felt sad for her. But then later, we all felt even *more* sorry for Helena. Underneath that rose-petal veneer, Curtsy Ann is strong. *And* willful. She may put up a fuss, but she invests her money and looks out for herself. Helena was the type who'd have loused up being married to the greatest guy in the world if it meant finding true love—whatever true love meant in that moment." He turned to arrange the dishes in the sink. "It's strange, isn't it? The way that going after the truly important things in life turns us into masochists."

"You do have a point there," I allowed.

He carefully poured some filtered water into the sink, and added a few drops of organic soap. "Small wonder that Helena would have turned to Bill."

"When you say turned to Bill, you mean—?"

"Of course." To scour the dishes, he used a spongy object that looked like it had once lived at the bottom of the ocean—though presumably that would have been very un-environmentalist. "You take a good-looking available guy and a good-looking available girl, and what do you think happens?" Basil wiped his hands on his apron, then undid the apron and neatly folded it on the counter.

"Bill is sort of like Brick with a gentlemanly twist. While Brick simply uses women for sex, Bill also compliments them on their minds." There was a bitterness in Basil's voice—even, yes, a bitchiness—that wasn't there before.

"Did Bill send many compliments Helena's way?"

"Helena didn't confide in me, Rick. But you know how it is. The guys get to talking and bragging, and you learn certain things."

"Did you have anything to brag about?" I couldn't resist asking.

Basil blushed to bright red. "Of course not. But anyway, Bill told Brick and me all about his encounters with Helena. I looked to see if there was some remote trace of jealousy or remorse on Brick's part, but there wasn't. He just sat there, drinking his beer and laughing as Bill would go on and on about how he and Helena tried it hanging upside down from a tire swing or whatever it was that they did."

"Did Bill mention anything kind of leather-ish?" I asked.

Basil stopped washing. "Why? What makes you ask that?"

I made a point of chuckling. "Just a rumor, that's all."

"Like I said, Helena didn't confide in me. Bill huffs and puffs in his guy kind of way. Nothing specific." He rinsed out the wooden salad bowl. "It's hard to know what the truth is."

Terry frowned with worry. "Did Ann-Margret know about Helena and Bill?" After all, according to the polygraph, Ann-Margret had it bad for Bill, and if Helena had kind of stolen him away . . .

"I have no idea. That would've been girl-talk stuff. Of course, she was super good friends with Helena, so even if she did know something, she would've kept their secret." He took a fresh linen towel from the drawer, and proceeded to dry the dishes.

"But why exactly was it such a secret, Basil?"

"Because Helena wanted Brick to think he was the only one in her heart. Which was true."

"Do you think Ann-Margret killed Helena?" I queried.

"Absolutely not."

"Do you know where she is?" Terry wanted to know.

"Hardly. It was utterly ludicrous to run away."

"What about a white room?" I asked. "Did Helena ever talk about something bad from her past having to do with a white room?"

"Gee, what is this—Twenty Questions? I don't remember anything about a white room. Except that one design she did." He smiled contentedly as he swept the floor.

"What about a rich old lady who helped Helena get started as a designer?" I queried.

Basil laughed. "We *all* have one of those in our past."

"Do you know Tippi Finkelstein?" Terry inquired.

He furrowed his brow in thought. "I'm afraid the name does not ring a bell."

"Brick never mentioned her when the guys were, as you say, confiding in each other?" Terry asked.

He looked up from his sweeping. "No. Should he have?"

"Yes, he probably should have," Terry replied. "What about Fernando San Marcos?"

Basil dropped a ceramic cup to the floor; it spun about but didn't shatter. "He's an actor. I remember hearing he was on the show."

"Yes, indeed," I confirmed, studying Basil carefully as he reached down to pick up the cup. "In fact, Helena built him an S-and-M torture chamber for a living room. Seems she knew his dirty secrets. In fact, we've been wondering if Helena didn't have this knack of airing the dirty laundry of all sorts of people whose rooms she designed."

"Oh, really?" Basil smiled in a pleasantly opaque, showbiz way.

There was a sudden rush of footsteps on the staircase.

*"Hi, Daddy!"*

Three kids, aged about seven to ten, ran to their father's arms, and he held them like a bunch of wildflowers. "This is Ben, this is Marley, and this is Shiva," he explained, pointing to them in order of their ages. Ben was black, Marley appeared to be Asian, and Shiva was either Native-American or from India or the Middle East. They smiled hello; they seemed like friendly kids.

Basil registered a kind of harried homemaker's resigned frown and sigh. "I'm afraid, guys, that the interview is over."

"Aw, shucks," I complained. "Just when we were getting to the good part."

Basil looked nervous. "What do you mean?"

"Nothing," I assured him.

"Rick likes to kid," Terry agreed.

As Terry drove us back to my place, I took out my trusted laptop, and started looking over the many *My House, Your House* files I'd downloaded.

"What do you know?" I commented. "It turns out that they were about to film a special episode in which one designer did a room in the home of another designer. Basil and Helena were going to trade."

"You mean—"

"Exactly. Next week, sweet Helena was scheduled to design a room in Basil's home. What do you want to bet it was going to have a theme pertaining to a detective show, or maybe another leather love nest?"

"I don't get it, Rick." Terry frowned in the rearview mirror.

"Jesus, Terry, how slow can you be? Does the name Fernando San Marcos ring a bell? It sure rang one with Basil."

Before he could tell me how much I had insulted his pride and wounded his dignity, the radio news came on:

"Fugitive Ann-Margret Wochinsky, wanted for the murder of controversial designer Helena Godiva, may well be the victim of genetics . . ."

"Holy cripes," Terry commented. "Turn that damn thing off."

"No, wait," I insisted.

"Rick, she's still at large, so there's no point in—"

"Terry, just listen, okay?"

". . . It seems that Ms. Wochinsky's cousin, Joseph "Zebra" Zobronsky, is currently on the FBI's Ten Most Wanted list in connection with the murder and kidnapping of fellow gangster, Kenneth "the Mole" Shultz. I guess it's true that the apple does not fall very far from the tree. On a lighter note, the sixth grade class of an Illinois elementary school—"

Terry turned off the radio. "Are you satisfied, Rick?"

"Terry, I had no idea you had a cousin in the mob."

"He's not in the mob. He's just a crook. And he's not really a cousin. He's like a second cousin to both Ann-Margret and me. I don't think either of us have ever even met him."

I could only assume that this was a real sore spot for Terry. Still, there was something I thought he should be told.

"Terry, you know your bedroom?"

"Of course. What about it?" Like a lot of men, embarrassment put him in a crappy mood.

"In Helena's original plans, you were going to get blow-ups of FBI wanted posters instead of crime-fighting heroes. In fact, I'm remembering now that one of the faces was of . . . you know, that cousin guy."

Terry pulled the car over to the shoulder of the freeway. "You mean to tell me that Helena was going to blab to the world about my being related to this no-good thug?" Cars and trucks whizzed by like arrows or comets.

"In a manner of speaking, yes. I mean, most people wouldn't have made the connection, but *you* would've."

"What a fucking bitch."

I gave his arm an affectionate squeeze. "Why Terry, I didn't know you had it in you."

# SEVENTEEN

TERRY WAS SPENDING SO MUCH TIME IN THE AUNT FERN ROOM—
and he felt so at home in it—that I had half a mind to simply chop it off
from the rest of the house and have it transported to his place. It would've
at least spared me the pain of having to get it redone.

Stretched on the recliner, he munched on his millionth donut of the
day. "Okay, let's recap. No one has all that great of an alibi as to where they
were during the murder. Curtsy Ann and Tippi both hated Helena's guts,
and either one of them could've done it, or else connived Brick into doing
it. Either through bribery or general weirdness."

"And let's not forget that it wouldn't be all that shocking if Brick was
hiding a skeleton or two, and wanted Helena dead for his own dumb-ass
reasons." What the heck—I helped myself to a donut.

"Fernando could've flipped out over the body piercing room," Terry
continued, "and Basil was maybe going to get similarly exposed to the
world. Who knows? Maybe they were in on it together. And we haven't
even checked out Koko or Bill yet."

I nervously chomped on my French crueller, dreading what I knew I
had to say next. "Of course there's at least one more person to consider."

"You mean Aunt Fern? Technically, I suppose we can't rule her out."

"No, not Aunt Fern," I gently replied. "I think the old dear's more into
killing people with kindness."

"Who, then? Tapioca? I mean— Tarragon?"

"No, not her, either. Though it *is* a female."

Terry thought for a moment, then stood up, crushing his empty donut bag in anger. "Jesus, Rick. I can't believe you'd even think such a thing."

"Terry, be fair." I tried to sound casual as I licked a fleck of chocolate icing from my finger. "You know you've even thought it yourself. Ann-Margret's in love with Bill. She could've heard something about Helena's involvement with him from the horse's mouth that last night in the motel room. They'd been drinking pretty hard. Maybe they started to duke it out a little. Things got carried away. Admit it, it's *possible*. Not likely, but possible."

He wiped a tear from his large brown eye. "You're right. We can't quite rule her out. But, God almighty, I hope she didn't do it."

I felt the urge to give him a hug. "Don't worry. I'm still sure she's innocent. It's just that we have to . . . well, you know."

As I was walking toward him, his cell phone rang.

"Hi, Boxer!" Terry looked at me with an expression intended to indicate his pleasure and surprise. "How great to hear from you. Just when I was feeling low."

And so the two of them proceeded to get utterly revolting over the phone. When my own phone rang a few seconds later, I could not have been more relieved.

"Rick—Chauncey Riggs here."

Needless to say, my relief was short-lived. If there was anyone on the face of the earth I never wanted to talk to, it was Chauncey Riggs. Yet as I glanced over at Terry so offensively turning to flotsam as Boxer no doubt told him something like "I had a really nice time the other night," I had little choice but to pretend to be delighted by my caller.

"Oh, it's *you*," I all but sang, careful not to mention Chauncey by name. "I'm *so* glad you called."

"Uh, Rick, you did hear me say who it is, didn't you?"

I gave a little laugh. "I'd know your voice anywhere."

There was a long pause. "Well anyway, Rick. I've been doing some snooping around on this whole Helena Godiva thing. I know you've been doing the same—don't even try to deny it—and I thought that we could meet for a drink and compare notes."

Normally, if Chauncey called to tell me this, I would've told him in no uncertain terms where he could stick his notes. I knew perfectly well he had no intention of sharing so much as a semicolon with me—and, for that matter, he probably didn't know much anyway. He was really just attempting, in his sleazeball manner, to steal what he could and then broadcast it first.

But I couldn't bring myself to say any of this. I wanted Terry—and by extension, Boxer—to have the sadly false impression that I had something approaching a personal life. It was ridiculously adolescent of me, but there you have it. Back in Iowa, there was begging little to do save watch old Gidget movies at the church basement on Friday nights, and Sandra Dee left her indelible mark on my consciousness.

"That sounds like *heaven*," I gushed, winking at Terry—who didn't seem to notice. "Shall we say dinner? Someplace small and quiet."

"Rick, I don't know what kind of shit you're pulling here, but if you think you can get away with—"

"Dinner it is then. Let's say eight o'clock at Zsa Zsa Baba's—that new place on North Robertson."

The devil in me couldn't resist picking a restaurant that I knew Chauncey would hate. It was very cruisy and way out of his league.

I could scarcely wait to tell Terry about my sudden and mysterious date—but I had to wait, since he wasn't about to rush getting off the phone with his beloved Boxer. Finally, after what felt like lifetimes—though it was only about ten more minutes—Terry said good-bye. I already inferred that he and Boxer were going to a hot new dance club on Hollywood Boulevard called Stomp.

"Wow, I think I finally met the One," Terry managed to sputter, all dewy-eyed and creepy.

"I couldn't be happier for both of you." I tapped my fingertips together in delicious anticipation. "Of course, I have quite a date myself this evening. No one you would know. He's . . . sort of in show business."

"Rick, don't tell me you've found another one of those hanger-on types who's going to spend all your money and then—"

"Nothing could be further from the truth." I couldn't help noting the irony of my words—Chauncey was in fact the dead opposite of my usual type. "He has his own career. Look, if something comes of it, Terry, you'll be the first to know. I promise."

"Fair enough." He stretched and yawned. "Mind if use the shower? I have to start getting ready."

"Me, too!"

Fortunately, I left before Boxer arrived—boringly on time again, no doubt—and so didn't have to watch them get all lovey-dovey. Still, my heart wasn't exactly skipping a beat at the thought of having dinner with Chauncey.

I was only about twenty minutes late when I got to Zsa Zsa Baba's, but Chauncey was so disgruntled you'd have thought I'd been keeping him waiting for twenty years. He was wearing one of his ill-fitting suits, the jacket buttoned as always—which made him look even more ungainly—and his bow tie horrendously out of style. As usual, he sweated profusely and self-consciously toyed with the two or three strands of hair that gallantly attempted to cover his badly-shaped bald spot. All about him in the crowded restaurant was the hum of traded phone numbers, and bottles of wine sent over to men seated across the room, who responded with smiles and winks and meltingly intense eye contact. Everyone but Chauncey was tanned and muscled and eager for sex and love, in that order.

"Sit down, Rick." He gave a huffy glance at his watch. "Your rudeness remains intact over the years."

"I was always taught, Chauncey, that the rudest thing of all is to call someone rude."

The hunky waiter took our drink orders, recited the evening's adjective-laden specials, and produced a pair of menus. I looked mine over with relish. The food was touted as quite good, in its snooty, novelle-cuisine way. "As I was saying, one properly grins and bears it, so to speak."

"Why did you invite me out to dinner, Rick? We both know it wasn't for the pleasure of my company."

"Boy, sun-dried tomatoes up the wazzoo," I commented, scanning the menu. "How eighties can you get? I think I'll try the trout poached in pheasant-egg sauce."

The waiter set down a vodka Martini in front of me while handing Chauncey his bourbon on the rocks.

"Cheers." I raised my glass for a toast.

"Very well, then." Chauncey obliged, touching his glass to mine. "I'll bet it's nothing all that diabolical. Probably you're just trying to make someone jealous."

"Oh?" I drank my vodka, careful to maintain a poker face.

"I'm right, aren't I? And to think you had no one to turn to but the likes of poor pitiful me. What's the matter, Rick? Did you already date every wannabe in town?"

"Better a wannabe than a common whore. Tell me, Chauncey, how often do they turn down your money because you gross them out too much?"

From the way he shook, I could tell he was fighting the urge to throw his drink in my face. I placed a steadying hand on his wrist. "C'mon, Chauncey. We're in public. Don't waste a good drink."

"You're right." He patted his face with his handkerchief. "You're a first-class SOB, but you're right."

Apropos of my comments, a waiter came over with a camera. "Mind if I take your picture, gentlemen?"

Chauncey and I jovially smiled for the camera, a couple of semi-celebs patronizing—and presumably endorsing—this new restaurant, and having the best time in the world. This drew attention to us, and several patrons sent over napkins for us to sign. Chauncey and I smiled and smiled like the best of friends.

When we'd finished signing autographs, we each ordered another drink.

"So Rick, what have you got?"

I shrugged. "Not much."

"I don't believe that for a minute."

"Believe whatever you want." I took a luxurious sip of vodka. "I've talked to a few people, but they've hardly been forthcoming." Technically, I was telling the truth—I *didn't* know all that much. Besides, I knew Chauncey well enough to be sure that he simply couldn't resist one-upmanship, especially when it came to me. Even if he were fairly well convinced I was holding out, he'd want to rub my face in his own superior knowledge.

"Are you working with that cute cop guy again?"

"Maybe a little." Through sheer force of habit, I found myself looking around the bar. "Why, did you want me to set you up with him?"

"Stop being cruel. The thing of it is, I'm *convinced* Ann-Margret is guilty."

"Do tell." I leaned forward, feigning more interest than I had. For all I knew, Ann-Margret *was* guilty, but I hardly expected Chauncey to be the one to figure it out.

"Well, besides all the police evidence, I found out something pretty amazing."

"Go on." A guy seated over at the bar caught my eye; he smiled at me.

"She's been—" He slapped my hand. "Stop cruising that guy, and listen."

I sighed. "Very well, Chauncey. I'm all ears, all for you."

"Ann-Margret has the hots for Bill McCoy. I spoke with a guy on the crew who swore it was true. But Helena was messing around with Bill on the sly."

"So what?"

"Do the arithmetic. Ann-Margret finds out about the affair—and whoops, there goes Helena."

"Chauncey, that's ludicrous. Ann-Margret's not some weirdo who would murder her friend just because she fucked some guy she had the hots for." Although of course, I'd suggested a remarkably similar scenario to Terry only hours beforehand. Somehow, whatever came out of Chauncey's slimy mouth automatically sounded like crap. If he told me my name was Rick Domino, I'd have had cause to believe I'd been lied to all my life about it.

Chauncey dismissed my argument with a sneer. "Accidents happen."

"Chauncey, if this was why you wasted my time by dragging me out—"

"Dragging *you* out? You're the one who insisted on dinner."

"Wait a second." The pretty picture I saw transpiring behind Chauncey was worth at least a thousand words: Fernando San Marcos and Basil Montclair were being seated at a table for two. They were done up in full black leather regalia. Once they sat down, Chauncey's considerable frame obfuscated them from view.

"Uh, Chauncey, I just remembered something. I have to run. I'm sure you won't miss me." I was careful to look away from the two men so that Chauncey wouldn't turn around and notice them. He presumably didn't connect Fernando to the dots leading up to the murder, but he did know who he was, and he would've recognized Basil Montclair as well. They were seated closer to the door, so it made perfect sense for me to walk in their direction—without arousing suspicion, I hoped. It wasn't just that I wanted to out-scoop Chauncey, I just knew he'd accomplish little if he monopolized their time.

The waiter was arriving with the food. "Here," I instructed, throwing down a wad of cash. "Something just came up." Chauncey muttered something about how an un-housebroken dog had better manners than I did, but I couldn't be bothered to respond. My plan, such as it was, was to go over to the other table, say hi, and take it from there. Fernando spotted me; he whispered to Basil, and the two of them stood up to leave.

"Shit." I ran past the waiter and followed them outside. Though it was still early in the evening, a couple of callboys were lurking about in their tight jeans, their gelled hair gleaming beneath the glow of the street lamps.

"Basil, Fernando—please wait."

But they kept on walking.

"Look, I can always say I spotted you both at a table for two in a gay restaurant." I hated having to say that—and in truth, I might well have not lived up to the threat—but it had to be done.

They stopped walking. "Okay, Rick, what do you want?" Basil asked, turning around to face me. Fernando turned around as well, as if to challenge me with his cold gaze.

"Just a few minutes of your time." I took out my cell phone to call Terry, feeling like a cop calling for backup. I wondered if Terry would tell me to handle it on my own—after all, he was in the middle of a date—but, ever putting duty before pleasure, he said he'd be right there, and was glad that I'd called. (As it happened, the dance club was only a few blocks away.)

And so Terry soon met up with us. I was curious, to say the least, about his date, but didn't have a chance to ask him anything. It was just as well, of course, since I hardly relished telling him about mine.

Fernando was totally pissed off to learn that Terry was a cop, and refused to calm down. He paced about in anger, his tall black motorcycle boots splashing in an oily parking lot puddle. A full moon rippled in the muddied reflection.

"I *knew* it," he kept shouting, though he looked at me and not at Terry.

"If you knew it, why were you so surprised?" I wanted to know.

"Okay, so I didn't know. But it was still a totally shitty thing to pull, Rick."

"Not as shitty as murder," I pointed out.

"I wouldn't know."

"Look, this isn't getting us anywhere," Terry finally stated. "Let's go someplace and talk."

"We might as well go to my house," Fernando offered. "It's close and *very* private."

"How gracious of you, Fernando. I expect the deluxe tour of your torture chamber."

"You certainly have turned into a prude in your old age, Rick," Fernando meanly commented.

"Not at all. I've been known to have some pretty kinky whims myself. Though nothing as a steady diet."

"Really, Rick?" Terry asked, all wide-eyed wonderment.

"Down, boy," Fernando admonished. "The word of mouth is that he ain't all that."

"I wasn't coming on to him," Terry protested. "And anyway, I'm extremely vanilla."

It came as a mild shock to hear Terry using some form of street slang to describe his sexual proclivities—albeit that the word in question was "vanilla." Maybe Boxer was helping him loosen up a little.

"How would you know?" I inquired. After all, in Terry's case, even vanilla-dom was more a matter of theory than anything else. Needless to say, Terry had no answer for me, save for a generally disgruntled demeanor.

"You are a feisty one, aren't you, Rick?" Basil, ever eager to play the peacenik, put his hand to my shoulder. Though not the actor of the two, he seemed to think he was playing a priest in a TV movie, taking a confession from one of his abductors.

"I have no idea how to answer that." I probably sounded hostile, and I didn't care. Condescension didn't deserve courtesy.

"Wow, Rick is at a loss for words," Terry commented. "This must be a first." He and Basil laughed, which irritated me all the more.

And so the four of us repaired to Fernando's Spanish-style home, which looked out onto Santa Monica Boulevard. By normal standards, it was an impressive, six-bedroom spread, with one of those swimming pools that jutted out to the breathtaking edge of a low cliff. But by Hollywood standards it was all kind of been-there-done-better. The décor of the home seemed to reflect his no-frills Detective Garcia style. I might have guessed that Basil had designed it, but it lacked Basil's flair. Everything was done in clean, modern lines, with creams, pale grays and beiges dominating—the kind of style that seemed to almost have a phobia about risking the bad taste of an actual color. In particular, it was hard to believe that the careful, ultra-tasteful living room had ever been the body piercing room designed by Helena.

But then, who knew what sorts of exotic furnishings could be found in some locked-off room of the house?

An all-purpose male servant greeted us, took out coats, and made us drinks. I always got a kick out of some rich guy in his kinky leather duds being called "Mister" or "Sir" by his hired help. Money, as they say, really does talk.

"That will be all," Fernando instructed. As the servant departed, Fernando carefully negotiated sitting on the white-and-gray sofa in his ultra-tight leather chaps. "Now, then," he continued, "I suppose there's no point in beating around the bush."

"That's one way of putting it." I took a hefty swallow of my vodka Martini.

"My wife and I have an understanding," Basil conveyed, taking a nervous sip of Bombay gin; apparently, he was off herb tea for the night.

"It works out perfectly," Fernando added. "I can't afford to be out to the world. And I do have my extracurricular pursuits, as you guys already know."

"When it comes to sex masters, one is never enough," I concurred. "Look, I don't really care. Basil, it's not exactly a shock that you and your wife have, as you put it, an understanding. If for you and Fernando, love means never having to say you're sorry after a flogging, all the more power to you. But who knows what else you're holding out on? And *that's* what we need to know."

"Or you'll out us?" Basil cringed, as if afraid to hear the answer.

"I'm afraid so." I was careful not to blink.

"Jesus Christ, I've got *kids*," Basil complained. "Have a little heart, Rick."

"And you can have a little heart toward an innocent girl accused of murder," Terry countered. "You both keep saying you know she's innocent. Then speak up, dammit. What else are you hiding?"

The two leather aficionados repaired to a corner of the room. They whispered urgently back and forth; at one point, Fernando raised his voice.

"We'll tell you everything," Basil finally declared. "Everything about Helena, that is."

"Good." I helped myself to the bar, adding an ice cube to my drink, followed by an extra shot. "Let's start then with the slight detail that Helena was about to do a room in your home, Basil."

"And you think—?" He flustered and swallowed hard. "Why, surely you don't think that I would ever, *could* ever . . ."

"Did you see her specs for the room?" Terry asked.

Basil swallowed his gin like good medicine. "Yes. If you must know, she was going to give my study a boot camp theme."

"Boot camp?" Terry registered puzzlement. "Oh, wait—now I get it. You like to . . . I mean . . ."

I was grinning ear-to-ear. "Basil, do all your politically correct friends know about your secret desire to be a drill sergeant? Especially when you have Fernando for a *buck* private?"

I was always intrigued by the way you indeed could not judge a book by its cover. Both Basil and Fernando were handsome, swarthy and black-haired; in their near-identical leather gear, they almost looked related. Yet it was bachelor Fernando who came across as conventionally masculine, while married Basil seemed "obviously" gay. Nonetheless, when the lights went down, something reversed itself, as if their shadows had lives unto themselves.

The macho star of *Badges of Philly*, whom we'd caught quite literally with his pants down in Fernando's dressing room, seemed much more the conventional master type—intensely masculine and no-nonsense in demeanor. Whoda thunk that fey, cooking-and-decorating Basil could've stepped into his boots, so to speak? But then I thought about Basil, who tried to be so exceptionally nice, but who was also so unapproachable in some nameless way. Or Fernando, who acted very pushy and bossy, yet who also liked to get bossed and pushed around . . .

"I refuse to dignify that with an answer," Basil flatly stated, as though he were royalty being asked to comment on rumors that he suffered from gastritis. "But it's true, Helena never could resist stirring things up." His drink polished off, he walked to the bar to make himself another. "In that inimitable, supposedly subtle way she had."

Terry surprised me by drinking a shot of Wild Turkey; maybe Boxer was having an upscale effect on his tastes. "What I just don't get is why people like Aunt Fern liked Helena so much, if she did all these crummy things to people."

"*I* liked Helena," Basil protested. He clearly was one of those people who had trouble admitting there were people he did not like. "With Aunt Fern, Helena was like the teacher's pet. Even when you had cold, hard evidence against her, Aunt Fern just wouldn't hear of it."

"Well, you do have to admit, guys, it was a remarkable stroke of good fortune," I reflected. "Just as Helena is about to wink to the world that Basil is more than just a devoted husband and father, she ends up hanging from a ceiling fan."

"We were with each other when she died," Fernando proclaimed. Basil sat on the arm of the light tan sofa, clasping Fernando's hand in a sign of unity.

"How touching," I commented. "Moreover, how convenient."

"I'm willing to believe you *were* with each other," Terry decided. "But so what? You both have enough money to pay to get the job done."

"Oh, come *on*, you know we didn't do it."

Terry shrugged. "I know nothing of the sort, Fernando. What do you think—because you happen to be gay, I won't consider you suspects?"

There was a large, tastefully whitewashed cabinet, behind which I guessed there was a wide-screen TV. On the top of the cabinet, I noticed a stack of DVDs—older episodes of *Badges of Philly*. Looking them over, the title of an episode jogged my memory.

"Look, if that bitch whore wasn't your cousin," Fernando shrieked, "you wouldn't even be here now."

Terry tried not to flinch, but I could tell he was deeply wounded—as much by his inability to respond as a good cop as by the words themselves.

"Fernando, please," sex master Basil urged, putting his hand to Fernando's shoulder. "Nothing can be gained by all this negative energy."

"I'm *right*, dammit." Fernando disengaged from Basil's touch, too irritable to want contact with anyone. "They're sticking their noses into everyone's underwear because this stupid cop doesn't know dick about his cousin."

Terry rose to his full, intimidating six-four. I knew he was struggling not to punch out Fernando, but Fernando stood defiant and unafraid, shoulders back and chin jutted out.

"Terry, wait." I wedged myself between them, holding up a DVD labeled *Episode Nine: Fans Do the Craziest Things*. "I'm remembering an episode of *Badges of Philly*. A soap opera star ends up murdered, hanging from a ceiling fan."

"I never saw that one," Terry despaired. "Was it good?"

I sighed. "It was *fine*. Obviously, that's not the point. Detective Garcia has a long speech—long for him, anyway—about how the body was hung from the fan in such a way as to evenly distribute its weight. That way, the fan didn't come loose from the ceiling. There was something about how if it had fallen to the floor, it would've woken up other people in the house. Eventually, they figure out that this crazed, dweeby teenager was a whiz in physics, so he would've known just how to hang the body."

Fernando turned pale, and sat back down on the sofa. Basil sat next to him, rubbing his back in a soothing, tender way.

"You know, in the back of my mind," I continued, "I always thought there was something weird about Helena's body swinging from the fan. Why didn't it fall to the floor, taking the fan with it? It was a crummy old motel. Surely the plaster had seen better days."

Actually, I'd wondered nothing of the sort, but it sounded impressive.

"And the material she was wrapped in," Terry thought out loud. "It was gold, wasn't it? Very similar to the gold you used in your house, Basil."

"I finished decorating the house years ago," he countered. "Besides, anyone could've bought some gold fabric. It's big this year. Curtsy Ann practically breathes gold fabric."

"We wondered about that," Terry allowed. "But as I think about it, her fabric is at least several hues lighter than the gold material that Helena's body was wrapped in, judging by the police photos. Which was more of a standard harvest gold."

"Lighter than harvest gold?" Basil pondered. "It's odd you'd say that. I should think it's more that Curtsy Ann's trademark gold contains traces of a pale, pale green."

"Green?" Terry scratched his bristly crew cut with incredulity. "No way is there green in there."

"I'm telling you, if you see the weave up close, you will make out a definite green thread."

"Since you mention it, I suppose it's possible there's a hint of ice blue," Terry allowed. "But never in a million years green."

"Look, guys, *forget* it, okay?" I slammed the DVD case on the cabinet for emphasis. "Green, blue, fuchsia, what the fuck difference does it make? Basil, we all appreciate your integrity. You might even walk to your lethal injection protesting if not your innocence then the true nature of Curtsy Ann's trademark fabric. But the thing is, guys—it doesn't look good."

"Millions of people saw that episode on TV," Fernando insisted. "You don't even know for certain if the body was hung the same way."

"But I can find out easily enough," Terry informed him. "Do you want to hedge your bets?"

"If you think I did it, arrest me." Fernando defiantly held up his wrists.

I couldn't resist laughing. "You'd like that, wouldn't you?"

"Now hold on," Terry urged. "No one said anything about arresting anyone. Guys, I really do hope you're both innocent. But as my cousin clears her good name—and she will—suspicions will turn elsewhere. And believe me, I'm the nicest cop you'll ever want to confide in."

"And I'm really not outing anyone," I promised, "as long as you stop holding back."

Fernando sighed, and put his face in his hands. After a moment, he looked up at us.

"Okay, I guess I've put this off long enough. Come with us."

Exchanging meaningful glances with Basil, he led us down his immaculate ice gray hallway—complete with a vase of fresh white tulips—to a room at the far end. Using a series of computer codes to open the door, he led us into a different sort of room that—among other things—hardly featured the same color scheme as the rest of the house.

Instead, within its black walls, floors and ceiling there was a small mock prison cell, stirrups, hanging handcuffs, a wall-length display of whips, chains and paddles, a black leather mummy sack, a torture rack, a kind of giant dog crate, and various electrical gizmos in all sorts of fanciful shapes and sizes. There also was a long rack of military uniforms and black leather accessories.

"For what it's worth, here it all is," Fernando informed us.

"I'm not sensing much enthusiasm from you," I couldn't resist commenting.

"This is, um, all very interesting." Terry could scarcely disguise how uncomfortable he was around this type of stuff. "But I'm not sure why you're showing it to us."

Terry had a point. It was as if they thought that showing us their X-rated sex world were somehow a fair trade-off and they now wouldn't have to tell us anything more about Helena.

"Patience, my friend." Fernando led us to another door. Once again using a complex system of computer codes, he opened the door and led us into pitch-blackness.

"Is this some sort of set-up?" Terry took the proverbial words right out of my mouth.

"I *wish*," Fernando made a sarcastic sigh as he turned on a light. We saw that we were in a nondescript utility hallway—probably near where the water heater was located. Fernando led us to yet another door. He punched in more codes, and we entered a kind of studio-bedroom. Besides a bed and TV, there was a small refrigerator, a stove and a sink; an open doorway revealed a stand-up shower.

"Normally he uses this room for the hired help," Basil explained. But we weren't much interested in what Fernando normally used it for. Lying blissfully on the bed, holding hands and watching TV, were none other than Bill McCoy and Ann-Margret Wochinsky.

Bill, I couldn't help noticing, had his shirt off.

"Does *this* help?" Fernando asked rhetorically. Then, to the startled Ann-Margret and Bill, he murmured, "I'm so sorry, but we had no choice."

# EIGHTEEN

TO SAY THAT TERRY WAS PISSED OFF WAS LIKE SAYING THAT ON occasion porn shops have been known to sell dildos.

"My own cousin," he kept repeating, pacing back and forth on the linoleum floor and seeming to wish he had hair he could pull out. "My own cousin goes on the lam to beat a murder rap, I just about shit in my pants with fear, and where do I find her? Sitting around, drinking a Diet Pepsi, and watching fucking *Buffy the Vampire Slayer* on TV."

I didn't think it politic to point out that she was actually watching *Angel.*

Ann-Margret could only lower her head in shame, her false eyelashes shutting like eyelids on a doll.

"Gee, Baby Cousin Terry, I'm like, you know . . . sorry?"

She loudly helped herself to another low-fat Wheat Thin from the box she'd been enjoying. "Uh, cracker, anyone?"

"Don't mind if I do." Bill eagerly dug his hand into the box.

"And you!" Terry pointed at him accusingly. "What in the name of fuck are you doing? Do you even *like* her?" Before Bill could speak, Terry added, "If you cared about her at all, you would've turned her in. For her own good."

Bill self-consciously reached for his black T-shirt, as if by putting it on he would atone for his sins. "Gee, man. No need to get so bent out of shape. I've been having feelings for Ann-Margret for a long time, and when I found out she was here, I figured it was now or never. I guess you could say it's the one good thing that's come out of all this." He slipped the tight black T over his head; the cotton fabric seemed to kiss every contour of his smooth beige skin. (Bill, I could tell, got his torso waxed.) That the shirt featured the words LOVE MAGNET did little to diminish Terry's ire.

"That's highly debatable," Terry decreed. "I fail to see what's good about your presence here at this moment."

Basil dared to gently touch Terry's shoulder with one fingertip. "Now, Terry—"

"And you two. You're the worst ones of all. Letting her stay in your home."

"It's not my home."

Terry mockingly slapped his forehead. "Right, I forgot. You have a wife and kids."

"But I told you, we have an understanding." Basil fretfully adjusted his leather chaps.

Terry walked over to the wall, and forcefully yanked out the plug to the TV. A spark flew out of the socket.

"That's a very bad habit," Basil scolded. "It wears down the appliance and could cause a short circuit."

"I *know*," Bill agreed. "My kid brother used to do that all the time. Finally, my dad told him—"

With his first and fourth fingers, Terry made a loud, police-sounding whistle. Everyone stopped talking.

"What is it with you people? Do you think this is all a joke?" He paced about like an army commander berating his sadly inadequate unit. "Ha-ha, I'm wanted for murder, but I think I'll go hang out with my leather pals. Ha-ha, we're the leather dudes, let's not tell her cop cousin we're hiding her. Ha-ha, I'm her new . . . I dunno, *boyfriend*? I think I'll just go watch TV with her and eat some mother-goddamn-fucking Wheat Thins. Well, ha-ha-ha, guess what? You're all under arrest. A real laugh riot, huh?"

"Arrested? Dude, you've got to be kidding." Bill was dumbfounded, as though he'd heretofore always been told he was immune to human law.

"We'll get through this." Basil clasped Fernando's hand with a partner's strength and assurance.

"But Baby Cousin Terry, it's not their fault," Ann-Margret insisted. "Go ahead and cuff me and take me in and do whatever you have to do. But these guys are my friends. They risked everything to help me. Please—can't you just give them a warning or something?"

"She was scared," Fernando related. "She thought the guards would rape her."

"We just wanted to give her some space," Basil explained. "Some quiet time to sort things out. We knew you guys were working on the case, so maybe she wouldn't have to go back to jail at all."

"Besides," Bill continued, smiling with all his charisma, "Aunt Fern gave us our marching orders. And how do you say no to a nice old lady like Aunt Fern?"

They looked up at Terry like kids hoping that the principal will let them go to the school dance even though they got caught playing hooky.

Terry took a deep breath. "Basil Montclair, Fernando San Marcos, and Bill McCoy, you are all under arrest for obstruction of justice and for sheltering a fugitive. You have the right to remain silent. You have the right to have an attorney present . . ."

Ann-Margret started to cry, her generously applied mascara running down her cheeks. Terry looked at her sternly, as though it were the only way he could get through what he was about to do. Ann-Margret, seeming to sense this, gallantly fought to stop crying as he placed her under arrest. I have to admit it kind of got to me, the way she could still care enough to try to make things easier for him.

After reading everyone their rights, Terry methodically called for backup. Fernando casually stated that he might as well go to the main part of the house for a drink, and Basil nonchalantly noted that it might be nice to change out of their leather gear. But Terry ordered them to stay put. Bill astutely remarked: "This blows. No offense, guys." To which Terry commented that the three of them had best just stand in the corner and not say anything more. Fernando, I noticed, was blushing as he stood with his hands in front of his crotch.

"Cousin Terry, please just listen for one minute."

"No, Ann-Margret, *you* listen. I know you didn't kill Helena. And I know you had good reasons to be scared. We could've taken care of all that. You probably would've even made bail. We're working on the case day and night. And you have a good attorney."

"*Had* a good attorney. He doesn't want to represent me anymore." She nervously picked at her white nail polish.

"Well, then I'm sure Boxer will take the case. And he's as good as they get."

I resisted the urge to disagree.

"Terry, I just *couldn't* go to jail. Why is that so hard to understand?"

"Because at the end of the day, that's still where you're going. And all you've done is make things worse for yourself. And for the people you care about. Not to mention the taxpayers, who now have to pay for an additional hearing."

Ann-Margret reached for her purse. Taking out her nail polish, she touched up the nail she'd picked at. "Well, I guess we can't all be perfect, like you. Never straying from the narrow path." She blew on her freshly polished white nail, looking away from Terry. Perhaps it was a coincidence that it was her middle finger.

"I've never said I was perfect."

"Do you have any idea what it feels like to be accused of *murder*? No, of course not. You just go around la-de-dah arresting people, and what's the big deal? You tell him, Rick. You tell him what it's like. What *he's* like."

Everyone was looking at me. Talk about feeling on the spot.

"Actually, folks, I hate to disappoint you. But Terry was right there for me, even when the world looked at me as one great big walking and talking social disease." I didn't like rehashing the past, but it was true that when I'd gotten myself in a heck of jam a while back, Terry was only person who helped me out of it.

"You're just saying that," Ann-Margret insisted. "You know perfectly well what I mean." She grabbed Terry's arm beseechingly. "I'm not asking you to stop being mad at me. I'm just asking you to understand. Do you know how important it can be to find out that the man you love loves you back, to need his touch and assurance more than anything in the world?"

Basil was sniffling; Fernando patted his hand. Bill reached to touch Ann-Margret's shoulder, but a warning look from Terry compelled him to stop. Instead, Bill and Ann-Margret made do with a tender exchange of glances.

"Look, I'm not a monster," Terry quietly stated. "I'm not a machine. Of course I have feelings. But I also have no choice."

"But Terry—"

I admonished Ann-Margret to give it a rest.

"The backup should be here any minute," Terry affirmed. "We're all going to walk into the living room. Basil and Fernando, I'll let you guys change clothes. But no monkey business."

And so it was done. Three carfuls of officers arrived to handcuff the motley crew of hooligans. Fernando had changed into a Detective Garcia-style suit, and, as if in character, said virtually nothing. Basil, though, acted like some sort of Quaker pacifist political prisoner. In his hemp shirt and jeans, he kept asking the officers if they were having a nice evening, and telling them how hard it must've been to be away from their families at night. Though the officers never asked, he was careful to assure them that the handcuffs weren't hurting him. Bill got all buddy-buddy with the cops, as if being arrested and placing someone under arrest were the same thing. "Hey guys, what's happening?" he inquired with a smile. He seemed to think that if he flattered them enough he might talk them into letting him go.

Just as Bill was being led off in handcuffs, he grinned winningly at Terry and me. "If you guys don't turn me in, I'll let you interview me."

Terry was less than amused. "How does this sound? I turn you in, but you still let us interview you."

Ann-Margret looked at Bill with narrow, angry eyes. "You mean to tell me that you've been holding back with them? When they're working to get me *off*, for chrissake?"

"Hey, baby, it wasn't like that." He looked at us beseechingly. "Tell her, guys. Tell her I've wanted to cooperate. But my lawyer told me not to."

"Your *lawyer*? You put your fucking lawyer above whether or not I get the fucking gas chamber?" Handcuffed though she was, she did her best to all but shred him into little pieces. It took two cops to keep her off of him. As fate would have it, at that precise moment the doors opened and various press cameras popped, clicked, and whirred as the crazed murderess tried to kick and scratch pitiable, defenseless Shirtless Bill. (Indeed, the headline of one tabloid the next day would read: HER NEXT VICTIM?) "You son of a fucking bitch!" she shrieked at him, as the cops led them off to what you might have called separate His and Hers paddy wagons. Or, as the expletives sounded on TV: "You son of a *bleep*ing *bleep*!"

But even had Ann-Margret gone into custody pleasantly trilling "Getting to Know You," the press would have had a field day: An actor on a hit TV series plus two of the designers from another hit show had helped her stay in hiding. The U.S. at large couldn't help but wonder: Were they all in on the murder? Was someone else on the show going to get whacked next? And most important of all: Was she banging all these guys at once?

Other cast members were interviewed in their respective homes. Curtsy Ann told reporters that she was "shocked, just so very shocked," by this recent turn of events, while Brick laughed and winked into the camera that he was sorry they forgot to invite him to the party. Koko Yee said she loved them all and was remembering them in her prayers. Only Aunt Fern had the temerity to offer no comment to one reporter after another— though she was also the one person who rushed to police headquarters to make sure they were all okay. It seemed classic Aunt Fern that she was indignant when told that she of all people wouldn't be permitted to see the prisoners.

As for Boxer Jones, he not only had his slimy lawyer hands full with Aunt Fern, but would also now be representing Ann-Margret. Needless to say, words could not have begun to convey my utter disappointment that he and Terry would not be able to spend as much time together as they would have liked. My pleasure in watching people age-regress, enact every banality known to humankind, and in general render for the onlooker an experience akin to fingernails scraping along a chalkboard knew no limit.

Still, when all the craziness died down, I saw Terry standing by himself in the police station, looking around at all cops and hookers and junkies as if watching it all for the first time. And my heart—that mighty, generous river that gives and gives so unabashedly—went out to the poor sap.

I put my arm around his shoulder. "How does a beer sound?"

"I don't like to drink when I'm unhappy."

"Then look on the bright side. You'll never be an alcoholic."

"The way I feel right now, crack wouldn't make a damn bit of difference."

We stepped out into the night air. It was unseasonably cool, in that deceptive California way that chills the bones. A few reporters lingered, vying for my attention, but I smilingly told them I had nothing to say.

"Maybe you'd like to be alone." I climbed into the driver's seat of the Cherokee. "I can drop you off at your place. Your Batmobile must be lonesome without you."

"You know what my mother told me?" Terry slammed his door shut; the seatbelt got caught, so he opened it and slammed it shut again. "My own mother told me I'd broken her heart. For betraying her sister's baby. Then my aunt told me I wasn't welcome in her house."

"So maybe being alone now isn't such a hot idea, either."

Actually, my tea and sympathy wasn't best served in matters pertaining to family. Personally, I would've been relieved if some relative back in Iowa told me to never darken their door again. In fact, I could scarcely remember the last time I'd been back to visit my parents and two younger brothers, and certainly none of them ever came to L.A. to visit me. But for Terry, all this family crapola was a big deal.

"Tell you what, Terry," I decided. "Let's go for a ride. You decide where."

He let out a quick sob that was part laughter. "Gee, Rick. That's awful nice of you. But probably we should just get some sleep."

"No, Terry, I mean it. Where's someplace you've always wanted to go? Within greater Los Angeles, that is. The ol' Learjet is in the shop again. Do you want to go out dancing? I know how you like to dance."

He thought about it. "I don't know. I don't pay attention to all that stuff."

Suddenly, I had an idea. "Well, let me pick the place, then."

He crossed his arms and looked out the window. "Sure. Wherever you say."

"Try not to act too excited," I cajoled.

The radio was all about news of Ann-Margret and her band of thugs. I offered to turn it off and put some music on the CD player, but Terry, resolute as ever, insisted that we listen to the news. It had nothing much to tell us—or at least nothing good. Ann-Margret was being "sedated." Boxer must have approved, since he told the reporters that she'd been under "an inhuman amount of stress" since being falsely accused of murdering Helena.

"I can't believe it." Terry shook his head. "Is he saying my cousin is nuts?"

"He's a lawyer. He's paid to do whatever it takes to get her acquitted."

"But what kind of drugs are they giving her? She's going to get all messed up."

"Terry, I don't know how else to say it. She seems like the type of person who probably has done some drugs in her time."

"Never. Not in a million years. Ann-Margret is smart enough to stay away." He looked at me with a fierceness of belief that would have made Mother Teresa look like an atheist. Whatever the truth was, I resisted the urge to argue about it.

"You're probably right. She just likes to act tough."

As for the accomplices, Basil told the press he missed his family and sent them his love. Fernando opted for that classic old chestnut, this-is-all-a-misunderstanding. He emphasized that he'd never broken the law in his life, and that in the morning it would all be straightened out. Bill skirted the issue at hand altogether, asserting that Ann-Margret was a terrific gal, and that he wanted to thank all the fans who'd come to the police station to show their support. When asked why Ann-Margret had attacked him, Bill replied, "Attack? I don't know what you're talking about."

Needless to say, Marion Goober was smugly insistent that now that everyone was brought into custody—as if his office had been any help whatsoever in bringing this about—they could proceed with what he promised would be a "swift enactment of justice."

I turned off the news, and maneuvered the Cherokee along Beachwood Drive, careful to say as little as possible.

"There are some things I just don't get," Terry shared.

"Like what, for instance?" I assumed he was going to say something about the case against Ann-Margret. But apparently, that was becoming too painful to dwell on.

"Like Basil. He seems like an okay guy, but how can he—I mean, he lives this double life. I don't see how people can do that."

"Well, Terry, you lived a kind of double life yourself. You were married to Darla Sue while you knew underneath it all you were gay." Irritatingly, the stick shift stuck at second, then loosened up.

"But I wasn't seeing anyone. If I had a thing for Fernando and he felt the same way and we did it and all, I wouldn't keep living with my wife."

"Me, either. But it's my decided impression that Tarragon does her own thing. She's not sitting home and knitting, crying into her flannel shirt that her hubby's getting his elsewhere."

"So you're saying you approve when people stay in the closest? Basil goes on and on about his family. What a fucking hypocrite."

"I'm saying that, ideally, everyone should come out. But I understand when people are afraid to. I'm sure Basil *does* miss his kids. And even Tarragon, for whatever his reasons. Besides, I wouldn't give up on him yet. He still might find his courage. I've seen it happen before."

Terry blankly rummaged through the CD case; he of course had no idea who sang what. "But Fernando—why does he put up with it? How does he stand it when Basil goes home to his wife?"

"Fernando plays the field himself. Thine own eyes have seen the glory of *that*. Honestly, Terry—the minute you see two people so much as cough in each other's direction, you hear wedding bells. You're worse than my grandmother."

"You showbiz people have no morals at all."

"You're probably right. That's why everyone wants to be in showbiz." A sports car swerved in front of me. I honked the horn and shot him the finger.

"Speak for yourself. I like *real* people."

I didn't bother responding. "Here we are," I brightly announced instead, pulling over shortly before the end of Beachwood. It was the best spot for viewing the famous Hollywood sign on Mount Lee. "What do you think?"

"Hey, what do you know? It's that Hollywood sign thing."

I could only assume this was an indication of approval. Terry clambered out of the Cherokee. "I've never seen it up this close before."

The tall white HOLLYWOOD letters that jutted out of Mount Lee seemed dizzily larger than life, like something out of a dream. If Hollywood was the world's new religion, then this sign was our Stonehenge, erected for purposes both sacred and profane, and ultimately more mysterious in its allure than any explanation could offer. The full moon glistened above the letters as if blessing them. And the relative quiet on the lookout point made it seem as if we were on the moon ourselves, in stark contrast to the lit-up city far below, glimmering in the faint night mist.

"Wow," Terry commented. "I didn't know it was that big."

"If I had a nickel for every time I'd heard those exact words, I'd be a rich man."

"Huh?" Terry registered a look of puzzlement. "I don't get what you mean."

"Never mind," I sighed. "Actually, each letter stands forty-five feet tall. And Mount Lee itself is the tallest peak in L.A."

"I never knew that."

"Oh, you learn a few things when you're a reporter," I allowed.

"Can we get up closer?"

"This is the best spot to see it. There's all these fences and alarms to prevent people from getting up close and personal with it, and doing something they might regret. You know—graffiti, suicide, whatever."

"It's so still and quiet, and yet so big and so . . . there."

"It is a bit surreal. You can get vertigo if you look at it too long."

Terry leaned against the Cherokee with his arms folded, looking up at the moon. "It must be fun to come up here with someone real special."

I walked over beside him, aimlessly kicking at the pebbles on the ground. "Maybe you can come up here with Boxer."

"Yeah, maybe. We had a great time tonight, but those things he said about Ann-Margret . . . I want to trust him. I want to believe he'll do some real good." He looked at me with his expressive dark eyes, his night-lit face brimming with earnestness. "Maybe I'm just afraid of really connecting to someone. That if I can't come up with an excuse to stop seeing Boxer, I might really be happy. Have you ever felt like that, Rick? Afraid of getting everything you've ever wanted?"

My cell phone rang. The fairly distraught person on the other line spoke so fast it was hard to understand all the words.

"So much for seeking the meaning of life," I declared, hanging up after a brief but intense conversation. "Koko is ready to talk to us. She says it's all gone far enough, and she can't eat or sleep knowing that all the people she loves are getting hurt."

# NINETEEN

KOKO YEE LIVED WITH HER AFRO-BRAIDED HUSBAND, J.T. REX, IN A 1960s edifice that from a distance looked like a flying saucer. It jutted out from a precipice on the outskirts of the hills above Benedict Canyon as if having crashed into it, and had stayed miraculously in place—thus far—despite periodic tremors and mud slides. This was due to some common principle of modern engineering that Terry explained to me as we walked up the driveway, and that I was unable to comprehend.

The doorbell played a cacophony of chimes going up and down the scales; besides being married to a record producer, Koko had been something of a child-prodigy novelty act as both a singer and musician. The front door slid open, *Star Trek*–style; I half-expected the person on the other side to be dressed in an *Enterprise* uniform.

Instead, we were greeted by Koko herself. She had long sleek black hair with grown-out bangs that she kept sticking behind her ears. Her normally petite frame was only underscored by her watermelonesque pregnancy. She wore an elaborate embroidered maternity top and colorful yet sensible string pants. Her bare feet were adorned with both an ankle bracelet and a toe ring, to go with the many rings upon her fingers. All twenty nails were painted purple. Koko wore makeup in that natural, I'm-not-wearing-any-makeup way characteristic of the granola crowd. Her fragrance was a predictable sandalwood oil.

"Hi guys." She hugged us as best she could. "It's so great to see you again."

For someone who only moments earlier had sounded on the verge of jumping off a cliff for her worries, Koko was amazingly ebullient. You'd have thought she'd invited us over for cookies and milk rather than to spill her guts about a sordid murder—assuming, of course, the guts were hers to spill.

"Are you digging your new rooms?" She led us into her round home. It occurred to me that she was the first person connected with *MHYH* who'd asked us how we liked our makeovers.

"Sure," Terry and I both obediently replied. But sincere or otherwise, we couldn't have said much beyond that, because Koko's house was leaving us both fairly at a loss for words.

There was a kind of circular indoor balcony that encompassed the circumference of the house. It was accessible from four different spiral staircases and featured four open bedrooms of a sort, including the large master suite. On the main level, the house was divided like slices of a pie; from the center area, one could gaze up at the impressive skylight shaped like the sun that spread out from the center point of the roof. The view from one side of the house wasn't much—the circular driveway and the small gardens it enclosed—but from the other side there was a dramatic view of a steep, wooded slope, as if the house were a roller coaster at the top of an incline, ready to swoop down into a magical forest. Even in the dark, it looked like something out of a dream, or a children's book.

The rooms themselves were open, save of course for the bathrooms, so that from the center point of the house, you could turn around and see right into the kitchen, dining room, billiards room, and living room—sort of like a doll's house. The décor was appropriately subdued—simple lines and pastel shades with a slight over-tendency toward Moroccan throw pillows. The house drew enough attention to itself, and the eye sensibly was spared what might otherwise have been overkill.

"We like to boogie. We have big dance parties here." Koko snapped her fingers and gyrated as best she could in her condition, grinning in her sunshine way. As sometimes happened with child performers, even as an adult Koko seemed to think her purpose in life was to spread joy and happiness at all times, as though either or both were evidently present when someone politely smiled back. The real hippies had happened long enough ago for their image to have taken on a relatively benign, almost all-American wholesomeness. And Koko's hippie-chick, peace-love-flowers demeanor was but a few steps removed from Shirley Temple.

"It must be fun, looking up at the night sky when you're dancing," I offered, though on this night anyway I could only see the usual L.A. haze.

"Uh-huh," the wide-eyed Koko agreed. "Let's get cozy, okay?"

She showed us into the living room, where we made ourselves at home on generous plush floor pillows amid a jungle of exotic plants. For the second time in recent history, I was forced to endure herb tea, as Koko poured a steaming beverage from a smoky, raku-glazed teapot. The tea, however, tasted much sweeter than Basil's had, as if it were a kind of organic herb punch for children. Her husband, J.T., she informed us, was busy working in the basement-level, sound-proofed recording studio, trying to rush out a couple of new singles.

"He does his best work at night," Koko explained with a wink. "Here, I'll give you a sneak preview of one of his hot new acts." She put a demo CD into the player, closing her eyes to sway to the music. It was a highbrow R&B group vocal, the harmonies veering off to both jazz and madrigal, and slightly too complex in nature—too *good*, one might have cynically stated—to guarantee a hit with the masses. If there was still such a thing as a college audience, I supposed it might become a kind of FM favorite. J.T. himself had a reputation for being a producer's producer, more interested in making good music than big money—although over time, his nickel here and dime there had clearly paid off.

All about the room were showbizzy photos: J.T.—or, as Koko called him, "Jate"—with the various minor and semi-major recording artists he produced (one of his vocal groups had been consistently scoring in the lower rungs of the Top Twenty now for some time), and Koko posing with each of the *MHYH* designers. There were also photos from her child performer days. Besides being a would-be soul singer, she was promoted as a classical and jazz pianist and comic impressionist by her widower father (her mother had died in childbirth) who was also her manager. There were shots of her at state fairs and old, low-budget cable TV shows playing piano and doing impressions of eighties icons such as Pee Wee Herman and Ronald Reagan. In one elaborately framed photo, she squealed with joy for being named a finalist on *Star Search* (though eventually she lost). Another photo indicated that her Asian features did not prevent her from starring in a straw-hat tour of *Annie*.

"It sure feels hip to have roots." Koko blew on her steaming mug of tea as I looked around at all the photos. "Dad's cool, but he lives in another era. Sometimes I felt like Baby Jane Hudson."

I laughed. "You seem to have come out of it all okay."

She joined her hands together, and gave her head a slight bow. "Thank you. It takes work to become a good person. Jate and I have been into yoga for years." Returning to her tea, she thoughtfully added, "But I'm blown away at times by how utterly normal it all turned out. I mean, you'd think I'd be crazy or dead, given all those horror stories about kids in show business. Maybe I was lucky in that I never quite made it. I was spared a million varieties of psychosis by only having to cope with mediocrity."

"Just out of curiosity, where is your father now?"

Koko smiled. "In South Beach. He has a nice little condo."

"And now your baby is on the way," Terry approvingly interjected.

"I couldn't have been any luckier than to get the *My House, Your House* gig. I'm not really trained for anything practical, and it's steady, no-brainer work. I want to stay with it as long as the show runs."

To the well-trained gossipmonger's ear, her last statement signaled the possibility that there were those intriguing for her to *not* stay with the show. I wondered if it was the *MHYH* producers, her husband J.T., or both.

"Well, I certainly can only wish you and the show the best of luck." I raised my tea mug spiritedly.

"Right on." She grinned ear-to-ear, raising her mug back at me.

"I almost hate to mention it, Koko, but we've been trying to set up a meeting with you for a while now. Some assistant to the assistant secretary was making it next to impossible."

"Really?" She couldn't have looked more surprised. "Well, guys, I'm so sorry about that, because I'm just about as approachable as you can get." She leaned back on her cushion, laughing. "Not approachable like *that*, but you know what I mean."

"Boy, these pillows sure are comfy." Terry indulged his hefty body in the layers of softness like a Saint Bernard.

She matter-of-factly nodded her agreement. "I like people to feel at home. Some of the designers on the show have offered to redo rooms for me, but I have to be honest and say that I like everything just as it is."

"As well you should," I agreed.

Koko held up her index finger. "Just listen to this next song." She scooted up to raise the volume, singing along in her tuneful voice to the upbeat lyrics, the upshot of which were that the singer would gladly wait forever to find her one true love. "God, that's amazing," she exclaimed after a moment. "Jate is *such* a great songwriter."

"So what did you want to tell us?" I tried to sound both friendly and businesslike. After all, we weren't there so that I could do a feature on J.T. Besides which, I flunked Hippie 101 back in college, and a little bit of sitting around listening to music went a long way with me.

Koko turned off the CD player. "So you're on to me. Shit, I guess I've stalled long enough." She closed her eyes and took a series of deep, yoga-like breaths. "My center. I must remember my center."

"Come again?" Terry asked.

"Just space talk." Koko smiled gently. "Okay guys, here goes. Ann-Margret *absolutely* did not kill Helena."

"Tell us something we don't already know."

"No, Rick, I mean it," Koko insisted. "She talked to me on the phone from about three to five that morning. Now, unless she has some sort of out-of-body powers, how could she have been chattering away while drowning Helena in a vat of acrylic whatever-it-was and then hanging her from the ceiling? I mean, supposedly that was the time of her death, wasn't it?"

After a pause, Terry asked, "Did you tell this to the police?"

"Of course. But I guess they didn't believe me. Or they must have some other evidence against her. I really don't get it."

Disgruntled, Terry shook his head. "The polygraph. Damn that stupid machine. It's not admissible as evidence, anyway."

"Ann-Margret flunked her polygraph? That's just plain crazy. She's such an honest person." Koko put the CD back into its jewel case, which she returned to its shelf; she seemed to take touchingly good care of anything belonging to her husband. "I'll have to let the defense attorney guy know about the phone call. No offense, Terry, but it drives me crazy when cops bust people when they haven't done anything."

"Don't confuse the police with the D.A.," Terry admonished. "We just do our job. The D.A. is a politician."

"That's true, I never thought of it that way." Koko took a reflective sip of tea. "I mean, like, he runs for office and everything. A crook, just like the rest of them."

"I wonder why Ann-Margret didn't tell us about the phone call. Why wouldn't she want us to know?"

Koko gave a thoughtful shrug. "Maybe, Terry, she just hasn't thought to say it, with so much else going on."

"Maybe," he allowed. "But that sounds unlikely."

"Do you mind if we ask what you and Ann-Margret were talking about?" I inquired.

"Oh, this and that. They were planning a baby shower for me. It was supposed to be a surprise, but Aunt Fern—who has this way of getting everything she wants—just kept on Ann-Margret's case to tell me about it. She said that if Ann-Margret told me, Helena wouldn't be mad at Aunt Fern for doing it. I know it all sounds nutty, but things get that way between friends. Especially when they're all highly opinionated cowgirls, like we are. Aunt Fern hates surprises, you know."

"So we've heard," Terry confirmed. "It's interesting, though, that even Aunt Fern was afraid of Helena."

"I wouldn't say afraid. It's just that when Helena got upset, she was a handful-and-a-half. Don't get me wrong. When she snapped out of it, no one was more fun. But boy, her bad moods were something else. In a way, I guess we used to take turns dealing with her, though of course we didn't spell it out that way. I guess Aunt Fern felt it was Ann-Margret's turn."

I set my tea aside. "So was the baby shower all you talked about for two hours?"

Koko closed the curtains, thought for a moment, and then drew them open again. "That's quite a lot right there. Ann-Margret figured that now that I knew about it, I might as well tell her everything I needed, so she could subtly hint to different people what to get me. Of course, it all became a moot point. None of us have been in much of a mood for a baby shower. Not to mention poor Ann-Margret can't even be there—except maybe in spirit."

I hated sounding like a broken record, but I had no choice. "Whatever you're hiding, we'll find out from someone else."

Staring out the window, she put her hand over her mouth to stifle a sob. "I guess I have to tell you. It's about my husband." She turned around to face us. "Since I've been carrying little Hiawatha here"—she lovingly patted her belly—"I haven't been real into, like, you know."

"J.T. must be getting some of his best work done in the studio," I reflected.

"That's one way of putting it." She grinned self-deprecatingly. "Really, it's been me, not him. I actually yelled at him one night when he came on to me. Hormones, I guess."

"So you're saying that . . . ?"

"I think you know what I mean, Rick. I just about handed my husband to Helena on a silver platter. I was *such* a bitch."

"So J.T. was in need," I summarized, "and Helena was a friend, indeed." She stepped away from the window. "That about sums it up."

Still, with all due respect that people could be different in private, it was hard to imagine Koko being all that bitchy. The more she protested that it was all her fault, the more convinced I was of her fundamental sweetness. Unless of course it was all an act . . .

"You must have been very angry at her," Terry sympathized. "A woman, supposedly your friend, has sex with your husband while you're pregnant."

Koko gently touched the hanging leaf of a potted fern, as if fascinated by its fertility. "It was a funny thing about Helena. She believed that women were superior to men. But *because* women were better, she had no sympathy for them. If a woman fucked things up, it was like she should've known better. Yet Helena felt sorry for men, as if they were too weak and stupid to be anything more than what they were. I think that's why she got so bent out of shape when a man could actually get under her skin. Like Brick. She hated that she needed him more than he needed her." She eased herself back onto the floor cushions. "No, I wasn't mad at Helena. I knew she meant no harm. Her attitude was that J.T. was just a man, anyway, so what did I expect? She'd been a good friend in a lot of other ways. She found my obstetrician. She found J.T. a great new singer to sign up."

My worldliness and Terry's naïveté rendered ironically similar looks of disbelief as Koko, in her laid-back way, kept trying to convince us that she didn't mind that Helena had screwed her husband. I wondered how much of Koko's protestations were to convince us that we shouldn't think she killed Helena, versus simply to convince herself that she had nothing to feel guilty about. After all, it can weigh mighty heavily upon the soul that you're glad someone got murdered—especially when you supposedly believe that the universe is love, or whatever crap she supposedly believed.

"Look at it like this, guys. J.T. could have found some other woman who'd try to break up our marriage. As it was, Helena helped him get his rocks off a few times and then gave him back to me, good as new. I got some much-needed space to deal with my estrogen OD, and J.T. got a few pointers in how to please a woman. It was win-win all around."

"If you say so."

"Crazy as it sounds, Rick, it's true."

"Just out of curiosity, what's the name of your obstetrician?" I remembered the slip of paper that Helena had dropped that last day on the set.

Koko looked puzzled that I would ask. "Dr. Mallory. Why?"

It was just like Ann-Margret said. "No reason."

"At least give me this much, guys—I'm why Ann-Margret didn't tell you about the phone call."

Terry shifted his bulky frame on the pillows. "I don't get what you mean."

"I mean the kid's too sweet for her own good. She didn't want to tell half the world about how my husband was banging Helena. At least not until she had a chance to talk to J.T. and me. I'm *sure* of it. That's just how Ann-Margret is."

"You're probably right," Terry affirmed. "I've known her all my life. But if you were so okay about it, why did you have to talk to her about it at three in the morning? You must have been crying. You must have been upset."

She clutched at her belly, feeling the baby kick. "I keep telling you, that's not how it was. It was more like I was being . . . philosophical. Sharing my thoughts about how it all fit into the larger spiritual picture. How Helena was proving to be an important teacher for me in the jigsaw puzzle of life."

"A *teacher*?" I asked sarcastically. "That's one way of putting it."

"Yes, a teacher," Koko insisted. "If you studied Zen, you'd know exactly what I meant."

"Fine. I give up."

"On the phone, you mentioned something about innocent people suffering." Terry looked at me like I should try to be nicer. "Do you also mean Bill and Basil and Fernando?"

Koko clapped her hands, leaning back in glee. "God, aren't they just the *craziest* guys? But they've done nothing wrong. All they did was help their friend. And they only did it because of Aunt Fern. Well, not only because of Aunt Fern. They really couldn't bear to see Ann-Margret in jail. But Aunt Fern is like the mother most of us never had. It's like she makes you feel that the world is this fragile egg, and if you disappoint her, the egg will crack."

"I know what you mean," Terry agreed.

"Maybe it's good that we *don't* all have her for a mother," I noted, which made Koko and Terry laugh.

"Anyway," Koko continued, "you need to know that they're all totally innocent. Bill had no reason on earth to want Helena dead. And there is nothing, absolutely *nothing*, to the rumor—in case you hear it—that Helena was planning on outing Basil to the world."

"Not even subtly, through her room design?" I asked.

Koko sighed dismissively. "Oh, what was that about, anyway? An in-joke that no one else would even remotely catch. Besides, I'd expect you guys to think it would actually be *good* for Basil if he had to come out. Isn't the truth always the best way?"

"More or less. But Basil might not have seen it that way. Murderers usually aren't the most rational folks in town."

"Surely you're not suggesting Basil murdered Helena?"

"No. But I'm also not suggesting that he didn't."

"Oh." She clearly was disappointed. If we weren't discounting Basil as a suspect, it meant we weren't discounting anyone else—including Koko herself.

"Do you know anything about Fernando?" Terry queried.

"I was sad when he didn't like his room. He was awfully nice. And Basil seems to have found something that works for him. I know they were out together the night of the murder, because Basil even called me to ask if they could bop over for a drink. I don't drink now, but you know what I mean—a drink in the general sense."

"But you don't actually know where they were at about four in the morning?"

"No, but why would they offer to come over if they were planning on killing someone?"

"What about Bill?" Terry asked.

"I'm sure he was where he always is on a Saturday night." She pulled her hair back, as if to make a ponytail, then shook it loose again.

"And where is that?"

"I can't tell you, Rick. But you have to believe me, it wasn't Helena's motel room."

"Gee, why am I less than convinced?"

Koko registered embarrassment at her own laughter. "Stop it. You know how these things are. Please, just believe me."

We heard the sound of rapid, even footsteps.

"Cool," Koko declared. "You guys will get to see Jate."

As her handsome dark-skinned husband opened a doorway and entered the main floor, Koko ran to his arms with the glee of a little girl. There were beads woven into his long black braids, and he sported a colorful African shirt, Levi's cut-offs, and Teva sandals. Though hip and casual looking, J.T.'s demeanor was of a man who put care into his appearance.

"Hey, Rick. My main man." With his arm still around his wife, he shook my hand.

I then introduced him to Terry. "Oh, right, the cop guy," J.T. smiled. "Nice to meet you."

"I enjoyed the music," Terry told him. "It must be a lot of fun to produce records."

J.T. laughed. "Fun is one way of putting it, I suppose."

"He works too hard." Koko wrapped her arms around his waist as best as she could. "But I forgive him."

"If you'd like, I could play you a couple of cuts." J.T. decided for us as he walked to the CD player and put the demo in. "Remember, you heard them here first."

Koko was highly animated, her eyes darting back and forth in anticipation, as the sounds came on. The first cut was by a male singer who had that basic Justin-Timberlake-trying-to-sound-like-Stevie-Wonder style that was already an epidemic. The second cut was a woman vocalist who, like so many others of late, sang in that all-too-familiar Whitney-Houston-trying-to-sound-like-Whitney-Houston voice.

I realized a fatal flaw in J.T.'s productions, highly proficient though they were: The music he liked was only marginally commercial. But when he tried to go mainstream—as he clearly was with these new singers—he didn't believe in it enough to make their performances convincing.

Koko grooved to the sounds like they were the hottest things ever, while J.T. stood with his arms folded, listening critically.

"Wow, those sound like big hits to me," Terry warmly offered.

"Thanks." J.T. managed an uncertain smile. "My bill collectors thank you as well."

I detected an undercurrent of urgency in his jocular tone, as if some corporate henchman had indeed told him it was time for a big hit or else.

"What did you think, Rick?" J.T. asked, as though daring me to tell him what I really thought—and sensing that it wasn't much.

"They've both got number one written all over them."

"See?" Koko waved a scolding finger, as if continuing a good-natured argument from before. She gave him a light kiss.

"Life is good every now and then," J.T. decided, kissing her back.

"True enough," I agreed. "Kind of makes you wonder if it's all just a crap shoot. Like Helena, for instance. How tragic can you get?"

He stared at me intently. "Yes, it's very, very sad. I was so shocked when Koko called me. I was in New York, but I cut my meetings short to be with my wife."

It was one of those things you couldn't exactly prove, but I was convinced that this was J.T.'s way of telling us he didn't do it, so leave him out of it.

Koko reached up to kiss his cheek. "My poor, sweet man feels things so strongly. He's really in touch with his emotions."

Maybe it was just her vulnerability from being pregnant, but I was getting the sense that J.T. was like oxygen to Koko. I wondered just how far she would've gone to hold on to him no matter what.

After congratulating him on his impending fatherhood, and promising to be in touch for an interview, we took our leave. It was Terry who said we should linger outside for a moment just in case we heard or saw anything. But the only thing we saw was a silhouette of Koko and J.T. locked in an embrace. They could have been posing for an ad selling faith in God, or a new deodorant spray.

"There's something there I don't trust," Terry murmured.

"Him?"

"No, her."

"I know what you mean." Our eyes met as we thought the same thing at the same time.

"Bill," we both declared, each of us knowing exactly what the other meant.

# TWENTY

BILL, HOWEVER, WOULD HAVE TO WAIT UNTIL THE MORNING. Once again, Terry crashed at my place—and in the morning, he once again took a personal leave day. I, in turn, predictably canceled my appointments with Max Headroom, my acupuncturist, a trained elephant in the new Tarzan movie whom the critics were raving about, and Sarah Ferguson, Duchess of York.

Just as familiar was our appearance in arraignment court. This time, the protesters outside the courthouse were carrying signs with messages such as: FREE ANN-MARGRET, FREE THE DESIGNER FOUR, HELPING THE INNOCENT IS NOT A CRIME, HELP US AUNT FERN, and BILL I LOVE YOU.

There were millions of reporters milling about—including Mitzi and Chauncey, both of whom were doing live broadcasts. I knew I could accomplish more by observing from afar, and was grateful to be spared the tedium of on-camera duties.

We watched as Curtsy Ann arrived, complete with full black veil, and was helped up the steps for her shaky countenance by a man whose dark blue suit all but screamed "attorney." She bravely managed to sign a few autographs at the top of the steps.

"And who should I make this out to?" she pleasantly asked the fan in question, smiling through her veil.

"Make it out to Carol," the fan replied.

"And is that 'Carol' with one or two Rs and Ls?"

The autograph complete, she patted her nose with her hanky as she resolutely continued into the courtroom.

Brick arrived but minutes later, rushing up the steps with guy-type impatience, his hair appealingly tousled as if to wink to his fans that he'd had one hell of a night. He wore an open shirt under a blazer. Some of the protesters squealed with pleasure at the sight of him. Hurried though he was, Brick paused at the top of the steps to smile and wave. He then cupped his hand around his mouth to call out: "We're going to win in here today." Everyone cheered.

"Win *what*?" Terry asked me. "And who's *we*?"

"Good question," I replied. "I guess he just means that everyone will get set free."

"Even Ann-Margret?"

"Nah, just the guys. I guess Brick will take them out for a beer to celebrate."

Tarragon, Basil's wife (ha-ha), arrived in a long, flowery hippie skirt. The friend at her side was introduced to Chauncey Riggs as "Winnie." According to Tarragon, Winnie was giving her some much-needed emotional support.

"I just don't know how I'd be getting through all this without Winnie," Tarragon gushed, as Winnie—a petite woman with a Dorothy Hamill bob—held her hand.

"Do you have any words for your husband, today, Mrs. Montclair?" Chauncey asked, with a foolish degree of seriousness. He had a distinctly humorless approach to interviews, as though every occasion were a funeral.

"It's *Ms.* Montclair," Tarragon corrected, in a compromise between tradition and liberation that struck me as neither fish nor fowl. "But I'd want my beloved husband to know that he's missed by all of us, his children especially, and to please hurry home, with God's help."

Nothing against Tarragon as a person, but she obviously was not accustomed to speaking to reporters. Her nervous little speech was like a teleprompter gone haywire. As in, it made no sense. Ironically, no-frills super-dyke Tarragon made me think of Marilyn Monroe's sweet nonsense in *Gentlemen Prefer Blondes*.

"Our oldest child, Ben," Tarragon glowingly conveyed, "takes after

Basil, and is adopted. But that doesn't matter. *Family* is what matters. Don't you agree?"

I nudged Terry. "Maybe when this is all over, they can all take a trip to Europe, France."

"Wasn't that in some old movie?"

I decided to give up on him altogether. It was like asking a corpse to tap dance. "Yes, with Francis the Talking Mule."

"Huh. I think I may have seen that. Is it the one where they sing, 'Que Sera, Sera'?"

"You got it."

Koko arrived with J.T., their arms linked together as a unified couple. He wore a linen suit, while she got away with a slightly more upscale version of her maternity threads from the day before. J.T. was extremely attentive as Koko slowly climbed the stairs. Given her condition, fans kept a respectable distance, though a few called out: "Boy or girl?" No one seemed to mind when neither Koko nor J.T. answered them, though they did give the fans a quick wave and smile.

With Boxer Jones's arm around her shoulder, Aunt Fern arrived to thunderous applause. Her granny-style dress featured a grape arbor pattern, and her Nikes gave her just the right eccentric touch. "Aunt Fern, we love you!" screamed a fan, and she turned to raise her militant fist in the air. As the fans went wild, Boxer gamely led her up the steps. He knowingly glanced over at Terry with what I had to admit was a cute roll of his eyes.

"I know someone who's blushing," I teased, which of course made Terry blush all the more.

I was surprised to see Tippi nonchalantly saunter up the steps in defiant jeans and sweatshirt. With her fingers, she combed a lock of disheveled hair from her eye as she told none other than Mitzi McGuire that she was there just to check things out.

"I thought the arraignment might be a kick," she elaborated. "Maybe it will give me some new material. Lord knows my audience would be grateful if it did." She mouthed the words "Hi, Mom!" into the TV camera, and Mitzi pretended to laugh.

"Tippi, you are simply incorrigible." Mitzi shook her head with mock resignation, her stiff wig remaining suspiciously unfettered. "Are you dating anyone at the moment?"

Tippi's hazel eyes unmistakably zeroed in on me. They were filled with hatred.

"No, Mitzi. The only man in my life is my pet goldfish, Carlos."

"Carlos? Tippi, you're simply too much."

"He's Mexican, you know. He glub-glubs only *en Español*. I've had to hire a translator."

"Oh, stop, stop!" Mitzi protested, as if hysterical to the point of wetting herself.

Predictably, the courtroom was packed with reporters. As Terry and I elbowed our way in, we saw Bill, Basil, and Fernando enter with their respective attorneys, for the benefit of the TV cameras. They were all wearing dark blue suits. Fans cheered and applauded until the judge banged on her gavel and ordered everyone to be silent. (Her Honor bore more than a passing resemblance to Judge Judy, though she chose to forgo the demure white frill around the neck.) Marion Goober methodically sorted his papers throughout, as if the ruckus were beneath his dignity.

Bill turned to the crowd to smile and mouth the words "Thank you," winking at this or that groupie, while Basil rather shyly pursed his lips together and bowed his head to likewise acknowledge the fans. Fernando, though, resolutely stared forward, as if not about to risk inspiring the judge's ire.

"How do the defendants plead?" asked the judge.

Bill leaned down into the microphone, and, glancing sideways to the audience like a true showman, replied, "Your honor, we have done nothing wrong. So we plead . . . not guilty."

The crowd erupted like Justin Timberlake fans at a Justin Timberlake concert. The judge banged on her gavel, and told the crowd it was their final warning, lest they all be cleared from the court. I looked over at Koko, who stared at Bill with luminous almond eyes, all the while clutching her husband's arm ever more tightly.

"Excuse me, Your Honor," Fernando interjected. "I'd like to plead no contest."

Basil frowned at him; Fernando frowned back. Fernando's attorney took the podium: "A moment with my client, Your Honor, if it pleases the court."

"Very well, but make it quick."

There was a brief, intense huddle consisting of Fernando and his attorney, plus Basil and his attorney.

"We all plead not guilty, Your Honor," Fernando's attorney amended.

"You're sure?" inquired the judge.

"Yes, Your Honor." Fernando shot a disgruntled look at Basil.

"Very well, then." The judge leaned back, her hands folded on her lap. "Any profound insights on the matter of bail?"

"The people object to bail," bellowed Marion Goober. "These defendants"—he always over-pronounced that word—"all have sheltered a fugitive from justice, and by so doing have shown a flagrant disregard for the law. The people have every reason to believe they present a flight risk."

"Your *Honor*," objected Bill's attorney. "My client is a respected member of the community who served in the armed forces, and who furthermore—"

"Spare us, counselor." The judge banged on her gavel. "I'm not wearing my hip boots. Bail is set at fifty thousand dollars for each defendant."

"But Your Honor—" Marion fumbled through his papers.

"Next case."

The crowd, never heedful of the judge's warnings, cheered yet again. Bill hammed it up for all it was worth, clenching his hands above his head like a champ. The judge gave the crowd yet another final warning. It was my distinct impression that she enjoyed being ringmaster at the circus and would never actually make good on her threats.

The next case on the docket was none other than our own Ann-Margret Wochinsky, on the silly matter of her having escaped from jail. (Bill had most chivalrously refused to press assault charges after her little attack the previous night.)

Ann-Margret wore a generic skirt and blouse, her hair tied back. But even without her usual flamboyant makeup, she might as well have been a stripper who, to tantalize the crowd, started off with a mousy librarian look. She was one of those dyed-in-the-wool sexpot types who, despite her sweet nature, was incapable of looking sweet.

"Don't tell me that counsel is going to ask for *bail*?" The judge shook her head in a boy-do-I-get-all-the-weirdos way.

Boxer cleared his throat. "Your Honor, I realize it might seem an inappropriate request under the circumstances. But my client has reason to believe that safety to her person is compromised by remaining in custody. She had no previous record before being falsely accused of the other crime in question, and furthermore—"

"Nice try," the judge interrupted. "You have chutzpah, counselor. I grant you that. Tell me something, Ms. Wochinsky. Were you safe last night?"

Ann-Margret lowered her head. "Yes, Your Honor."

"Speak up, please. And look at me when I ask you a question."

"Yes, Your Honor." The redness of her eyes betrayed some earlier fit of tears.

"Then there is no problem at all with keeping the defendant in custody."

"But Your Honor—" Boxer protested, while Marion Goober smarmily threw up his hands in an in-your-face shrug. Curtsy Ann most conspicuously began to sniffle as the fans erupted into a unified, prolonged hiss, followed by a boo.

"Oh, spare me." The judge banged her gavel repeatedly. "Next case."

Aunt Fern stood up, and spoke completely out of turn. "Please, Your Honor. Can't she be released into *my* custody?" The crowd applauded wildly.

"Madam, may I remind you that you yourself have been brought before the court for helping the defendant to escape from prison. Released into your custody? I don't think so."

"You have to hand it to Boxer for trying," I whispered to a despondent Terry. "I can tell he's really going to fight for her."

"Yeah, I guess." Terry forced a smile, as if thinking wonderful thoughts would magically help his cousin's case. "Boxer's great. I . . . I like him a lot."

Since Terry was a cop, we got to leave out of a side exit and bypass the crowds.

"This isn't your fault, Terry. Don't deny yourself a shot at some happiness."

"I don't know what you're talking about, Rick, but I'm sure it's a bunch of highfalutin' hogwash."

"What I'm talking about," I explained as we stepped out into the glaring, smoggy sun, "is that your almighty family could have, I'm sure, lived without your being gay. And now to top it off, they're mad at you for turning in Ann-Margret. You start to have a nice little thing with her attorney, and now, lo and behold, you're losing all interest in him. What a startling coincidence."

At the corner, Terry impatiently pushed on the Walk button. "It's funny, hearing this coming from you, Rick. Because I'd gotten the distinct impression that for one reason or another you didn't like that I was dating Boxer."

"I didn't. But I don't want to see you break up with him over so shitty a reason as family guilt and shame. Break up with him for a *good* reason, dammit." We had to run across the street for the shortness of the Walk signal.

"A good reason being . . . ?"

"Any reason I give you, dummy. As I subtly plant diabolical seeds of doubt in the tradition of all the great soap opera bitches who have come before me." Spying the Cherokee, I unlocked it with my key chain remote.

"Oh, I get it. Well, okay, then." He flashed his big goofy grin as he climbed in the passenger side.

"So you won't break up with him— yet?" I revved up the ignition.

"Not until you've successfully brainwashed me against him. In fact, I'll call him about meeting for dinner tonight."

"Good. I'm glad we've gotten one thing solved." I checked the rearview mirror to maneuver out of the ridiculously tight parking place. "By the way, where are we going?"

"How about a quick burger and then a visit to Bill? Assuming he'll finally talk to us."

"I think he's ready to do just that." I honked at the idiot behind me trying to inch into the parking place before—minor detail—my own vehicle had even pulled out from it. I flipped him the bird, just so he'd remember me in his will. "After all, think of the bad press I could direct at the unfortunate Bill after the way he treated my bosom buddy's beloved cousin."

"Would he be thinking that far ahead?"

"Are you kidding—Bill? All he *does* is think a few steps ahead of the game. It's what gives him that endearingly irresistible fake depth."

"Koko, for one, might find it irresistible."

"Or let's at least hope she did the night of Helena's murder. That would give them both an alibi." Though of course it was with no small amount of irony that I hoped this or that person was innocent—because another person's rock-solid alibi was like one more knot in the noose around Ann-Margret's neck.

"It is kind of weird, when you think about it." Terry rolled down his window to feel the hot, muggy breeze.

"Well, I might do a better job of thinking about it if I knew what you were talking about."

"You always have to be such a smart-ass. I mean the way that just about everyone is managing to get arrested and stuff. Like it's a mob family, and when one goes down for the count, they all do."

"Kind of makes you wonder, doesn't it? It's as if a little bit of jail or probation or whatever is preferable to the truth coming out." I pulled up in front of a fairly decent, family-style burger joint—one that I could eat at without suffering indigestion. "But maybe it just seems that way. Curtsy Ann and Brick haven't gotten in trouble. Not to mention Tippi."

Terry held the restaurant door open for me. "Give them time."

"Thanks, I owe you one." The waitress showed us to a pink-and-orange booth, and handed us plastic-coated, technicolor menus.

"I suppose the chef's salad might be edible."

"I have a surprise, Rick." He took out a rolled-up document from his black leather jacket. "The polygraph."

I set down the menu, and looked about the restaurant furtively, to make sure no one was listening. "How did you . . . ?"

"I promised someone a favor." Before I could say anything, he added, "Nothing like *that*, I can assure you. I swear, Rick, your mind goes straight to the gutter every time."

"So what were the results?" I glanced hopelessly at the graphs and numbers and things.

Terry sighed. "Not good, I'm afraid. She flunked a couple of very important questions. Her feelings about Bill, which she already told us about, plus the small matter of what she was doing at the time of the murder."

"What about the question, 'Did you kill Helena?' "

"Inconclusive. Hard to read."

"I hate to say it, Terry. But the case against her doesn't seem as far-fetched as it did about thirty seconds ago."

"She's hiding something, protecting someone. Maybe even more than one person."

The waitress took our orders. Terry asked for the Super-Triple-Decker-Burger with everything on it, and the Mountain of Cheese Fries.

"It's nice to see that your worries over Ann-Margret have not affected your appetite."

"Actually, worrying makes me more hungry."

"Does anything ever make you less?"

"Be careful what you say to an officer of the law." He made a face upon hearing his cell phone ring. "It's my aunt," he complained, looking at the number. "Sorry, Auntie, but I'm just not in the mood." He let the phone keep ringing.

"Good for you."

"Aw, what the hell." He answered it. "Yes, Auntie. *Yes*, I will do that. Yes, I understand. Of course I'm not mad at you. Yes, I know everyone loves me. Yes. Yes. Good-bye." He put the phone back in his jacket pocket. "They want me to make sure Ann-Margret has a toothbrush, *and* that she's brushing with Crest. My aunt has this thing about brushing with Crest."

"Can you blame her? Don't four out of five dentists—" My own phone was ringing. "Yes, Aunt Fern," I spoke into the phone, grimacing at Terry, who smiled back. The waitress appeared with the tons of food we ordered; this was one of those places where a small dinner salad could feed an entire Third World nation. Everything was piled high and coyly arranged and garnished—the kind of food that looked best under orange lights. "Yes, we're already on it, Aunt Fern." I hung up the phone just as Terry was digging in. "She wants us to talk to Bill, big deal. She says she thinks he's hiding something."

"You should have made it sound like she was giving us the idea for the first time. Let her feel important." He generously proffered the mound of cheese fries; I declined to try one.

"I see no reason to encourage her." I picked at my chef's salad.

"Have a heart. She's just a harmless, meddlesome old lady."

"Who harmlessly enough just got three people arrested, after she harmlessly helped a fourth break out of jail."

"You *know* what I mean, Rick. Stop showing off."

"Look, shut up, okay? Just let me eat in peace."

# TWENTY-ONE

WHEN I CALLED BILL MCCOY ABOUT MEETING WITH HIM, HIS RE-
sponse could not have been more encouraging.

"Dammit," he remarked cordially. "I guess I have no choice. Might as
well get it over with."

"I'll bet he takes his shirt off, just for us," I confided to Terry upon
hanging up.

Among other things, I was more than a little curious to see how Bill
actually lived: Did his home feature the theme park funhouses and the like
that he foisted so egomaniacally on other people? I was hardly surprised
that the answer was no.

In fact, Bill lived in an old warehouse that he'd converted into a very
upscale loft. The warehouse was located in one of those new cutting-edge
neighborhoods close to downtown that had heretofore been considered
seedy and industrial. The loft wasn't far from the freeway, and the traffic
constantly roared in the distance, almost like a lulling ocean.

The walls had been sanded back to their original brick, and the high
ceiling featured a vintage safety-glass skylight and industrial ceiling fan—
the lattermost element being, of course, the cardinal sin of *MHYH* designers when on camera. The living space was mostly open, with an occasional
dividing wall to give the area focus and style. Bill's private master bath—
his pride and joy—featured a Jacuzzi made to resemble a vintage porcelain
tub, complete with claw feet. As Bill pointed out, the tub could easily hold
three—though one could only assume he wasn't intimating anything

about Terry and myself, since recent issues of *Playboy* and *Penthouse* were scattered liberally about the loft. The furniture throughout was faux thirties modern, all steel and geometry and no-frills cushions.

"So, where should we do this?" Bill asked. Now more or less forced to talk with us, he politely made an effort to be an agreeable host. He looked great—with his gelled jet black hair and his pale cotton pullover and pants contrasting vividly with his brown complexion, he easily could've been a model in a TV commercial for the Gap.

"I guess the living room would be fine," Terry replied.

"I kind of like the Jacuzzi," I countered.

Bill forced a laugh. Like a lot of showbiz-type guys—especially those in fields dominated by gay men—Bill came across as very at ease around gay stuff, and probably even engaged in a bit of "marvelous darling" talk now and then. And since Bill was a real looker, he no doubt had to fend off his share of sleazy passes from gay men. In a way, it was like women in showbiz needing to get used to a certain amount of sleazy passes from straight men.

"I think the TV room would be best," Bill decided.

"What's this bit about not having a TV in the living room?" Terry complained. "What is it with people like you and Rick? It's like you're ashamed of having a TV. Don't you know that there are people in other parts of the world that would give their *lives* to own a TV?"

Terry's little digression into patriotism reminded me of a time long ago when Aunt Fern had never set a hook to my living room. As much as I hated to admit it, it *was* mighty comfortable to lean back in the recliner and dumb out with the tube. Still, one does have standards to maintain.

Bill grinned with amusement. "It certainly is refreshing, Terry, to meet a gay man who isn't quite so . . . fussy as some. Although my own tastes owe a huge debt to the gay world. After a while, things like a TV in the living room start to seem so . . . what would be the word, Rick?"

"Normal?" Terry suggested.

Bill chuckled. "Normal's as good a word as any." He gestured for us to take our seats. The chairs were squat, charcoal gray boxes consistent with a particular form-follows-function look, but were far from the world's most comfortable seating experience. However, Bill himself reached for his acoustic guitar and then stretched out on a geometric divan that looked far kinder to the body. He did not offer any refreshments. Bill had impeccable, even pompous manners when it struck his fancy, so I could only assume that his rudeness was intentional. He would meet with us because he had to, but he would stick it to us every chance he got.

His own paintings dominated the walls—abstractions on butcher paper, the paint splattered on through a straw. Uniformly mounted behind glass and plain steel frames, the pictures were all called things like *Untitled #5* or *Composition #6*. Behind what used to be the steel security doors to a freight elevator was a wide-screen TV. The black-looking TV blended in well with the white, gray, and black theme of the room.

"I thought this would be casual, and put us at ease," Bill explained, though sitting in the chairs felt a little like being strapped in a torture chamber.

"It's great." Terry squirmed to make his hulking frame fit. "Though I guess we're not going to be watching any TV."

Bill picked at his guitar and laughed. "I hope you guys aren't too disappointed."

"It was just a joke, Bill," Terry protested.

I couldn't help thinking, though, that even if Terry said he needed to watch TV because his mother was on *Oprah*, Bill wouldn't have turned it on if so doing destroyed his mood.

"Do you like my paintings?"

"Very much," I politely lied. I didn't think they were terrible, but they didn't leap out at me, either.

"I like more realistic art," Terry confessed. "I don't get this modern stuff."

Bill closed his eyes as he picked away at the strings, feeling the blues of the moment. "Ah, yes. The curse of the modern artist. Always misunderstood."

I didn't think it a wise move to point out that *some* modern artists sold very well indeed. "Have you had any shows?"

"A few. Nothing that would put me in the *Encyclopædia Britannica*. Let's just say that painting is my first love, but I'm glad to have a second career." He did a playful little flamenco riff. "Poetry is my third love."

Remembering Helena's memorial, I resisted the urge to ask him about his poems. "Just out of curiosity, how did you end up becoming an interior designer?"

He set aside the guitar. "I was doing theme parks. I studied architecture and interior design in school. Then the TV gig came along, so I figured, why not? No, I'm not from the ghetto, and no, I didn't go to college on an athletic scholarship. My family was middle class. My father was an accountant and my mother taught fourth grade. And anyway, that's not why you're here, so why don't we just get to the point?"

So much for trying to set the guy at ease. "Okay, Bill. For starters, tell us where you were the night of the murder."

"I was busy." He reached for a cut-glass container, took off the lid, and helped himself to a handful of gourmet jellybeans, putting the lid back on when he'd acquired a handful.

"Busy with Koko?" Terry inquired.

"Why, what did she say?" Bill shifted his weight on the divan, adjusting the throw pillows as if to remind us how much more comfortable he was.

"Nothing," Terry conveyed. "That's the point."

"Okay, we were together. But it isn't what you think." He tossed a jellybean in the air and caught it with his mouth.

"That's what they all say," I couldn't resist quipping.

"Very funny, Rick. But it's true. Koko is just a friend. She worships J.T., in case you haven't noticed. The *only* reason she was there was to talk."

"Well, what did she talk about?"

"Helena, *duh*. What else? J.T. had, as they say, fallen prey to her charms, and Koko wasn't what you'd call a happy camper." He sat up on his elbow, deep in thought. "It's strange, but sometimes I feel like there are two kinds of people in the world—those who are okay with multiple sex partners, and those who aren't. If you think about it, isn't that what ninety percent of people's problems boil down to? Who knows, maybe it's something in the brain. Maybe someday they'll isolate what it is, and you can know in advance if you're with someone who likes to mess around or someone who can't deal with it."

"Many would no doubt feel that the person who discovered this would deserve the Nobel Prize," I opined. "If not coronation as King of the World."

"Make fun of me all you want, Rick. But I'll bet you know exactly what I mean. Some people can go to a shrink and go to college and take drugs and find Jesus and who knows what else, yet they just can't get past the idea of their partner diddling around with someone else. And then other people have no problem with it at all."

"Yes, I have noticed," I agreed. "And I've noticed something else, too. The person who doesn't mind is usually the one who's getting the extra nookie."

Bill considered my observation, rubbing his chin in thought. "Not always. I know any number of people who are cool about their partner being with other people, regardless of whether or not they're getting some themselves."

"Well, anyway," Terry prodded, "as you were saying about Helena?" Besides wanting to stay on task, Terry was of course ill at ease discussing the relative merits of a nonmonogamous lifestyle.

"Right. Koko was just about losing her mind over J.T. being with someone else. She . . . well, I guess I might as well say it. She even said she'd—you know—kill that fucking bitch and what have you, if she didn't stay away."

"And what time was this?" Terry asked.

"From about midnight to whenever. I didn't really notice what time I crashed. I often don't. That always gets me on TV shows, like people are supposed to have it burned into their memories what time they fall asleep every night. But she was here for a *long* time. It must have been at least several hours."

"No doubt," I observed with a certain skepticism. "So what did you do while she ranted and raved?"

"Not much. I listened." He reached for another handful of jellybeans. "The thing of it was, J.T. was out of town on business, so Koko kept saying how things would be different when he came back home. But don't get the wrong idea, guys. I think she just meant that she'd try to be a better wife, or some shit. I don't think in a million years that Koko could ever—you know, kill someone. I mean, she's *pregnant*, for chrissake."

"So you just sat there and listened like a good friend?"

"More or less, Rick. Oh, and she asked me to do something for her, but I turned her down."

"And what was that?" Terry asked.

Bill stifled a yawn. "She wanted me to seduce Helena. I told her it was a little late in the day for that. Helena and I had already done the foul deed on a number of occasions. 'I mean sleep with her again,' Koko said. And I laughed—I guess I shouldn't have—and told her that I already intended to. Koko then said, 'This is my life, Bill, not a joke. How can you be so cavalier?' Which of course proves my earlier point about there being two kinds of people in the world. Well, what she said after that just about floored me. 'Then seduce me, Bill. Make J.T. jealous.' I couldn't believe what I was hearing. Leave it to Koko to make even adultery sound squeaky clean."

"So did you make good on her offer?" I inquired.

"Of course not. Not because of me, but because of her." He put his finger in his mouth, presumably to deal with a jellybean caught in his teeth.

"You mean you didn't want to take advantage of a desperate, pregnant woman? How noble."

"Actually, Rick, it was because pregnant women turn me off. Call me weird, but it's like having a *kid* in the room. But just so she could test herself, I did kinda pretend to make a play for her. I wanted her to realize that she couldn't cheat on J.T. in a million years. So I grabbed her and kissed her. She's a great kisser, if I must say so."

I leaned forward in my chair. "What did she do?"

Bill laughed. "Well, for a second or two she struggled. Then she kind of melted in my arms, like she was digging it. I'm not trying to say I'm all that, but that's exactly what happened. But then, when we surfaced for air, she broke away. 'I can't go through with this,' she told me. I told her that I already knew that. She let me hold her in my arms while she put her head on my shoulder. It wasn't sexual, just tender. I told her that J.T. was nuts about her, and that guys just did really flaky things sometimes and to try not to let it bother her. Then I started getting tired, so I gave her a peck on the forehead and sent her on her way."

"But you didn't notice the time?" Terry inquired.

"No, I already told you that I didn't."

"And that was really all she said to you?" I asked.

Bill studied the hem on one of the throw pillows, looking at it critically for its apparent shoddiness. "Pretty much."

"What do you mean, pretty much? That's like saying you pretty much didn't rape somebody."

He took a deep breath. "Look, Rick, I really don't want you guys taking this the wrong way. But who knows, maybe she said it to someone else, too, and I don't want anyone thinking that I'm a liar. The thing is, Koko made one other request."

"This eensy little request being . . . ?"

"That I kill Helena for her. She even offered me a shitload of money. A hundred grand, to be exact."

That made both Terry and me sit up and take notice. "To which offer you replied . . . ?"

Bill punched the throw pillows to increase his comfort. "That I wouldn't of course. What do you take me for, Rick? I'm no killer. I told Koko that she needed help if she was getting *that* bent out of shape. I gave her my shrink's number. She screamed at me that she already had a shrink—who didn't?— and that the only thing she needed to feel normal again was to know Helena was dead. Actually, she phrased it more colorfully than that, but I'll leave it to your guys' imaginations to fill in the blanks."

My mind was reeling with possibilities. "Was this before all the touchy-feelies?"

He sat up to stretch. "You got it. So by the time she left, she was calm again. I don't think for a minute that she meant any of it, anyway. She didn't have a hundred grand to spare, let alone that she's just too nice a kid to ever follow through on something like that. She was just being over the top. I guess that happens sometimes when you're pregnant."

For a moment or so, no one said anything. Some sort of extra-loud rig whizzed by on the freeway, hitting a bump and then honking.

"By the way," Bill finally added. "I hear you've been asking about some white room that Helena talked about. I have no idea what it could've meant. And I also know less than nothing about how Helena got to where she was. She was very evasive when it came to her past. There was supposedly some connection to British royalty, but I never believed it."

"What about my cousin?" Terry asked.

"What about her? She's great." Bill flashed his best thousand-watt grin. "What is this, the Middle Ages? Are you going to ask if my intentions are honorable?"

"That, too. But do you know if Koko talked to her that night?"

Bill considered. "She might have, after she left. Why?"

"Never mind." Terry got up from his chair, and stood over Bill. "So, since you raised the subject yourself, what *are* your intentions?"

"What Terry means," I quickly interjected, "is what did she tell you about her involvement? Did she mention anything that we should know about?"

"*And* why did you get involved with her?" Terry added.

Bill laughed. "Hey, that's cool that you look out for her. It's like I said the other night, once Ann-Margret got in big trouble, I realized how important she was. I poured my soul out to Basil, and he told me she was at Fernando's. So I saw her there in that tiny servant's bedroom, and we just kind of looked at each other, and that was it. Neither of us had to say anything."

"*What* was it?"

"Geez, Terry, do I have to spell it out?"

I sighed for my impatience. "They *did* it, okay, Terry? But did she say anything important?"

"Truth be told, guys, we made every effort to talk about everything but the murder. It was just one of those unspoken things where we both knew not to spoil the moment."

"I'm touched. But tell us, does she have any idea who really did it?"

"Why is she holding back?" Terry interjected.

Bill clasped his hands behind his head, and looked up into the industrial skylight. "If you ask me, guys, every woman on the face of the earth is the Mona Lisa. They're all so fucking mysterious. Who knows why they do what they do, or say what they say? All I can really tell you is that she was very sad but very brave. She didn't have a bad word to say about anyone, other than that jail guard who made a play for her. She even went out of her way to talk about her future. She lay there in bed, kind of playing with my hand, going on and on about how someday she was going to marry a real nice guy and have a bunch of kids and her own DIY show. 'I'm going to have it all, Bill,' she told me, in this very sad but very determined way. It was funny the way she said it, though, because I never felt like she was trying to trap me into marrying her. It's like she was completely in the moment with me while still going on about this great future she would have with the right guy, whoever that was."

Terry shook his head sadly. "Your kind of person. The type who can fool around without a care in the world."

I've never understood that routine some guys pull about their female relatives. If I'd had a sister, I could've cared less who she diddled. But Terry had a bad case of whatever-it-was, and I could see him struggling to not blow his cool.

Bill smiled genially at him, as if to lighten up the mood. "The way you phrase it, you make it sound pretty silly. But yes, essentially, that's my impression. Not that I don't want to get married someday. I want it all, too. It's just that I'm in no great rush."

"What about Basil and Fernando?" I queried.

"What about them? Basil's my buddy. What they do together is none of my business."

"That's big of you. But did they say anything that would lead you to believe—"

"Look, Rick. Let me put it to you like this. I have no idea who killed Helena. But believe me, if anyone said anything that sounded even remotely suspicious, don't you think I would've reported it? Do you think I want the new lady in my life to be in *jail*?"

"Well, your new lady was pretty upset with you back at Fernando's," Terry reminded him. "Just why was it that you didn't want to talk to us?"

Bill stared at him evenly, as if so doing were the equivalent of passing a polygraph. "Because I really have no idea who killed Helena, and everything I just told you accomplishes nothing besides make a certain innocent party look guilty as all get out."

After an uncomfortable pause, I asked, "So, do you miss theme parks?"

Bill laughed in spite of himself. "Hardly. The stress level was through the roof. Everything has to get inspected by about a million different safety boards. It's a miracle that anything gets done at all." He sat up and stretched. "Well, is that it?"

"Just one more thing, Bill," I promised. "I'm curious about your designs on the show. Why do you give people rooms you'd never want yourself?"

"Because I want my clients to have something *better* than what I provide for myself. That's my level of dedication. And that's the honest truth." He said all this as if there were a TV camera in the room recording his words for posterity.

"Does it bother you when all you accomplish, though, is people having to spend money on changing what you did?"

"I jumpstart the process of change. I do them a favor, even if they don't see it that way at the time." He grinned sheepishly. "Besides, they *do* sign a contract."

"What about Helena? Was she ever troubled by people's reactions?"

"You know, the one thing everyone tends to forget is that *most* of the time, the homeowners like what we do."

"Or so it seems on camera."

"Well, that's really all we have to go on, isn't it?"

It seemed futile to pursue the matter any further. No doubt if I'd asked him why he always took his shirt off on camera, he would've replied that it was for artistic reasons.

"I guess maybe what I really want to know is what you thought of Helena. Did you love her? Do you miss her? Because you sure don't seem too broken up about her death."

Bill stood up and stared at me with a look that was inscrutable. "I thought you said that you had no more questions."

Just as he was showing us to the door, I noticed a photo of Bill shaking hands with a prominent producer who was known to have what you might call a fancy for handsome young men of color.

"Interesting," I commented. "I assume that he asked you to do more than just decorate?"

"I don't decorate, I design. If you want decoration, go to Aunt Fern or—" He caught himself before he said anything more. "But yeah. Of course he made a play for me. I get a lot of fan mail from gay guys, if you want to know the truth. Even a few marriage proposals. They like it when I take my shirt off."

"And did you take it off for our producer friend?"

"Of course not. Why would I do that? I'm not into guys. If I wasn't an interior designer, the question would never even come up."

"Bill, I believe you're straight"—and I did—"but we both know what this town is like."

"He was my first important client. *Someone* had to be. But that's the end of the story. I'm where I am because of my talent, not because of who I fucked. My designs speak for themselves."

"Why, of course they do, Bill." I shook his hand. "We'll be in touch."

Terry felt like driving, so I let him take us back to my place. "Do you really think Bill had sex with a guy just to get a job?" He asked this rather like a child hesitantly inquiring as to the truth about this Santa Claus thing.

"That, my friend, is a question that can never be answered. Though it's interesting that out of everything he said, that's the first thing you want to talk about."

"Ha, like it doesn't interest you just as much. More, probably, since you're so much more into sex than I am."

"Who wouldn't be?" I aimlessly searched the radio for news updates.

"Very funny. But seriously, Rick. Do you believe everything he said?"

I thought about it. "I dunno. What do you think?"

"It seemed pretty consistent. But of course, lies can be just as consistent as the truth."

"Sometimes even more so," I affirmed. "So when are you going to call Boxer?"

"None of your business. But let's get back to Bill. Koko doesn't smell so good right now, does she?"

"She stinks to high heaven. In fact, I think that maybe another visit with her would be just what the doctor ordered."

"What about Curtsy Ann? We still have a lot of crap on her, too."

"*And* Brick, and just about anyone else, if we use a little imagination. Who knows? Bill could be lying about where he was that night. Maybe Helena was getting to be a real pain in the ass. Maybe there *was* something that happened with our friend the producer, and she was going to—" I stopped myself, having remembering something I saw at the *MHYH* web site.

Terry gazed intently into the side mirror, as always a hyper-vigilant driver. "What are you doing?"

"Just taking another look at those files I downloaded." Like zillions of other people, I had zero patience when it came to waiting for my computer to turn all the way on, and I snapped my fingers in agitation waiting for all the hard drives or whatever to upload. A long minute or so later, I eagerly opened one of my files on Helena.

"Here it is, plain as the nose that used to be on Mitzi McGuire's face."

"What is?"

"A little friendly message from Lady Godiva. A few ancient days ago, I wouldn't have thought anything of it. But now that I've lost my innocence, it really hits me between the eyes. Helena was asked by a fan what she thought of Bill, and she replied, bless her heart, 'Bill is my spiritual brother in design. I've been a huge fan of his ever since he first designed the home of a famous producer, which led to his job at Disneyland. I don't want to spoil it by telling you what the designs were, because someday soon I want to copy them for some of my own *My House, Your House* projects. But the experience changed his whole life, and it showed in his brilliant work.' One can only wonder if she was just getting warmed up or if she was going to let the sleeping dogs lie, so to speak."

"You'd think they'd update the web page now that she's dead." He carefully rolled down the window to look behind him before changing lanes, never one to trust the possible blind spot in the side mirror.

"Probably they're trying to figure out what on earth to say. But don't you get it? She was going to let the cat out of the bag about Bill." I quickly amended, "Or at least maybe she was going to, assuming there's a cat in a bag at all."

"I'm sorry, Rick. I was distracted for a minute. Could you read that thing again?"

I sighed. "Too much Boxer on the brain, I see."

Terry's face reddened. "Will you *stop* it?"

# TWENTY-TWO

WORKING FROM THE BASIC PREMISE THAT AT THIS POINT, SOME folks might not exactly be standing in line to talk to us again—especially if they were guilty of a little thing called murder—we figured that Koko Yee's would be a good place to start making a few surprise visits. After all, pregnant as she was, there was a good chance we'd find her at home.

We were far from disappointed. Not only was Koko at home, but as a kind of added bonus, she had some mighty interesting houseguests.

Finding Curtsy Ann in the living room was not a big surprise—they did of course work together on the show. But finding Tippi there as well, the three of them apparently having a perfectly chummy girl-talk kind of afternoon, was indeed unexpected. The big, floppy floor cushions of the living room made it seem like they were having a slumber party. Had I suddenly morphed into Jane Powell, I'd have sung "It's a Most Unusual Day" in a heartbeat.

Koko was effervescent with giggles when she greeted us at the door, and she seemed to regard our calling on her as the pleasantest of surprises, just one more glorious gift in this magical experience called life. The dime-store shrink in me wondered if the giddy creature was a teensy bit manic-depressive.

But her girlfriends matched her in silliness. Curtsy Ann wore a delicious look of mischief as she greeted us with wide open arms and called out, "Rick, Terry, my best friends in the whole wide world." For some reason, this made all three women crack up laughing all over again. Even

Tippi was all sweetness and light as she beamingly tilted her head, gave a little wave with her fingers, and cooed, "Hi there, you big strong guys." There were no telltale signs of drinking strewn about the room—or for that matter, on anyone's breath. It crossed my mind that they might've smoked some dope or whatever, especially given Tippi's sudden lovey-dovey about-face. But getting high didn't seem like Curtsy Ann's style—nor Koko's, not while she was pregnant, anyway—and I had to conclude it was just the contagious mood of the moment. (Unless of course it was all just an act.) As a Hollywood reporter, I was well accustomed to sudden mood swings in celebrities, and for that matter even back in high school in Iowa sometimes people responded differently to me in groups than they did one-on-one. In any case, I figured we'd lucked out—not only to have three suspects at once, but to find them in such agreeable spirits.

"Can I get you guys anything?" Koko asked, which rather inexplicably caused yet another round of giggles. Curtsy Ann even picked up a pillow and zanily hit Tippi with it while Tippi called out for mercy. The afternoon sun shone through the curtains onto their hair, and the whole scene almost looked like a Renoir painting.

"We're fine," Terry replied. "By the way, what's so funny?"

The three women looked at one another, and predictably enough started laughing again.

"Nothing," Koko managed to tell us. "We're just being silly."

"I didn't realize you were all such good friends."

"Oh, sure," Curtsy Ann answered. "We met Tippi when she did the show, and we've been huge fans ever since."

"It's like we've known each other all our lives," Tippi insisted.

It occurred to me that when we met with Tippi, she'd bad-mouthed Helena to kingdom come, but never even mentioned Curtsy Ann. It was, after all, a long couple of days ago, and we hadn't known yet about Tippi and Brick. In fact, we still did not know for a fact if Curtsy Ann knew about Tippi and Brick—or if Tippi knew about Brick and Curtsy Ann.

Oh well, time to have a little fun. However the cookie was about to crumble, it might just tell us something about who murdered Helena.

First, though, we needed to find out some things about Koko. Terry got things off to a rollicking start when he asked her, "What happened with you and Bill on the night Helena was murdered?"

Talk about a shift in moods. For an interminably long couple of seconds, Tippi kept giggling, as if the question were part of the jocular continuum, but she wised up soon enough when she saw the color drain not only from Koko's face but from Curtsy Ann's as well.

"I don't know what you mean." Koko aimlessly toyed with the rings on her fingers.

"I think you're upsetting her," Curtsy Ann protested. "And in her condition."

"I think we're upsetting *you*," I countered.

"It's okay, Curtsy Ann," Koko insisted. "I might as well tell them. I went to see Bill that night. I knew that he was good friends with J.T., plus—well, you know—there's that way in which guys understand other guys."

"What did you talk about?" Terry sat himself down on the floor cushions, and I figured I might as well join him.

"Not much." She picked up a porcelain vase on an end table and moved it over a few inches; then she moved it back to its original spot. "J.T.'s birthday was coming up, and I wanted to—"

"Have him murder Helena for you?" Terry interrupted.

Koko dropped the vase. It shattered into a seemingly infinite number of tiny pieces.

Sniffling, she held her belly and vainly attempted to bend down to pick up the shards, but Tippi and Curtsy Ann rushed over to stop her. "We'll get it," Curtsy Ann announced sharply, as if to suggest that this broken vase was somehow the major problem at hand.

"You have to believe me, guys." Koko urgently walked about the room. "Haven't you ever felt one way in your guts while your brain tells you something else? I knew that on some lofty spiritual plane I wasn't supposed to be hating Helena with every cell of my body, but I couldn't help myself. I just *did*. I said so many terrible things that I didn't mean. Things I still can't face up to."

"According to Bill, you seemed pretty cocky in the moment."

"Rick, I didn't kill her. And neither did Bill."

"Guess you were too busy doing other things."

"Like what?" Koko looked genuinely scared, almost more so than when we were hinting at the possibility that she was a murderer.

"Suppose you tell us," I encouraged. I felt pretty tacky doing this, but we needed to see if her story jibed with Bill's. Though I have to say I was reasonably confident that this particular aspect of the story would prove to be PG-13 at most. I believed Bill was telling the truth when he said that he and Koko stole but a lone kiss.

Koko stared at the sad pile of shards in the wastebasket. "Look, I can't help it if Bill wanted her dead just as much as I did. But I guess making love is a great equalizer. We both needed something the other had to give. I never in a million years thought I'd cheat on J.T., but one thing led to another, and there we were. And somehow, lying in each other's arms in those quiet moments before the sunrise . . . I mean, don't get me wrong, I'm very much in love with my husband. But I knew then and there that I could never be part of a murder. And neither could Bill. Sometimes it works that way, doesn't it? A small bad thing keeps you basically good."

"Say what?" Terry asked, taking the proverbial words out of my mouth.

Koko covered her mouth to laugh. "I guess I need to rewind. What did Bill tell you?"

"He was a gentleman, sort of," I conveyed. "He didn't kiss and tell, or at least not make a full disclosure. But what's all this about Bill wanting her dead?"

"Why, that *bitch*," Koko observed. "That's really the only way to put it. Here I was, holding out, to protect his ass as much as my own, and he leaves out half the story. I'll bet he couldn't wait to talk about how *I* wanted her dead."

"He told us kind of reluctantly," I recounted. "Like he had no choice but to tell us, since we'd find out anyway."

She walked about in agitation. "I *can't* believe it. What did that mother-fucker think? That you'd take his word for it and not even check out his story with me? What an ego. What a goddamn, no good—" She stopped herself. "Name calling will get us nowhere. So let's just say that that prick told me a neat little story about how Helena was about to dig up some dirt on him for all the world to see, so he wanted to stop her in a big way, if you get what I mean."

"Was this by any chance about a famous producer who gave Bill his first big break?" I shyly asked.

"Smart boy. I see you've been doing your homework. Bill insisted that there wasn't a speck of truth to the innuendo, but who knows? I think the SOB bastard would've sold his mother's soul to the devil for a chance to make a buck. Anyway, Bill's pride was such that he was ready to kill her— or at least kinda ready to kill her—rather than have her suggest to the world that he was anything other than the hetero stud of the western world."

I clasped my hands together in thought. "Helena sounds like a frustrated gossip columnist. Only much worse. Just why did she get off on spreading all this gooey dirt?"

Koko sat down on the floor pillows. "Helena was very into TV as a power trip," she explained. "She was blown away by how many millions of people you could reach. So she used it as a way of getting back at people. She was very aggressive."

"Don't you mean *passive*-aggressive?" Curtsy Ann interjected. "She wore those godawful pearls and white pumps, like she was *so* dignified. And then she'd ever-so-smilingly stick it to you."

"But she was upfront about it, too," Tippi contributed. "I mean, sometimes she'd just really let people have it."

"Sounds like she was a lot of things to different people," I concluded. "Most of them shitty."

Curtsy Ann nodded sadly. "I guess that about sums it up."

"But I still don't get it," I admitted. "I can see how she might've wanted revenge when it came to her personal life. Maybe for good reasons, maybe for not-so-good reasons. Sure, it's human to *want* to get back at people when you think they've done you wrong. But what about those total strangers whose rooms she'd design? Why would she ask around or whatnot to get the dirt on them, too?"

Koko put her arms around her belly. "Well, think about it, Rick. There she was, designing for these strangers, and she was shy around people she didn't know—I don't know if you picked up on that. And all she knew how to do was this way-out stuff. So what insurance does she have that they won't badmouth her before millions on TV?"

Suddenly, it all made sense. "She kind of blackmails them."

"Smart guy."

"She did it to all of us," Curtsy Ann affirmed. "Right there on the airwaves, she presented me with an ice sculpture of the Virgin Mary."

"Or during our show in Whitefish, Montana, when she gave me a copy of a book called *Wife Swapping Made Easy*, supposedly as a joke," Koko added. "And so many of her rooms hurt people the same way. Like the couple who got the igloo bedroom."

"Or the bachelor—ahem—who got the dog-kennel bedroom," Curtsy Ann recounted.

"Or the lesbians whose play room was made to look like a Monte Cristo sandwich," Koko contributed. "Although frankly, I never did get what that one was about."

"It *is* a toughie," I agreed.

"The thing is," Curtsy Ann added, "what do you do when someone you know gets brutally murdered, and in a way, you're relieved? Even . . . well, *happy*? Believe me, we all know it wasn't Ann-Margret. But when we know who really did do it, there's a part of me that would like to kiss that person and say, 'Thank you kindly, sir.' Or 'ma'am,' as the case may be. Yet when someone dies, period, there's all those obligatory nice things we all have to say—"

"That *you* have to say," Tippi interrupted. "Me, I'm too honest. I hated the bitch's guts, and I don't care who knows it. I'm *proud* of my hatred, even."

"Well, except of course for you, dear," Curtsy Ann amended. "But really, guys. I'm sure we've all had to tell little fibs, because the truth just ain't pretty. You couldn't possibly have known Helena for more than about five minutes without conjuring up images of how she might've looked treading water in concrete shoes. It simply was the nature of the beast."

"What about Aunt Fern?" I asked. "What about Ann-Margret? They seemed to think she was great."

Koko shook her head, perplexed. "Aunt Fern had a blind spot when it came to Helena."

"So I've heared."

"But why not?" Curtsy Ann offered. "Aunt Fern's past the age where Helena's shenanigans could've affected her. It's not like the two of them were after the same guys. And the thing about Aunt Fern that people don't get right away is how self-absorbed she is. She makes it seem like she's baking cookies just for you, but she's baking them for herself. She doesn't want you to be happy, exactly. She wants to *make* you happy. She's that old-style woman who only feels good when she's butting into other people's business."

"Helena reached out to her in this mother-daughter way," Koko continued. "It was music to Aunt Fern's ears."

"Not that she confided all that much," Curtsy Ann stated. "Helena wanted the world to know the truth about everyone else, like she was some sort of oracle. But when it came to the lady herself, mum was very much the word. I'm sure she told Aunt Fern the same half-truths and tall tales she told the rest of us. But Aunt Fern was probably very deeply touched. Not to mention flattered."

"She *loves* attention," Koko observed. "I think she's been very lonely since losing her husband and her son."

I brushed aside the pang of guilt that despite my better judgment had possessed me once again—maybe I *could've* been nice to Aunt Fern. "But what about Ann-Margret?"

"A question of class, pure and simple." Curtsy Ann gazed into the silver bowl on the coffee table and fussed over her hair. "For Ann-Margret, Helena was an aristocrat. Of course, Helena was actually about as aristocratic as a garbage truck, but no matter. Ann-Margret is still pretty wet behind the ears. To her, Helena was a goddess."

"It's true," Terry admitted. "My cousin is really just a kid."

"She lacks your worldliness," I couldn't resist pointing out.

"Very funny, Rick." Terry threw a small pillow at me, and the girls chuckled.

"I still can't get over that Grade-A number one fuckhead, Bill McCoy,"

Koko spat out. "Like I was the only one who said I wanted her dead. What nerve."

Tippi gave an amused shrug. "What do you expect? All men would've done the same thing. They're physiologically incapable of thinking about anything or anyone but their own beloved cocks for even a single instant of existence."

"Right on," agreed Curtsy Ann.

"Would you say that's true of Brick?" I asked.

"Of course," Tippi bragged. "I don't discriminate against a guy because he knows how it's done."

I glanced at Curtsy Ann, who trembled slightly as she ran her fingers through her blond hair.

"And would you say that to his face?"

Tippi stared at me dead-on, as if rising to a challenge. "I say what I please to anyone, anytime. And if people don't like it, then I guess they just don't like me."

"I'll have to remember that, the next time I see Brick. I'll tell him that Tippi thinks he's . . . What? A narcissistic prick? Is that close enough?"

"You tell him anything, and I swear I'll—" She cupped her hands to her mouth. "I mean, c'mon, Rick. Give me a break, okay? Sure, it's harder to walk the walk than to talk the talk. Brick gets under my skin, I admit it. I know he's totally full of shit, and he must be banging everything with tits in L.A. But I . . . care about him a lot. I can't help it."

"Why didn't you mention him the other night?" Terry inquired. "You only told us about Helena and that other man. Hoover Swann."

"You're lucky I told you that much. I didn't have to say anything. And I still don't."

Terry stood up, and walked over to her. "But you knew Helena had also had a thing with Brick, and quite a serious one from her point of view."

Tippi barely came up to his chest, but she wasn't about to be stared down. "What are you saying?"

"I think it's pretty obvious," Terry answered. "You didn't want us sniffing in the direction of you and Brick. Because it just might implicate either or both of you in Helena's murder."

"Ha! What a joke." Her thick dark curls swayed to the rhythm of her head as she turned away from him.

"Then what about a check you made out to him for ten thousand dollars?" Terry asked.

"A personal loan. The emphasis on the personal. It's none of your business."

Curtsy Ann was making a point of avoiding eye contact with me. I got the impression that this was the first she was hearing about Tippi and Brick, but she wasn't about to betray her surprise. Maybe it was a matter of pride, but maybe it was also to avoid exposing very much of herself to the likes of us.

"Tell that to Brick," countered Terry, doing his tough-cop shtick. "He left the check lying around in plain view, on the kitchen table. He told us you were paying him to remodel your house—after you told us that you were good as broke. But I guess there's always a few extra bucks kicking around when it comes to bumping someone off. Unless it was merely for services already rendered?"

There was a faint sound of rhythmic music filtering up from the floor—J.T. must have been working in the studio down below.

"Brick has that machismo thing happening," Tippi admitted. "Of course he didn't own up that I loaned him money. But what do you think—I'd pay him to knock off Helena and then leave the fucking check on the kitchen table? That I'd even be stupid enough to write him a check in the first place? Maybe I should've written a memo on it that said: 'One hit, Helena Godiva.'"

She crossed her arms, searching for words. "Can't you see, guys? It's just like Curtsy Ann said. Helena wasn't Eleanor Roosevelt. Or even Nancy Reagan. We *all* wished her dead, and I guess you could say God has been kind, because we all got our wish. But none of us did it. I'm sure of it."

"Then who did?" I asked.

"Anybody could've," Tippi replied. "Who knows how many other people wanted to off her? There's all those people whose homes she ruined. We've maybe only seen the tip of the iceberg when it comes to her personal life. Maybe it was even just some hideous coincidence. Someone went into the wrong motel room and bumped off the wrong person. Or someone wanted to rob her."

"I doubt that," I replied. "Everything about the murder was too obviously about who she was."

"You have a point there," admitted Tippi. "But still, it could've been a crazed fan. A stalker."

"Maybe," Terry considered. "But we doubt it."

"But why?"

"Because it was far too personal," Terry explained. "Because whoever it was knew just where Helena would be. Because Helena herself was acting nutty the entire day, and if it was only over a crazed fan she wouldn't have been so secretive about it. She would've been a full-scale drama queen diva and never shut up about it. Because we're not going to eliminate all of you from the list of suspects just because you tell us that sure, you wanted her dead, but golly gee, we wouldn't have done it because that would've been icky."

Terry could talk turkey when he had to, I'll give him that much. Like a real bear, he wasn't just for cuddling.

"I'm sure we don't sound *that* incapable of it," Tippi haughtily replied. "Typical man, putting down women on general principle. Even when you think we're murderers, you can't take us seriously."

Terry held up his hands defensively. "Now hold on. This has nothing to do with being a man or a woman."

"I disagree." Tippi stood with her hands on her hips. "I think this entire mess *is* about being a man or a woman. It's about men thinking they can walk all over women."

"Now *I* disagree." Curtsy Ann looked haughtily at Tippi. "I think what it's really about are whores versus decent people. Some of the whores are men, and some of the whores are women. But a whore is still a whore, no matter how you slice it."

"And what does that mean?" Tippi wanted to know.

Curtsy Ann sauntered over to her. "It means that in the end, whores get stuck with other whores."

"I still don't know what you mean." Tippi turned to the rest of us with a kind of Woody Allen befuddlement. "What's she trying to say?"

"She means," Curtsy Ann scornfully answered, "that Brick was once upon a time her fiancé. *My* fiancé. Until Helena spread her whore legs as open as a drawbridge on the Mississippi River. I'll bet Brick never even mentioned me, did he?"

"Uh, truthfully, no," Tippi replied.

Curtsy Ann emitted a bitter, sad laugh. "And to think I still see him. God, am I stupid, or what?"

"About as stupid as me, I guess." Tippi touched Curtsy Ann's shoulder, but she pulled away.

"Thank you, Tippi. I appreciate your concern. But tell me something. Even knowing what I just told you, do you have any intention of no longer seeing Brick?"

Tippi considered the question. "Truthfully, no."

"I thought so." She held up her hands to preempt all protests. "Hey, relax, everyone. I'm not putting myself on a pedestal. I'd do the same thing. Hoping that somehow, out of it all, Brick would see the light and come back to me for keeps."

Tippi smiled self-deprecatingly. "I'll tell Brick you said hi when I meet him for dinner."

"Yes, do that." Curtsy Ann put her finger to her chin, as if deep in thought. "In fact, tell him I said . . ." She sighed. "Never mind."

"Friends?" Tippi extended her hand.

"Why the hell not?" Curtsy Ann vigorously shook her hand.

"Hooray," Koko cheered, clapping like a cheerleader.

"What about Brick?" I asked in my quietest, most concerned tone. "Are you through with him now, Curtsy Ann?"

"What do you care?" Tippi shot back. "You're a tacky reporter who drags people through the mud."

I shrugged. "You know me—I'm just curious."

Curtsy Ann laughed through her tears. "I think I've been through with Brick since the moment I met him. I've just had trouble accepting it."

"Then you'd tell us if he were hiding anything?" I asked.

"Hey, what is this shit?" Tippi hit herself on the forehead in exasperation. "Brick has nothing to hide. He's too stupid."

Curtsy Ann looked down at her manicured pink fingernails. "Actually,

I agree with Tippi. Brick isn't nearly clever enough to have pulled this off."

"Or at least not by himself," Terry amended.

"Don't tell me we're going *there* again," complained Tippi. "I already told you, the money was a loan."

"I think they're talking to me," Curtsy Ann corrected. "As in, did *I* somehow get Brick to do it?"

"You did say something kind of ominous the other day at Brick's," I pointed out.

"The other day at Brick's?" Tippi repeated with disbelief. "It blows my mind that you were at Brick's the other day."

Curtsy Ann rested her elbow on her bent leg as she stared out the window. "If I know Brick, it was about an hour before you were. And he had another girl there, too. Some bikini type, minus the bikini. I said a lot of things. All I meant was that I'd put my life, my pride, my everything on the line for Brick time and time again. And that I'd gotten—big surprise—a great big zero in return."

Everyone grew quiet.

"You guys probably need to get going," Koko finally stated.

Curtsy Ann looked at her watch, and melodramatically shook her head. "They're not the only ones. God, what was I *thinking*?"

"Are you *sure* she wasn't wearing her bikini?" Tippi half-joked.

"Just one last question," Terry promised. "Curtsy Ann, we know Helena didn't exactly confide in you. But did she ever mention anything about a white room?"

"Or a rich old lady who helped her get established?" I added.

Curtsy Ann frowned. "I don't know anything about a rich old lady. But once, on a location shoot, Helena and I had to share a motel room. You can imagine how delectable that was. In the middle of the night, she woke up screaming. She was saying something about a white room. I held her and told her everything would be all right. I mean, at the time, she was hurting, so just as one human being to another, I reached out. Well, the next morning, I asked her what she meant by the white room, and she denied ever having said it—or ever even having a nightmare. She actually tried to say that I was making the whole thing up to make her look bad. Needless to say, I dropped it like a hot potato. But it always seemed weird to me."

"What do you think it meant?" I asked.

She shrugged. "Who knows? I figured it was probably some kind of hospital room. Maybe she had an operation as a little girl. Or maybe—you know—she got herself into trouble somewhere along the way. An illegitimate baby, or even . . . well, even worse. I do know that Tippi's room was the first and only white room she ever did on the show. Helena actually had this thing against white, I guess because it reminded her of whatever gave her nightmares."

"Gee, lucky me," Tippi remarked, "that she bravely set aside her phobia long enough to ruin my house."

Curtsy Ann smiled with irony. "Helena had many fears, but when it really counted, they never got the best of her."

"It's weird, then, that she would always dress in white," I observed.

"We're talking Helena," Curtsy Ann shrugged. "Go figure."

Driving home a short while later, Terry skillfully maneuvered the Cherokee around a hairpin turn in the canyon and told me, "You looked disappointed when Tippi and Curtsy Ann didn't have a catfight."

I hit the Find command on the computer screen of my laptop. "I'm sure I have no idea what you're talking about." I was disappointed but not surprised when file after file on Helena made no mention of a hospital stay. "Besides, who's to say they aren't having one now? Maybe they were just waiting for us to leave."

"You kind of like it when people don't get along, don't you, Rick?"

"Hardly. There are few things I despise more than being in the same room with people not getting along."

"But do you like it when they *do* get along?"

I thought about it. "A little more, though not much."

Terry's cell phone rang. "Why, Boxer, I was just thinking of you." He smiled over at me with intentional exaggeration. "Sure, sounds great. Uh-huh. That's good, yeah. Oh, really? *Really?* Okay, see you then."

"Well?" I tried another search through the Helena files, this time for "mentor" or "first design," or "first job." Once again, the search came up empty.

Terry smiled like the proverbial cat with a canary feather hanging out of its mouth. "We're having dinner at eight. And Ann-Margret is doing better. He says she's opening up a little more, and he thinks he can logically convince a jury that the evidence is circumstantial."

"That's great."

"Oh, and one more thing. He got a message from Fernando. It seems he remembers the name of the rich old lady after all."

# TWENTY-THREE

"SO, I WONDER WHAT MRS. CREIGHTON WESTPORT WILL HAVE TO say about Helena," I thought out loud as Terry and I journeyed that evening to what was called the dowager's Malibu beach house. I patted his shoulder and added, "Sorry about your dinner date."

"I wouldn't have enjoyed myself," Terry insisted. "Besides, maybe it won't take long. Maybe the old biddy's in Europe. Maybe she'll have nothing to say."

I thought for a moment before speaking. "Does it bother you that Boxer opted out of joining us?"

Terry shrugged. "You know how lawyers are. He doesn't want to get his hands dirty."

"But you still like him?"

"So far, so good." He irritably tapped on the steering wheel; the driver in front of him changed lanes without using blinkers. "Now *that's* how accidents happen," he muttered. Terry would've been the perfect cop to visit a kindergarten class to lecture on why the police officer is your friend.

"Jesus, where *is* this place, anyway?"

I thought I knew the coast highway pretty well, but the map directed us to a steep, winding side road that was particularly treacherous in the dark. The Cherokee wound around the windswept Monterey cypress trees and sparse beach grass; no guard rails protected us from the jagged coastline straight below. The moon was barely visible through the layers of fog.

We came to a wide plateau. A row of pine trees had been planted to make a kind of natural gate, but the fierce coastal winds had tortured them to grow at a twisted angle. Driving past the trees, we were surprised by how long the sandy, wooded road was, and it led us deeper and deeper into the coastal fog and darkness. Even with the high beams on, Terry was driving at something like one mile per hour—not just because he was a lunatic about safe driving, but because we literally couldn't see a foot in front of us. It felt like we spent a lifetime inching our way through the pitch blackness.

"Daddy, are we almost there?"

"Hell if I know."

"Did I ever tell you my life story?" I quipped. "I was born to a humble family—"

"Shut up, Rick. Things are bad enough."

When, after an interminably long, silent drive, a pair of flashlights shone in our eyes, it came as a relief. Better to get robbed or kidnapped than have to keep enduring this monotonous, seemingly pointless drive.

"Take me, I'm yours," I joked, while Terry rolled down his window to greet the two approaching figures.

"What the . . . ?"

"Terry? Rick?" Holy shit. "It was Bill, and the guy standing next to him was Brick. "What the fuck are *you* doing here?"

"Couldn't have said it better myself," Terry replied.

"Did the old bag want you to help?" Brick asked.

"Why would she do that?" Bill replied on our behalf. "What can *they* do? I think they followed us here."

"But how?" Brick wanted to know. "No one else even knew. Unless you blabbed it all over town."

"Me? You're the one with the big fucking mouth. You should be a *girl*, the way you're always blabbing to every asshole walking down the street about how you got laid."

Brick gave Bill a shove; Bill shoved him back.

I wondered if Fernando had some Machiavellian reason for happening to "remember" the name of Mrs. Creighton Westport on this very day. Whatever Bill and Brick were up to, they clearly did not appreciate bumping into us at this particular time and place. Not that they necessarily would've wanted to bump into us at *any* time or place, but this did appear to be an especially inopportune happenstance. One could only hope it wouldn't lead to one of them killing the other—or us.

"Time out—okay, guys?" Terry stepped out of the Cherokee and stood between them. "Look, we're only here because of Fernando."

"Fernando?" Bill narrowed his eyes and shook his head to express his disbelief. "Brick, why in the name of fuck did you tell *Fernando*?"

"Easy, now." Terry held up his hands to restrain Bill. "Fernando never mentioned you guys. We've been trying to learn about Helena, is all. And apparently this Mrs. Creighton Westport helped her get going as a designer."

"Oh." Bill extended his hand to Brick. "Sorry, man."

"Hey, buddy, no sweat." They gave each other a syrupy, sensitive-guy hug, patting each other on the back for good measure.

I got out of the car to join them in the foggy darkness, zipping up my black leather jacket against the cold. The strong wind tasted of salt, and it howled in a mournful chorus with the crashing ocean, which I couldn't see through the dim shadows of the trees. I felt like I was in some expressionist stage set, in which the world was intentionally blacked out and unseen. "I hate to interrupt this magic moment, but what exactly are you two doing here?"

"My car died," Bill explained. "It's parked back over there. We were walking to the main road to flag down the AAA truck."

"Small wonder it died," Brick scolded. "You'd think someone above the age of five would know that when the oil light comes on, it means it's time for an oil change."

Terry threw up his hands in unutterably wretched perplexity. "You mean to tell me that you *knew* you needed an oil change . . . *and you put it off?*" For Terry, this was tantamount to cheating on your spouse, or not trimming your mother's hedges when she asked you to. Only the lowest of the low would engage in such reprehensible behavior.

"I'm an artist," Bill stated in his own defense. "I don't relate to all that mundane bullshit."

"Excuse me, guys," I interrupted. "Okay, so your car broke down. But that still doesn't explain what you were doing here in the first place. Unless, of course, you saw an ad on TV for a repair shop conveniently located here in the middle of nowhere."

"I got a phone call from this weird old lady," Bill told us. "Actually, it was from her butler or some shit."

"Me, too," Brick interjected. "She feels really bad about Helena, I guess, because she wants us to work on a room in her house."

"I'm not sure I get it," I commented.

"She wants to make like this shrine to Helena," Bill explained. "She picked me to do it, because she said I understood Helena's design vision best. That my work was closest to hers."

There was no arguing that one, though whether it should be taken as a compliment was subject to debate.

"And she picked me to be the carpenter because . . . well, I'm the one she picked. She said she wanted to watch us work with our shirts off."

Bill gave him a buddy-type nudge. "And anyway, Ann-Margret's in *jail*, you peabrain. So who else is she going to pick? See, she wants it to be like an episode of the show, as part of the tribute. So she's using us guys who worked with Helena."

"Among other things," I noted.

"Hey, yeah—I hadn't thought of it like that." Brick held out his hands in a *gimme-five* gesture, which Bill returned in true dudelike fashion.

"So anyway," Bill went on, "we were here tonight to start coming up with drawings and specs. The lady's loaded up the wazoo, so the sky's the limit. I'm thinking about something along the lines of an ancient temple, complete with pillars, only some of them are knocked over, like it's all in ruins. There'd be these frescoes of Helena—a nice close-up of her face in the middle, and then in all the panels around it she's like directing people to make this or that room. Sort of like telling the story of a mythic goddess through pictures. There'd be lots of candles and stuff like that."

"Sounds very ambitious," I tactfully commented. "Did Mrs. Westport like your idea?"

"We'll know in a couple of days," Bill replied. "See, that was what was kind of weird. We never actually met her."

"The butler dude was the one who talked to us," Brick conveyed. "He asked all these questions from a list and made notes. Then he told us madam would be in touch, with like one of those English accents."

Bill rubbed his shoulders for the brisk night air. "We left, and then a little ways from the house, the car died. I called AAA on my cell and then we ran into you."

"I doubt that you'll be able to see anyone but the English butler guy," Brick advised.

"You could be right," Terry admitted. "But no harm in trying. When did AAA say they'd be here?"

Bill shone his flashlight on his watch. "Probably not for another half-hour or so."

"Tell you what," Terry suggested. "Let's have a look at your car. If we can't fix it, it'll only take a few minutes to drive you down to the end of the road."

It was difficult to believe that the end of the road was only a few minutes away. As my eyes adjusted to the dark, I saw that on either side of the unpaved road was a kind of thicket. Off to the left side, like a furtive moon, a single electric light shone through the trees. I could only assume it was the one lit room of the house, but I couldn't make out even the darkest, faintest outline of the house itself.

We walked directly into the wind, the cold sand stinging our faces, as we found Bill's car—a jazzy vintage red Corvette. "Whoa," Terry exclaimed. "How great is *this*?"

"It's fun to drive." Bill affectionately tapped on the hood as if petting a dog. "The new engine, though, needs to get broken in."

"Are you having trouble *really* getting into third?" Terry asked.

"Some," Bill admitted. "But it's getting better."

Call me a weirdo, but whatever is supposedly so interesting about cars frankly eludes me. I could appreciate the look and feel of certain models, but going on about miles per gallon or tune-ups just didn't do for my testosterone what it was supposed to do.

Terry and Brick opened up the hood and launched into this long discussion that might as well have been in a foreign language about how, given the make and model, this or that was probably what was overheating or stuck or frozen or whatever. Brick turned on the ignition and Terry listened and felt around as attentively as a doctor with a stethoscope. "Yep, she definitely needs oil," he concluded. "But I wonder . . . maybe we can try something."

"I'm game," Brick eagerly volunteered, rubbing his hands together. Give Brick something to do with his hands, and life was beautiful to him.

As the two of them chattered and poked away, I told Bill what Koko had said about Helena's murder being on his own list of things he wanted for Christmas.

"Oh, she said that, did she? Well, I'll have you know that the *only* reason I said what I did was to cheer her up."

"You have an interesting way of, as you say, cheering people up. If conspiring to commit murder is how you brighten someone's day, then the only thing I don't understand is why you haven't been hired by Hallmark."

Bill flipped up the collar of his jacket to protect his ears from the cold. "Very funny, Rick. But you know what I mean. Koko kept going on and on about what a bad person she was to be having these thoughts about Helena, so I tried to say that hey, it was *human* to be feeling that way. You know—I felt the same way myself, and blah-blah-blah."

"How big of you." We walked maybe a hundred feet away from the car.

"Look, I was trying to help. That's all I'm saying." Squatting down, he absently toyed with a stick, scribbling into the sand.

"But what about the slight detail of *why* you wanted her dead?"

"You're jumping to conclusions, Rick. You're adding two and two and coming up with Einstein's Theory of Relativity. Yeah, okay, Helena was going to hint at some stuff from my past. She was hurt. She felt like I slighted her for not becoming her devoted lover. But I knew she had no proof of anything with that producer. Because I knew it wasn't true."

I stuck my hands in my jacket pockets. "Still, if people started wondering certain things about you, it wouldn't exactly have been a press agent's dream."

Bill's laughter echoed. "You mean if people thought I was gay? Hell, some people are convinced I must be funnier than a pink flamingo. If I were hung up on that stuff, do you think I'd even *be* in this line of work? Let alone on national TV."

"You do have a point," I admitted. "Still, are you saying that even if I sniffed around in the direction of Mr. Producer, I wouldn't smell anything reeking of Bill McCoy?"

He picked up a pebble and threw it; we heard it hit a tree branch. "Absolutely." He turned to look me in the eye. "I have *nothing* to hide."

We heard footsteps crunching down on the pine needles and mulch. Someone was in the woods.

"Shh," Bill instructed, which annoyed me. I didn't like the implication that I didn't know enough to keep my trap shut.

Bill whispered, "Whoever it is is kind of stooped over. Like they're hiding from the guys fixing the car. I don't think they've seen us."

All of a sudden there was a small, blazing fire. Almost as quickly, there was a sound of splashing water, and the fire was doused out. There was a faint, lingering smell of smoke. The person, whoever he or she was, scampered away.

"C'mon." Bill nudged me. "Let's go see."

Hunched over, we ran across the road, ducking for cover as soon as we got to the other side. I felt like I was in a children's mystery story about an old house and a buried treasure.

With his flashlight, Bill led us along the trail of smoke.

"Here we are." He pointed with his flashlight to a small hole where the fire had been.

"Better throw a little more sand on it, to make sure it's out." True to my word, I knelt down and scooped some sand on the remnants of the blaze. "I used to be a Boy Scout," I explained.

Just off to the side of the firepit was a stray scrap of paper that hadn't quite finished burning. Bill and I both spotted it at the same time, and in some *Boy's Life* way that even I apparently hadn't quite gotten over, we both reached for it.

"*I've* got the flashlight," Bill haughtily reminded me, reaching down to read what it said. " 'Helena in the hospital,' " he read, shining the light so I could see it.

"Actually, it literally says, 'elena in the hospita,' " I noted, "but I think you grasped the general idea."

"Lord only knows what that means," Bill commented.

"Yeah, who can say?" I figured I'd leave it at that.

We wandered back over to Terry and Brick, who were deeply enmeshed in the grim task of getting the car to run, as though it somehow were cheating to leave the matter to AAA.

"Looky here." I brandished the scrap of paper in front of Terry.

He shined a flashlight on it. "I can't read what it says."

Impatiently, I told him. "Holy shit," Terry commented. "Do you think that maybe . . . ?"

"Who knows? But what else do we have to go on at this point besides a hundred fifty million people denying everything?"

"I resent the implication of what you're saying," Bill complained.

"Me, too." Brick intently studied a dipstick that he had removed from the engine. "Whatever he just said goes double for me."

Bill looked at his watch agitatedly. "We should really get down to the main road. I don't want to be stuck here all night."

Terry shut the hood of the car. "This does seem to be a lost cause. The car, I mean."

A cell phone was ringing. "That's me," Bill told us. "Sorry, we'll be right there," he spoke into the receiver. I could tell it was AAA.

I was thinking fast, which in my experience is the best way to think. "Call them back. Tell them you don't need them after all. We'll give you a ride, don't worry."

"Why?" Bill asked.

"Because," I explained, "we can use your help."

"I don't get it." Brick shut the hood of the Corvette.

"Look, if you're as innocent as you say you are, don't you want to help us figure this thing out so that we'll leave you the fuck alone?"

"I resent that," Bill protested. "I want the case solved *only* so that Ann-Margret gets out of jail. I need her."

"Suit yourself. The thing is, we just might be able to use your help."

Terry looked at me with this wary you-better-know-what-you're-doing expression. For in fact I was asking Bill and Brick to help us solve the very crime that either or both of them might well have committed. But, like the great Vanna White herself might have uttered, you use what you've got. Besides, as I thought about the whole thing, if Bill and/or Brick did kill Helena, they'd want to play along to keep close tabs on us.

"Yeah, we can use your help," Terry assured them. "Think of it as helping with police business." I had to hand it to Terry for trusting me enough to give me the benefit of the doubt.

"Well, gee—when you put it like that." Brick gave a guy-ish sort of crooked grin.

"Lay it on me," Bill agreed.

"Okay, guys, here's what we do . . ."

A few minutes later, we stood before an enormous fieldstone mansion, complete with turrets and spires. It loomed over the misty night Pacific like a black hole in space. The fury of deafening waves far below almost seemed like the moans of the house itself, as if someone were being endlessly tortured yet at the same time warning all who passed by to stay away. I thought I had a good working knowledge of the various mansions in L.A., but I'd never even heard tell of this strange, isolated monstrosity before.

The gargantuan front door was made from ornately carved oak, tinted green from years of abuse by the salt air. Bill grabbed hold of the heavy iron knocker that was fashioned into the head of Medusa.

"Not exactly a Martha Stewart touch," I noted as Bill banged on the door.

The house was completely dark save for a single light coming from the second of four stories. We watched as a figure carrying some sort of lamp descended the stairs.

A few moments later, an elderly gentleman in full livery opened the door—though only partially.

"Hi!" Bill brightly greeted him. "Remember us?"

The butler cleared his throat. "Yes," he allowed, then looked at Bill for more information—with an air that simultaneously signaled he didn't really want any.

"Our car broke down," Bill explained. "And my cell phone is dead."

"And we don't have another cell phone," Terry lied.

"And you are . . . ?" the butler asked.

"These are my assistants." Bill gestured smilingly at Terry and me. "I'm afraid we got our wires crossed, and they thought they were supposed to meet us here."

"We can get a ride to a phone with them," Brick conveyed.

"And we'd be happy to drive them," Terry added.

"But the thing is," Bill continued, "we'd still have to get the car fixed anyway, and we just figured that since we were right here, why not do it now?"

"It *is* hard to find your way back up here," Brick noted.

"So we were wondering if we could use your phone," Bill cheerfully concluded.

The butler stood there for a moment, thinking. "I suppose. But there is really only need for one of you to come inside. The rest of you gentlemen can enjoy the pleasant sound of the ocean surf. Madam always says she finds it most soothing."

"Uh, but I need to come in, too," Terry insisted. "I need to use the rest room."

"Me, too." Brick put his hands over his squirming legs to get the point across.

The butler looked at me. I nodded my head to signify a similar desire.

"I really think," the butler stated, looking furtively at something or someone on the other side of the door, "that you gentlemen should attend to your needs elsewhere. One of you may make a quick phone call, but that is all. The house is closed for the night."

Brick did a double take to express his disbelief. "What is this bullshit, anyway? You act like we're Mary and Joseph and there's no fucking room at the inn. What do you want me to do, take a dump on your front steps?"

"Uh, thank you anyway, sir." Terry tugged on the sleeve of Brick's jacket. But Brick squirmed free and punched the butler squarely across the jaw, knocking him out cold.

"What the fuck did you do that for?" I wanted to know. "If the butler didn't let us in right away, we were supposed to—"

"Fuck the plan." Brick blew on his hand, presumably because it smarted it a little. "I can't believe some creep would actually tell someone they couldn't take a goddamn crap in their house. When we find that snooty old battleax, I'm giving her a piece of my mind."

"Shouldn't be worth very much," Bill joked, as we all stepped inside the cavernous house. The foyer alone must have had a thirty-foot ceiling. The walls were made of stone, and the place was cold and drafty as a medieval castle. A winding grand staircase stood before us, the newels carved in the shape of gargoyles. The stone floors echoed from even the slightest foot-step. There were only a few candles lit here and there, and the imposing, old Gothic furniture seemed ghostlike in the throbbing amber glow.

Terry knelt down to examine the butler. "This is hardly by the book," he complained, gently tapping the butler's face to bring him back to conscious-ness. The older man moaned, coughed, and eased himself up on his elbows.

"Are you all right?" Terry asked him.

"Sir, please." The butler rubbed his jaw, fleshy with age. "Spare me. I'm . . . I'm only following madam's orders. If you want to steal something, please just be quick about it."

"We're not here to steal anything." Terry helped the man to a carved teak-wood chair. "We should get some ice on this." He felt around the man's jawline. "Tell me where it's most tender."

"I'm sure it's nothing that a brandy wouldn't fix." The butler gave a wink.

"Nothing's broken," Terry determined. "Now, please just tell us where we can find madam. We really only want a few minutes of her time."

"But *sirs*," the butler pleaded. "My job, first and foremost, is to make certain that madam is never disturbed."

"We can tie him up," Brick offered. "The old bag's gotta be around someplace."

"I don't think she'll want us to do the commission after this," Bill sadly noted.

*"On the contrary."*

We followed the booming voice to the grand staircase. Suddenly, an eight-tiered electric chandelier lit up above us. As we struggled to adjust to the unexpected burst of light, we saw, at the top of the stairs, a regal elder-ly woman in a long black hostess gown, decked out in what were probably her stay-at-home diamonds. She had that assurance about her that people often get as they grow into having tons of money—as if she deserved to have every last penny, and more.

"You boys *will* be working for me. Although I also should send you the doctor's bill for hurting poor Holloway."

Everything about her was so haughty and authoritative that, as she descended the staircase and came closer, it was almost impossible to believe she was Aunt Fern. Yet she was.

# TWENTY-FOUR

"GEEZE, AUNT FERN, I'M SORRY FOR CALLING YOU . . . LIKE, ALL
those things." Brick was extremely solicitous as he helped her into an
antique William and Mary chair. Its imposing Gothic arms and legs punc-
tuated the general mood of the musty sitting room, where our shadows
loomed like nimbus clouds. "If I knew it was you, I would never have said
what I did."

Aunt Fern laughed. Her long black dress blended in with the dim light-
ing, making her face, hands and diamonds eerily bright by comparison.
"That's quite all right, Brick. Aunt Fern may be a right-on old woman, but
Mrs. Creighton Westport *is* a stuffy old drag."

Terry, who had gone off with the butler to tend to his needs, stepped into
the room. "Mr. Holloway is sitting up with a brandy. I hope he'll be okay."

"Okay?" Aunt Fern laughed. "You made his day, if not his decade.
Holloway—not Mr. Holloway—has become such a fretful bore over the
years. It's high time something happened to him. Besides, he should have
let you in as my guests. I *wanted* you here. I'm afraid age is catching up to
the poor man."

As she kept talking, Aunt Fern—or Mrs. Westport—drifted back and
forth between her high society snobbish voice, and her down-to-earth,
unpretentious, Aunt Fern one. I noticed that the changes often occurred
upon the clearing of her throat, like an actress uncertain of the part she was
being asked to play.

Certainly nothing about the house yodeled "Aunt Fern." It was all about stale Oriental rugs on dark ceramic floors and gold-leaf doorways and cracked ceiling frescoes and formal draperies and scrolled furniture in dark wood tones. It was a Victorian-like clutter of vases and bowls and crystal lamps. There were grandfather clocks and suits of armor. Even more so than the difference in the woman herself, it was hard to imagine down-home-howdy Aunt Fern being at home in all this stuffy opulence.

"I suppose you'd all like to know what's going on," Aunt Fern commented dryly, as if the explanation were as simple and sensible as could be. "I expect that my other guests should be arriving shortly, so you'll all get to hear what I have to say at the same time." She dabbed her eye with a fine linen handkerchief. "I am willing to tell my story. But I have always disliked having to repeat myself."

"When you say other guests, Aunt Fern—I mean, Mrs. Westport—"

" 'Aunt Fern' is fine, Rick. As for the guests, I'm sure you know them all. Koko and Curtsy Ann and Basil from the show. And Tippi and Fernando. You see, a while ago, I heard a commotion outside. Men arguing. It was hard to see much in the fog, but when the flashlight shone on Rick, I recognized him right way from the fast way he walked. I realized that if Rick and Terry were going to be snooping around, they just might uncover some things that I would rather everyone heard from me. So I sent a limo to scoop everyone up." She smiled at Terry and me admiringly. "I must say I am impressed. Aunt Fern is very good at getting people to do whatever she asks. But you two remained firm. You didn't let me in on much of the goodies, so I couldn't control the situation to the extent I am normally accustomed to."

Terry threw up his hands in frustration. "Aunt Fern, I can't believe I'm asking this. Do you know who killed Helena?"

"Certainly not." She toyed with her long string of pearls.

"Are you *sure?*"

"Do you think I'd let that poor child suffer in jail for another minute if I *did?*" She rang her little hand bell for the butler. "Shame on you, Terry."

"Gee, sorry." He shifted his feet around, his huskiness belying his childlike embarrassment.

The butler appeared, with a big bruise under his right jowl. He stared straight ahead, giving no indication of having had an altercation with us.

Despite what Aunt Fern had said, I felt sorry for the old man—not only that Brick had punched him out, but that he'd been given all of thirty seconds to recover from it.

Aunt Fern counted intently on her fingers. "Brandies for . . . ten. And leave a full decanter, Holloway."

"Yes, ma'am." The butler turned on his heels.

"How do you know they're all coming?" Terry asked.

"I told the driver to tell them all it was an emergency. I'm sure that did the trick." She made a rather crude snort. "After all, I *am* Aunt Fern."

Needless to say, I had about a zillion questions, but it seemed the best thing to do was wait. We exchanged innumerable pleasantries over the house and its appointments. Brick wanted to know how everything was made, Terry wanted to *explain* how everything was made, Bill wanted to know where everything was from, while I, in my subtle way, tried to ask how much it all cost.

Finally, the limo pulled up. And sure enough, Holloway led into the sitting room the three women and two men that rounded out our tawdry list of suspects.

Any sort of customary greetings—or even the displeasure of seeing Terry and me yet again—got lost in the pervasive shock that this rich society matron in her imposing, dreary mansion was our own beloved Aunt Fern. Even Tippi and Fernando—who only knew Aunt Fern from watching her on TV, plus whatever else people said about her—were stunned to realize that Aunt Fern apparently lived some sort of bizarre double life. We all helped ourselves to brandy and settled into the ornate sofas, divans, or various chairs in a circle round the room. Aunt Fern's chair was the most regal of all, and the floral silk dividers framing the gilded mantle and walk-in fireplace behind her made it look almost like her throne.

"I've lived a long, dull life," Aunt Fern began. "I came from silly old Eastern money, and I married silly old Eastern money. My son, Leo, bless his soul, took a job as a CEO for a corporation located in Los Angeles. When my husband died—big deal—Leo coaxed me into moving out here. I didn't know what else to do, so I had this white elephant of a house constructed. It didn't go according to my plans at all. As you can see for yourselves, it came out so ominous and stuffy. I couldn't help thinking that it reflected something about *me*—that even when I wanted a fun beach house, I created the House of Frankenstein.

"One day, I turned on the TV, and there was a show about how to crochet. I can't explain it—but I liked what I saw. I started crocheting like there was no yesterday, today or tomorrow. Suddenly, I felt *lighter*, like maybe there was a drop or two of fun left in me after all. I knew that what I was doing was very good indeed. So that was when Aunt Fern's Homespun Originals was born. It was a lark, a hobby—at first. But soon people were writing about how much they enjoyed my latest pattern, and I realized that in my small way, I was finally making a difference in people's lives. I started a cable-access show that I paid for out of my own pocket. Then a legitimate sponsor picked it up, and I was on my way. And at my age! I knew of course that it wouldn't do to be Mrs. Creighton Westport. So I became Aunt Fern. My first name *is* Fern, though I'd always gone by my middle name of Marjorie. When need be, as Aunt Fern I use my maiden name. At first, I figured that if a reporter asked about my life, I'd tell the truth. But I found I quite enjoyed having two lives. I could retreat into being Mrs. Westport when I felt like it, and get away from everyone. People do tire me, you know. But then, when I wanted to be warm and social in a way that Mrs. Westport could never be, I could become Aunt Fern. My friends back East—the sort whom Brick would call a bunch of old biddies—probably don't even know that there is an Aunt Fern, and here in California I didn't know that many people anyway. None of them were my sort. And so the secret was easy to keep.

"I started branching out into design almost by accident. In my newsletter, I'd describe how a particular pattern would look on a particular sofa, and soon people were writing with questions about decorating. I knew that what they wanted were simple, country-looking rooms, so I learned what I could about country-style design and folk art. Before you could say 'Jane Hathaway,' I was getting offers to redo rooms and houses. I guess I just have a knack for getting money to follow me around like a Pekinese. Then *My House, Your House* came along, and I was bigger than ever."

"But what does all this have to do with Helena?" I asked.

"Mercy, Rick. You are *so* impatient." She took a medicinal swallow of brandy and poured herself a hearty refill. "I met Helena as my alter-ego—I mean, as Mrs. Westport. Through a friend of a friend who slept with some-body or whatever, I heard her work was worth taking a look at."

"Was it?" I asked.

She put her bejeweled hand to her bejeweled chest. "It was horrible. Awful. The most derivative garbage I'd ever seen. And yet, there was jaun-tiness to it, like a smart, stylish French girl wearing a beret. There was a *line* to it, a sense of color. Aunt Fern, of course, would not have gone *near* what Helena was doing, but as Mrs. Westport, I thought she was on to some-thing. I told her I'd die before I'd let her redesign so much as a loose thread in my house. But I took one look at her, and I did something I'd never done before with anyone, outside of my son—and Holloway, whom I knew could be trusted. I told her I was Aunt Fern."

"And she kept your secret?" Terry inquired.

"Positively. I made it expressly clear from the outset that she was to tell no one, that I guarded my privacy religiously. And Helena was always true to her word. That in itself was a continual source of comfort to me. No matter how tempting it became, Helena could be trusted to not tell a soul who I really was."

Tippi gave a sarcastic little spatter of applause. "Big fucking deal. She told a hell of a lot of souls things about other people,"

Aunt Fern sat up even straighter in her chair. "That may very well have been, Miss Finkelstein. But one does tend to judge others subjectively. Your problems with her were none of my concern. It was certainly not my fault if Helena simply liked me better than other people."

"Whatever." Tippi took a generous swallow of brandy.

"As I was saying," Aunt Fern continued, "I trusted Helena absolutely. She went to work for me. Opening my mail, working on new patterns, a lit-tle bit of everything. Through my son, she started getting some important designing jobs. I'd go over her plans with her, and make suggestions and improvements. Really, much of her eventual style came from me—Mrs. Westport, that is."

The reality of what she was saying was only now sinking in. It was one thing to believe that Aunt Fern had meant well when she was desecrating my living room. But to find out she wasn't even sincere about it made me more pissed off than I'd been in quite a while. "You mean to say that you could've given me a totally different room?"

She smiled wisely. "Not as Aunt Fern. Only as Mrs. Westport. And she, I'm afraid, designs rooms for no one."

I wanted to say a great many things in response to this—all of them rude and insulting—but decided it was best to let things slide for the time being.

"So when I say I loved Helena like a daughter," Aunt Fern assured us, "it was much more than a figure of speech. I nurtured her. I shaped her. I couldn't have been more proud. She was descended, you know, from *royalty*. And my, how it showed."

"Yeah, it showed, all right," Tippi remarked.

"A royal pain in the wazoo," Curtsy Ann added.

"Girls, really." Aunt Fern extended a warning index finger that dripped with diamonds. "This entire matter is most difficult for me. As I was saying, Helena was a true Mandarin in every sense of the word. Most of all, I watched most approvingly as she and my Leo fell in love. She made him *so* happy."

Aunt Fern started to cry. "Excuse me, children." She blew her nose into her handkerchief, and regained herself. "Then there came . . . the most terrible car accident. Leo was killed instantly. His neck snapped. One of those stupid doctors actually told me I should be *happy*, because the end had come so quickly." As she cried all over again, Koko and Curtsy Ann rushed over to comfort her. Curtsy Ann squeezed her plump arm, while Koko, less able to move about, made do with resting on the wooden arm of the chair, holding her hand. "Bless you, child." She stroked Curtsy Ann's shiny hair and beamed at her through her tears. Given her loyalty to Helena, Aunt Fern hadn't exactly been Curtsy Ann's idol, but then and there it didn't seem to matter. "And you, dear sweet Koko." Aunt Fern warmly squeezed her hand. "Isn't love all there is?"

In truth, it gave me the creeps when old people in particular said this type of thing. It always made me think that the person declaring it believed it the least of all, and it was disturbing to think that a lifetime of experience could add up to so little. But I obediently nodded my endorsement of what she'd just said, along with everyone else in the room.

"I'm afraid my horror was not over," Aunt Fern continued. "In my youth of course we did things differently—or at least we pretended to. But Helena was a modern girl, and she and Leo did apparently get familiar with each other. She was carrying his child. Not only did she lose the baby in the accident, but was told she could never get pregnant again. After that, of course, she became nothing but work-work-work. I imagine she also became quite envious of other people's happiness. But I couldn't blame her. Not really.

"We kept our secret for all these years. Even if I hadn't wanted to protect my privacy, I think we both just found it too painful to dwell on Leo and all that might have been. We of course did not get along to perfection. Who, I ask you, did not have their moments with Helena? But underneath it all, we of course felt nothing but love for each other. Love, as pure as the sea water outside my bedroom window." Aunt Fern stared at her brandy in the golden light of the authentic Tiffany lamp. "I asked Bill and Brick over tonight to build a memorial tribute for Helena here in my house. I was hoping I could keep myself a secret from them, but then the sight of Rick and Terry snooping about convinced me that would be futile. So here you all are. I must say, it's been such a long time since I've had any guests over. Everyone thinks of Aunt Fern as being so hospitable. No one notices that she doesn't say where she lives. She's just another old person, to be forgotten about as quickly as possible. And so I come clean before you all. I'm the worst kind of fake, because who I really am is so much more than who I pretend to be. I am also one very rich, very lonely old lady."

For quite a while, everyone was speechless.

Finally, I felt the need to say something. "Aunt Fern, that was a very moving story. But it doesn't bring us any closer to knowing who killed Helena."

"Did I say it would? I thought that was your job." Aunt Fern had always said these kinds of things in a manner suggesting that she regarded virtually everyone she met as a hired hand. Only now it seemed less impishly eccentric and more a snob's assumption of entitlement.

"Well, somebody has to wrap this up." Terry assumed his military demeanor, pacing about like a sergeant trying to shame one of his G.I.s into volunteering for a dangerous mission. "Curtsy Ann," he scolded, towering over the former Miss Texas, who avoided looking at him. "It's hard to figure out what's the real story with you. But one thing we know for certain is that you hated Helena. Your alibi is flaky. The maid could easily have lied about where you were that night. You're exacting, yet you twist things around. A dangerous combination, to say the least. And you're unforgiving—"

"Unforgiving?" Curtsy Ann protested. "My religious values have always taught me that forgiveness is the greatest virtue. 'Judge not, lest ye be judged.' These are the words I live by." You'd have thought she was speaking to the pageant judges.

Terry sipped his brandy. "Do tell. The thing is, when it comes to Helena and Brick, your piety goes right out the window."

Curtsy Ann put a hand to her flabbergasted chest. "Are you suggesting I'm . . . unbalanced?"

"We wouldn't dream of it," I put in. "We're merely saying that you might be a murderer."

"Well, that's just ridiculous. I deplore all forms of violence. I even step out of the way of an ant." She patted down the edges of the antique lace antimacassar on her overstuffed chair. "Unless, of course, it's inside my house."

"Speaking of Brick." I raised my drink in his direction. "You, my good man, most decidedly did *not* hate Helena. But you don't hate money, either. Since you're not exactly Mr. Conscience, maybe, just maybe, you were willing to do Helena in. With a little prompting from Tippi. Unless we're back at square one, so to speak, with the beautiful Curtsy Ann."

Brick chuckled to himself and shook his head, for want of knowing how else to respond. Tippi, though, was not about to take the accusation lightly.

"You love it, don't you?" she hissed at me. "You walk up to someone's entire life and then you flick with your thumb and forefinger and watch the whole thing collapse like a house of cards. Who cares if it's a lie? Who cares how it makes them feel?"

The odd thing about her belligerence was that she didn't appear concerned with being accused of murder *per se*, but some larger principle about reporters and gossip. I imagined her getting strapped down into the gas chamber, and, when asked if she had any final words, saying something like: "Yes, I object to the innuendos and attacks on my dignity that have hounded me throughout this ordeal."

"So I take it you aren't the president of my fan club. Nonetheless, you might have killed Helena."

Tippi stared at me challengingly. "I thought you said I paid Brick to do it."

"Same difference."

"Well, I didn't do either. Kudos, though, to whoever did." She stood up to pour herself another drink.

"In that case," I pronounced, "perhaps the congrats should go to Basil and Fernando, either or both." I winked at them as they sheepishly squirmed about the antique aubergine divan. "So many secrets, so little time. How much simpler life in the closet would be if only Helena's big mouth could get permanently shut with acrylic glaze."

"You should know that I'm contemplating a lawsuit," Fernando told me.

I stifled a yawn; the mellowness of the brandy was going to my head. "I guess that'll have to take a back burner to the criminal charges you're facing. Plus somehow I don't think you'll want to risk putting me on the witness stand."

"Well, maybe not," Fernando admitted.

"I oppose violence as a solution to any problem," Basil insisted. "I'm a pacifist."

"Easier said than done," I replied. "I've never known a peacenik who, underneath it all, wasn't the same total shit as everyone else."

"Rick, that's such a negative thing to say." Basil frowned with concern for my well-being. "If I were you, I'd try to find where inside me that kind of attitude is coming from."

I was tempted to reply "Yes, Master," but then thought the better of it. "Basil, since you're so into exploring your true feelings, tell us how you really felt about Helena. Tell us how you feel knowing that she didn't live long enough to out you to the world."

Basil swallowed hard. "I'm devastated, of course."

"I can tell. The thing I still don't get is why you guys were so certain that Ann-Margret is innocent. Certain enough to even risk going to jail yourselves."

"Did *all* of you know about that?" Terry asked, like a stern schoolteacher. "Were all of you in on the secret of where my cousin was hiding?"

Like contrite children, they all shamefacedly raised their hands—everyone but Aunt Fern, that is. Terry glared at her, and soon her hand went up, too.

"What else is everyone hiding?" Terry wanted to know. "Whatever it is, my cousin is hiding it, too. She's sitting in jail right now, because she knows something about the night of Helena's murder, and she won't come clean."

Tippi twisted her hair around her finger. "Well, maybe she *did* do it." When this assertion was met with a thick, hostile silence, she hastily added, "It *is* possible, isn't it?"

"So much for having the audience in the palm of your hand," I remarked. Tippi shot me a dirty look as she polished off her brandy.

"Then there's Koko," Terry continued. "And then there's also Bill. And then there's Koko and Bill. Koko said she wanted to kill Helena. No wait, *Bill* said he wanted to kill Helena. Or they both did. And get this—it was on the night Helena was murdered."

Koko gave a wan smile. "Gee, small world, huh?"

Bill, who sat next to her on the Sheraton sofa, reached over to clasp her hand. "Don't even listen to them, babe. How ungentlemanly can you get, accusing a woman in her condition of such a terrible thing?"

"Bill, you're forgetting one slight detail. We're also accusing *you*. As you may recall, there was a small matter of Helena letting the cat out of the bag about a possible incident from your wild, impetuous youth."

"Rick, that's really low. After our time together in the woods—"

The look on everyone's face made him stop. "Hey, I don't mean anything like *that*. I'm just saying that Rick and I found that burnt scrap of paper thing."

"What scrap of paper?" Aunt Fern seemed to grow ever more powerful in her imposing chair as she demanded an answer.

"A scrap from the papers you had the butler burn," I evenly answered. "It said something about Helena being in the hospital."

"I cannot believe you would rummage through my private things." She said this as though I had dressed all in black and then picked the lock on her jewelry box. "I can still see Helena sitting in that hospital room. I ordered Holloway to burn everything I wrote in my diary from that awful time. I just couldn't have it around anymore. That Bill and Brick would be lurking about seemed as good excuse as any to get rid of the thing."

Plus of course she'd already admitted that she knew Terry and I were hanging around, but I didn't think it prudent to go there just yet. Besides, maybe it was after the burning of the diary that she spotted us.

"Was it a white room?" I asked instead.

Aunt Fern dismissed me with her hands. "I imagine so. It was a *hospital*. Why?"

"Just wondering."

"It *wasn't* a white room," Basil confirmed. Everyone turned to look at him. "We were talking once about design. I said I was all about what looked pleasing to the eye, but Helena told me it was all about what a color or fabric reminded her of. She said she had a terrible memory about being in a hospital, and so she never did anything in what she called 'hospital green.'"

"Why didn't you tell us this before?" Terry inquired. "We *asked* you about the white room. It might have helped."

Basil looked at the silver ring on his finger; it was shaped like a crescent moon. "But you didn't ask about a green room. Look, I was trying to not get involved. I wanted you guys to go away."

Terry sarcastically applauded. "Finally, a little crumb of truth. Look, what is it with you people? What are you hiding, what are you trying to—"

His cell phone rang. "Damn this fucking thing," he rather uncharacteristically commented. Sighing, he quickly added, "Please excuse my French."

"Yes, *hello*, Darla Sue." He rubbed his temples for her excruciating interruption. "I can't talk now. Yeah, okay, I'll take a look at the lawn mower." He shook his head in aggravation. "Look, I really have to . . . did who *what*? . . . Are you sure? *Really* sure? . . . Well, you should've said something . . . No, that's not what I mean . . . Yeah, okay . . . I'll call later . . ." Almost as an afterthought, he murmured, "Thanks."

He shut off his phone, staring blankly, as if in a daze.

"Maybe it's hypnosis," I suggested.

"Maybe what is?" Terry asked, still not completely back to normal.

"This strange hold your ex-wife has over you. Maybe there's some secret word she says—'donut' would be my guess—that sends you into this mad swoon of devotion."

I was waiting for him to tell me to fuck off as per usual, but instead he turned to me and stated, "Rick, we need to talk. *Now.*"

"Uh, nobody go anywhere, okay?" I flakily insisted, as Terry grabbed my arm to lead me out into the foyer. The grandfather clock behind him told me it was nearly midnight.

He put his hands on my shoulders. "Darla Sue," he whispered meaningly.

"Yes, I recognize the name." I pulled away from his grip. "How's for making sense?"

"She said that she lost a cigarette lighter, and had you or I found it? Because the last time she remembered using it was when she heard about Helena and Dr. Murphy. I didn't know what she meant. It turns out that over the weekend, Darla Sue heard Aunt Fern on the phone. Aunt Fern said the name 'Helena,' and she said the name 'Dr. Murphy,' and something about how Helena would have to tell her what Dr. Murphy said, and how this was wonderful news. When I asked her why she didn't say anything about this sooner, she said she hadn't wanted to bother me about the lighter right away."

"Darla Sue said all *that*?" I could scarcely believe that Terry's ex could form whole sentences, let alone recount a conversation with names and everything.

"Give it a rest, Rick. But this Dr. Murphy must have been the 'Dr. M' on that list that Helena wrote. Not Koko's Dr. Mallory, after all."

"Ergo, there might be a connection here as to what was making Helena so upset that last day of her life. Even if Aunt Fern did think it was 'wonderful news.'"

"Well, duh." He gave me a supposedly good-natured slap across the head. "What was this wonderful news? Obviously not that she was pregnant. That would've come up in the autopsy."

"Obviously." I rubbed my temple in pain, feeling around for my dislocated cerebellum. "Besides, Aunt Fern said Helena couldn't have kids after the accident."

"And the drunk driver who caused the accident was in prison." Terry snapped his fingers. "I can get his name."

"And I'm remembering something else." I got out my cell phone. "A bunch of things, actually. Something that Helena said when she almost electrocuted herself. Then something Ann-Margret said in your kitchen after we found the body."

Terry was clearly on the same wavelength. "And then Aunt Fern, in Boxer's office. Or Curtsy Ann telling us about Helena's dream."

"Plus, I'm remembering the fabric that Helena's body was wrapped in. And let's not forget how Fernando claimed he got onto Helena's hit list."

I made a few quick phone calls, and so did Terry. A few minutes later, we walked back into the oppressive, Gothic living room.

"We know who killed Helena." I tried to sound low-key about it all. I've always hated overacting.

"Backup will be here any minute," Terry interjected. "So no one try anything stupid." He marched into the room, waving a pair of handcuffs. "Jesus, I hate doing this." But he took a deep breath and stated: "Aunt Fern—I mean, Fern Westport—you are under arrest for the murder of Helena Godiva."

# TWENTY-FIVE

IF LOOKS COULD KILL—IF YOU'LL PARDON THE EXPRESSION—THEN Aunt Fern would have added Terry to her list of victims. She said nothing while he cuffed her, but stared at him with an indignation that would have made Queen Elizabeth II look like a Hollywood Boulevard hooker by comparison. When the horrified butler hurried in to intervene, Aunt Fern smiled bravely and scolded him to mind his own business. "Really," she insisted. "Madam is fine, Holloway. Just see to it that our guests have more brandy."

"Dear Aunt Fern." Koko touched her shoulder as the butler tearfully refilled the decanter. "Those handcuffs must really hurt. Guys, can't you at least . . . ?"

"Don't look at me," I replied. "I ain't no cop."

"Sorry, Koko," Terry answered. "I had no choice. She put these handcuffs on herself."

"This is obscene." Basil stood up, indignant, though Fernando tugged on his pants that he should sit down again—and presumably stop trying to get involved. "If Aunt Fern murdered Helena," Basil decreed, "my name is Sophia Garbo."

"It's *Loren*," Fernando corrected.

"What—his name is Basil Loren?" Brick pondered aloud. Curtsy Ann guiltily bit her lip to keep from laughing, while Tippi flushed with embarrassment for her boyfriend's lack of mental agility.

"*Whatever,*" Basil continued. "I can't believe you guys would treat this poor old woman so heartlessly."

"She's not poor," I tactfully replied, "and not too old to be a murderer."

Aunt Fern held her head imperiously high. "I'm old-fashioned. I prefer the term 'murderess.' But what on earth would possess you boys to think I murdered Helena? I *told* you, I love her like a daughter."

"Yeah, damned right," Brick affirmed. "What gives with you guys?"

"Say it and get it over with." Bill poured himself another brandy. "Whatever it is, it has to be wrong."

"We only wish it were, Bill," I replied. "But we found out a few things. Things that Aunt Fern was hoping would never come out. She had us all come over tonight not to come clean, but to stay dirty in selective places. She left out numerous choice tidbits. Such as the fact that Helena went to see a doctor during her lunch break on the first day of shooting."

"A fertility specialist, to be exact," Terry elaborated. "She saw a Doctor Murphy, seeking his counsel on how to get pregnant. Aunt Fern knew all about it. Darla Sue heard her on the phone talking to Helena, gushing on about what wonderful news it was."

I looked to see if there was some telltale response on the part of Bill or Brick, some flicker that suggested Helena might have discussed having a baby with either or both of them. But neither one betrayed any such notion.

"Well, what does that prove?" Bill asked instead. "Aunt Fern thought it was wonderful. You said so yourself, Rick."

"I said she told Helena it was wonderful news. Ain't the same thing as believing it. But then, Helena knew what nobody else knew—that jolly old Aunt Fern wasn't someone to fuck with."

"Rick, *please*," Aunt Fern bristled. "Such language."

"I'm not following," Brick admitted.

"I hate to say it, but I feel the same way," Tippi interjected.

I poured myself a hefty refill. "Look, be patient, okay?"

"Hey, maybe some of the rest of us would like some brandy, too," Brick lectured. "Ever hear of sharing?"

Though my mind reeled with retorts, I remained focused on the task at hand. "You see, gang—way back when, Leo got into an accident, all right. But it seems that our friend, the drunk driver, was suddenly released from prison the day Helena was murdered. Talk about a coincidence. But then, Aunt Fern herself said something odd the other day in Boxer Jones's office. She said how ever since the accident she had a special concern over people being killed, or the wrong person being put in jail. But what exactly *did* this accident have to do with putting the wrong person in jail?"

"Ironically," Terry continued, "the man owes his freedom to Aunt Fern. She got a high-powered lawyer to grant him clemency from the governor in nothing flat. But her good deeds extended only so far that day."

I walked over to her. "What was it, Aunt Fern—or I guess I should say, Mrs. Westport? What did Helena tell you that made you get the poor guy released from prison? It must have been something about Leo, because he's the only other person who could've caused the accident. Because Helena was not in the car with Leo, was she? She was already in the hospital, suffering a miscarriage. You see, I heard her trying to confide in Ann-Margret, after she saved her from electrocuting herself—for all the good it did her. Helena said it was a dream she kept having—and once she almost told Curtsy Ann what it all meant—but from what we've learned about her, maybe it was more than a dream. Maybe it was her furtive way of trying to talk about something she was forbidden to talk about."

"A man kept beating her," Terry continued, "only it was a nightmare based on an actual memory, wasn't it? That's why she told Fernando back when he tended bar that the father took care of it for her. And also raped her. But it wasn't that he gave her money, was it? Did she tell him she wanted to keep the baby? And what—Leo responded by beating the crap out of her? Is that why she couldn't have children?"

Aunt Fern stood up, and, for want of being able to slap me, spat in my eye. "My son was an angel," she hissed. "He would never have forced himself upon her. They were *dating*."

"Or so you wished to believe," Terry corrected. "After all, you were giving Helena everything she ever wanted for her career. How could she tell you that she didn't like your son? Especially when you kept forcing him on her."

"A most uncouth young man, despite his breeding," I added. "Wasn't there an incident of him being accused of raping—"

"Those charges were dropped!" Aunt Fern pounded on her lap with her cuffed wrists. "The girl was a gold digger. We paid her off handsomely for her troubles, I can assure you."

I stood over her, and set down my brandy. "Whatever. But that was the white room, wasn't it? A room she was designing when he beat her."

Aunt Fern stared back at me with pure contempt in her eyes. "It was Leo's child. *My* grandchild. She had no right to decide for us all. I even tried paying her to marry him. I mean, what was so *wrong* with him? He had money. A good career. Any girl should've felt honored." A tear rolled down her cheek. "I don't blame him. I'd have done the same thing myself."

"Your sense of family loyalty is touching," Terry noted. "So what happened—did you pay Helena off in the hospital to keep her mouth shut?"

"In the end, they all want money," Aunt Fern insisted. "They say it's the principle of the thing, or they say it's their grief and sorrow. But in the end, they take your money. Helena was no different. She could have been a common *demimonde*."

"A common *what*?" Brick asked.

"A *whore*," Basil explained.

"Yeah, you would know what that meant," Brick answered back, pleased as always by his own cleverness.

Aunt Fern could not help rolling her eyes. "Anyway, I never believed for a minute Helena really wanted to keep the baby. Or have *any* babies. She'd even thought about . . . doing away with it with *him*."

She looked right at Fernando—which caused everyone else to, as well. "Hey, I didn't do anything," he reasoned. "It's not like I knocked her up. I didn't even go with her. What's everyone on my case for?"

"Why *indeed*?" Aunt Fern asked haughtily, as though it were Fernando's indifference that set in motion all the tragedy that was to follow—as though he should have known his ultimate purpose was to accommodate her needs.

Terry paused to drink his brandy. "But anyway, Leo beats her, and drives off before the medics arrive. There's no record of anyone else in the car with him. Was the accident really his fault? Was it road rage? Was he drunk? Stoned? Or just careless, speeding along at a hundred miles an hour to not be around if anyone asked questions?"

Aunt Fern looked away from Terry. "There was never any proof about that. He was dead, for God's sake. While the other driver was drunk as a skunk. He'd even had two DUIs. It was a blessing to have him behind bars."

"Then why the guilty conscience? Why get him released the day you killed Helena?"

"I'm sure I have no idea what you mean."

"Anyway," Terry went on, "a few years go by, and Helena decides to have a baby. So she makes an appointment to see what can be done. The doctor must have told her that there was reason to hope she could get pregnant. But she knows she has to take care of some old business first. Because part of the pay-off was over the fact that she could never have children."

Aunt Fern sadly nodded her head, causing her earrings to jangle. "It's true. I was generous to Helena. And all I got in return was one lie after another." Koko attentively wiped the older woman's tear-stained face.

"So there the two of you were," I conjectured. "Face to face in the motel room. Helena stood up to you, didn't she? She was determined to finally live her own life. That's why she was so preoccupied all day. She told you to fuck off. Maybe she even paid you back the hush money."

Aunt Fern swallowed back a round of sniffles. "She did nothing of the sort."

Terry touched her shoulder and quietly advised, "Please, Aunt Fern. Stop denying the truth. You'll only keep making it worse."

Aunt Fern laughed bitterly. "Oh, poppycock. You and your 'truth.' You have it completely wrong. You think that conniving little wimp had principles? She blackmailed me. She called me that afternoon and told me about the doctor and said she was planning on having a baby and living her own life, and I was to stay out of it. She said that if I caused her any trouble, she'd go public about Leo's accident. That he caused it—as if she even knew if that were true. Well, to stall for time, I pretended that it was all just the jolliest news about possibly getting pregnant, and that I was *sure* the other matter could be worked out. But I knew there was a simple way out for me. The man in prison was due to be released in another year, anyway, and I don't much appreciate being blackmailed. So I made a call or two, and had him released."

"That was big of you. I suppose you also tossed a bone or two his way to make him willing to publicly contradict Helena, and say he really had been at fault."

"Rick, don't even think about getting holier than thou. Not after the smut you print about people." She shifted about uncomfortably on her chair; nothing like being handcuffed to put a damper on the illusion of elegance. "But as I was saying, later that night, I was driving around for more fabric like I always do. I bought some lovely gold material that I was going to use in your living room. And so I thought I might as well surprise Helena at her motel room. I knew she'd still be up—she never slept during a taping, either. I told her to forget about blackmailing me—the man had been released, and yes, given some money for his trouble.

"She did the oddest thing. She started crying and said, 'Very well, then. I always knew it would come to this.' She wrote out a check for the same sum of money I'd given her years ago. 'I'm buying back my freedom,' she told me. 'I'm going to go public with what Leo did to me. I should've done it years ago. I never should have let you pay me off.' She acted like I was some sort of *monster.*" Aunt Fern started crying again; after a moment, she recovered herself. "Well, I couldn't let her say that about my Leo. I could barely stand hearing it, let alone sit back and watch it become . . . common gossip. 'Everyone will know,' she kept saying, with that smug face of hers. There was a big tub she'd brought from the work site, along with these bottles of acrylic glaze. I had no choice. My son's honor was at stake. *My* honor. I grabbed her by the throat. At first I thought I'd choke her with my bare hands, but I dragged her over to the bucket of glaze.

"It was the oddest thing. She offered no resistance—or none that I remember. I *am* stronger than people may realize. Still, there was this look in her eyes. It was as if she was telling me that she's always known that it would come to this, and so I might as well get it over with. Or maybe she was gloating, because she knew somehow I wouldn't get away with it."

"Or maybe," I suggested, "it's hard to fight back when you're being choked."

Aunt Fern paid no attention to what I'd said. She wasn't crying now. If anything, she was elated—like she was the star of an opera, and no one was going to spoil her big aria. "I held her down into the bucket, I just held her and held her, until I knew she was dead."

Strange as it may seem, Aunt Fern was actually smiling. "My only regret is that the timing was off."

"Come again?"

"Well, you see, Rick, if only Helena had gone to that fertility doctor sooner. Leo, bless his heart, had had some of his . . . you know, seeds frozen before he died. For posterity."

"Don't tell me that you—"

"Why, of course, Rick. If it had happened a few years ago, when she still was minding her place with me, maybe she finally could have had Leo's baby. As it was meant to be."

"But he raped her, dammit!" Tippi stood up, her face flushed to bright crimson. "How can you even—"

"No, he did not rape her," Aunt Fern replied evenly. "My son was not a rapist."

I could barely believe what I was hearing. "And you'd go to any lengths to convince yourself, wouldn't you? Even if it meant . . . never mind."

"But you weren't quite done," Terry pointed out. "Why the gold fabric?"

"I had the fabric in my car, and I figured, why not?" She conveyed this like a naughty grandma who'd mischievously bought her grandchild a toy, despite the parents' admonishments not to do so. "It served her right, after doing such awful things to people's rooms."

"Why not indeed?" I poured myself a hefty refill. Of course, the same charge of questionable taste could have been levied against Aunt Fern herself, but it seemed a minor point under the circumstances.

"I thought you liked her rooms, that you liked Helena?" Terry asked.

"I admired her spirit. But when I realized she had none, there was nothing left. Sometimes I think all those fancy new terms like 'cutting edge' are just a chicken-shit way of saying someone's nuts."

"I declare, she can swear."

"Shut up, Rick," Terry instructed. "That's unnecessary."

"Still, the gold fabric seems less than coincidental."

"Whatever do you mean, Rick?" Aunt Fern squirmed about, full of indignation.

"Leo, a name of royalty, combined with gold, the color of royalty. It was your way of getting back at Helena. Doing to her what she'd done to other people, with all her symbolic colors and theme rooms and whatnot." I didn't bother to add that it was precisely the kind of crazy subconscious imperative that was so often the earmark of more psycho murderers.

"Oh please," Aunt Fern sighed. "Spare me your mumbo-jumbo. It was the material I happened to have in my car, pure and simple."

"What about the fan?" Terry asked.

Aunt Fern shrugged. "What about it? I tied a rope around her neck, stood up on the bed, tied the other end around the fan, and made a pulley. Don't they teach those basic things in school anymore? I swear, the level of education has declined so tragically since I was a girl. We need rigor. We need the three Rs."

"And that was it, then?" I inquired.

"Well, you'd better believe I put some real elbow grease into cleaning up after myself."

"What about Ann-Margret?" Terry wanted to know. "Why did she fail some of her polygraph?"

"You'll have to ask her," Aunt Fern replied, seeming a bit insulted that we would inquire about someone else. "I haven't the *slightest* idea."

"But I guess we know why you helped her escape," I shared. "To make her look bad. In fact, I'm sure you scared her into it in the first place."

Aunt Fern stared at me without blinking, her voice neither loud not soft. "I only wanted to help her. She was frightened of the guard. I saw no reason for her to be in prison, since I knew perfectly well she was innocent. I can't tell you how horrified I was when it turned out her fingerprints were on the container."

"I think you were out to frame her," Terry insisted.

*"I told you, I only wanted to help her."*

The sound of a police siren told us that the backup had arrived. Koko and Curtsy Ann were crying in each other's arms, while Fernando put his arm around the perturbed but dry-eyed Basil. Tippi yawned, stretched, and rested her head on Brick's shoulder. Brick, for his part, appeared to be way out of his depth, as if he couldn't even imagine how to react. Bill drank up like it was last call in the bar, and shook hands with Terry and me. "Nice work, guys," he sportingly told us. "Sorry I doubted you."

Terry ludicrously turned to me, and in dead seriousness asked, "Do you think you would have liked the solid gold fabric more than the yellow gingham we ended up using?"

I sighed from exhaustion. "I'm sure the yellow gingham is fine, Terry."

As the police led off Aunt Fern, she paused to look at us. "I'm sure you'll have plenty of time to talk to Ann-Margret now."

# TWENTY-SIX

THE MURDER CHARGES AGAINST ANN-MARGRET WERE DROPPED that same night. As for her having escaped from jail, even the likes of Marion Goober was shrewd enough not to push his luck. As Boxer succinctly phrased it, "Fuck off, or we're talking lawsuit." (Indeed, the charges were likewise dropped against Basil, Bill, and Fernando.) As Ann-Margret hurriedly left the courthouse, followed by a swarm of reporters, she cried in Terry's arms, then in mine, and then in Boxer's, thanking all of us about a million times over. Savoring her freedom, she ignored the reporters and camera operators completely, as if they were flies to be shooed away, and confidently walked toward the Cherokee with Terry and me.

But otherwise, Aunt Fern got it wrong. We didn't have much time to talk to Ann-Margret. By the next morning, she decided to climb aboard her Harley and take off up the California coast. "I need to clear my head," she explained, revving up in front of her upscale Malibu condo. But as she put on her helmet, she told Terry and me, "I was with someone in my motel room when Helena got murdered. That's why I failed the polygraph."

"Who were you with?" I asked.

She gave a kittenish smile. "J.T. Rex. He came back to town at the crack of dawn. I was trying to keep Koko from knowing about it, especially given her condition. She'd been on the phone with me, freaking out because he'd been with Helena. I didn't want to add insult to injury, if I could help it."

Terry was utterly dumbfounded. "How could you? His wife is going to have a baby."

"I didn't." She flexed her manicured fingers on the handlebars. "Not ever. But it turned out he kind of admired me from afar. When he called me from the airport, he said he'd had a few, but would I please meet with him because it was very important. I had no idea what to expect. But he . . . what the hell, it's the truth. He asked me to marry him. Just like that. I was floored."

"What did you say?" I asked.

"I told him that he just had cold feet now that he was starting a family, and that he was drunk, and that he should go home to his wife. Not long after that, I went to wake up Helena."

"That's my girl." Terry kissed her on her helmeted forehead.

"But anyway, I was really trying to avoid Koko finding out about it."

"That makes sense," I assured her.

"Later, guys." She waved to us. "Tell Bill I said to fuck off."

We watched as she sped off down the highway. "I told you she's really a good girl," Terry proudly gushed, wiping an errant tear from his eye.

"I know. How boring."

"Shut up, Rick. Why do you always have to spoil everything?"

Aunt Fern's trial wouldn't be starting for another year. The fickle crowds in the courtroom, however, cheered when she was denied bail, given what the newly assigned D.A. called the "exceptionally heinous nature of the crime."

"Then I'll just have to make a nice home for myself in jail," Aunt Fern defiantly told the judge. As if getting the last word in a crazed, Bette Davis sort of way, Aunt Fern from then on out gave all her exclusive interviews to Chauncey Riggs, and refused to meet with me again.

In the meantime, some of the other folks from *My House, Your House* made some news on their own. Nothing like being connected to a sordid murder to make your name a wee bit more recognizable to the general public. Aunt Fern, it could be said, was like the Tonya Harding of DIY—her evil made superstars out of everyone else.

Basil soon announced to the world that he was a) gay and b) leaving his wife. When he started getting hate mail about it, Tarragon, to her credit, came out herself. The producers of *MHYH* insisted that Basil would not get sacked for his revelations, though coincidentally enough he left the show shortly thereafter over what were termed "creative differences." Basil issued a statement to the effect that he felt he'd be happier working as a private designer. He and Tarragon agreed to share custody of the kids. Basil got to keep the remarkable underground home, since Tarragon was designing what she described as a "tree house" for Winnie and herself.

Fernando, alas, dropped Basil like a hot potato, given that he certainly could not afford to be seen in public with an openly gay man. *Badges of Philly* was still a hit show, however, so presumably Fernando found other things to occupy his mind. Basil, last I heard, was still wistfully single, scouring the leather bars for that special someone.

Curtsy Ann remained on the show, but she wasn't one to rest on her laurels. Instead, she published a self-help book entitled *Designing Your Way to Happiness*. In it, she explained how to become one with God, lose weight, find happiness in marriage, make millions, and overcome all addictions through learning the fundamentals of good interior design. Though it made little logical sense, the book included many full-color photos of her as Miss Texas. As one would have expected, the book was a runaway best-seller, and soon all sorts of Miss Texas wannabes were standing in line to attend Curtsy Ann Thomas seminars on "Designing a New You." To date, she still wasn't married, though she often winked at reporters and told them her work kept her too busy to think about men.

Bill McCoy went through a phase of arriving at a house with his shirt already taken off, but somehow the fans preferred the element of tease, so he reverted to his old ways. He was commissioned by a new theme park called "Dinosaur Disco" to design the dancing cages for the robotic triceratopses. The scandal sheets linked him to a couple of TV starlets here and there, but he still had to keep denying rumors that he was gay. A highlight of Bill's career was his acting debut on *7th Heaven*, playing an embittered interior designer who had to choose between paying for surgery to save a little girl's life and paying for a fixer-upper mansion that he'd always wanted to redesign. PS: The little girl got her new liver. Those of us fortunate enough to have known the real Bill truly were impressed by his courage in letting himself be cast so dramatically against type.

Yet, on the other hand, Bill eventually did construct a tribute to Helena much like the one he described to us that cold, windy night along the coast. It was like a small-scale Parthenon, and was on permanent display at the lobby of IDTV headquarters. There was a tiny fountain off to one side into which hopeful souls could toss a coin and make a wish. The coins were periodically donated to a local homeless shelter.

Brick cropped up frequently as a judge on cable wet T-shirt contests and the like, and published a book of his own entitled *Carpentry A to Me*. On the dust jacket was a ditzy photo of a befuddled Brick looking into the camera while pointing at himself. Tippi broke up with him not long after the murder, and presumably he was making mischief pretty much as he had before.

Tippi, for her part, got her own short-lived sitcom called *Tippi!* in which she played a struggling East Village performance artist who moonlighted as a hot dog vendor. The conspicuous failure of the show gave her plenty of kvetchy new standup material. She married—and divorced five weeks later—a struggling screenwriter whom she'd earlier fired from her show. Before *Tippi!* got the ax, I called to set up an interview for her to plug it, and she hung up on me.

Koko and J.T. are expecting their second child. He became a judge on a popular teen karaoke show called *You're All That*, which made him richer than all his years in the recording studio. Koko still emcees *MHYH*, admonishing the designers to hurry up and finish and to stay within their budgets.

None of these people kept in touch with Terry or me, save for Basil, who sent me a postcard from the Yucatan. He wrote he'd had a dream that Helena was designing a new house made entirely from clouds, and she wanted him to help her paint them every color of the rainbow. I wasn't sure why he told me this, and could not think of how to respond. (When I later said hello to him at a gay rights fundraiser, he walked passed me without saying anything.)

My own feelings toward Helena had shifted quite a bit. I thought about how beholden she'd been to crazy Aunt Fern all those years, and her brief, dark victory in standing up to her in the motel room. Maybe Helena's diabolical designs weren't just about a lack of confidence, after all. Maybe some of it was a festering, unconscious drive to make other people feel the same pain she did over the secrets that life burdens us all with. As for why someone with such a phobia of white rooms would go out of her way to wear white, I could only chalk it up to Helena's strangely defiant nature—so frightened and yet so bold.

Stopping by the fountain Bill made to toss in a silver dollar, all the mess she'd made didn't seem to matter, and I found myself missing her.

But otherwise, I guess the whole thing was pretty much something everyone wanted to forget. Getting caught lying and wishing someone dead who really does die—not to mention people digging around for the relative kinkiness of your sex life, or lack of it—is not exactly the proven Dale Carnegie method for making friends and influencing people.

Helena's last episode never aired. By the time Aunt Fern got busted, the whole thing had become so sordid that it no longer bespoke the wholesome image of IDTV. Lord knows the ratings would have gone through the roof of Mount Olympus, but every now and then even money-grabbing producers give a token nod to what used to be called decorum. Moreover, some closed-door meetings between the bigwigs at HNTV and IDTV and a slew of lawyers resulted in the banning of my behind-the-scenes documentary on the filming of a supposedly typical episode of *My House, Your House*. So all that final footage of Helena and Aunt Fern has been laid to rest in a vault someplace, to decompose or get mislabeled or whatever else happens to sad old news stories.

*My House, Your House* itself obviously needed some replacements, seeing as how one of its designers had murdered another one. First to come on board was Happy Logan, a New Age type who found inspiration not in major themes like Bill or Helena but in odd little everyday things she encountered. "Design is *everywhere*," she was prone to comment. And so Happy would turn to her feta cheese salad as the inspiration for her latest design, or the design on her mouse pad. One could only wait with eager curiosity for her to use, say, her last pap smear as the focal point for someone's kitchen. Happy's other main distinction was her dogged fanaticism about staying under budget. What exact measurements were to Curtsy Ann, saving money was to Happy. Her designs would come in at, like, seven hundred dollars, and rather than take the extra bucks to buy something nice for the room, she would leave it at that, as if having won a contest.

Basil's replacement was a foppish Englishman named Maurice (pronounced "Morris") Branford-Norris, although an erroneous rumor persisted that his name was *Maurice-Branford* Norris. He dressed in that mod Edwardian style from the sixties, and some people on the *MHYH* message board called him Austin Powers, but in truth he was the prettiest thing on the show. Like Basil, he created sumptuous rooms that were mysteriously under-appreciated by the masses. Again like Basil, there were constant rumors about his sexual proclivities off the set. As if to make him more Basil than Basil, there were even some low-rent jokes on the show about "Miss Norris" or "lovely Maurice." Still again like Basil, Maurice insisted he was happily married. Whatever the truth about his personal life, he and his wife were generous participants in AIDS-related charities around town.

The powers that be at *MHYH* decided against hiring a replacement for Aunt Fern, and elected instead to leave things at four designers. I got the sense that they were superstitious about replacing Aunt Fern, though maybe the cheap bastards simply wanted to save a few bucks.

Ann-Margret did whatever she needed to do in Big Sur and rejoined the show to considerable brouhaha. The promo ads showed her from behind, pulling up on her Harley; there was a close-up of her spike-heeled boots stepping off, and then the camera droolingly panned up her curvy, black-leathered body. As she took off her helmet and shook loose her long, big hair, she purred into the camera: "I'm back," and brandished her power drill. But the fun ended once she got to work. As always, she toiled relentlessly to prove herself as a woman carpenter, while Brick the practical joker glided by, putting devil fingers behind people's heads and protesting that he had too much work to do.

As for Terry and Boxer, their place in the sun soon clouded over when Boxer told him he wanted an open relationship. I did, however, infer that things had progressed to what might discreetly be called the next level, whereby the break-up was even more tumultuous for Terry—albeit he was the one who initiated it. Terry turned to me for comfort, but his approach to these sorts of things was, to put it mildly, lachrymose, and a little bit of drama-queen antics go a long way with one as unpretentiously down-to-earth as myself.

We were at a bar when the you-know-what hit the fan. After about the millionth time that he lectured me (as a stand-in for the rest of the universe) about what was wrong with people nowadays, and didn't anyone want an honest commitment to another person, it seemed to me it was time for a reality check.

"Get over yourself," I firmly yet sympathetically encouraged, my eyes darting about the bar in search of some possible action. "You think you're the only single fuckhead on the face of the earth?"

"Gee, thanks a lot, Rick." He moodily turned away from me. "You really know how to cheer a guy up."

"I haven't been told that since last night."

"Very funny." He grabbed his leather jacket. "I'm glad my problems seem so silly and unimportant to you."

"I accept tips," I shouted cheerfully, as he stormed out of the bar.

Although our paths hadn't crossed since that ominous occasion, I had heard via the grapevine that he was still very much in the junior league as a detective. When, after solving this high-profile murder, he went to the LAPD bigwigs to ask for meatier cases, they all but yawned in his face. Apparently, it was the usual seniority argument, combined with some predictable good old boy politics. Terry could crack a murder case as easily as flipping open a can of beer, yet I wondered if he was up to playing the hardball required of a homicide detective in such a high-crime, high-profile city as L.A. Maybe, ironically, Valerie Bertinelli or whoever was his guardian angel was looking out for him in mysterious ways.

Terry also ended up changing his bedroom pretty much back to how it started. I guess the novelty of a Batmobile for a bed wears thin after a while. I offered to pay the expenses, but Terry wouldn't hear of it.

Needless to say, I, for my part, seized the moment, and most understandably started getting my Aunt Fern living room dismantled immediately. I told Terry it had nothing to do with him, but that I certainly couldn't live with a room designed by a killer. On reconsideration, my Ralph Rapson rocking chair, hand-dyed Jack Lenor Larsen throw cushions, and Andy Warhol original lithos didn't seem so bad. So I more or less returned to what I had started out with, sort of like in those kiddie stories where happiness turns out to be right there in your own toy box or what have you.

I continued to endure the omnipresent Mitzi McGuire, and Chauncey Riggs kept trying to make my life as miserable as possible. Max Headroom got fired when our overall ratings slipped by something like half a percentage point. Since then, the antics of my coworkers and I have been akin to those of the von Trapp children in their pre-Julie Andrews phase. A few different corporate henchmen have come and gone, but I'm proud to say that none have been able to tough us out for long.

It was about two months after the murder and a month since Terry so pathetically overreacted to my harmless teasing in the bar that, on a Saturday night, my doorbell rang. And there stood Terry, looking as good as he was able to in his black leather jacket and 501s.

"How did you know I'd be home?" I asked, inviting him in out of some sort of automatic reflex to be polite.

"It's Friday night," he shrugged. "You're watching *My House, Your House*, right?"

In point of fact, I never did miss a new episode, but I had my pride to consider.

"The show ends early, and then I go out on the town." I led him to the TV room. "After all, I *am* Rick Domino."

"What did I miss?" He negotiated his large, bulky frame on my casual Danish sofa, unlacing his construction boots to put his big feet up on my marble slab coffee table. Then he opened a paper bag, tossed me a can of Bud, and opened one for himself. Dasher, who had a way of appearing whenever Terry came over, suddenly leapt onto the arm of the sofa. He magnanimously granted Terry permission to scratch him under the chin; Dasher even emitted a sound that suggested a kind of half-hearted grouchy purr.

"The show's really just getting going," I told Terry. "Bill is going to make a kitchen into Santa's workshop—and, to top it off, I think the couple whose house it is is Jewish. He wants the table and chairs to become the sleigh with reindeer. Meanwhile, Happy is designing a children's bedroom around the spaghetti squash she had for dinner last night."

"Oh, I meant to tell you. That guard who hassled Ann-Margret got fired. I made a big stink about it."

"Good for you."

"What's spaghetti squash?" He scratched his foot unself-consciously.

I felt, as I sometimes did, the need to simplify when explaining something to Terry. "It's health food." I scrunched up my nose. "You wouldn't like it."

"You're probably right." He stretched his massive, hairy arm across the back of the sofa. It felt warm and bristly as it brushed against my neck.

"Say, Rick. You must not be used to drinking beer. Your face is getting all flushed."

It was true. I had that disconcerting dizziness people sometimes get, almost as if you're leaving your own body. "Maybe I should cool it." I set the beer aside.

"Oh my God," Terry commented. "*Why* is she making the bed pillows look like hazelnuts?"

"Because, silly, there was hazelnut cream sauce on her spaghetti squash."

"Well, it looks pretty weird, if you ask me."

"Oh, God," I cried. "*What* are they doing to the walls of that poor kitchen?"

Terry shook his head with sad disbelief. "They're not even doing it the right way. If they really have to put cut paper snowflakes on the wall, they need some sort of sealant. Especially in a kitchen. I mean, just hanging over the stove like that? It's a fire hazard."

Sure enough, the couple working on the room with Bill complained that the snowflakes were a fire hazard. Bill dismissed their arguments. "Aren't most people *careful* when they cook?" he asked. When the couple replied that accidents could still happen, Bill scoffed and told them: "Look, kitchens are just for show, anyway. No one really cooks in them anymore."

"You know, Rick, I really am over Boxer." He kind of playfully rubbed my neck with his fingers.

I heard myself laugh, never before realizing I was ticklish in that spot. "That's nice."

He tucked his thumb under my chin and gave me a quick kiss.

"Thanks for being . . . you know, like, such a good friend and all that."
I guessed the beer was getting to Terry as well, since he was looking pretty
red-faced himself. Some men really do have a hard time expressing what
they're feeling. I always found it challenging to deal with, needless to say,
since I confronted what I was feeling head-on. But over the years I'd gotten
used to it.

"That's . . . well, nice of you, Terry. I'm glad I'm a good friend." I
counted to three and still felt like I had no choice but to add: "You're, like,
a good friend, too."

"Do friends do this?" He put his arm firmly around my shoulder.

"Sometimes. Yeah, sometimes I guess they do."

I nuzzled my head against Terry's powerful forearm as we cursed Bill
and Happy and prayed for the two couples. Sometimes he kind of squeezed
my shoulder with his hand, or I'd find myself lightly breathing onto his
neck. And, during the commercials, we sort of kissed a few more times. The
last time, it was even a real, deep kiss, and as I came up for air I had to
admit that it felt kind of okay. Terry wasn't the worst kisser I'd ever known,
I'd give him that much.

Not that he was my type, or anything like that.